SHIRLEY PALMER

LIONESS

MIRA™

First Published 2000
First Australian Paperback Edition 2006
ISBN 1 741 16409 5

LIONESS © 2000 by Shirley Palmer
Philippine Copyright 2000
Australian Copyright 2000
New Zealand Copyright 2000

Published by
Mira Books
3 Gibbes Street
CHATSWOOD NSW 2067
AUSTRALIA

Printed and bound in Australia by
McPherson's Printing Group

For Dan Palmer

My thanks go to Peter Miller of PMA Literary Management
in New York, who first read this novel and loved it.
Thanks, too, to Ken Atchity of AEI in Los Angeles,
who nurtured the first draft.

The people of MIRA Books, Dianne Moggy and
Amy Moore-Benson, have been, as usual, terrific.
Thank you both.

If the elephant vanished
the loss to human laughter,
wonder and tenderness would
be a calamity.
—V. S. Pritchett
reviewing *The Roots of Heaven*

The slaughter of the elephant on the plains of Africa has
slowed in recent years, but has never been eradicated.
It still continues. The elephants who once visited the caves of
Kitum are no more.

Prologue

British Airways Flight 283 from Nairobi stood outside the hangar, its cargo doors open. Cat Stanton was aware of activity inside the cavernous building, the whir of machinery, forklifts moving containers into place, men's voices. Nothing seemed real.

Joel's coffin inched into view, alone on the platform that descended from the bowels of the 747 toward the wet, shiny tarmac. As it cleared the protection of the giant aircraft, rain bounced off the gray metal carrying case.

He would like that, Cat thought. Joel loved the rain. She started toward the open doors of the hangar. A restraining hand touched her arm.

"Honey, you don't have to go outside, you'll get soaked," John Rifken said. "They'll bring him in."

Cat took a moment to process his words—they sounded hollow and distant—then said, "It's okay, John. It's only rain." A cold storm had barreled down from Alaska, unheard of in September, and still hovered over Los Angeles.

She started walking again and felt John keeping pace with her. She heard the whisper of wheels on the cement floor and turned to him.

"John, I…" She glanced at the black-suited men behind him trundling a wheeled cart and fumbled for words. "John, keep them here for a minute. I'll be all right."

John looked at her face. "Okay, honey."

Silently he motioned to the two attendants from the mortuary, and they stood back with the casket carriage they had brought to transfer the coffin to the waiting hearse.

Alone, Cat walked out into the rain. She tried not to think of Joel in the darkness, his bones crushed, his body mangled.

One

Cat stared into the eyes looking back at her from the mirror of the bathroom attached to their office. Her office now. She forced herself to form the word, say it aloud. "Dead." She made herself go on, "Joel is dead." Her twin brother, the other half of herself. Dead.

She heard Mave Chen open the outer door and turned on the faucet, ran her hands under cold water.

"Cat, are you okay?"

These days, that was Mave's constant question. What did it mean, okay? What was okay? She had a payroll to meet, an architectural practice to keep alive. Ongoing jobs had to be supervised, anxious clients reassured that nothing had changed now that The Stanton Partnership was just one architect, a thirty-two-year-old woman at that, running a crew of twenty draftsmen. The hotel job—the job that had killed him—had been put on hold, and for that she was grateful. She never wanted to hear of it again.

Was that what Mave meant by okay?

"Sure," she called back through the open door. "Just washing my hands."

"There's a letter," Mave said. Her voice sounded strained.

Cat dried her hands quickly, dropped the paper towel into the wastepaper basket, reentered the office. "What letter?"

Mave held out a large brown envelope.

Cat felt her heart thump twice against her chest then start to race. Suddenly light-headed, she stared at the envelope. It was battered, water-stained. The stylized lettering of the address jumped out at her.

"It was among the rest of the mail," Mave said. "That's Joel's architectural lettering."

Cat took the envelope, sank into Joel's chair behind the partner's desk they had shared. Since his funeral, she had alternated between her own side and his, otherwise she found herself staring at his empty chair, lost to time and grief. His clutter was still in place—piles of books on architecture and art and wildlife photography, some fossils he'd found interesting. A few pieces of modern sculpture. A framed picture he'd taken of Jess the year they had all turned seventeen—the year he and Jess had become lovers.

Cat slit open the envelope, extracted half a dozen sketches. A note fell from between the drawings, a page ripped from the sketching pad, and Cat picked it up with trembling fingers. Joel's printing ran together as if he'd scribbled the note in haste. She took in the words at a glance, then read them again to make sure she understood what they said.

"Cat, what is it?" Mave reached to take the note from Cat's shaking hand. She read it aloud. "'Need to talk to you. Will call as soon as I can get to a phone. There's something odd going on here, nothing's what it seems to be. Don't worry, I'm on top of it. Will get the film developed in Nairobi. J.'" Mave looked up, her eyes wide. "There's no date. What do you think he meant?"

Cat shook her head. Joel must have written it around the time of his phone call seven weeks ago. The call had been garbled, breaking up without making any sense. But she'd known it was Joel and had not been surprised she couldn't understand what he was saying. She'd figured he was calling from a village phone somewhere and would call again. That was the last time she had heard his voice. A week later, Jock Campbell had called their client and friend, John Rifken, to say that Joel was dead. And John had come to tell her in person.

Cat picked up the envelope, studied the blurred postmark. She could make out the year, 1986, but not the month nor the place where it had been mailed, and she reached for a magnifying glass, bringing the postmark closer. It could be Nairobi, but according to Jock Campbell the accident had happened in the remote bush. Joel had never returned to Nairobi. And if he had, he would have called her.

So who had sent it?

She put the envelope aside, picked up the sketches.

They'd been done from a mountainous point, high above golden grassland dotted with grazing animals. They were good. In a few lines, he'd caught the drama of the landscape, but something was missing. Cat knew Joel's work as well as she knew her own, and these had an unfinished quality, as if he'd left out the core of each scene.

So why had he sent them?

She looked up at Mave.

"Get John Rifken on the telephone. I need to see him, now, today."

While she waited for Mave to make the call, Cat spread the sketches over the desk. Four washed with colour and a couple merely thumbnail sketches, done in a hurry, but still small works of art. She traced the lines Joel had drawn with her fingers. He had been so good at what he did. . . .

"Cat." Mave came back into the room. "I spoke to Charlotte, Mr. Rifken's assistant. She says he's in Houston meeting with his investors in Bluebonnet Development."

So he was moving ahead on the Kenya project. "Try him in Houston."

"I already did. I left word at his hotel and at the Bluebonnet office."

"Did Charlotte say when he'd be back?"

"He'll be in his office on Friday."

Two days. "Okay Mave, thanks."

Cat waited until Mave left, closing the door softly behind her, then punched out the number she had for Jock Campbell in Nairobi. Eleven hours ahead of Los Angeles, it was already midnight there, and she listened to the ringing tone, then a click and a terse message in a hard male voice.

"You've reached Campbell Safaris. Leave your name and number, we'll call back."

Cat gave the information requested and added, "It has been six weeks since my brother's death and I have not yet received a police report, or his cameras or film. I'd appreciate it if you would look into this, Mr. Campbell, and get back to me." She gave the time and date, then said, "I'll expect a call from you tomorrow."

Cat hung up, swiveled Joel's chair so that she could look into the dark green leaves of the coral trees outside on San Vicente. Then her eyes picked up her own reflection in the window.

At a quick glance, it could have been Joel sitting there; they'd been so much alike, more than was usual for fraternal twins. Both tall, though he'd been taller and heavier. But the same toffee-colored hair, the same straight dark brows and greenish-gold eyes. Feline eyes, their father always said, followed by how like their mother they were, nothing like him, what they needed was to toughen up— Quickly, Cat slid her mind away from Derek Stanton.

From their birth, they'd been like two sides of the same coin, answering each other's unasked questions, finishing unspoken thoughts. Even now when Joel was dead, she heard his voice in the drafting room, the clatter of his feet taking the metal stairs outside their office three at a time, as only he did. Not her imagination. She actually heard it as if Joel were still here, alive.

And every night she awakened moaning and terrified, the nightmare images gone the minute she opened her eyes. All that remained was the horror and the knowledge that it was the same dream, night after night.

She swung the chair back, flipped on the intercom.

"Mave, would you check flights to Nairobi, please. Flying time, availability, that kind of thing. I'll let you know the date later. And find out about hotels. Something large and anonymous."

She was going to retrace Joel's route, see what he had seen, go to the place where he'd died. And once in Nairobi, she would start asking a few hard questions.

Two

"So, sugar, what's the urgency?" John Rifken asked. He leaned back in the black leather chair behind a desk only slighter smaller than a tennis court. He sounded as if he'd come out of the Texas hill country, which he had—he just hated to mention that it was by way of Harvard Law School. Liked to refer to himself as a simple Jewish hillbilly, but to his credit, he always grinned when he said it.

For answer, Cat lifted the bag she'd brought with her, placed it on the desk in front of him.

"What's this?" he asked.

"Joel's cameras. They came yesterday." They'd been in transit before her call to Jock Campbell. "And they're empty. No film, no photographs. And this came the day before that, while you were still in Houston." Cat handed him the battered brown envelope.

John looked at her, then opened the envelope and removed the drawings. He riffled through them quickly, then went back to study them.

"These are pretty good."

"Did you see the note?"

He picked it up, read it. "Yeah, well, you know what Joel was like—" He stopped, then said, "I'm sorry, honey, you know what I mean."

"No, I don't."

"Well, I mean he could be pretty goddamn difficult with people. It's a good thing you were there to smooth the ragged edges, sugar, or I'd probably be your only client."

John Rifken had known them since childhood, encouraged them to form The Stanton Partnership as soon as they'd received their licenses to practice architecture, given them their first commission five years ago. He'd once been a client of their father's.... She pulled her thoughts back from that path. Cat looked out of the floor-to-ceiling windows. Seventeen stories below, Los Angeles again sweltered under a copper-colored October sun and smog hazed the distant hills. The fire season this year threatened to be long and dangerous.

She turned back to face him. "He was brilliant and he didn't suffer fools easily. But he wasn't paranoid. If he said something wasn't right, then it wasn't."

"Honey, Joel was like a son to me, but that don't mean I was blind to his faults." He shook his head. "That boy had a hell of a burr under his saddle."

Cat felt her gut clench. Of course he'd had a burr under his saddle. They both did. Joel just hadn't bothered to hide it as well as she did.

"What's that got to do with his note?" she asked. "Something's not right about his death, John." A freak accident, Jock Campbell had said. The Land Rovers had run into a large herd of buffalo, the most dangerous and unpredictable beasts in Africa. Joel had been killed in the ensuing confusion. *A shutter in her mind opened on long-horns streaming over the hill in Malibu.* She shook her head, and the image was gone as quickly as it had come.

The police investigated Joel's death, Jock Campbell had said. Their report would follow. But it hadn't.

"I should have had an autopsy—"

"Whoa. Steady. Your imagination is really runnin' with the cattle here." Rifken shifted in his chair. His fingers went to the patch over his right eye. He'd lost it in his wildcatting days in the Texas oilfields—or in a barroom brawl over a woman. The story varied according to his mood. "Let me give Jock Campbell a call—"

"I've already done that. He says the police report is on its way. He said the same thing last week and the week before that."

"Sugar, you gotta remember you're dealing with a Third World bureaucracy. I warned you about that. Did you tell Jock about this note?"

"No." She left the word hanging.

Rifken frowned. "Why not?"

"I wanted to talk to you first."

He stared at her, then nodded. "So, I'll get him to fax the report."

"I did that yesterday."

"Then I guess we just have to wait until it arrives. Meantime, I'll call, ask him about the missing film." He picked up a sketch, studied it. "Okay?"

"No. Not okay. John, I don't think Jock Campbell was even on that safari with Joel."

His answer surprised her.

"'Course he wasn't, honey. Jock doesn't deal with clients. He's got a farm upcountry. Occasionally he takes an old friend like me out on safari, a few days to drink some good whiskey, tell tall stories, sleep under canvas. His son does the hard work."

"Why didn't you tell me?" She thought of the phone conversations she'd had with Joel while he was in Nairobi, trying to remember whether he'd mentioned that. They'd talked mostly about the jobs they had under way in Los Angeles, some general comments about the trip. He'd been thrilled with Nairobi, but had not yet connected with his old college friend Stephen N'toya and was still trying. After he left Nairobi, she'd had only that one garbled call from the bush.

"It wasn't important, sugar," John said. "The kind of country we want for this hotel is remote and wild. That's the attraction. I didn't expect Jock to take charge of Joel's expedition himself. Joel knew that."

"Okay." She let it go. The office had been busy and she'd paid only cursory attention to the details of Joel's trip. The start of their international reputation, she thought bitterly. She pulled her Day-Timer out of her briefcase. "While you were in Houston, did you settle on a new time frame for the project? The sooner the better for me."

"Honey, wait a minute."

The tone in his voice caught her attention. She looked up.

John got up, made his way around the desk and over to the bar in the corner of his office. She caught the rich smell of good bourbon, heard the clink of ice cubes. He turned, a glass in his hand, and held it up in invitation.

Cat shook her head. "Thanks, but I still have a lot of work tonight." She waited for him to say what was on his mind.

"Honey," he said finally, "you gotta know that Joel's death has changed everything."

Cat closed the Day-Timer. "No. I don't know that. An architectural practice doesn't fold when one partner is—" she stumbled over the word "—killed. Why should it?"

"Okay," John said. He took a breath, then said it again. "Okay. Cat, honey, without Joel, there is no Stanton Partnership. Alone, Bluebonnet doesn't think you can handle the deal."

"What?" She felt as if she had taken a body blow. She'd expected it from other clients, but not from him. John started to speak, and she said, "No, wait a minute. Joel and I did everything together. Design, supervision. Everything. Could you ever, even once, tell where Joel's work ended and mine began?"

"Honey, that's not the point. You weren't born yesterday, you know what these Third World deals are like. You gotta have iron *cojones*." He looked at the glass in his hand as if uncertain how it got there. He swirled the whiskey without drinking, then walked back to his desk. Abruptly, he said, "We're going with Raul Guitterrez."

Her first thought was that she hadn't heard the name right. But she knew she had.

"You can't," she said. "John, you can't do that."

Guitterrez. They had competed for the same jobs for years, and it had not been a friendly rivalry. Joel hated what he called the Disneyland School of Architecture, thought it made a joke of an honorable profession.

"I can. I have to. Raul's put his time in with Gehry here in Los Angeles, and he's in Houston now in his own practice. He's tough. And he's a Texan."

"And that's the qualification for this job? He's a Texan who designs like Gehry?"

"Don't knock it, sugar. Anyway, that's it. I'll see to it that you don't suffer financially."

"That's not the issue." She could barely hear him through the roar in her ears. She and Joel had learned early never to trust anyone but each other. Now, she realized, somehow over the years, in spite of everything she knew, she had come to trust John Rifken. How could she have allowed herself to do that?

He went back to the bar, poured another drink. Cat pushed her Day-Timer back into her briefcase, reached for the sketches, started to stuff them into the stained envelope.

John watched her for a moment, then said, "Sugar, listen to me. This is not the only job—"

She did not let him finish. "It's the only job that matters to me." She turned away from him to pick up Joel's cameras.

"I've got a lot of other work for you, Cat. Honey, wait a minute."

His words registered. If she left now, she thought, she had no hope of getting what she really wanted: the legitimacy this hotel job would give her in Kenya.

She left the cameras on the desk, turned to face him.

"Let me spell this out, John. Because one of the partners of The Stanton Partnership was killed searching for a site for the hotel Bluebonnet Development is committed to build in Kenya, the firm is going to lose the commission. Do I have this right?"

"Yeah, well, sounds pretty raw put like that. But I guess that's about it." He looked at her. "Honey, you know this business. We risk millions before we make a dime. And these Third World deals are even tougher to pull off. With a woman in charge—"

"Oh, stop it," she said impatiently. "This is the 1980s, for God's sake. Even in Texas."

"Yeah, well, we're not talking about Texas. We're talking about investing millions of American dollars in some remote, goddamn beauty spot in Kenya we haven't even found yet."

"But Joel *did* find it. I have the sketches. I just need to find where they were done." She took a beat, then said, "I also have this deal, John. You were there when Bubba Nelligan shook hands on it after Joel's funeral."

"A handshake deal ain't exactly carved in stone, honey."

"John, I need to do this job."

"Christ's sake, honey. I did my best for you. I was outvoted."

She wanted to believe him. She glanced out the window, took a second to gather herself. Below, on Century Park East, a silver stretch limo had been broadsided by a delivery truck. Ant-size men threatened each other with tiny waving arms.

"Well, you'd better tell the guys that the surviving partner of The Stanton Partnership has a handshake deal and she is going to hold them to it." The word *lawyer* did not have to be said. "I intend to finish what Joel started."

"For Christ's sake, Cat! What is this? You don't give a shit about this job—"

"What makes you think that? I'll get you that site—"

"Sugar, you're not interested in any site. I've known you kids all your lives. You think I don't know you've got some cockamamy idea that Joel's death was not an accident? That you're going to go over there, dig something out that'll back you up? Some goddamn conspiracy theory?"

"Don't make me into a nutcase, John. My brother was killed and I'm not satisfied with the explanation. I just want to follow his route." It was out in the open, and she was relieved. "But I'll also get you the site." She shook the sketches out of the envelope again, spread them across John's desk. "The guys at Bluebonnet Development have not seen these. Time is money—in this business, a lot of money. And every day, the clock is running on the interest on loans you've already got. Millions of American dollars."

He grunted, and Cat pressed her advantage. "With Guitterrez you're back to square one."

"Sugar, you ain't making a shitload of sense here, you know that? And you're not gonna find that Joel's death was anything but what Jock Campbell said it was." For a moment, John stared at her silently. Then he said, "Okay." He reached over, patted her hand. "Okay, sweetpea. You go clear your head of this nonsense or it's gonna eat you alive. You got three weeks. Then Guitterrez takes over."

"Even if I get the site?"

"I thought we'd settled that. You're not going for the site. You're going to get clear about Joel."

"But suppose I do get it?"

"Then I guess we'll talk about it. Now, you'll be using Campbell Safaris. They're the best at what they do—"

"And what's that? Letting their clients get trampled to death?"

"Oh, Cat, for God's sake! They work with film companies, the BBC, National Geographic, the documentary stuff you see on television. Mostly they do research work. They're trackers and hunters, so they know the country like their own backyard."

She stared at him, stunned. Hunters! Joel and a party of hunters? He must have been crazed!

She found her voice. "Well," she said, "I guess you'd better let them know I'm on my way. Thanks, John." She went over to him, pressed her lips to his cheek, a rare display of affection. She shouldered her bag and the cameras, started toward the door. His voice stopped her.

"Cat."

She turned in the doorway, waited for him to continue.

"You're not Joel, remember," he said. "Go easy on the attitude."

Three

Cat awoke in the icy room, the reek of blood in her nostrils, the images of the dream already gone. Dread pressed against every surface of her skin. She lay still, waiting for her pounding heartbeat to return to normal—it usually took a few minutes. An unfamiliar drone filled the room. She wanted to turn on the light, but didn't know where it was. Where she was.

A toilet flushed on the other side of the wall and automatically she registered the thought, "cheap construction." And remembered. Nairobi. The Inter-Continental Hotel.

She pushed aside the blanket, padded across the carpet to turn off the air conditioner, silencing the drone. In the bathroom, she bent over the sink, bathed her eyes with cold water. The sense of dread still pressing down on her had the weight of ages behind it. Holding a wet towel to the back of her neck she crossed the room and swung back the drapes. The sliding glass doors opened easily, and she stepped onto her small balcony. On the other side of the square, windows of the Jomo Kenyatta Conference Center shone with the reflection of the midmorning sun. From his pedestal, Kenyatta threw his shadow across the canna lillies edging the public garden. Cat breathed deeply, hoping the spicy fragrance in the air would dispel the odor of blood. Even though it was a trick of her mind, it lingered.

Five stories below, cars clogged the road, a lone bicyclist among them hugging the sidewalk. Cat clung to him with her eyes as he pedaled slowly out of sight, as if concentrating on his wobbling progress could keep at bay the dreadful image of Joel being lowered into a plain wooden coffin, silence the sound of the lid sliding into place, the deafening blows of a hammer sealing his crushed body forever into darkness.

She turned back into the room, glanced at her travel clock on the table beside the bed.

Ten-thirty. Time to get ready.

"Campbell Safaris does not work with women." Dan Campbell looked at his watch, clearly eager to be gone. "I'm sorry."

Cat made herself take a few seconds before answering. She was jet lagged, exhausted after traveling for two days halfway across the world, arriving in Nairobi at an ungodly hour and checking into the hotel by 7:00 a.m. that morning.

And now this.

"Well, I guess you are going to have to change your policy," she said. "You have a contract with Bluebonnet Development Co. for this job."

"With Bluebonnet, Miss Stanton, not with you. I'm afraid you've had a long journey for nothing."

The coffee shop of the Inter-Continental Hotel buzzed with conversation, the clatter of china, bustling waiters filling orders, pouring coffee. He'd been late for their eleven o'clock appointment, and he was dirty and unshaven, his clothes filthy. He stunk of oil and smoke and heavy male sweat, and something else, an odor she recognized, but for the moment couldn't name. His eyes were bloodshot and watchful.

"You do realize this puts you in breach of your contract?" Cat asked.

"Oh, the hell with that. Anyone familiar with East Africa knows that Campbell Safaris never takes women as clients."

"Well, you must find that quite limiting. Anyway, I'm sorry I'm not as familiar as I could be with East Africa." She spoke pleasantly. It seemed to escape him that East Africa was not exactly the belly button of the universe. "I'm surprised it did not occur to you to inform John Rifken—" She stopped. John Rifken couldn't be unaware of this, he'd known these people for thirty years. For some reason, he'd chosen not to tell her. To cover her confusion, Cat picked up the pot of coffee on the table, refilled Campbell's cup, then her own.

Campbell shrugged. "We simply did not expect a woman, and when we found out, it was too late. You were already en route." He drained the cup, his third.

"I don't think you understand," Cat said. "I'm here to take up where Joel Stanton—"

"Listen, I've just said there is no way I will take you into the bush."

"There is no one else." Deliberately, she allowed a plaintive note to enter her voice, but to get what she wanted, she'd plead with the devil himself.

"Well, we could go around and around on this, but I don't have the time. I'm sorry. It's best if you return to Los Angeles. I'll talk to Bluebonnet."

"Don't bother. If I have to get another outfit to do this job, I will. And I'm quite capable of explaining the reason to Bluebonnet myself."

"Good. Well, that's settled." Campbell retrieved a few crumpled Kenyan pound notes from a pocket, dropped them on the table. For the first time Cat noticed that the rolled sleeve of his khaki shirt was stiff with dried blood and seemed laminated to his skin. Suddenly she realized that the elusive stink was cordite. She remembered it from a construction site she'd been on.

Campbell rose to his feet and Cat stared up at him. "Wait a minute," she protested. "You can't just—"

"Yes, I can. Have a good trip home." He turned, walked toward the lobby.

Cat stared after him, unable to believe what had just happened. He'd walked out. The man who had been with Joel when he died had turned her down and walked out.

She gathered up her bag and the briefcase containing Joel's sketches, got herself out of the booth and started after him, hurriedly threading her way through the tables.

The lobby was filled with tourists sporting stiff new safari gear and hats from the hotel shop, and in his filthy, blood-stained khakis, Campbell's tall figure would have stood out.

But somehow he had managed to disappear as if he had never been there.

Back in her room, Cat threw her briefcase on the bed. She'd left the doors to the balcony open and a warm soft breeze entered, ruffling the papers on the table. She crossed the room, stepped outside.

For a few minutes she leaned on the balcony to watch the cars jockey for position as they tore around the square, unable to summon the strength to move. A mud-encrusted Land Rover with a heavy winch mounted on its front bumper bullied its way across three lanes of traffic, and Cat tried to make out the driver. A muddy Land Rover was exactly what she imagined Dan Campbell drove, but the Land Rover disappeared, and Cat turned back into the room to retrieve Stephen N'toya's card from her Day-Timer.

She wasn't without resources here, she told herself. She had a copy of Joel's itinerary. And she had Stephen N'toya. They'd met at Harvard. She and Joel were studying architecture, and Stephen was in the law school, but the two men discovered they shared a passion for wildlife photography. Stephen had returned to his homeland, but he and Joel had remained in touch over the years. And now Joel's old friend was a rising star in Kenya's Ministry of Justice.

The card showed a number, but no address. Cat picked up the telephone, got an outside line, dialed. It started to ring, and she waited. No one answered. She let it ring a dozen times, hoping at least for a machine so that she could leave a message. But the ringing continued, and she finally replaced the phone. A call to information got her the number of the Ministry of Justice and she dialed again.

A male voice in her ear said something that could have been "MinistryofJustice." All one word.

"I'd like to speak to Stephen N'toya, please."

"One moment, *memsahib*," the voice said. Then, "No one of that name, *memsahib*."

"Is this the Ministry of Justice?"

"Yes, MinistryofJustice."

"Mr. Stephen N'toya works there."

"No Stephen N'toya, *memsahib*."

"Well, would you mind checking again, please. Stephen N'toya." She spelled it.

"Yes *memsahib*. Stephen N'toya. No record of that name."

"Thank you." Slowly, she put the phone back into the cradle.

She shrugged off her disquiet. She still had the number on the card, and he'd have to return home sooner or later. If it was his home.

She picked up the phone book, found it offered a daunting display of safari companies and, more to get an idea of what was available than anything else, she made a list of those that sounded most likely. Stephen would be sure to know whom she should hire, but meantime, it would not hurt to do some homework. She dialed the first number.

A male voice answered. "Singh Brothers."

"Hello. My name's Catherine Stanton. I'm an architect from the United States, and I want to make an expedition into the bush to do research for a hotel site. Can you help with this?"

A silence, then, "Well, I'm sorry," the voice said slowly, "there is not much call for that kind of thing, you see. We can show you some fine places close to the game parks, but you'll have to talk to the government, you know. You can't just decide to build hotels and such, willy-nilly."

He sounded as if he thought he had a child on the phone, Cat thought. "No, I realize that," she said patiently.

"Well, then, I can probably come up with something within the next couple of weeks."

Cat thanked him, hung up, dialed the next number on the list.

Just after two o'clock, she put down the phone and sorted through her notes. Several companies had dismissed her request, others knew exactly the place she was looking for. When pressed, they'd trotted out the usual game parks and waterfalls, the beach resorts. Out of the fourteen companies she had called, only one sounded possible, and she'd made an appointment for the following day.

Then on impulse, she dialed Paul Neville's number. It was 1:00 a.m. in Washington, D.C., but time meant nothing to Paul. He could sleep standing up, party all night, leave the country at a moment's notice.

They'd met at an art opening in a gallery in Santa Monica. It had been packed with the usual mix of impossibly slender girls, encased in minute black spandex dresses, and black-clad young men, their slicked-back hair clubbed into tiny bullfighter's pony-tails. Paul had stood out in rumpled tweeds, working his way through the crowd toward her, a couple of glasses of white wine held high. He'd thrust one of the glasses into her hand and said, "Here, you look like a woman with all the right moves. How would you like to get out of here and go dancing?" She'd laughed at his effrontery, but had been taken by his lanky good looks, the lock of straight brown hair he constantly swept off his forehead, the humor in his light blue eyes. They'd danced at Vertigo, eaten at the Pantry downtown. Since then he'd been part of her life, leaving without notice to cover foreign wars, returning as suddenly by way of Los Angeles whenever he could. They'd worked out a relationship that suited them both. No complications. No commitment. No questions.

Before leaving Los Angeles, she had left a note for him with Mave in case he returned from Myanmar while she was away.

"Gone to Nairobi," she'd written. "See you when I get back." Except for Nairobi instead of Rangoon, it was word for word the note he'd sent her three months earlier, attached to a papier mâché cactus with a suspiciously phallic shape.

She had pinned her note to his tie—a bright blue Thai silk he'd had embroidered by a woman in one of the refugee camps on the Cambodian border. White daisies with green centers. She'd found it hanging over her bedroom door after he'd left the last time. It had surprised her. He never left his things, he knew she hated it. He never stayed overnight, either.

On the fifth ring, his machine picked up. "Paul Neville. If it's urgent, call the bureau. They usually know how to contact me."

Cat hung up without leaving a message, but the sound of his voice had brought a comfort she had not realized she needed.

She ordered a salad from room service, ate on her balcony, then dialed Stephen's number again with the same result. Finally, she picked up her purse, left to kill time with some sight-seeing until she could call him again later in the evening.

She smiled at the doorman, enjoying the flourish with which he opened the heavy glass doors, and turned toward Kamathi Street. The afternoon sun was bright, but the streets were not oppressively hot. Nairobi, her guidebook had told her, was the Maasai word for "cool fresh water." The city was a mile above sea level, its temperature always moderate. A handful of wooden buildings surrounding a railhead only a hundred years ago, it was now a modern city.

Ignoring her exhaustion—this might be the only time she'd have to look at the city—she walked aimlessly, soaking up the atmosphere. The buildings left over from colonial times were interesting, a few of the hotels were excellent, but most new construction looked as if it had been thrown together, and she wondered how local architects made a living.

The streets teemed with people. Beggars crouching in the shade of buildings. Men in three-piece suits and jeans and T-shirts. Fresh young girls in colorful saris and immaculate makeup. Pregnant women who looked already worn-out by childbearing, small children clinging to their legs, babies suckling at the breast.

Easy to believe Kenya had one of the fastest-growing birthrates in Africa.

For the first time in her life, Cat was conscious of her color, a white face in a sea of black. Even to her untutored eye, tribal differences were obvious. Fine Nilotic features and slender-boned bodies, heavy faces that matched strong square figures, skin colors from pale ivory to a rich blue-black.

Joel had seen this tumult of life and color, she thought. His artist's eye had caught every detail; he'd probably taken a thousand photographs, each one with his unique take on life. And all lost. She would never see them.

She stumbled, then realized a skinny hand was clamped around her arm, pulling her off balance. Deep in thought, she had not been aware that a beggar was keeping pace with her until he grabbed her.

She gagged at the smell of his rags, his unwashed body. Incoherent words burbled from his throat. His temples were sunken, the bones of his face barely covered with flesh.

Cat pulled her arm free and backed up, reached in her bag for a few Kenyan pound notes. Trying not to shudder, she pressed them into a clawlike hand, then attempted to step around him. Still mumbling, the man blocked her path. White foam flecked his lips, flew from his mouth. Cat jerked her head back, trying not to think of the AIDS epidemic sweeping through Africa.

The beggar clutched her arm again, shouting now, his face thrust into hers. She struggled to free herself, but his long bony fingers tightened.

Then a tall heavy woman with skin the color of ebony stopped and began to yell. More people gathered, calling out questions to which the woman shouted answers. Within seconds it seemed, Cat was the center of an angry noisy crowd, she and the crazy beggar alone in the middle of a circle, the crowd carefully keeping its distance.

Heart pounding, Cat looked from face to face.

"What's going on here?" A loud, authoritative voice rose above the din. "Let me through."

Still shouting, the crowd drew apart.

"What's happening? Are you all right?" The voice had a strong European accent. A priest in a black cassock peered at her.

"Yes, but they're shouting so loud I can't understand what they're saying."

"Ah." The priest turned to the woman who'd started the noisy exchange. "What is wrong here?"

"This diseased person is stealing," the woman answered. Her voice was loud, but at least she no longer shouted. "He should be arrested by police." The woman stabbed an accusing finger at the beggar while the rest of the onlookers yelled their agreement. No one seemed inclined to back off.

"They seem to think this man was robbing you," the priest said to Cat. "They are determined to hold him for the police, but they will not touch him because he probably has AIDS and they don't want to catch it." He spread his hands, gave a Gallic shrug. "They are good people but frightened, you understand."

Cat let out her breath in a small puff of relief. She smiled at the woman. "I gave him the money, but he seems to be sick in his mind. I think we should let him go."

The woman looked doubtful. She turned to the crowd, the discussion continued. Seeming to enjoy the excitement, the crowd did not disperse, and the priest took Cat's arm.

"There is nothing for you to do here."

He drew her away. Reluctant to leave the beggar to their judgment, Cat looked back and was relieved to see that somehow he had managed to slip away.

She turned to the priest. "Things were really getting away from me there." She gave a small laugh to cover her embarrassment. "I couldn't understand their accent. I'm sorry. I feel pretty stupid. Anyway, thank you."

"No, no. I am delighted to have been of service. People here hate thieves, they'll always hold them for the police. Only the fact that he looked as if he had AIDS prevented him from being handled very roughly."

He was staring at her. Cat smiled uncertainly, and held out her hand. "Well, thank you again."

He took her hand, hesitated, then said, "Forgive my impertinence. You look quite pale. Perhaps you would allow me to give you a cup of coffee?"

"Well—"

"Come," he said. "A brief rest, a cup of coffee. It will be good for you."

Cat found herself nodding. "Yes, thank you, that sounds wonderful."

The priest guided her across the street, weaving expertly through cars that made no attempt to slow down. Miraculously, they reached the safety of the sidewalk, and he led her to tables outside a hotel. He waved to a white-jacketed waiter, then seated her in the shade of a blue and white umbrella.

He took the chair opposite, and said, "Allow me to introduce myself. I am Father Yves Gaston."

Before she could give her own name, the waiter was at the table, and Father Gaston said, *"Mademoiselle?* Coffee?" He glanced at his watch. "Ah. After five. Perhaps you would prefer something a little stronger?"

"No, thank you. Coffee would be fine."

He gave the order in Swahili, then smiled at her. "I did not get your name, *mademoiselle.*"

"Catherine Stanton. From Los Angeles."

"California. Beautiful I am told." He reached across the table and they shook hands once more. He hesitated, then said, "Mademoiselle Stanton you say, yes?"

Cat nodded.

"Ah."

Cat looked at him expectantly. Long bony face, fierce dark eyes, olive skin. A wonderful mane of unruly iron gray hair, over which, she would guess, he waged a losing battle with vanity. She tried to pinpoint his accent. It was attractive, but not French.

"Forgive me if I intrude, *mademoiselle*, but are you by chance the sister of the young American, Joel Stanton?"

The noise and color of the street receded, leaving her alone with the man on the other side of the table. It seemed an age passed before she could respond, but it could have been only seconds.

"Yes. Joel was my…" Her voice strangled.

Father Gaston allowed a moment of silence, then said, "You have my deepest sympathy, mademoiselle. I read about the accident. It was a terrible thing."

Cat fought to find words, but could only nod her thanks. The waiter arrived, set out the coffeepot and sugar cookies, filled the cups. The interlude gave her a moment to recover her equilibrium, and she picked up her cup with a steady hand and drank, feeling gratitude as the caffeine hit her system.

Father Gaston replaced his own cup and said, "I had the pleasure of meeting your brother, you know. Of course, now I see the strong resemblance between you."

"You met him?" Cat stared at him in astonishment. "Did you rescue him, too?"

Father Gaston gave a small laugh. "No, no. We met quite by chance when he was visiting the Cathedral of the Holy Family here in Nairobi. We walked around the Cathedral together, and I invited him to visit my own little church."

"Oh, I see."

Smiling, Father Gaston shook his head. "No, my dear. He was not getting religion."

Cat smiled back. "No, I didn't think so."

"He was a fine young man, nevertheless. We discovered we shared an interest in church architecture."

Cat felt a small stab of amusement. Joel had studied just enough church architecture to get him through his exams. As far as she knew, he had never looked at it again. But Joel always knew when to be kind.

"He mentioned our little meetings, perhaps?"

"No, I'm afraid not." She stared out at the passing crowd, felt Father Gaston's eyes on her and looked at him. "What did you hear about his death?"

"Hear? Well, the same thing you did, I imagine. Just what I read in the newspaper. I understood he was caught up in some sort of rampage. Buffalo, was it not?"

"Isn't that unusual?"

He seemed startled. "Well, I don't know. What do you mean?"

"I mean, how many people do you hear about getting killed like that?"

"I don't know. I didn't think about it, *mademoiselle*. You must forgive me, I confess to having little interest in the wilderness. Pastoral work among a rather wild flock is about all I can manage. You are troubled by this explanation of his death?"

Cat hesitated, then said, "I just can't imagine how this could have happened to my brother. He was experienced in the wild. He was a very good wildlife photographer. He knew how to handle himself."

"My dear." Father Gaston reached across the table, placed his hand over hers. "The loss of a loved one is hard to accept, especially someone so young and so talented as your brother."

Alone in the middle of this city where she was unknown, the

touch of the priest's hand was oddly consoling. She couldn't imagine seeking out such contact in Los Angeles. She allowed her hand to stay where it was.

"Well, I think there is something—I don't know—wrong about his death." The words just slipped out.

Father Gaston nodded. "With our limited understanding, we always believe it is wrong for someone so young to die, but we cannot know the divine plan. What good does it do to question God?"

"I mean the way he is supposed to have died. I don't think he would have been caught like that, in the open where he could be trampled by buffalo." She could feel the sweat building where the priest's palm touched the skin on the back of her hand. But his dark eyes were warm and sympathetic. "We were twins," she said. "We were born twelve minutes apart. I would know..." But she didn't know. She had only nightmares she could not remember when daylight came.

"It is very human to struggle against the finality of death by raising questions," he said gently. "At first it can provide a connection of sorts to our loved one. But do not, I beg of you, dear *mademoiselle,* allow it to continue. Do not torment yourself with these thoughts."

Cat removed her hand, reaching for her cup to make the withdrawal seem less abrupt. "You're right, I guess." For a second she had been about to tell him of her disquiet about the missing film, the lack of a police report. The urgency Joel seemed to have felt, somehow managing to send a note and unfinished sketches even though he'd been deep in the bush, miles from civilization. But the moment passed, and she was glad she had kept silent. She glanced at her watch.

"So, what brings you here, Miss Catherine?"

"Please, I'm usually called Cat." Only Derek Stanton called her Catherine. She had learned to hate the name.

"Yes, of course, Joel mentioned that. I'd forgotten. So I, too, will call you Cat. So, what brings you here?"

"I'm sure Joel told you about the site for a hotel. Our clients still need it."

"Ah. You will be traveling into the bush, then?"

"Yes, I expect to be leaving in a day or two." She glanced at her watch again. "I'm sorry, I hope you will excuse me. I have some calls I must make tonight."

"Ah, young people, always working. You will be taking the same route taken by Joel?"

"Yes. That's the plan." She felt under her chair for her purse.

"You must be very careful. The bush can be very dangerous—" He stopped. "But, of course, you know the risks more than most. Forgive me."

Cat stood and the priest jumped to his feet.

"Well, I must not keep you. Perhaps before you leave you will give me the pleasure of showing you my little church? Some tea, perhaps, one afternoon?" He smiled. "I promise I will not ask you for a donation."

Suddenly, she was eager to be gone. "Yes. Thank you," she said. "I'd like that. Thanks again for rescuing me."

Father Gaston took a small notebook from a pocket in his cassock, scribbled a few lines. "This is the address of my church and my telephone number. Regard me as a friend while you are in Kenya. Call if you need, just to talk, you understand. Sharing your grief will help. Especially with one who knew your brother."

Her throat tightened. "Thank you." She folded the note, slipped it into her pocket although she knew she would never call. She had neither the time nor the temperament for pastoral counsel.

Four

She called Stephen's number again from her room. This time, after only one ring, a voice said, "N'toya."

"Stephen." A spurt of gladness warmed her at the sound of his voice. Someone who had known Joel as a student, who'd laughed with him, argued, fought sometimes. An old friend and irreplaceable. "This is Cat."

There was silence. Then a click, a faint mechanical hum. She could hear him breathe.

"Stephen," she said. "It's Cat Stanton." At Harvard they'd all spent hours together arguing until dawn over pizza and jug red. "I'm here in Nairobi."

"Cat. What are you doing here?" There was no greeting, no lilt of pleasure in his voice at hearing from her. He must have realized the starkness of his words because he gave a small strained laugh. "What a surprise."

"Yes, I suppose it is—"

"Wait. I'll call you back."

"Oh. Okay. I'm at—"

But he'd hung up. Frowning, Cat replaced the phone and wondered how he would know where to reach her. She sat staring at the telephone. Fifteen minutes ticked by. Then it rang, and she snatched up the receiver.

"Stephen?"

"Yes. How are you, Cat?" He sounded more relaxed.

"I'm fine. How did you know where to find me?"

"I guessed. I'm sorry about Joel."

"Yes." He'd written a note and she had responded, but it had been in a fog of grief, and she could hardly remember it. He had not mentioned meeting up with Joel. Nor leaving the attorney general's office.

"So, how are you, Cat?"

"Okay." Behind his voice she could hear traffic noise, the shouts of a street vendor. It sounded as if he was at a public phone. Certainly no place for a long cozy chat with an old friend. She got right to the point.

"Stephen, I need some help. I have some questions about Joel's death."

A beat of silence, then, "What kind of questions?"

"I wonder if we could meet for a drink, or if you haven't eaten yet, maybe dinner. We could talk."

"Cat, I don't know what I can do to help you."

Her gut clenched and she realized how much she had been relying on him to come through for her. She said, "If this is not a convenient time for you, Stephen, I can call tomorrow. We could meet for lunch."

"I'm afraid I can't tomorrow."

"Do you have a new job?"

"No, same old grind, you know how it is."

"Stephen, I called your office today. They didn't seem to know your name."

"Typical. Government offices, can't find anything."

She waited for him to continue, but he didn't. She said, "Well, when can we get together?"

"Cat, I feel terrible about this, but you've caught me flat-footed. I have to go out of town on a case upcountry. You should have let me know you were coming."

"I can come to your office tomorrow and wait until you have some time, if you like. Any hour. I don't mind waiting. Just name it."

He was silent.

"Stephen," she said. "What's going on? Joel was killed in Kenya. He said he was going to see you while he was here, and I don't know whether he did, but I'm here and I need some help. I can't believe you can't squeeze me in, no matter how busy you are. Do you want me to just park myself in your office? Because I will."

She heard him expel a loud breath. "I'm sorry, Cat. I really am going out of town. Let's make it tonight. I'll meet you at the Kenyatta statue in the square. Ten o'clock."

"Stephen, for God's sake! What's wrong with the bar in the hotel?"

"It's better this way. If you leave the hotel at three minutes to ten, you'll be at the statue at ten." He hesitated, then said, "Be discreet. Do not draw attention to yourself." A warmer note crept into his voice. "I'll be glad to see you, Cat."

"What do you mean by discreet?" Cat asked. But the dial tone hummed in her ear. He'd hung up. Cat stared at the phone in her hand. What the hell was that all about? She looked at her watch, saw that it was only seven o'clock. She called the front desk, waited forever until they answered and asked if they had a list of safari guides they could recommend.

* * *

Downstairs, she pushed into the crowd surrounding the desk and leaned over, trying to catch the eye of a harassed desk clerk. Failing, she raised her voice, adding to the clamor.

"I'm Cat Stanton. I just spoke to you about a list of safari outfitters." Her words were lost in the cacophony of a dozen different languages. She felt herself sag, suddenly drained of the strength to compete.

"G'day. Fierce bloody lot, eh?"

The voice, full of laughter, belonged to the enormous young man at her side. Bright blue eyes, bloodshot from exposure to the sun, looked down at her. Sandy hair, ruddy skin, the top half of his forehead white where it had been shaded by the battered Australian bush hat now pushed to the back of his head. He grinned. One front tooth was slightly crooked.

A charmer, Cat thought, and not unaware of it. She smiled back at him. "About as fierce as a bunch of kids at a Sunday-school picnic."

An elbow thrust into the middle of her back and she catapulted forward. Laughing, he held her until she put her hands against his chest and pushed away from him. His grin was contagious, and she found herself laughing with him. He put an arm behind her, interposing his big body between her and the crowd.

"See. A bunch of savages. What you need is a strong right arm." He slammed a fist the size of a boulder on the desk. "Hey, mate. Lady here needs a list of safari outfitters. And pronto. Doesn't do to keep a pretty lady waiting."

A desk clerk started their way but was waylaid by a man in white robes shouting insistently in Arabic.

"Now just a bloody minute." The young Australian shot out a long arm, grabbed the clerk's shoulder.

"Peter! Oh, mate, this is right crook," a voice called from the middle of the crowd. "What d'y'say to getting a couple of tubes, come back later?"

"Yeah, right." Peter relinquished his hold on the clerk, who moved rapidly out of range, and turned to Cat. "Come have a beer until this lot clears. Name's Peter Stone. That's Bobby Watson over there. We're a harmless couple of blokes. You'll be safe with us." Looking anything but harmless, he grinned down at her.

Tempted, Cat smiled back. A drink, some food, certainly some laughter. Or she could eat alone and run over in her mind every permutation of the words Stephen had uttered—and those he hadn't—and wait for the hands of the clock to move to three minutes to ten.

"Come on, you'd be doing us a favor," Peter said. "We've been out in the bush too bloody long. We need the company of a lady to civilize us."

Bobby Watson shoved his way into a slot next to them. Tall, lean, bush hat tilted rakishly on dark curly hair, he leaned over the desk on the other side of Peter.

"I don't know what this bloke's been telling you, but don't trust him, whatever it is," he said seriously. "Now, I'm a much better bet."

Cat found herself laughing again, her mood already lighter. It felt as if she hadn't laughed in months. "He's saying something about being in the bush too long."

"Well, for once he's telling the God's honest truth." He reached a hand across his friend. "Howd'y'do? Bobby Watson. Adelaide."

She took the calloused hand. "Cat Stanton. Los Angeles."

"Before you pushed your ugly mug where it definitely wasn't wanted, I was trying to persuade her to take pity on us," Peter said. "Now she's going to take one look at that kisser of yours and run screaming from the place." He turned to Cat. "We just got back from a hunting trip. Dropped a ruddy great tusker—"

"Ol' Pete here only hunts so he'll have something to impress the ladies with," Bobby said. "Loves to tell tall stories, this bloke. Now, my tusker was worth talking about. Carried ivory you wouldn't believe." Bobby raised an imaginary rifle to his shoulder, tracked the movements of the unseen elephant. "Took this difficult shot right behind the ear. Pow!" He reenacted the recoil and grinned. "Dropped him like a ruddy tank."

Cat's amusement drained away. "You mean you've been killing elephants? You shot them?"

"Well, only two. One each. Not here, of course, it's illegal." He flicked his eyebrows, including her in a conspiracy of lawbreaking, and grinned. "No, we had permits in Botswana. But they were ruddy giants. Take some finding nowadays, good tuskers. Place is getting shot out, not much left now. Ivory's worth a fortune on the black market. Poachers have already taken the best."

"Got some other stuff, though, not only tuskers," Peter said. "Some good trophy heads. We'll sell them to some punter, make a few pounds." He nodded toward the desk clerks. "Look, let's get a jar. The rate these blokes move, this place won't clear out for another hour."

Suddenly depressed, Cat shook her head. It was stupid to be shocked, but she was. This is Africa. People come here from all over the world to kill. Joel's face came into her mind, his look of total absorption when he bent over his camera, waiting for the right light, a flock of birds or an animal to move into place. She frowned at the sudden stab of pain across her eyes.

"Cat?" Peter Stone was looking at her quizzically. "You coming for that beer?"

"No, thanks, I have work to do. Don't let me keep you."

He started to press her, and she said sharply, "No, really, I'm busy. Thanks, anyway. Good night."

The two Australians lingered for a moment, but she turned her back, and finally they retreated. She could hear them arguing as they left.

"What did you say to her, you silly bugger?"

"Nothing. Swear to God. She just suddenly turned off…"

Their voices diffused, blended into the general hubbub.

Cat leaned against the counter. Extracting the promised list of outfitters from the busy desk clerk seemed more than she could manage. And if she did get it, she could not face one more call tonight. Not one more discouraging reply about borders and routes and logistics. She'd done enough homework.

She pushed her way out of the crowd and took a circuitous route to the coffee shop, avoiding the busy Safari Bar with its shields and spears, its woven leather furniture and Australian hunters.

The waiter found her a corner table and Cat ordered coffee and chocolate cake, and heard Jess's voice in her mind, chiding her for indulging what Jess called her chocolate habit.

Joel should have trusted Jess, Cat thought. Jess waited for him until she thought her biological clock had ticked for too long, so she married Mike and had Rosie. But Joel would always be the love of her life. Maybe if he'd married Jess, he would have found some peace. Maybe then, he'd still be alive.

She toyed with the cake, watched the crowd. Thought of how her own life paralleled Joel's. His work had been everything to him, as hers was to her. Neither of them had anything left for babes clustered around the knee.

But she did have Jess as a friend, and she had Rosie. Cat softened at the thought of her godchild.

Time dragged. The hand on her watch seemed immobile. Finally, at seven minutes to ten, she signed the check and rose to her feet. The whole affair seemed unnecessarily melodramatic, skulking around statues at night, but the palms of her hands were clammy, and in spite of two cups of coffee, her mouth felt dry.

The lobby was quieter, and the same uniformed doorman who'd been on duty earlier opened the glass doors with a flourish. The night air was cool, and she shivered.

"*Jambo, memsahib. Teksi?*"

"No, thanks."

Spotlighted on his pedestal, Jomo Kenyatta was almost opposite where she stood. All she had to do was cross the road, enter the square. But for whatever reason, Stephen had said, "Be discreet." She turned left.

"*Memsahib!*"

Cat turned. The doorman was coming toward her.

"You walk, *memsahib?*"

"Just a stroll, it's such a nice evening." She glanced at her watch. Three minutes to ten.

"Not good, *memsahib.* Nairobi not like it was. Plenty bad people now. Not good at night in the park."

"I'll just go to the end of the hotel block then. Not far."

"I watch you, *memsahib.* You be okay you stay in the light."

"Thank you."

Halfway down the block, she turned. The doorman waved, nodded. She waved back, then glanced at her watch. Couple minutes to ten. She'd have to hustle. She picked up her pace. The sound of voices reached her, and she looked over her shoulder. Her guardian angel was bending over the open door of a taxi, helping a couple to climb out. They were laughing loudly, more than a little drunk, the man was trying to push money into the doorman's pocket, and he was cooperative, smiling and nodding.

She darted across the road, away from the protection of the light from the hotel, and kept her eyes fastened on the golden beacon that lit Jomo Kenyatta in the center of the square while she cruised the edge of the park, looking for a path. An opening appeared, a trail worn by people taking a shortcut through the trees. No other path was in view, and time was passing. She turned onto the trail, half expecting to hear a shout of warning from the doorman.

The track was narrow, and a few feet in, the undergrowth blocked out the comforting view of Kenyatta on his plinth. Then the bushes closed around her, and the ground underfoot was suddenly rougher. She realized that somehow she had lost the track. A breeze she hadn't noticed until now rustled through the trees. A hand grabbed her hair. Heart pounding, she jerked her head free, whirled. It was only a branch brushing her face. She forced her way through, hoping she was not going in circles. Then the trees thinned, she stepped onto a graveled path, and there, to the right, twenty feet away, was Kenyatta, bathed in light.

She walked to the statue and looked around. She checked her watch, found she was late, but not as late as she'd thought. It was still only seven minutes past the hour. Uncertainly, she stared around.

"Cat," a voice said softly.

"Stephen, where the hell are you?" she hissed back.

N'toya stepped into the light. "*Jambo,* Cat. How are you?"

"What's going on, Stephen? Why are we meeting here?"

Even in the light, it was hard to make out his features. His skin was black, he wore black. All she could really see was the outline of him and the glint of his eyes a couple of inches below the level of her own. He was as thin as he'd been when they were students.

"Come on," he said. "Let's walk while we talk." He took her arm.

"Stephen, are you in trouble of some kind?"

"What makes you say that?"

"Well, I've been skulking around the bushes for the last ten minutes, and that's not the usual way I go to meet a friend. Then you say you work for the ministry, but they say they don't know you. You were always a political animal, Stephen, and I know that opposition to the government is discouraged in Kenya. And I think your telephone could have been bugged and that's why you left for a public phone booth. I guess I'm putting two and two together."

"And coming up with the wrong number. Those clerks in the ministry couldn't find their mothers in their own kitchens. You said you needed help with something, Cat."

He was trying to put her off. "Okay, I'm sorry," she said. "You're right, it's none of my business. I want to talk to the men who investigated Joel's death. Can you arrange that for me?"

"Why do you want to do that?"

"Why are you surprised? Isn't it a normal sort of request from the family after an accident where someone is killed?"

"In Los Angeles, maybe. Anyway, when I read in the *Nairobi Times* that Joel had been killed, the first thing I did was find out who was investigating. The officers did a good job. It was a terrible accident, Cat, but really, unavoidable."

"Maybe. But think about it, Stephen. You and Joel spent enough time together in wild places. Would he be caught, as Jock Campbell said he was, unaware of what was going on around him? It's not possible."

"Well, it happened very fast. He just could not get out of the way when that herd started to move. That's what the police were told by the people who were there. The bureaucracy moves very slowly here, you'll just have to be patient like everyone else—"

Cat felt her anger rising. "I'm all out of patience," she said. "Now I want some answers. I want to see the police report."

"What you have to understand is that getting out written reports is not a top priority." He put up a hand to stop her protest.

"I know Joel's an American, but he's just one man. There are a lot of other matters that have to take precedence."

Cat stood still, forcing him to look at her. "I'm not talking about an unknown American. I'm talking about my brother. I'm talking about your friend, Joel Stanton. And I am going to get some answers. I'll turn Nairobi upside down if I have to. I'll start tomorrow at the Ministry of Justice. I'll go to police headquarters and demand they speak to me. I'll go to the newspapers. I'll go to the goddamn Parliament Building. Whatever it takes. I will make a lot of noise."

He looked away, then nodded. "I'm sorry. Of course, you're right. I'll try to find the men who investigated, but you will have to be patient. I'm sorry. They could be reassigned by now."

"Why would they have been reassigned?"

"I said I'd try. It will take time."

"How long?"

"Give me two or three weeks—"

"Stephen, I don't have two or three weeks. Listen. I don't know how things work here, but if you have to grease a few palms, do it. And I'll go to wherever they are." She struggled to see the expression on his face, but they were far from any light that came from Kenyatta's statue, and it was impossible. "And I want a copy of the police report. I was trying to get Jock Campbell to move on that before I left Los Angeles, but I think he's stonewalling."

Stephen gave an exclamation of disbelief. "No, no. Jock Campbell is beyond that kind of suspicion."

"You know him?"

"Well, I know of him. Everyone in East Africa knows Campbell Safaris."

"So I'm told. Anyway, can you get it?"

"Maybe. But I can tell you right now that if you haven't received it yet, it doesn't mean anything."

"I think it does. Joel wrote me a note that I received after he was dead," she said. "He sent some sketches and said he had a lot of film. When I got his cameras back, they were empty. You know Joel, he would have taken hundreds of pictures."

"What sort of sketches?"

Something in his tone made her wary. Why was he not mentioning the missing film, suggest it had been misplaced, the unexposed film stolen? That was the first explanation that had jumped to her own mind. Except, who would bother to remove exposed film from the cameras? It would be of no use to anyone.

"Wildlife, birds," she answered carefully. "You know the sort of thing Joel did."

"What did he say in the note?"

They had been walking as they talked, and Cat noted that Stephen kept them to the deepest shadow. A cool breeze riffled through her hair, and she caught a whiff of raw sewage drifting toward them.

"Just that he'd call me from Nairobi. But he didn't get back to Nairobi. Jock Campbell called to say Joel had been killed."

"I'm truly sorry, Cat. It's a terrible loss."

From the old Stephen, she would have welcomed the words of sympathy. She realized how much she had been longing to see him, to talk to someone who'd known Joel when they were both younger. Not carefree exactly, but for the first time in their lives, they'd at least begun to leave the shattered landscape of their childhood behind them.

As if that were ever possible. The thought wriggled beneath her defenses.

Cat glanced at the man beside her. "Yes," she said in response to his sympathetic words. Her throat was tight, and she had to struggle to give voice to the words. "It is."

She could see the lights from the hotel through the trees. They had come full circle. The breeze had died, the air was still and warmer, and the fragrance of plumeria had replaced the stink of sewage.

"As soon as I know something, I'll be in touch, Cat," Stephen said. "It might be a couple of weeks. You'll be staying around Nairobi?"

"That's the other thing I want to ask you. I still have to find that hotel site. It's a big job for us, we can't afford to lose it. I thought I'd use Campbell Safaris and retrace Joel's route, but I met with Dan Campbell and he refused to do the job. I need someone else. I thought you'd know of a reliable outfitter."

"Cat, this is not a good idea. Not for a woman—"

"Oh, come on, Stephen, I'm tired of this. Kenya is full of tourists, half of them women."

"On established tourist routes. And even they run into trouble with bandits. There are a lot of poachers, well armed, ruthless. Whole armies of them. In the remote areas you're talking about, you would not be safe, Cat."

"Well, safe or not, I have to do this job. People are relying on me. And I'm going to follow Joel's route. Anyway, do you know of a good outfit?"

"Not offhand. I'll ask around and call you."

Disappointment was a pain in her heart. She realized she'd been hoping for more from him. Time together catching up on the past ten years. Maybe a chance to meet his family. She didn't even know if he was married, or whether he had children.

"Stephen, let's meet again soon," she said impulsively. "Somewhere we could sit and talk."

"Sounds like a good plan." He squeezed her hand, dropped a light kiss on her cheek. "Good night, Cat."

The old Stephen she would have trusted. But this shadowy figure was not the old Stephen. Cat stared after him, but he had already blended into the night.

Five

Dan Campbell turned out the desk light, plunging the room into darkness. A shoe scraped the brick edge of the path. He was not expecting visitors, and whoever was out there did not want to be heard. He picked up the hunting knife he kept on his desk—a surer kill than a gun, more silent. Through the shuttered window of the office, he could see the main house sixty feet away shrouded in trees, and closer, the outline of a figure only slightly darker than the night.

Without conscious thought, he took in the intruder's size and height, judged the point of entry for the knife. On silent feet, he crossed to the door, waiting for something to tell him the position of the intruder. A breath of sound—a foot placed carelessly, a pebble dislodged—reached him.

He slammed open the door. With one motion he had the dark figure backed hard against his chest, left forearm across the throat, right hand pressing the knife to the sternum. A quick upward push, and he would be holding a corpse.

"Dan!" The voice was strangled. The man was careful not to move.

"Jesus!" Campbell relinquished his hold. "Don't you know better than to come creeping around here at night like that?" He was sweating. "You came bloody close to perdition."

Campbell closed the door, switched on an overhead light that threw the mounted heads crowding the walls into harsh focus. Animals, heads, horns, entire bodies of smaller creatures covered every available space, hung without much care, as if they'd been there so long no one noticed them anymore. Campbell tossed the knife back onto his desk.

"What are you doing here tonight?"

Stephen N'toya put a hand to his bruised throat. "Don't you ever relax?"

Without answering, Campbell went around the desk, opened the bottom drawer.

"Something's come up," N'toya said. "We need to talk face-to-face. I thought it wouldn't be wise to use the phone to call for an appointment."

"Sit down." Campbell took a bottle of scotch from the drawer. "Want a drink?"

N'toya massaged his throat. "Thanks." He sat in the visitor's chair across from Campbell's desk, took the glass Campbell handed to him. "I saw Cat Stanton tonight."

Campbell grunted. "She gets around. I saw her this morning."

"So she said. You turned her down."

"I told her to go home."

"She's not going to do that. What she is going to do is start asking a lot of questions. You are going to have to take her on this safari."

"The hell I am."

"Dan, listen. She's going to stir up an ants' nest if we allow her to poke around, looking for information about her brother's death. She doesn't believe that it was an accident."

"Stephen, I dealt with one Stanton, and that's enough for me. Anyway, I don't take women into the bush."

N'toya looked into his glass, swirled the liquid gently, raised the glass to his nose, inhaled the aroma of the single malt. He looked up. "That's an old story, *n'duga*—"

"And not your business."

"Until your past impacts our present—"

"Stephen, stop. Right there." Campbell's voice was soft but lethal. "You are now way out of bounds."

N'toya let a moment pass before saying, "She says she is going to hire an outfit and retrace Joel's route."

"Let her try. It's wild country. Give her a week and she'll be back in Nairobi eager to get on a plane to Beverly Hills."

"I don't think so. I know her. If she says she is going to do it, she will."

Campbell got to his feet, went to the window. Through the trees he could see the house, its occupants sleeping safely in their beds. "She can't know he died over the border."

"No, of course not. There's no way she could know that."

The house and the trees had vanished from Campbell's sight as another house, another time appeared in their stead. He could feel the trap closing. He was going to have to revisit a decision with roots almost two decades in the past.

Without turning, he said, "What's the news on that bastard Reitholder?"

"He's lying low, but the word's going to reach him that she's here. When it does, he'll go looking for her. You know what he'll do when he finds her."

Campbell did not reply. He knew only too well what Reitholder would do. He'd roast her men over a slow fire, and she'd die wishing that was all he'd done to her.

"And he'll leave her body for the scavengers," Stephen said. "She'll probably never be found."

"N'toya, that's enough." Campbell held himself very still. *Another house, another time.* "If you've said what you came to say, you know the way out."

"There is something else," N'toya said.

Campbell returned to his chair. He leaned back, propped his feet on the open drawer. His eyes never left N'toya's face. "I'm listening."

"I'm picking up word of a load of ivory going down to the coast," N'toya said. "I'm not yet sure when, or the route it will take, but it's by far the biggest load in years. And you will never guess who's behind it." He looked at Campbell expectantly, waiting for his reaction.

Campbell stared at him, then brought both feet to the floor and sat up. "General bloody Francis," he said slowly.

Stephen lifted his glass. "The very same. Is Tom here? He should hear this."

"Tom went home. We got back late this morning."

Stephen glanced at the bandage visible beneath Campbell's rolled-up shirtsleeve. "You lose any men?"

"Yes," Campbell said. He did not elaborate.

Stephen got up, wandered around the office, stopped in front of the head of a large kudu. He leaned forward to examine it. "Marxism being no longer the driving terrorist force it once was in Africa, funds from Francis's usual sources have completely dried up. Even the Cubans have retired from the field. General Francis needs a large infusion of cash to keep his organization from collapsing."

"So he's trading his ivory for what he can get."

"Our self-styled general still has fantasies of creating a Marxist paradise, but he needs cash. He's going for broke."

"What about the Afrikaner Broederhood?" Campbell asked.

"They've financed his poaching activities for years—they certainly won't be standing aside while he dumps ivory onto the Hong Kong market."

"No, they're not standing aside. Political destabilization is still their number-one priority, and they need large amounts of cash for that. They'll have to recover what they've spent for recruiting, training, directing the actual killing operations, to say nothing of the concealment of the tusks. They are going to demand a massive return on their investment."

"So that means Reitholder will be watching Francis on behalf of his masters in Johannesburg." Campbell gave a short grunt of unamused laughter. "Those bastards are going to go cross-eyed watching each other. Reitholder would sell his mother to a whorehouse for a fiver, but he won't dare cross the Broederhood." He thought for a moment. "If there's as much ivory being moved as you say there is, it will be well protected. This is going to be a risky operation." Campbell leaned back in his chair, his hands clasped, peaked forefingers to his chin. "Still, it's too good to pass up."

"Then you'll do it? You and your people will take the ivory in transit?"

Campbell nodded. "Just find out the route and the time. We'll do the rest."

"Good. That's settled, then. We take out Reitholder and Francis, inflict some damage on the Broederhood. And we get the ivory."

"I like the we, Stephen. You planning on joining us on this one?"

"Figure of speech. Anyway, that brings us back to Cat Stanton. She's threatening to crash around Nairobi with her questions. If she reaches the wrong ears, we could find ourselves caught in a very dangerous spotlight, *n'duga*. Campbell Safaris cannot afford that."

Campbell picked up the hunting knife, turned it around in his fingers without speaking.

Stephen went on. "Just get her out of Nairobi, keep her under your eye and get her the site she wants. Set her mind to rest about Joel's accident, and she's on her way home before all this starts." He waited for Campbell to reply. When he did not, he stood, replaced his glass on the table. "Well, I'll leave her to your conscience."

"She's in poor fucking company then."

"Good night, *n'duga*." Stephen crossed to the door. He opened it, then turned. "Oh, and give my love to Morag."

The door closed behind him. Campbell replenished his glass with the single malt, raised it in salute to the head of a lion that occupied the center of the wall opposite the desk.

"Poor fucking company, indeed," he said.

Six

Cat tucked the telephone against her shoulder and picked up a pen, doodling absently. "So if we do come to an arrangement, Mr. Ward, when could we leave?" she asked.

"Rather depends on you, Miss Stanton. Do you have all the documents required for travel close to the borders?" The voice of Brian Ward, Trackers, Ltd., was throaty.

Cat stopped her pen abruptly without finishing the span of tiny horns, the triangular body, the stick legs of a cartoon buffalo, part of the herd Cat had drawn without noticing what she was doing.

"No. I don't have anything like that."

"Didn't you make any arrangements at all before you left Los Angeles?"

Cat restrained a spurt of irritation. "Of course we made arrangements, Mr. Ward. They just haven't worked out."

"I understand, my dear. Heard what happened, don't y'know. Well, least said, soonest mended, as the old saying goes." He laughed, a short barking sound. "Just the same, you must have the proper documentation. That's sensitive country, all those borders. Doesn't do to tangle with the border chappies. Touchy blighters, some of them. Hold us up for ransom as soon as look at us. Now, if you'd let me show you a few nice spots with good road access, I think we'd find something to suit you."

"We've been over all this, Mr. Ward. Easy access is precisely what I am *not* looking for. As I say, I already know the route I want to take. I guess I'll just have to get the paperwork that's already been done."

She was beginning to regret her decision to go ahead with the appointment she had made with him on the phone yesterday, but it seemed prudent in case Stephen did not come through. After last night, she was not certain that he would.

"Well, you could get them signed over, I suppose," Ward said.

"Signed over to me, you mean?"

"No, no. To me. I would be in charge. Brian Ward, Trackers Ltd."

"Yes, I've made a note of the name," Cat said. He'd mentioned it several times. "I'll see what I can do, Mr. Ward."

"You do that, my dear."

Before hanging up, they made an appointment for that afternoon at three—he was willing to forgo his siesta, Ward said with a laugh, and her heart sank. She was not at all sure that he was joking. But even if she didn't continue with Brian Ward, Trackers, Ltd., she would need whatever documents Dan Campbell had. She found his business card and dialed the number. He answered at the first ring.

"Campbell."

"Cat Stanton, Mr. Campbell. I understand I will need the paperwork you have. I'd appreciate it if you would make whatever changes are necessary and send everything over to me at the hotel."

"Good morning, Miss Stanton. Have you signed another outfit for your safari?"

"Not yet, but I'm talking to some people. I just need that paperwork."

"I can't get away just now, but you have my address—"

"Just send the file over by messenger."

"We need to talk, Miss Stanton. You have my address. It's only ten minutes by cab." He hung up.

Astounded, Cat looked at the phone in her hand. She considered the idea of sending a messenger to the address on the card to pick up the documents, then dismissed it. He wanted to talk. Good. He could talk about Joel.

The cabdriver stopped on what could have been a country road. Grass verges instead of sidewalks, the ground littered by fallen leaves. Ten minutes from downtown Nairobi, as Campbell had said, and a different world. Houses set back and glimpsed through thickets of shrubbery, the still air filled with the scent of the blue gum trees lining the road and the song of unfamiliar birds.

Cat asked the female cabbie to wait—to her surprise a good number of the cabdrivers in Nairobi were women—and after a friendly negotiation, an agreement about the fare was reached. The woman brought out a battered magazine and settled down to wait.

The driveway was a luminous green tunnel of flame trees. A small silver car blocked access to the back of the house. The building itself was a low rambling structure surrounded by a deep veranda with rattan chairs and glass-topped tables, fringes of crimson bougainvillea drifting from the roof.

Cat mounted the steps, crossed the veranda to the carved front doors. She looked for a doorbell, but found only geckos clinging to the walls, raising and lowering themselves on tiny legs, reptilian athletes doing push-ups.

"Hello," she called. Her voice faded in the stillness.

One of the doors was ajar. She pushed it open, called again with the same result, then stepped inside. The entry was large, with a dark, polished wooden floor, but it was filled with sunlight. A corridor to the left was lined with French doors into a garden and seemed to run the depth of the house. Cat hesitated, then crossed the hall to a wide arched doorway on the right.

The room could have been in an English country house. Sofas piled with pillows in front of a fireplace filled with unlit logs. Chintz-covered armchairs, old oriental carpets.

She called again. "Anyone home?"

Only silence greeted her. A vibrant silence, as if someone had just left and the room was waiting. Feeling like an intruder into another woman's life, Cat crossed the room to examine the silver-framed photographs on top of a closed grand piano. Sepia-toned pictures of men in uniform, many with large sweeping mustaches, veterans of colonial wars the United States had probably never even heard about. Young women of earlier generations, alone and with children, black and white alike dressed in shorts and not much else, squinting against the sun and grinning as they clung to the women's skirts.

Then the sound of voices shattered the silence—a woman's voice first, raised in anger, then Campbell's deeper tone, overpowering it.

Cat put down the silver frame she had in her hand, crossed the room quickly, hoping to get out before she was discovered.

A door slammed, the sound of heels drummed on the bare wooden floor. A woman emerged from the corridor. Sunlight caught silvery-blond hair, golden skin. Maybe in repose she would be lovely, but her face was twisted with rage.

"Morag!" A door bounced against a wall and Campbell's voice was a roar from the back of the house. "Don't you run out on me."

"I hope you die," she screamed back.

Cat hovered, frozen in the doorway, caught between the living room and the front door. The young woman stormed across the entry, grabbed a bag on the hall stand as she passed, disappeared through the front door and slammed it behind her. From the end of the garden corridor, glass rattled in a French door as it, too, was hurled closed. The sound of an engine revving too high invaded the house, then faded rapidly as the car raced down the driveway.

An uneasy silence descended.

Uncertainly, Cat waited for a moment, then crept toward the front door.

A soft female voice behind her said, *"Jambo, memsahib."*

Cat turned to find a stout African woman watching her. Her hair was cut close to a round head, revealing small delicate ears. She wore a dazzling green and orange dress, and was barefoot.

"I'm sorry, I didn't mean to intrude," Cat said. "No one heard my knock. The door was open."

Unsmiling black eyes regarded her and Cat felt like an insect pinned to a board for scientific study. "I'm Cat Stanton," she said. "I think Mr. Campbell is expecting me."

"You come, please. Bwana Dan is in the office."

The woman led the way along the corridor, opened a French door, its glass still intact. "Through the trees." She pointed to a long, single-story building that appeared to be built of the same handmade red bricks used for the main house.

The brick path, blue with fallen jacaranda blossoms, wound through trees under which flourished the carefully planned disorder of a traditional English garden, a riot of delphinium and daylilies and veronica. The scent of roses and lavender mingled with the smell of the blue gums outside.

Cat was not sure what she had expected, but this civilized establishment was definitely not it.

The office door was open, and Campbell rose to his feet and came from behind his desk, his hand outstretched in greeting. He was not smiling.

"Jambo," he said. "No trouble getting here, I see."

"Good morning." Cat shook his hand briefly. He looked less worn than he had yesterday and was clean and combed, dressed in fresh khakis. But his was not an easy face. Straight heavy eyebrows, long narrow eyes, dark blue, with a fan of lines at the corners showing white against brown weathered skin. His hair was threaded liberally with silver. There was a grim, forbidding set to his mouth and jaw, but that was not surprising. He'd just been faced with a meltdown. A woman with guts, whoever she was, Cat thought. This was not a man who would take kindly to being crossed.

Cat looked around. One wall was covered in photographs, the rest were crowded with trophies of the hunt. She expected the whole place to reek of death, but the shutters to the garden were open, and the office smelled surprisingly fresh.

"Doesn't it make you uncomfortable to work with all the creatures you've killed staring at you?"

Campbell closed the door. "Not a bit. Should it?"

Cat walked over to read the small plate below the head of a black-maned lion, muzzle wrinkled in a snarl, ferocious even in death. "'December 23, 1899. Tsavo Station,'" she read aloud. "'Dan Campbell.'" She looked at the man watching her. "Not one of yours, obviously."

"No. That chap's a victim of my great-grandfather. Gave the old man no sport at all, you'll be glad to know." He studied the lion. "Bloody lazy hunter, not worth a moment of your enlightened sympathy. Acquired a taste for human meat, killed and ate forty men building the Tsavo railway before the old man was brought in to bag him."

"You don't need to be defensive, Mr. Campbell. I am not accusing you of anything. Anyway—" she could not resist the dig
"—I haven't come here to discuss the decimation of Africa's wildlife. I just need the documents you have."

"Sit down." He pushed a chair toward her. "Have some coffee."
He went to the door, opened it, yelled in a language Cat thought
was Swahili. The sound of a female voice answering in the same language floated across the garden. "Mary clings to the old ways," he
said in explanation. "She won't use the intercom." He gestured impatiently to the chair he'd placed for her. "Sit down, for God's sake."

Reluctantly, Cat did as he asked and he resumed his own seat
in an ancient swivel chair behind his desk. He leaned back, peaked
fingers pressed to his chin, and stared at her. "I hear you're talking to Brian Ward."

"How did you hear that?"

"This is a small town, Miss Stanton. Have you engaged him?"

"Not yet."

Mary shouldered open the door and Campbell rose to take the
tray from her. He murmured a few words in Swahili and placed
the tray on his desk.

"Safari simply means journey in Swahili, did you know that?"
he said. "Interesting language, Swahili. Arab slavers brought it
down the coast and along the old slaving routes. Sugar?"

"One, please."

The cups were English bone china, the teaspoons sterling with
the lovely patina that only age and use and care give to silver. She
took the cup he handed her and shook her head at the plate of
homemade cookies.

"Mr. Campbell, I'd like to talk to you about my brother."

"I've nothing to add to what's already been said. I was hired for
this job because I know the bush, and my best advice to you now

is to return to Los Angeles. Send a male colleague and I promise you I will do all I can to get a good professional—"

She interrupted. "That's not going to happen." She leaned forward, placed her cup on his desk. "You seem to think you're the only game in town. But you're not. If I have to, I'll get Land Rovers and hire a crew myself. And I'll leave Nairobi as soon as that is done. I'll follow the route Joel worked out with you. Borders or no borders. Papers or no papers."

"You think you can follow that route?"

"Why not?"

"Fools rush in." Grim-faced, Campbell picked up a folder from his desk. "All right."

Cat reached into her bag, tossed a pen onto the table. "Sign the papers over to me personally.

"I mean, I'll take you myself."

She stared at him, startled. She wanted to tell him she didn't need his help, she could do it alone, but she left the words unspoken. *There was no Joel anymore to stand steady when she needed it. No one to bail her out.* "Thank you. Why the change of heart?"

He shrugged. "It's a job."

"Did Stephen N'toya call you?"

"N'toya? I don't recognize the name. Why would he call me?"

"He's a friend, and I just wondered if he might have called to ask you to change your mind."

He shook his head. "I don't change my mind because someone asks nicely, Miss Stanton. Right, then. Let's talk about the conditions of this offer."

"What does that mean, conditions?"

"It means that out in the bush, you will do exactly as you are told. Whether you understand or not, I want you to do as you are told, by me or my men, without argument or hesitation."

"Are you serious?"

"I never joke about life and death. I won't have you endangering the men's lives, or my life come to that, because you can't handle yourself in difficult situations."

Cat looked at him. "You're not talking about me. You're talking about Joel—"

"I'm telling you we travel hard and Pax Britannica is a thing of the past. We'll be getting into harsh country. Remember that."

"What happened to my brother?"

"We've been over this. Jesus." He threw the pen onto the desk. "This is going to be a bloody hard slog. I cannot keep on about your brother—"

"Then answer my questions."

"For God's sake." Campbell's chair protested as he got abruptly to his feet. It rolled back, crashed into bookshelves behind the desk. Two large volumes fell to the floor. "He was killed. No one could have prevented it. No one."

"Isn't that why you were there? To protect him?"

"I was there to show him some pretty spectacular country and help him find a site for a bloody hotel."

"You say yourself you're an expert. Your job was to see that he could do his job safely, that he didn't get into trouble, even if he was rash. But you didn't. You didn't protect him."

"Why the hell do you insist on knowing the details? What good will it do you?"

Cat stared at him without answering.

"All right," he said. "It happened about sunset. We suddenly ran into a herd of buffalo, and they're testy buggers at best. The herd was spread out and bloody nervous. Something was obviously wrong. It was early in the season but calves had already been dropped, and lions were about."

Campbell had moved and was standing in front of the Tsavo lion as if to draw attention to its fangs, the size of the enormous head. Cat could hardly breathe. Whether it was true or whether Campbell was completely self-serving, this was the first eye witness account of what had happened.

Campbell went on. "There's no way to get around them and we were driving slowly so's not to spook them. But then we came across a group of cows starting to calve." He stopped. Then he said harshly, "Your brother got out of the Land Rover. In spite of being warned, he grabbed his camera and he jumped out. We couldn't shout to warn him for fear of starting a stampede. He got too close, that bloody camera clicking away. The herd was restless, and something—lions or the camera, who the hell knows what—something set them off. A couple of the big bulls charged, then everything was moving at once. We couldn't reach him, and he couldn't get out of the way. That's about all. I'm sorry."

"Why didn't you stop him?"

"You mean, why didn't I tie him down?"

"No, I don't mean tie him down." Suddenly she was damp with sweat and cold, her nerve endings rippling. Joel had too much experience in wild places. He would never have taken such a chance. Something was not right here. "What happened to the film?" she asked.

"The film? The bloody film? Who the hell do you think cares about film at a time like that?"

"Afterward you could have thought about it. His cameras were returned empty, and all the exposed film is missing."

"The cameras were turned over to the authorities with the rest of his gear. I spend about ninety percent of my time in the bush, so I'm not up to date on the details. I have no idea what the bloody bureaucrats did with the film."

"Obviously someone tampered with his cameras."

Campbell shook his head impatiently. "Do I look as if I need to pilfer a client's bloody cameras? What more can I tell you?"

Cat stared at him. "You didn't like my brother, did you?"

"No, I didn't. And the feeling was mutual."

Cat nodded. "Let me ask you something. Why are you doing this? Helping us get a site for a hotel, I mean. I don't see you as a man who'd appreciate luxury hotels being built in remote areas."

"Kenya needs hard currency. Tourism brings it in."

"But you'd prefer to keep Kenya the way it is."

"No. I'd like to have kept it the way it was." He bent to pick up the two large books that had fallen. Cat caught the titles. *Hunting Big Game in East Africa,* by John Giles Bingham. *Memoirs of a Hunting Man,* by Lord James Percheron. Old books, written when the white man was supreme in Africa. "So," Campbell said over his shoulder, "what's it going to be?"

"What do you mean?"

"I mean, if you are not capable of following orders, let's not waste each other's time."

"Okay, I'll try to remember to jump when you shout. *Bwana.*"

Campbell shook his head. "Christ, I need my brain tested."

"I want to go first to Mount Elgon—"

"Not this time of year. We'll go west toward the Mara—"

"We have to follow Joel's route exactly."

"Why is that so important?"

"Part of the design work has already been done and accepted by the clients." Cat said. Not true, but he'd never know that. "To fulfill that initial concept I have to see what Joel saw. Experience the same things. It's absolutely essential."

Skepticism writ large on his face, Campbell said, "That sounds to me like a load of artistic codswallop."

"Really. So you're an expert on art and architecture as well as a great hunter? Well, a lot of time and money has already been spent on this work. I need to follow that route."

He regarded her for a moment. "All right. Mount Elgon. We can't linger, we're getting into the rainy season. Eventually we'll have to cross part of the Mara, and it can turn into a bog overnight."

He got up, thumped once on the wall with his fist. A single thump came in answer. A moment later, the door opened, and the man who entered seemed to fill the doorway. As tall as Campbell, six-two, she'd guess, as broad, with skin black enough to have a blue cast to it. Long eyes set in a square, high-cheekboned face. Wide flaring nostrils, well-curved prominent lips. He looked aristocratic, aware of his blood.

"My partner, Tom M'Bala," Campbell said. "Our client, Tom. Miss Cat Stanton."

M'Bala turned his head sharply. Not quite a classic double take, Cat thought, but close. The look on his face was more than puzzled. He looked stunned.

"Yes, well, you'll get used to the idea," Campbell said.

M'Bala recovered quickly. He took the hand Cat held out, bent over it. The old-fashioned gesture sat easily on him.

"*Karibu.* Welcome to Kenya." His English was fluent, but clearly not his mother tongue.

"Thank you. I'm glad you've decided to make an exception in my case."

He looked at her carefully as if uncertain of her meaning.

"I'm told Campbell Safaris never take women into the bush," Cat said blandly.

"Ah," M'Bala said. He glanced at Campbell.

"She was about to engage Brian Ward. Or get a crew together and follow Stanton's route alone."

Tom answered in Swahili. The two men exchanged a few sentences, then Tom turned to Cat. "I'm sorry about your brother. He was a good man."

"Yes. He was. Thanks."

"Have another cup of coffee," Campbell said. "I need a few minutes with Tom." The two men left, closing the door behind them.

Cup in hand, Cat turned to examine the photographs. Through the open window she heard the men talking, but not in English. The voices faded. A door closed. Cat studied the pictures, her eyes sliding over them until her attention was caught by a group of recent snapshots stuck in the frames of the older, sepia-toned prints.

Morag, laughing and holding the neck of a large bay horse, her windswept hair tangled with the animal's mane. No wonder he's captivated, Cat thought. She felt her own thirty-third birthday pressing closer.

"Those are very old pictures." Campbell was at her side. He had entered with the soundless tread of an animal. "A record of the hunting skills of several generations of Campbells and M'Balas."

All of the framed photographs were of trophies of the gun. Groups of men, black and white, grinned triumphantly into the camera as they stood over dead bodies. Elephants, lions, buffalo, rhino. Antelope too numerous to count.

"I see the way the guns are held," Cat said. "Interesting."

Campbell leaned forward to see what she meant. Then he grunted. In every photograph, the guns were braced against knee or hip, rampantly upright. "You think that's significant?"

Cat shrugged, picked up her bag. "Am I going to meet your father?"

"Unlikely. He runs a farm upcountry."

"I'd like to thank him for the arrangements he made for Joel."

"I'll tell him."

"While you're about it, ask him what progress he's made getting the police report."

"Right."

Campbell walked with her to the cab, talking about their departure. He insisted on leaving the following morning, and she hesitated before agreeing. It would afford no time for her to pursue the questions about Joel's death here in Nairobi, but she could do that when she returned.

They passed a pair of double doors that had been closed earlier. She glanced into the room, a comfortable masculine retreat of leather couches, an armory of hunting rifles in glass-fronted cabinets. Zebra skins scattered on the dark polished wooden floors.

A large portrait of Morag hung over the fireplace, a snow-capped mountain in the distance behind her.

When she got back to the hotel it was lunchtime, and she had missed a call from Stephen. He'd left a message.

"Everything in motion. Take a few days."

She called him right away, but there was no reply.

She'd have to wait until he called again.

Before she left, she would make her daily call to her office in Los Angeles. But suddenly it seemed important that someone in Nairobi should know that tomorrow at dawn she would be leaving the city with Campbell Safaris. She picked up her bag, left the hotel.

Seven

Father Gaston's church was Gothic, steepled, and looked as if it would be more at home under the soft sky of an English village than baking in the heat of an African sun. With the noisy crowded slum pushing against its fence, the church reminded Cat of a rather grand lady who found herself in reduced circumstances, but was still holding her chin—and her skirts—high, trying against all odds to keep up appearances.

Cat knelt beside a grave in the shadow of an unfamiliar African tree. The graveyard seemed filled with small graves; so many children had died before reaching their first birthday. She pushed back the tangled growth of weeds concealing a headstone.

"'Henrietta Gilmour,'" she read. "'Born April 18, 1915. Died January 9, 1916. An English rose faded on foreign soil.'"

The British had paid a heavy price for Empire, she thought. A weight in her chest welled into tears, and she took several deep breaths, knowing the grief was not for Henrietta, dead these seventy years.

Joel should not be in that impersonal necropolis in Los Angeles, she thought, crisscrossed with roads, filled with the activities of urban death. But nor would he rest in a quiet graveyard like this. He should be in the wilderness somewhere, his ashes strewn where he would feel the most peace. She sat back on her heels, remembering. He was buried close to their mother's grave—he'd always adored her, made excuses for her. Something she had never been able to do, even after her mother's suicide. The hot African day faded, and she was back in that terrible bathroom in the house in Malibu, the blood filled bath, her mother's pale drained body. She heard a whimper and knew it was her own voice, and she wrestled her mind back to the present.

Cat bent forward, and with a shaky hand, swept another headstone free of overgrown weeds, leaned closer to read the inscription.

"Memsahib!"

Cat looked around. From across the graveyard, a tall, thin black man waved some sort of gardening tool. He shouted at her in Swahili.

Cat got to her feet. It was clear he was warning her.

"I'm sorry," she called. "I don't speak Swahili. I'm just looking at the inscriptions." She started toward him. "I really came to see Father Gaston. Is he here?"

As she got closer, the man stopped shouting, and Cat looked at him, puzzled. Something about him tugged at her memory, but she knew she was mistaken, she knew no one in Nairobi. He turned and ran across the graves, leaping over headstones, baggy khaki shorts flapping around skinny black legs. He disappeared behind the corner of the church.

"Wait," Cat called. She hurried after him, keeping to the path, but when she turned the same corner, he was gone, and Father Gaston was emerging from a long, single-story building on the far edge of an untidy garden. Carefully, he pulled the door closed behind him and came to meet her.

"Miss Stanton! What a pleasant surprise."

"Father Gaston. I should have called first, but I came on impulse. Just got into a cab and came over. I hope you don't mind."

The priest took her hand and held it in both of his.

"No, no. It is fortunate I am here today, not about my pastoral duties. Your presence gives me much pleasure. A chance to show you my little church."

"I'd like that. I was looking at your graveyard." She glanced over his shoulder. The windows of the room he'd just left were covered by shutters, but she sensed a dark shadow behind one. "I think I upset your gardener."

"Poor Isaac. When he realized you did not understand him, he came to get me. You had your hands in the undergrowth. Here we have to be very careful. There are many snakes. A quiet undisturbed churchyard is as close to heaven as a city-dwelling cobra is going to get."

Cat laughed with him at his little joke, allowed him to usher her toward a tree-lined path.

"Come," he said. "First we walk, then some tea. Yes?"

As they walked, Father Gaston pointed out several statues in the florid, weeping-angel style. He seemed rather proud of them, and she made appreciative noises, sure that Joel had been as tactful when he'd been given the same conducted tour.

"Your brother particularly liked this tiny corner," Father Gaston said.

He paused in front of a strikingly awful baby angel. Cat smothered a grin. She'd seen clients back down from Joel's imperious manner, his stubbornly held opinions. But there was never any reason to be concerned about his sensitivity. He would have been more gentle here.

The church itself was musty, smelling of old incense and the sadness of a glory long past. Dutifully she admired the baptismal font, rich with decoration that was vaguely Norman in character. The walls bore the same tablets and inscriptions she had seen in English churches, mostly commemorating men fallen on distant, long-forgotten battlefields. But it was the Christ figure behind the altar that dominated.

"That is stunning!" she said. No gentle Jesus, meek and mild. This huge figure was a black Christ, arms bulging with muscle. "Who is the artist?"

"A native carver. I don't know his name. I brought it with me from the Congo."

"How did you become pastor of a British church?" she asked. "You're a long way from France."

"No, no, I am not French. I was born in Bruges. In Belgium."

"Still a long way from home."

"A Jesuit has no home but the church. We are the shock troops of Christ." His voice rang through the silent church.

The militancy in his voice reduced her to silence. There seemed nothing to say.

Father Gaston smiled, ran a hand through his magnificent hair, then modified his voice. "Of course, we go where we are sent. Since most churches in Kenya were British, we do what we can for the few Catholics who are left and try to stem the tide of Islam." He led her back up the nave, opened the door to the outside, allowing sunlight to flood into the building. "Now, I think some tea would be welcome."

His small house was one-room deep, but half-a-dozen-rooms long, a design similar to Campbell's office. A deep veranda ran the length of the building, sheltering a few battered wicker chairs, a couple of tables piled with shabby magazines, one that bore a loaded tea tray.

Father Gaston busied himself with the teapot.

"So, how are you enjoying your stay in Nairobi?" He glanced up, frowning. "Ah, stupid of me. This is a sad time for you, of course. Better to ask what you are doing with your days here." He handed her a cup. "Have you found out anything more about your brother's last days, his sad death?"

"No, and I'm leaving tomorrow, so I won't have time to pursue it until I get back. I was hoping you could tell me something about Campbell Safaris. I am leaving with them tomorrow. Do you know them?"

"By reputation only."

"He seems a hard man, Dan Campbell."

"Yes, I have heard that. A famous hunter, as was his father before him. Jock Campbell."

"It was Jock Campbell who made the arrangements about Joel. Sending him home, you know..." Her voice trailed.

"Ah. The Campbells have been a power in Kenya for a very long time," Father Gaston said. "From the early days, a hundred years ago."

"This must have been a paradise then."

"For the Campbells, yes, most certainly. They fought at the head of their own troops in the Boer War, two world wars. They brought men in from their holdings upcountry, joined them up in the King's African Rifles on condition they be kept together under Campbell command. Remarkable even then. Of course, nothing like that could be done now. Those days are over."

"I imagine they are."

"Yes. And at one time they were famous for their racehorses. Sent their bloodstock all over the world. Then they lost everything." Father Gaston flung up his hands as if tossing treasure to the wind. An odd, almost joyful gesture. "Rinderpest. They lost everything. Many of the old colonial families did."

"What is that, rinderpest?" Cat asked.

"Cattle plague. Highly contagious. But the Campbells have managed quite a financial recovery. Astonishing when you consider the political climate in this country." He fumbled in a pocket of his cassock, produced a pack of Gauloise cigarettes and a lighter. He selected a cigarette and lit it. "I hope you don't mind. A small indulgence."

"One that will kill you, Father."

"One way or another, something will. I would like to know the secret of the Campbells' success. Perhaps I could use it to repair the fortunes of my poor church." He laughed as if to show he wasn't serious. "Of course, the Campbells' power will never be what it was. That time has gone."

She wanted to ask about Dan Campbell personally, find out about his young wife, but couldn't bring herself to ask a Catholic priest to engage in idle gossip. And she sensed that she was about to outstay her welcome. She gathered her bag.

"You've been very kind. I've enjoyed my tea, but I mustn't keep you any longer."

Father Gaston rose to his feet without protest. "If I can help you with inquiries about your brother's death, please, you must call upon me."

"Thank you. I met a friend last night, and he believes that it was an accident. I wish I could agree with him."

"A friend? I thought you knew no one here."

"An old college friend of Joel's and mine."

"And who is he, this friend?"

"A lawyer in the Ministry of Justice." As she said it, she wondered suddenly. Joel had said nothing was as it seemed. Maybe he meant Stephen N'toya, too. "Anyway, he said he can put me in touch with the policemen who investigated. At least then I can get a police report."

Father Gaston walked with her to the gate. On the other side were the teeming streets of a shantytown. She was reluctant to leave the peace of the small churchyard and Henrietta, the tiny English rose sacrificed to Empire. She took a last look around, noticed the gardener under a tree on the far side and waved to him, but he melted back into the shadow without response.

Again, he tugged at her memory. Someone at home, she thought. It had to be. She knew no one except Stephen in Nairobi.

Before turning in, she called Stephen again. There was no reply. By now, she was not surprised.

Eight

Awake long before dawn, Cat was ready, her bag packed and in the lobby by daybreak, determined to start out on the right foot, to give no opportunity for patronizing remarks about women in the bush. She sat in the poolside restaurant that was just gearing up for the morning rush, leafing idly through the *East African Times*. Few people were about, and she looked up, surprised at the throaty voice booming her name across the terrace. A hugely overweight figure was making his way purposefully toward her.

"*Jambo, memsahib,*" he called.

"Good morning." She put down her coffee cup, returned the smile of the red-faced man looking down at her. "I'm sorry, I seem to have drawn a blank."

"Brian Ward, Trackers, Ltd." He placed a business card on the table in front of her, then thrust out a large hand. Cat found her own hand lost in its moist, cushiony folds. "Wanted to meet you before you go off." He pulled out a chair, looked inquiringly at her. "May I?"

"Please." In shock, Cat folded her newspaper and moved her coffee cup aside. Even in the cool of early morning he looked ripe for a heart attack. Out in the bush, this man would be a catastrophe waiting to happen. She'd had a lucky escape. "How did you know I'd be here?"

The chair creaked under his bulk as he sat. "Picked up the message from the old thorn tree." He raised his eyebrows, looked playfully mysterious, an odd expression on such a large red face.

"I don't think I'm following you."

"The thorn tree. Messages."

"A riddle," she said. "I give up."

"Thought everyone knew about Nairobi's famous thorn tree. Our little bit of local color, don't y'know." He gave two curious, guttural barks of laughter. "One of East Africa's traditions, left over from the days of the great white hunter of blessed memory. Used to leave messages for each other about game movements, where to trade their ivory, reports when anyone was killed. That sort of thing. Pinned to the thorn tree over at the New Stanley. The hotel, don't y'know."

Surreptitiously, Cat glanced at her watch. Not yet six, and already his safari jacket was damp with sweat.

"All that's gone, of course." He shrugged large, soft shoulders. "Tourists use it now. Train times." He assumed a squeaky soprano that he seemed to think sounded like a female voice. "'Jeremy, meet me in the museum at noon.' 'Amanda, let's lunch at the Norfolk.'" He resumed his own voice. "Seen better days, the old thorn tree."

As had Brian Ward, Trackers, Ltd., Cat guessed. She noticed he hadn't really said how he knew she'd be here. "I'm sure you didn't come out this early just to tell me about the thorn tree, Mr. Ward."

"No, no. Wanted to make sure you had this before you went off." He indicated his card. "And never pass up a chance to meet a pretty gel, don't y'know." He gave his two odd barks.

"Well. Thank you. Would you like some coffee?" They'd

brought two cups with the pot she'd had with breakfast. "Not too hot, I'm afraid."

"Thank you. No."

Barely able to twist his girth in the small chair, Ward turned to beckon the waiter. Cat averted her eyes from the flash of white belly discernible through gaping jacket buttons barely holding together under the strain.

"Fresh coffee. Right away," he said to the waiter. He turned back to her. "Speak better English than I do, these fellers, nowadays. Time was when only Swahili would do." He shook his head. "Times change, I suppose. Got to change with them. They say it's a good thing, but I don't know. They don't seem any happier now than they were when we ran the show. At least things got done then, and done right, by God."

The waiter placed a large white cup in front of him, filled it with coffee, smiled as he placed the pot of coffee on the table. "You order now, *bwana?*"

Ward waved him away. "I'll take the buffet, later." He spooned sugar into his coffee, followed it with a liberal amount of cream, gulped eagerly, then leaned back. "Aah. New man. Well, now, Miss Stanton, so you're off this morning."

"Yes, I'm waiting for Campbell Safaris now. I'm sorry our plans didn't work out. Perhaps next time."

"Yes. Campbell called me yesterday, professional courtesy and all that. Guessed you'd be off very early. Must say, Miss Stanton, bit surprised you decided to go off into the bush with a man like that."

Cat was taken aback. "A man like what?"

"Unpredictable chap, Campbell. Tough, though. Give him that." Ward opened the napkin wrapped around the basket of warm rolls brought with Cat's breakfast of juice and poached egg on dry toast, squeezing each one with fat fingers. "Cold." He reached for her unused knife. "D'you mind?"

Cat shook her head, and he tore a roll apart, slathering butter onto each piece before popping it into his mouth.

"You don't seem to like Dan Campbell," she prodded. She'd be willing to bet what she couldn't bring herself to pry from Father Gaston would be food and drink to Brian Ward.

"Wouldn't say that. Not at all. Tough as nails. But just you watch yourself, m'dear. Word to the wise." He looked around, then tapped a forefinger greasy with butter against his nose. "Word to the wise."

"What do you mean?"

Looking virtuous, Ward held up a hand. "I'll say no more. Just be warned."

"You can't say something like that then just drop it."

"Campbell's got a reputation, m'dear. That's all." He slid his eyes significantly toward a group of black businessmen waiting to be seated. "He's close to the right people. You know what I mean." Spite lingered in his voice.

"I'm not sure that I do."

"Oh, knows what palms to grease, among other things." Ward held up a hand again. "Enough said. Hate to gossip, don't y'know." He reached over and patted her hand. "Tragic business, the young man who was killed. Knew he was a relation of yours immediately when you said your name. To be killed like that..."

He seemed to be repeating the word, rolling the word around in his mouth. Killed. Killed. Cat looked into tiny, stupid eyes sunk in layers of fat.

"What do you know about his death?"

"Caused quite a to-do here in Nairobi, you can imagine," Ward said. "Bad for the safari business, I can tell you, that kind of thing. Frightens off paying customers."

"What did you hear, Mr. Ward? What were the rumors?"

"Well, of course, they said it was buffalo." He smirked.

Cat stared at him. Her heart lurched in uneven beats. "Is that what you mean by greasing palms? Did you hear that Campbell paid someone to cover up something about Joel's death?"

Ward seemed suddenly alarmed. "Now I didn't say that, m'dear. Not at all. No way to prove..." He stumbled over his words. "I'm just saying that might be why Campbell's taking you out—"

"That isn't what you said."

"I'm saying he feels he owes it to you. He never works with women, don't y'know. Not since that old business years ago—"

"Old business, Ward?" a voice said softly. "What old business would that be?"

Cat turned. With his noiseless tread, Campbell had entered the terrace from another door and stood behind her. Both hands grasped the back of her chair. She could feel the hostility radiating from him.

"Just telling Miss Stanton here how competent you are, Campbell, don't y'know. Filling her in, you might say." Malice sparkled from Ward's small blue eyes. He stood, drew himself up to his full height. Cat could see the effort he made to pull in his stomach. He glanced at the buffet where waiters clattered with chafing dishes. "Ah, my pancakes. Been waiting for them. Excellent, excellent. You'll join me for breakfast, Campbell?"

"No, thanks," Campbell said. "Ready to push off, Miss Stanton?"

"Yes, my luggage is in the lobby."

"Right." He picked up the soft leather jacket hung over the back of her chair, held it while she slipped it on.

Brian Ward leaned forward, picked up the business card still on the table and handed it to her. "Tuck this away," he said. "You never know, you might decide you need it one day." He patted her hand, nodded to Campbell and turned away.

Cat watched his retreating figure waddling off to the buffet table and again sent up thanks. She felt the stillness behind her and turned to look at Campbell over her shoulder.

His eyes were fixed on Ward's back, and the muscles in his face seemed to have flattened, smoothing all expression. He caught her glance and bent to pick up her kidskin carryall. Without comment, he led the way through the empty tables.

Nine

The mud had been cleaned off, but the Land Rover looked exactly like the one she'd seen intimidating traffic in the square the day before. A winch was mounted on the reinforced front bumper, and behind the driver's seat was a gun rack loaded with weapons. Large gas cans were built into the back, and she guessed it was also fitted with an auxiliary tank.

Tom M'Bala, standing beside an identical vehicle, waved a greeting. "Good morning, Miss Stanton."

"Good morning, Tom. Is it okay if we go to first names?"

Tom smiled. "Good morning, Cat."

She glanced at Campbell, but he did not look up from stowing her two bags among the gear in the back of M'Bala's Land Rover.

"You'll travel with Tom," he said curtly when he'd finished. "I'll be ahead of you. When you get tired, Tom will let me know and we'll stop."

"Don't worry about me," Cat said. "I can keep up."

"Don't try to prove anything. This is your first day. We can stop when you need to."

"I won't need any concessions, thanks."

"Oh, for God's sake, relax." Campbell put a hand under her elbow and almost tossed her into the passenger seat.

Without comment, Tom M'Bala slid behind the wheel, turned on the ignition, and her irritation melted into a thrill of excitement. The country was unknown, the future uncertain, but whatever happened during the next couple of weeks, she was committed.

They left Nairobi on the main road to Uganda. The heavy traffic seemed to be mostly gasoline tankers and enormous trucks loaded with Tusker beer. Small, open-sided vehicles overflowing with brightly dressed men and women recklessly opened up space for themselves, slipping in and out like tropical fish between whales.

Cat craned to read the names painted in brilliant colors in both English and Swahili on the sides of the little vehicles.

"'Prince of Darkness'," she read aloud. "'Heaven's Helper,' 'Gateway to Paradise.'" She turned to Tom. "'Gateway to Paradise'?"

He laughed. "They're called *matatus*, they're a sort of rogue bus service. They've got a deadly accident rate."

Cat laughed, turned to watch the passing scene. The landscape became increasingly African as Nairobi was left behind them. Tiny villages encircled by thornbrush stockades, small round huts thatched with straw. Children tending goats and skinny cattle ambled along by the side of the road.

And the women. More and more, the heavily laden women.

Cat caught her breath. "My God!" Ahead, Campbell had just swerved to avoid three women, babies bound to their chests with bright cloth, loads of firewood on their backs. "Where are the men? Women shouldn't be carrying stuff like that. They must be worn-out before they're thirty."

"Men don't carry firewood."

"Why not?"

"It is not in our tradition."Tom's face was tight, lips pressed together, nostrils flared. "These women do not consider themselves exploited. They cling to the old ways as much as the men."

"Really? Did anyone ask them?"

He was silent, eyes fixed on the road. Cat closed her mouth. She expected him to be an American, and he wasn't. She had to remember she was the stranger here.

The Land Rovers emerged from a belt of thin forest, and the road hugged the edge of an escarpment.

"The Great Rift Valley,"Tom said.

Cat stared in awe. A checkerboard of sparse cultivation merged into a distance dappled by soft patches of green forest. A changing pattern of light and shade faded to a nebulous rim of purple lining the horizon.

"I never dreamed it would be so beautiful."

"The Great Rift splits Africa from the Dead Sea to the Indian Ocean. It's two thousand feet deep, thirty miles to that far rim." Tom changed to a lower gear, slowing their pace to give her time to appreciate what she saw. Campbell was lost to sight ahead of them. "The first true humans were African. Before you leave Kenya, you should pay the museum in Nairobi a visit. They've got a number of skulls recovered from the Rift."The grade of the road flattened, he accelerated and they swept down the escarpment. "The oldest, Lucy, is from Olduvai in Tanzania. Females, apparently, last longest, in spite of their burdens."

Cat caught his sidelong glance and grinned. "Well, their bones did."

By noon, Cat felt she had been battered for a lifetime from traveling in a Land Rover that seemed to hit every pothole in Kenya.

For the twentieth time in the last half hour she changed her position in an effort to ease a bruised spine. Then ahead, Campbell's directional signal blinked and he took a sharp turn onto an unmarked track no different from countless others they had passed. Reluctantly she relinquished the fantasy of the Kenyan equivalent of Denny's and Howard Johnson. The Land Rover jolted and swayed for another hour before they ground over a rise. And suddenly, aching muscles were forgotten.

Rolling grassland, dotted with wide, flat-topped trees, stretched toward an unrestricted horizon. A small group of giraffe rocked in a strange undulous canter, heads eighteen feet above splayed hooves, and in every direction was the constant motion of browsing herds of antelope and zebra.

Cat held on to her seat with both hands, braced herself against the jolting Land Rover and turned to Tom, smiling.

"A fraction of what it used to be," he said. "Even in my time."

She nodded. But nothing she had seen or read or imagined had prepared her for the impact of these wild herds grazing on golden grass under a sky that stretched into infinity. Carl Jung's words when he visited Africa in the twenties came into her mind: "The stillness of the eternal beginning." Too much had changed, was still changing, but the words held true. Maybe Joel was right. Maybe the more people could experience what was left, the more they would be willing to pay whatever it took to help preserve it.

Lunch was a brief stop in the shade of a thorn tree. Tom handed her a can of Tusker's—the ubiquitous local beer that filled the trucks on the highway they'd left behind—and a sandwich. Both men were alert, leaning against the Land Rovers while they ate, binoculars to their eyes, quartering the surrounding country.

"What are you looking for?" she asked.

"Anything that moves," Campbell answered.

She rummaged in her bag, produced the binoculars she had brought with her. She focused until the antelope were close enough for her to see the large limpid eyes, the rough patches on what had appeared to be smooth bodies. Only animals were out there. Nothing else that she could see.

Within half an hour they were back in the Land Rovers, leaving behind them nothing but a few scraps of bread. And those were probably gone, Cat thought, before the engines had turned over. African ants were at least half an inch long and looked capable of eating the Land Rovers.

As they pushed northwest, the track petered out, the grassland became drier. Dust swirled in clouds around them. In the lead, Campbell drove without hesitation—across dried streambeds, around rock outcroppings, through scrubby forests of thorn. Tom answered her endless questions. The smallest gazelle, the dik-dik, was the size of a spaniel, lived in woodland and mated for life. The largest, the eland, weighed a ton and roamed the open plains. Richly striped kudu, without doubt, were the most beautiful. Zebra did not bray like a donkey, but barked like a dog.

As the hours passed, she lapsed into silence. By four, the glory of the massed herds no longer held her as rapt as it had earlier. Tom asked if she wanted to rest. Cat shook her head.

"You are going to feel this in every muscle tonight," Tom said. "I should have brought you a nice fat pillow."

Beyond words, Cat had to force herself to smile.

By five-thirty, she knew there was no way she could go on. The breeze lifted her lank, grit-laden hair. Dust itched in the pores of her skin, caked uncomfortably in the sweat. Concession or not, she was going to have to call a halt. She clenched her teeth. She worked out at the gym four times a week, ran three miles every morning. She was in great shape. She could stand anything thrown her way.

"Here we are," Tom said.

She wanted to cry with relief. Campbell was inching between tumbles of rock; a shallow cleft in the land flattened, and they stopped in a grove of thorn trees. The ground was littered with pods bursting with seeds the color and shape of kidney beans. Zebra ambled unhurriedly from their path. Birds swept low over a stream not too far distant. The heat had gone out of the day, the air smelled cool and green.

For a moment, she allowed herself to sit in the Land Rover, feeling the peace, before seeking terra firma with one tentative foot. Holding on to the door, she pulled herself erect.

The two men were already working, a practiced team, unloading the vehicles.

"I'll start a fire for cooking, if you show me how," she called. "I'm not much at woodcraft."

"You'd better have a drink before you attempt anything more than standing up," Campbell said. "You've had a hard day." He produced a bottle of scotch and a stack of plastic glasses, took water from the cooler, placed everything on the camp table already set up. "I know I could do with one. Tom?"

"Parched," Tom said.

"I'll pour," Cat said.

Campbell glanced at her. "Good."

He went back to his Land Rover. Cat mixed three drinks, took Tom's over to him on legs that felt like india rubber, then picked up Campbell's drink and started toward him. He had lifted a long green canvas bag from behind his seat, unzipping it as he turned. A polished stock, telescopic sight.

Her father had had a gun like that. Exactly like that.

Campbell took the drink from her hand. She looked at him, knew he was speaking to her. When would it end? she thought. It was all so long ago, but it would never end. *Not for Joel, not for her.*

"What?" she said. His voice was fuzzy.

"I said you'll be able to get cleaned up pretty soon," Campbell repeated. He zipped the case, replaced the gun behind his seat. "Listen."

A distant hum she'd heard only as background became the murmur of an engine, increasing in volume. Then a Land Rover bumped through the stand of rock. Back wheels skidded on dry grass, skewing the vehicle before it came to a lurching stop beside the other two.

"Who is it?" Cat said. Whoever they were, they were lousy drivers.

"The Maasai," Campbell said. "They're joining us."

Cat looked at the Land Rover with a surge of anticipation at her first sight of the legendary warriors of East Africa who still carry shields and spears and ignore the twentieth century. Nomads who live with their cattle, and drink blood tapped from their living veins.

Three men, each closer to seven feet tall than six, their hair braided in cornrows, climbed from the Land Rover. A fourth man, not short except in comparison, more squarely built, his hair cut close, followed. All wore khaki bush pants and shirts in military style, well-worn and travel-stained. No traditional red cloaks. No spears or shields. Just another gun rack loaded with automatic weapons. And a Land Rover loaded mostly with gas cans.

A sudden stab of misgiving caught her. She was miles from civilization with heavily armed men she didn't know or trust. And now they'd been joined by yet more armed toughs.

Campbell greeted his men in a language that was not Swahili, spoke again in answer to what sounded like a question from one of them.

Cat watched the exchange, the eyes that swiveled her way as

Campbell spoke, the heads that remained motionless, their concentration on Campbell's words. Their limbs long and slender, the Maasai towered over him.

"This is Moses," Campbell said. "Olentwalla. Sambeke." He indicated the shorter man. "And this is Thomas."

"Hi." She smiled at Thomas. His answering grin revealed extensive gray metal dental work outlining square white teeth. "Moses. Olentwalla. Sambeke." She shook each long-boned hand in turn, and they nodded without speaking. Dark, almond-shaped eyes flickered slightly. As much surprise as they would show, she'd guess. They had not expected to find a woman here. Certainly not someone called Stanton.

Tom called to them, and the men turned away.

"What language was that you used to them?" she asked Campbell. "Not Swahili." She could already recognize the cadence of that language—like a dark torrent tumbling over rock.

"Maa," Campbell replied. "The word *Maasai* means 'speaker of Maa.'"

"They are very impressive."

"They are warriors. The Maasai believe they own all the cattle in the world by command of Engai—God—and they still raid to gather them in. They also raid for the sheer hell of it. These days it causes them no end of trouble."

"Thomas isn't Maasai, surely."

"Kikuyu. Maasai are proud buggers, won't do camp chores. Thomas is as tough as they come, but he'll also turn his hand to anything."

She looked over Campbell's shoulder at the armory of weapons racked in the Land Rovers. "So what is the function of heavily armed Maasai warriors on this little expedition? If they don't do camp chores?"

Campbell looked at her with what seemed grudging respect. "Well, you don't miss much, I see. I should have said *most* camp chores. They make themselves useful."

"Doing what?"

"Heavy work," he said. He looked over to where the men huddled in conversation with Tom. "I'll get Thomas to bring up some water for a bath for you."

"Will he also bring water for you and Tom?"

"No. We scrub off in the river."

The sun had turned the stream into a ribbon of gold. "Is it safe?"

"The river? Safe enough. But for a woman straight from Beverly Hills—"

"Being from Beverly Hills is not a physical handicap," she said. "If it's safe enough for you, I'll use the river, too."

"The sun will be gone in about forty-five minutes."

"I won't be that long. Where's my bag?"

Campbell considered her for a moment. Then he drained the last of his drink. "I'll take you down." He glanced at her face. "Don't worry, you'll never know I'm there. Your gear's in your tent."

Cat approached the one small tent that was already in place. Inside, the light was a dim, cool green, the air rich with the smell of dust and crushed grass. A white mosquito net twisted into a large knot hung from the roof pole over a narrow camp bed, and a small table and canvas chair had been set up.

Cat pulled Joel's old terry-cloth robe from her bag. She held it to her face for a long moment, imagining his warm, comforting smell.

Careful not to shake loose the red dust gathered from the day's travel, she stepped out of her clothes, slipped into the robe, stuffed the pockets with shampoo and soap, then found her sandals and picked up the dark brown towel laid across her bed.

Rifle in hand, Campbell led the way upstream. A bend in the

river quickly hid the camp from view, and for the next five minutes they exchanged few words, mostly terse warnings from Campbell about rocks underfoot, thorn-covered branches reaching out. Had it been Tom ahead of her, she would have been full of questions about plants and birds and wildlife. Campbell had an uncanny ability to wrap himself in a solitude difficult to penetrate.

He stopped before a wedge of rock that sloped down into the water.

"There's a decent-size pool on that far side. You should have it to yourself, it's not deep enough for hippo."

Hippo? "Oh. Thanks."

Campbell sat on his heels by the side of the stream, scooped a handful of water over his face. He looked up at her.

"Better get to it. The sun'll be going soon."

"Yes. Okay, I will." She hesitated. "Should I watch for crocodiles—" she gave a small shrug "—or anything?"

He laughed. "No. But if you do see anything that moves, give a shout. I'll be over before you draw another breath."

Suddenly her insistence on bathing in the wild seemed stupid. She cast around for a reason to change her mind, but it would mean backing down, admitting she was frightened. She couldn't do it.

She clambered over the boulders, Campbell disappeared from view, and she was alone. Hurriedly she dropped Joel's robe onto a bush, turned to step into the water and felt the pressure of watching eyes. She looked up sharply. On the far bank, strange creatures stared back at her. Long sad faces decorated by straggly beards. Heavy in the shoulders, almost frail in the hindquarters. Their horns were curved and menacing.

Cat shivered in sudden terror. The shutter in her mind opened onto Bony Ranch in the hills above Malibu.

* * *

Longhorns pouring down the hillside, bawling and tossing their heads, Ed Mueller and two other horsemen behind them. Cat could hear them yipping, whistling.

Their father wheeled his big chestnut gelding. "Come on, kids." *He was whooping and laughing.* "Let's help bring them in."

She clutched her pony's mane, looked at Joel's white face. Her father leaned over, grabbed her reins—he already had Joel's. He urged his chestnut into the oncoming herd, dragging them both with him. Cattle pressed against her pony. She closed her eyes, shutting out the horns that were going to stab into her, make her bleed, sure she was going to fall under their feet and make her daddy mad at her.

She clung to Buttercup's mane, trying not to cry. The steers made so much noise, they smelled, and the dust choked in her throat. It went on and on; she felt so small, so frightened. Then the noise was gone, the steers were gone, and Ed Mueller was lifting her down. The saddle was wet, her pants soaked. She'd peed in her pants like a baby. Their father laughed, and her chest was jerking with sobs she tried not to let out. She looked at Joel for comfort. But he was crying, and her breath wouldn't keep still in her chest. She couldn't breathe, then she couldn't stop it anymore, and she started to sob, too, choking with fear.

Their father's face was red as he shouted, "Stop it. Stop that noise. I hate that sniveling."

"Chrissake, Deke," *Ed Mueller said,* "Give it a rest, they're only kids."

"They're my kids," *he shouted.* "They're my kids, and she's ruining them. Their mother's ruining them, making them as weak as she is." *He spurred the chestnut, beating him with his whip, jerking back on the bit to force the big horse to rear and dance, squealing in fear, the saliva dripping from his damaged mouth turning red with blood. Shouting, their father looked down at them.* "I'll teach you some guts. Every week you'll work this cattle. You'll learn."

Ed Mueller had protested, but their father had a large interest in the ranch, so he got his way with Joel. He told Joel nothing could be expected of girls, anyway. But she'd had to watch, and if she cried, her father yelled, "Catherine. Every time you snivel, your brother does another fifteen minutes. You're both going to learn something from this."

That summer they were five, she and Joel had thrown up all the time, and they'd both started to wet the bed. But every weekend, Joel was on his pony among the longhorns, and she was there, holding his hand on the car ride to and from the ranch.

They learned a lot that summer. Not to cry. Never to trust anyone but each other. And they both learned how to hate their father.

Cat rubbed shampoo into her hair, massaging her scalp while she counted rapidly to twenty-five instead of the usual slow fifty, then plunged her head underwater. It was dumb, but she kept her fingers in her ears so that nothing could wriggle in. The guidebooks talked about bilharzia, parasitic worms that infested water and could lodge in the brain.

She pulled herself up onto the platform of rock, twisted a towel around her hair and slipped into her robe, then climbed back over the rock.

"What are they, the animals on the other side?"

Campbell was leaning against a small tree, studying the sky. His hair was damp, his shirt clung to him where he'd put it on over his wet body. "Wildebeest. They're also called gnu."

When she reached him, he pulled down a branch of the tree. "Kikuyu detergent." He crushed a few leaves between his fingers and held them out. She bent to smell a faint, pleasant pungency. "Mwethia tree. Kikuyu used it for soap." He brushed the leaves from his fingers. "Ready for dinner?"

"I am."

She followed him along the riverbank. The water was a deep rose in the western sun. An intermittent chorus of frogs was beginning to tune up. She was tired and hungry, but she'd met every challenge thrown at her, had asked for nothing. The water had gone a long way to restoring her sore muscles, and with any luck, she'd sleep, maybe tonight without the nightmare.

"What are we having for dinner, anyway?" she asked.

Then suddenly she found herself walking into him.

He was motionless. Reaching behind him, he pulled her tight against his back. The brush ahead was noisy; he did not have to tell her to be quiet. She hardly breathed. Slowly, Campbell brought up the rifle. She heard the click of the bolt and inched her head cautiously until she could see around him.

Thirty feet away, enormous black bodies moved slowly. Heads bearing a distinctive heavy bar of horn over the eyes swung low in their direction.

She sagged against Campbell's back.

Buffalo. The animals they said had killed Joel....

"Don't make a sudden move," Campbell said softly. "There's no danger, they're going down to drink."

The bovine stench stung her nostrils. Her nightmare punched into her mind...Joel falling, crushed beneath hooves, his blood spreading... That's what she dreamed... that's what she couldn't face.

Campbell reached to steady her. "They've gone. There was no danger—"

"You let him die...you let him die...where were you...?" Words staggered out of her mouth. "Why didn't you stop him...shoot them—" She was shaking.

Campbell kept his hands on her shoulders. "All right, all right."

He did not argue, or defend himself. Cat bit back the hot words she wanted to hurl at him. She tightened the belt on Joel's robe, took a breath, forcing herself into a shaky calm.

"Let's get back."

"Wait a minute. You're wound up tighter than a bloody watch spring—"

"Campbell, thank you, but I don't need any advice from you about the state of my nerves." She thrust her hands deep into her pockets among the tubes of shampoo and soap. "What I need from you is a hotel site I can use. That's all. Let me worry about the state of my nerves." Pain shot through her head, and she had to force herself not to put a hand to her eyes. "Now, please, let's go. I'm hungry."

He started to turn away, then turned back to face her. "You are just like your brother, you know that? You insist on making everything a bloody sight harder on yourself than it need be. Thomas would have brought water up for you, it's no problem, but no, you had to prove you can do it. Whatever 'it' is to you." He swung the rifle in a small arc. "You can't control any of this. This is my backyard, and I can't, either. But I know it and you just have to trust me."

"Like my brother did?"

Campbell opened his mouth, then closed it without speaking. He turned abruptly and led the way back to camp.

Ten

Smoke from Tom's cheroot scented the air, mingling with the smell of coffee and brandy and wood smoke. Two days had passed without incident. Each morning they left the men to break camp and did not see them again until evening.

They had stopped at several possible sites, a couple that were wonderful—a waterhole surrounded by waist-high golden grass, with banks churned into blood-red clay by countless hooves, the contrasting colors of sky, grass, water, mud, dazzlingly beautiful; a rocky promontory that gave limitless views over the grassland. Each different from the others, each spectacular. None of them matched Joel's sketches. She'd taken pictures, made notes and some thumb sketches of her own.

While she poked around with Tom as escort, Campbell quartered the countryside with his binoculars and kept radio contact with someone—the other Land Rover, she guessed, riding point somewhere out of sight.

Cat leaned back in her chair, staring at the millions of stars hanging just above her head. But the perfect peace was an illusion. Weapons were always within reach, leaning against camp chairs, and hunkered down around the kitchen fire she could see the three heavily armed Maasai.

"If we eat like this all the time, I'll have to be rolled onto the plane home," she said. "What was the name of that soup again?" A thick and unprepossessing brown, it was surprisingly tasty.

"Brown Windsor," Campbell answered. "Inflicted upon the defenseless every Sunday in every boarding school in the British Isles. Thomas was taught by missionaries, and for some reason known only to God and the British Baptist Society, that was part of his education."

Cat laughed. "Well, it's very good." She felt caught in a time warp. The table lit by a blazing fire, heavy, horn-handled silverware that looked a hundred years old, worth a fortune to an antique dealer, the four-course meal served impeccably by Thomas, his Uzi put aside for the occasion. Even the formidable Thomas found it difficult to juggle Brown Windsor soup and an Uzi.

"You said we'd be traveling hard. I hadn't expected such luxury. Do you always do this?"

"Not anymore," Tom said. "But we thought we'd give you a taste of what safari used to be."

A glass suspended from his fingers, Campbell leaned back, stretched his feet toward the fire. "My great-grandfather always dressed for dinner on safari," he said idly. "Took a hip bath with him and his evening clothes wherever he went."

"Yes, and my *baba* carried them," Tom said.

Campbell made an amused grimace. "Now, you know that's not true, Tom. Your great-grandfather was so bloody dignified, no one would dare suggest such a thing. He was the one bossing the other fellers who carried his gear, too."

Tom laughed and blew a series of perfect smoke rings. Firelight threw the high ridges of his cheekbones into sharp relief, gleamed on blue-black skin. Even lounging in his chair, he seemed poised to spring into action.

"I heard that in two world wars the Campbells raised their own companies, joined everyone in the King's African Rifles and marched them off to do or die for Empire," Cat said.

Campbell grunted a half laugh. "Good God! Who told you that?"

"I have my sources." A small breeze rustled through the branches of the thorn trees and the weaverbird nests swayed gently. A large night bird swept low on silent wings. "I even heard about the famed Campbell bloodstock. In demand in racing circles all over East Africa, I'm told. Very impressive."

"Who've you been talking to? Ward?"

"No. I had tea with a friend of Joel's. Father Gaston. He's a parish priest, been in Kenya for years. Do you know him?"

There was a beat of silence, then Campbell said, "I know him. Your brother never mentioned he was a friend."

"Didn't he? He's a nice man. Full of information about the Campbells."

"Mostly claptrap, no doubt. What more did he say?"

"Well, he would certainly like to know how you've managed to recoup your fortune. He'd like to do the same thing for his church."

Cat intercepted the glance that passed between the two men before Tom leaned forward, threw his cheroot into the fire. "I bet he does. Well, I have to check a few things with the men, so I'll say good-night." He picked up the Uzi leaning against his chair. "Sleep well, *memsahib.*"

Cat murmured a good-night and watched Tom walk to the kitchen fire and hunker down with the men. She could just see the outline of them beyond the smoke and flame, the gleam of fire, a glint of metal as firelight touched a weapon. Tom spoke at length, gesturing to either side of them, the men nodding as they listened. It was the nightly ritual. Then one of the Maasai, usually Moses or Sambeke, disappeared into the darkness.

"What else did the estimable Father Gaston have to say?" Campbell asked.

"Nothing much." A soft drumbeat reached her ears. "Who's the musician?"

"Olentwalla. It's a finger drum. Listen."

Another, deeper note twined around the rhythm. The tattoo progressed, weaving a complex pattern of sound, loud then soft. A gentle, high-pitched chorus of tree frogs was in counterpoint to the boom of bullfrogs in the marshy ground by the river. Overhead a sliver of moon hung against the glittering backdrop of stars.

"Tom's English is very good," Cat said. She spoke to fill the silence between them. "Not his native language, though."

"No. His mother's from the Cameroons. His first language was an obscure dialect. He's multilingual, several African languages, French, of course. Swahili, English."

"An educated man."

"Better scholar than I ever was. Graduated with honors from the University of Nairobi."

She almost asked him where he went to school but stopped herself in time. She was not interested in a friendly relationship with this man.

For a few moments, she listened to the night. The cry of a far-off bird and the closer rustle of dry grasses as the breeze shook them, or a small animal passed, the gurgle of the river, and the frogs. A series of yelps Tom had said earlier were made by spotted hyena. Laughter from the men. Beneath, she felt rather than heard the repetitive, insistent rhythm of the drum.

Campbell left his chair, stood with booted foot on a log bordering the fire and threw more wood onto the coals. Sparks exploded through a diaphanous silver veil of smoke, and shadows danced against the canvas walls of her tent. Beyond the ring of firelight, Cat could feel the pressure of a limitless Africa. She was alone out here. Out of touch with all she knew. And very conscious of how vulnerable she was, surrounded by armed men.

"I think I'll turn in," she said.

"I'll walk you home."

Totally unnecessary as far as she could see, but either he or Tom always walked her to her tent, a matter of half a dozen paces. And the fire was kept up all night, a watch always posted. Tonight it looked like Moses, a shadowy figure watching the darkness from the cover of the Land Rovers parked on the other side of the grove of trees. She started to ask Campbell what he was watching for, when coughing grunts cut her off. An answering roar seemed to come from only yards away. Hair on the back of her neck prickled. The sound faded into a rumbling growl.

Lions. And at least one seemed to be sharing their campsite.

"They're not as close as they sound," Campbell said. "There's nothing to worry about."

"I'm not worried, Campbell. I'm too busy trusting you. That's what you said I should do. Remember?"

"Well, I'm glad to hear it." He picked up the weapon leaning against his chair. "If you're ready?"

Cat sat bolt upright, staring around at her white-shrouded bed, a restless, dream-filled sleep shattered by voices. Men's voices, shouting. Gunshots galvanized her into action.

She scrambled from the cot, fighting with a mosquito net that fought back. She dropped to her knees, crawled beneath it. She ran to the door of the tent, fumbled with the zip fastener with fingers that would not work.

The voices were louder, and she heard the drum of hooves increasing. They were real, not part of her nightmare. The zipper door opened and she burst through, almost running over Thomas standing outside, a snub-nosed weapon held across his chest.

"What's going on? What's happening?"

Both fires were blazing, and in the flickering light she could see clearly. Buffalo were stampeding between the Land Rovers. Only Campbell and Tom, arms spread, prevented them from invading the camp. A fusillade of shots came from the direction of the river, and she could hear men's voices.

"Thomas, what's going on?" It sounded as if someone was deliberately driving buffalo into the camp.

Suddenly she was living her nightmare. All she could see was lowered heads, horns, huge black beasts dappled with firelight. Confusion and death. Campbell shouted, Tom answered, but she could not understand what they were saying. She screamed at them to speak English, but her voice was lost in the din of a volley of shots they fired over the heads of the rampaging animals.

Thomas shouted at her, and uncomprehending, she stared at him. He shoved her down and stood over her.

"What is it? Who's out there?"

Then Moses and Olentwalla appeared at the edge of the firelight, herding the buffalo away from the camp. The jostling animals melted into the darkness, the sound of their hooves faded.

It was over.

Thomas pulled a camp chair forward. "You sit, *memsahib.* I get you *chai.*"

She was shaking. "Yes. Just a minute." She went back inside the tent, groped for Joel's robe, pulled it on, then stepped outside into the night. Campbell stood there, waiting.

"Sorry for the disturbance," he said. He held his rifle loosely in one hand. "This sort of thing rarely happens, but you never know on safari—"

"Someone was out there."

"No. You simply never know—"

"I'm not a fool, Campbell. Animals don't stampede at night for no reason, and I heard the shots—"

"That was Moses and Olentwalla," Campbell said. "It was their shots you heard, trying to turn them."

She could see Tom and Sambeke prowling through the grove where the Land Rovers were parked. Thomas was bending over the kitchen fire. "Where are they now?"

"Making sure nothing more happens tonight."

"Campbell, I saw which direction the men came from, and it wasn't from the river. The shots came from the river—"

"I'll have Thomas bring you some tea." He cut her off, his voice curt. "Unless you'd like something stronger."

"Tea's fine. Thomas is already making it."

"Right. Well, stay here, please, until he brings it." He shouted to Thomas in Swahili.

"*N'dio,*" Thomas shouted back. He straightened, waving a teapot in one hand. In the other was an Uzi.

Campbell turned to leave. Cat watched him until he was beyond the ring of firelight. Buffalo, the animals that had killed Joel, had been deliberately stampeded into camp.

Why? And for whom were the Maasai trackers searching?

By eight the next morning they had broken camp and continued their drive toward the northwest and Mount Elgon. Tired—

sleep had been impossible for the rest of the night—Cat was willing to let the hours pass without much conversation. Tom had already made clear his reluctance to talk about what had happened. Cat did not insist. The last thing she wanted was to put him on his guard. Instead she watched the herds, already able to identify the curved horns of the Grant's gazelle and the black-striped sides of the much smaller Thomson's.

"Why are they jumping like that?" The little Tommies sprang into the air, bouncing forward on stiff legs like rubber balls thrown by an unseen giant hand. "It's a strange way of getting about."

"It's called stotting. Dan's made them nervous." Campbell was a cloud of red dust fifty feet ahead of them. "They do it when they're anxious." Tom waved toward the west. "Could be that, though. Lions will be hanging about."

In the distance, a solid line of black bodies moved purposefully.

"Wildebeest," Tom said. "About a million and a half go down every year to the Serengeti in Tanzania, following the grass. Back again July to September, after the big rains. One of the last great animal migrations left on earth."

Bracing herself with one arm against the dash, Cat watched through Tom's window. Red dust hung low over the herd, drifting toward the Land Rovers on a hot breeze that carried a harsh, acrid smell of animals. Flat-topped thorn trees dominated a landscape that was drier, more forbidding, than yesterday. She thought of Joel, dying under the crush of hooves. They'd never even said goodbye, she'd just dropped him off at LAX, rushing as usual to an appointment, concerned about the traffic piling up around the airport.

Ahead, Campbell's arm appeared out of his window, gesturing upward and to the north. Acknowledging with a wave, Tom leaned out to see where Campbell pointed. Cat followed his gaze. Birds hung in the sky, circling lazily on giant wings.

"Are they what I think they are?" she asked.

"Vultures," Tom said.

He wrenched the wheel, following Campbell across the savannah toward the circling birds.

"Tom, they must be circling a kill."

He didn't answer.

"Why do we have to detour to look at it?" These men had spent a lifetime slaughtering animals. One more kill could be of no interest to them.

"Well, it's on our way," Tom said.

"No, it's not. We've changed direction. Tom, I don't like this. It's gruesome, and we don't have the time. We have a lot of ground to cover today."

Tom slowed, following Campbell. Out of the haze of dust kicked up by the Land Rovers, large, immobile forms appeared. Six or seven—it was hard to count in the thick dust. Overhead, vultures circled.

Elephants.

A sick dread rose like bile in her throat. Campbell had stopped and was climbing out of his Land Rover. He reached behind his seat, wrenched a rifle from the gun rack. The elephants did not move.

"Cat, stay here." Tom got out, unracked a rifle.

The animals seemed in shock, heads low, trunks trailing on the ground. And they were small. None of them seemed fully grown. Even to her untutored eye there was a look about them that the young of any species had. The dust was settling. For the first time she saw blood trickling from the faces of two of the larger animals. Gunshot wounds.

Campbell walked slowly toward them. They turned, dispersing but giving no ground. As they parted, Cat saw an enormous prostrate body lying in a pool of dried blood. The trunk had been slashed, hacked from the body, and shreds of dirty white tissue hung into the ghastly wounds. Where the tusks should have been were gaping, bloody holes. A tiny elephant, no larger than a Saint Bernard dog, nuzzled at dry teats, squealing weakly as it butted a small head against its dead mother.

What felt like an iron fist closed over Cat's heart, squeezing tighter and tighter. She couldn't breathe. Sweat was icy on her skin.

She opened the door of the Land Rover, got out. The dazed animals did not look in her direction. Their eyes barely left the dead cow.

The skull beneath the wrinkled gray skin was prominent, cavities sunk deeply over the eyes and temples. Cat tried to keep her eyes away from the terrible mutilation. A sweet, sickening smell hit the back of her throat, and she gagged, then swallowed the rising bitterness.

For ivory. For carvings and jewelry and piano keys and mahjongg tiles and chess sets.

She turned to look at the vultures circling above the little party of stunned survivors. Three birds landed, waddled forward, wings outstretched. Squealing with anger, a half-grown elephant ran at them. The vultures flapped huge wings, keeping just out of range until the elephant lost interest in them, then they turned back toward the corpse.

"Campbell." Her voice was hoarse. She ran her tongue over her lips, tasting the grit of drying dust. "We've got to help somehow."

"Get back in the Land Rover."

"That baby needs milk—"

Campbell raised the rifle, slammed a clip into place. The sound cracked through the silence.

She realized what he was going to do. "Tom, don't let him. For God's sake, we can radio for help—"

"There's nothing to be done here, Cat," Tom said.

"We can give it water, then get it back to Nairobi. It's not that far, we can keep it alive—"

"Tom," Campbell said.

Tom took her arm. "Come."

"No. Wait. We can get it to Nairobi. I'll foot the bill if that's a problem—"

Tom placed himself in front of her. A shot crashed, echoed across the plain. The vultures rose into the air.

She wanted to kill him. Joel would have wrenched that rifle from his hands. Joel would have tried to kill him. *The shutters in her mind opened onto her father's face, the surprise as the bullet hit him.* She forced her mind away. She could not think of that, not now…not now…

Cat turned and walked to the Land Rover, opened the door, sat down, drew her legs inside, reached out, slammed the door. She couldn't look at Campbell, at the dead calf she knew was at his feet, at the shocked, pathetic herd.

Tom opened his door, replaced the rifle in the rack. She continued to study the map she had pulled out of the pocket on the door. The lines blurred, the colors ran together. The Land Rover swayed under Tom's weight as he slid behind the wheel.

"Cat—"

"Not now, Tom." Her skin was clammy, the edge of her vision seemed to be closing in. She felt as she had that day in Zuma Canyon. Her blood pressure must be dropping—that's what they'd said then.

Tom backed in a large arc to avoid the small, traumatized herd of elephants, then threw the gear forward.

Cat kept her eyes on the map, trying not to think of the animals fading into the dust behind them. The tiny calf lying dead beside its mutilated mother. The youngsters lost and leaderless.

Nothing she could do. Nothing she could do. The words became one with the grind of the engine.

Eleven

For two nightmarish days they followed a trail of death. They found no more survivors, just carcasses bloated in the sun. Entire herds wiped out, adolescents killed for tusks so small, Tom said they would be worth only a few dollars on the markets of Hong Kong. The animals looked as if they'd been blown apart by machine guns, the mutilations that had been inflicted on them feeding some terrible lust for killing.

Tom tried to reassure her about the youngsters they had left—they would be all right, they would soon leave to find water. Cat had read enough to know the words were meaningless. Young elephants have to be taught about waterholes, where they are, how to get to them. Like children, they have to learn survival skills. Their social structure is matriarchal, the dead female had been their leader. Now they were alone.

She had known the slaughter was happening, read the occasional newsmagazine story, hardly noticed among the enormous human catastrophes of Africa. But what she had seen—the mutilated bodies, the pathetic survivors—was, she knew, forever burned into her consciousness.

They skirted the bodies without stopping. Today they'd traveled hard, and the sun had long passed its zenith when Campbell called a halt for some food. Yesterday he had shown her another site, a perfunctory stop. She was certain now that a different agenda, not hers, was being followed. Campbell's contact with the men, if that was whom he spoke to, had increased. He stopped every hour now while Tom continued driving. Campbell caught up within a few minutes, so whomever he was talking to, the conversations were brief.

Cat looked over to where he stood by his Land Rover, radio mike in hand. His back was to her, but she wouldn't be able to hear, anyway. He always made sure of that.

"It is Reitholder," Campbell was saying. "I've got the men keeping close watch."

"Has he made any more attempts to kill her?" Stephen N'toya's reply crackled with static.

"It was a few buffalo, Stephen, not a serious attempt. He was just playing silly buggers, testing our strength. What have you heard about the ivory? Over."

"Nothing firm yet. Should know more within a few days. But trucks are being assembled, everything you can think of. They've got ivory coming out of Uganda, as well. It's the biggest thing for years. Worth every risk we have to take going after it."

Every risk he and his men had to take, Campbell thought. Not Stephen. "Why is he here, then, not watching Francis?"

"Ahmed's in the area—" Stephen N'toya's reply was faint.

"What about Ahmed? You're fading. Repeat. What about Ahmed?"

"Ahmed's in the area—" Static crackled.

Campbell swore.

"...the *askari* was probably bribed." Stephen's voice was suddenly clearer. "Reitholder is after those tusks."

"You mean the fucking guard has lost him? He doesn't know where Ahmed is?" Campbell contained his rising anger. "Does the old man know?"

"It doesn't matter—" The static had miraculously cleared. Stephen's answer was distinct.

"Does the old man know?" Campbell repeated.

"What does it matter?" Stephen's voice blasted from the mike. "Keep out of the way. Let it happen. Let Reitholder do what he has to. It'll keep him busy until we're ready."

"Jesus, you're a ruthless bastard, N'toya—"

"What's the matter with you? We're talking about one damn elephant—"

"No. We're not. We're talking about a national bloody treasure." Years ago Ahmed, with his fourteen-foot tusks, his immense size, his age in a culture that revered age, had been placed under the protection of the president of Kenya and was venerated for the wiliness that had enabled him to evade trophy hunters for all of his adult life.

"One more elephant, what difference does it make? Just keep your priorities straight."

Campbell thought rapidly. Ahmed was experienced, he'd know he was being hunted. But he was also getting old, slowing down. Weakened by old wounds, even he must be tired of carrying those great tusks. "My priorities are straight. I've done what I said I'd do. I've shown this woman four sites, enough for her to make a choice. I'm sending her back to Nairobi. Get a plane here today."

"You can't do that—"

"Don't tell me what I can't do, N'toya." Ahmed had avoided the best hunters in the world in his seventy years, including two generations of Campbells. He'd outsmarted Tom and Campbell more than once. "That old bull is not going to be taken down by a team of butchers like Reitholder and his men, blown apart with AKs, I can promise you that. I'd rather do it myself." One clean shot. A hunter's shot. The wily old devil deserved that.

"Are you mad? Let Reitholder do it. Don't go near him. We're too close. In a few days I'll know where that ivory's being moved—"

"Just get this bloody woman out of here. Today." He gave N'toya the coordinates. "I'll give you until sundown. Then I'm going to find Ahmed before Reitholder does. If a plane doesn't get here, I'll be forced to take her with me. Cheer up, Stephen. Fourteen-foot tusks. Sixty kilos each. Think of that. It'll make you feel better. Campbell out."

Twelve

Deiter Reitholder kept the glasses trained on the Land Rover. Campbell's Maasai had been out there for days, following, watching. He settled his back more firmly against the sun-warmed rock of the *kopje*. The *kaffirs* stayed well out of range, making no attempt to conceal themselves. No attempt, either, to attack. At night they peeled off, but every morning they picked up the trail again as easily as catching a bus in the middle of Johannesburg.

Reitholder turned the binoculars toward the southeast, sweeping them across the grassland. Campbell was there, somewhere, but with a woman on his hands. Good. That was good. By now Campbell would have heard about the bribed *askari*. That would bring him out. Reitholder laughed out loud. And that black bastard M'Bala would be frothing at the mouth.

The binoculars bounced against Reitholder's chest as he dropped from rock to rock, scattering the baboons whose home it was. He reached the small flat ledge to find his own *kaffirs* lounging in the shade, smoking and laughing. Just a brief stop to scan the countryside, and they'd lit fucking fires! But at least the bloody white men no longer shared fire and food with the Bantu. He'd finally prevailed on that issue. They'd been too damn friendly by far.

"What is this? A bloody rest camp?"

Bobby Watson shoved his bush hat farther back on his dark curly hair. "They're still out there, then? Have a cup of tea, mate. It'll settle your nerves a bit."

Reitholder looked up at the sun. "There's no time for goddamn tea."

"There's always time for a brew-up, mate." Watson lifted a blackened billycan, filled a tin mug with tea. "What's with you and this bloke Campbell? He's sent his abos to keep an eye on us because we're on his patch, that's all. If he was going to interfere, he'd have done it by now. We've taken enough ivory to keep us like white men for a couple of years. Let's get that ruddy tusker and get out of here." He grinned, showing perfect white teeth. "Like they say, enjoy our ill-gotten gains."

"That's a beautiful woman out there with Campbell." Reitholder tested the water. "Yours, if you like." He watched for the Australian's reaction. The twitch of a muscle. The tongue touching his lips. The bob of his throat. But the Australian just shook his head.

"Nah, mate. Not my style. She turned me down already, me and old Pete." He turned and shouted to Peter Stone, sitting in a patch of shade, his back against a tree, cleaning a rifle. "Tea's up, Peter. Butcher boy here's itching for the off, so you'd better get it quick."

Reitholder watched the two Australians drinking their everlasting tea, joking with each other. He'd picked them up in the casino in Nairobi, known what they were the minute he laid eyes on them. Hunting bums, owning nothing but well-kept weapons, living high when flushed with cash, sleeping bags in the rough when broke. But two extra guns, two white men to watch the *kaf-*

firs so that they couldn't kill him while he slept. He'd played next to them while they gambled, watched them lose heavily. He'd followed them to the bar, struck up a conversation. Hunting. Trophies. Gambling losses. They'd been easy to recruit. He'd held out the trophy elephant Ahmed as bait, mentioned a fortune in ivory and rhino horn if they could find some, for sure a load of skins as a bonus. There was always a market for the big cats, cheetah, leopard, lion. The more endangered the beast, the higher the price a good skin commanded.

They'd canceled their flights home the next morning.

They'd been squeamish with the first herd of elephant, bullshit about sport, wanting to leave the calves. Gone a bit quiet when they'd arrived at the hunting camp and smelled the stockpiled skins. But they came around when he reminded them about the cash they had coming. If they stayed alive, they had possibilities for the future, Reitholder thought.

Reitholder found his own patch of shade, well away from the *kaffirs,* and lowered himself to the ground. He took off his wide-brimmed panama, wiped the band with a bandanna, dabbed gently at his face. Goddamn skin was peeling again, sweat running into the open cracks. He hadn't been able to shave for days now. He was going to end up like his father—a good, tough Boer, a farmer who loved his country, who never shirked his duty and taught his sons the same. He had seen his father beat more than one of his thieving *kaffirs* to death with his *sjambok* and never lose a night's sleep over it.

Reitholder tried not to think of him, tall and beefy as he was himself, healthy as a horse except for the cancer eating through skin like his own, thin pale skin never meant for the sun of southern Africa, the light blue eyes so reddened they looked filled with blood. The same eyes he saw every morning in his own shaving mirror.

He called out to the two white men. "Tell me about the Stanton woman." He hadn't known they had met her until after he'd had the *kaffirs* stampede the buffalo to test Campbell's strength. He stayed alive by being cautious, so he'd left the Australians in camp—not sure they were in deep enough to ensure their silence. He'd hoped for a chance to kill the Stanton woman that night, and they certainly weren't ready yet for that kind of work. But every day, they slipped a little deeper, and soon they'd be in too deep to get out. Then they could be useful to the Broederhood. "Tell me exactly what she said."

"Christ, don't you ever let up? We've told you half a dozen times. Nothing. She said bloody nothing," Stone said. He dumped powdered milk into a chipped white enamel mug filled with strong black tea, stirred it with a twig. "I stood next to her at the desk. She wanted a ruddy list. I tried to get it for her. I asked her to have a drink. She said thanks, you're a smashing pair of blokes but I'm busy. Me and Bobby went to the bar. Then we went to the casino and lost our ruddy shirts." He laughed, swigged the tea, rubbed a grubby sleeve across his mouth. "Then we met you and got a chance to recoup our fortunes. And now we're going to get this national treasure and a picture standing on top of him to show our mates back in Adelaide. That's it."

Reitholder had had to promise them that. A photograph to prove they'd killed the famous Ahmed, who had been hunted by the best in the world and survived. He shook his head. The pleasure of trophy hunting eluded him. He'd never understood it. The conquest of enormous beasts, bellowing as they faced your guns, their power seeping away as they went down. The scream of the herd as they took the bullets, the smell of hot blood. That he could understand.

"She said nothing about her brother?"

"Christ, mate! Will you listen to yourself? Nothing about her bloody brother. She said, thanks, I'm busy, good night." Stone tossed the dregs of tea from his mug. "Come on, Bobby. Let's get these buggers on their feet. We can earn a few more dollars before nightfall."

Reitholder watched the two Australians join the *kaffirs* squatting on their heels twenty feet away. The usual scum, dregs from the armies of a dozen African wars, he'd been forced to recruit without knowing their backgrounds. His own devils—not one he'd trust, but at least devils he knew—had scattered halfway across Tanzania after Stanton's death, fearing the Americans would insist on a manhunt. But they hadn't, of course. These days, the Americans were too eager to be the friend of every black bastard in Africa. They had no fucking balls anymore.

So the sooner the Stanton woman went to join her brother, the safer they'd all be. And Campbell and his black brothers with her.

While the two Australians chivied the men into action, joking with them, checking rifles, dousing the fires with earth, Reitholder reviewed his last meeting with General Francis.

The plane had brought Francis close to the base of the hills, close enough to the hunting camp, but the man had had to climb the rest of the way under his own steam, grimly determined as usual to check the amount of ivory personally. Reitholder grinned at the memory: Francis, dressed in combat fatigues, black scarf covering his face—as if that could hide his identity—puffing and struggling his way up the hillside to the hunting camp.

As soon as he'd posted his two bodyguards, Francis had loosened the black scarf, pacing slowly along the rows of tusks, counting. He'd stopped, hefted one of the tusks. "Twenty kilos, maybe. They're smaller than the last lot."

"Four months' hard work, General. Not many mature beasts left now," Reitholder said impatiently. But he intended to make up the shortfall. Trophy tusks from the famous Ahmed would bring a premium. He didn't mention that plan to Francis. The general would just carp about the uproar there'd be if a bloody national treasure fell to poachers. Reitholder hadn't got the patience to listen. "You just need to make sure you got enough trucks laid on to move this stuff down to the coast."

"That is being done. My own men will be with them—"

"Working under my orders."

"Working with you, Colonel Reitholder. Under my orders. How much more ivory do you expect to add before we move it?"

Reitholder grunted. "I don't know. The beasts are wary. We have to search for herds now, and Campbell and his fucking Maasai have been following me for days."

"He shouldn't be a problem, surely. He has the Stanton woman with him."

"Yes, I've seen her. That's good. There will never be a better time, General, to put an end to them. Campbell, that black brother of his and the woman." He clapped Francis on the shoulder. "A clean sweep, my friend."

Francis looked at him in alarm. "We must move the ivory first, Colonel. Nothing must endanger that."

"Don't worry. The woman makes them vulnerable."

A small breeze brought the stench of the skins toward them more strongly, and Reitholder smothered a grin as Francis put his scarf to his nose.

"But now is not the time for that, Colonel," Francis insisted. "We must concentrate on getting the ivory to the coast. Nothing more."

Reitholder was losing patience. It was Campbell he wanted, and M'Bala. The woman was a bonus. "The woman is dangerous, man. You said so yourself."

"In Nairobi, yes, asking questions. But what damage can she do here in the bush with her questions? What will Campbell tell her? The truth?" General Francis shook his head. "No. Let them be."

"And when she goes back to Nairobi, asking the same bloody questions again, what then, eh?"

"In Nairobi, we have friends. She'll be taken care of. A car accident—"

"I'll feel safer if I take care of this myself. Campbell and the woman and that *kaffir* of his, M'Bala. And the fucking Maasai." He glanced at Francis. "Maybe I'll give the woman to my *kaffirs* to play with." Inwardly, he grinned at Francis's impassive face. The bastard had seen enough of that kind of thing in the wars in Africa, but only with blacks. The young girls were the best. They fought hardest. The women were passive, seen it all before, those that had survived. Reitholder toyed with the images conjured up, itching to stroke the engorgement in his loins. His breath quickened. He caught Francis's knowing eyes and laughed. "On second thought, I'll share her with my Australians."

He told Francis about the two young men. For the sake of security, he'd sent the Australians out to track a small herd of elephant before General Francis arrived. "They're good. They'll do what they're told. White men. Extra guns. No, my friend. Trust me. Now is the time to finish Campbell."

"I will not be able to control an investigation if Campbell and this woman die—"

"Ach, man. With all those black palms greased?" Reitholder lifted one hand, rubbed two fingers against his thumb. "Just remind some of your tame Bantu what they owe us. Talk to that minister you own. I'll make sure there are no survivors. No one to tell a tale. No bodies. No cock-up this time. How long before you have all our ivory in Kenya gathered together, then on its way to Hong Kong? A week?

Ten days? The end of a good two years' work, eh?" He clapped Francis on the shoulder again. "You worry too much, man."

"Colonel, this is against my advice—"

Reitholder allowed the smile to leave his face. "Then I think you should reconsider your advice." He laid his arm across Francis's shoulder, forced him to pace along the edge of the plateau, away from the stink of the drying racks. "A word from me to Johannesburg and your funds dry up. Who will finance your People's Party for the Liberation of Kenya then? Provide the arms and training for your men? The Russians are finished, *ja*? The Cubans don't have a pot to piss in. Maybe a few crumpled marks from the Red Brigade? The Shining Path? But you're a long way from Peru." He laughed. "No, you need us. We have the same goals."

For twenty years, Marxist and Afrikaner had found themselves fishing in the same troubled waters, destabilizing the same shaky governments. Mozambique, Angola, the front-line states. Now the traitorous government of South Africa was selling out to world fucking pressure and the *kaffirs* were going to run the country—into the ground like they had everywhere else in Africa. Only the Broederhood was stronger than ever, men flooding to the banner, ready to do whatever they had to, use whoever they needed, to restore the homeland when the call came.

"Well, Colonel, you know your business as I know mine," Francis said. "Be sure you leave no trace. I'll do what I can in Nairobi."

Reitholder had squeezed the shoulder under his hand. "I knew you'd see it my way, General," he said.

Thirteen

Campbell filled Tom in quickly, running through what N'toya had just told him. He did not mention the bribed *askari*—Tom would get that point without him having to drive it home. Besides which, Campbell did not want to add to Tom's anguish over what had happened to his brother. It was bad enough that Cat Stanton's presence kept the whole episode raw.

"I told him we'll take Ahmed down ourselves. The old devil deserves better than Reitholder's butchery. We'll put his ivory with the rest."

"We'll never be able to disguise fourteen-foot tusks," Tom said. "If we're found with them—"

"We won't be."

"What about——?" Tom nodded toward Cat sitting in a canvas camp chair in the shade of a thorn tree.

"N'toya's sending a plane." Head back and eyes closed, she looked young and strangely tender, bare throat vulnerable. Campbell looked away. "Tell her to get her gear together."

Tom blew the air from his cheeks. "And while I'm doing that, *n'duga,* what will you be doing?"

"I'm going to have to go to the *engang,*" Campbell said. The Maasai village was close by but they had intended to avoid it—with Reitholder in the area, a visit from them could put the people there at risk. But N'toya's news had changed all that. "They'll know exactly where Ahmed is. And they'll be able to save us some time tracking Reitholder. He's moving fast."

"You tell her to get her gear together. I'll go to the *engang.*"

"Tom, just tell her."

"What? What shall I tell her?"

Campbell climbed behind the wheel of his Land Rover. "I don't know. Tell her something that will shut her up." He grinned. "Tell her we're tired of all this civilized pussy-footing and we're going hunting." He wheeled the Land Rover and roared toward the distant hills.

For the last few minutes, Cat had been watching them through half-closed eyes, wondering about the glances in her direction, the sudden air of purpose, the very apparent lifting of their spirits. As the breeze changed direction, it brought her snatches of their conversation, nothing that made sense, but Campbell's last comments were clear.

They were going hunting. Her heart jumped against her rib cage. Hunting had been banned in Kenya since 1977.

A flutter of panic stirred in her belly. That's how the Campbells had recouped their fortune, she thought. That's why Campbell and Tom had been so tense when she'd mentioned Father Gaston's comments. They were poachers.

She felt rigid, too frightened to open her eyes in case they realized she had overheard what they'd said. Was this what happened to Joel? Had he been killed trying to prevent it? He wouldn't have hesitated to use a weapon against them.

Campbell's Land Rover was a rapidly receding speck on the grassland. Without thinking, Cat ran to Tom's vehicle. The keys were in the ignition, as she knew they would be. She climbed into the driver's seat, turned the key. The big engine came to life, she slammed into first, gunned the engine. She leaned on the horn, the alien shriek spooking zebra and antelope into a mad gallop.

Campbell's vehicle stopped, the dust around it slowly started to settle. Cat pushed her foot down, the wind bucketing noisily against the Land Rover.

Campbell wheeled, raced back to meet her. He drew alongside. "What's up?" he shouted.

"You are not going to do this." She yelled the first thing that came into her mind. "Not on time bought and paid for by my clients."

He started to slow and Cat took her foot off the accelerator. The Land Rovers stopped and he leaned from his window. "What are you talking about?"

"I'm talking about hunting on my time."

"For God's sake! Hunting's illegal in Kenya—"

"I know that. Too bad no one seemed to have told them—" She pointed to the great arching skeletal ribs of dead elephants littering the grassland around them. "And them and them."

Campbell climbed out of his Land Rover, came around to lean against her door, blocking out the sun. "And you think you're going to stop it and protect the rest?"

"No, I don't think that. I know all this is beyond my control." She kept her voice even, quelling the need to yell, to shriek at him about the blood he spilled so casually. "I just want to finish my work and get out of here. If you want to go hunting, do it on your own time. Not time bought and paid for—"

He cut her off. "Jesus, you really are like your brother. Your safari is over. A plane is being sent for you—"

She stared at him. Fingers of terror touched her spine. Faced with this, Joel would never have backed down. *He'd have died first.* She found her voice, forced herself to speak. "You've been paid to get me a hotel site—"

"I've shown you enough. Make a choice."

"Nothing's suitable."

He slapped the top of the Land Rover and turned back to his own vehicle. "Get your gear together. A plane will be here before sundown."

She climbed out, put one hand on the top weapon in the gun rack. "I'm not going anywhere—"

"And I'm not bloody arguing with you. You're going back to Nairobi."

Around them, the endless grassland was peaceful in the sun. But nothing was what it seemed. Joel had said that. The savannah was a place of slaughter, hunter and prey.

"Oh, Christ," Campbell said. He turned back to her. "I don't have time for this." He put a hand on her arm, started to move her back into the Land Rover.

Cat wrenched the top rifle from the rack.

"Don't touch me," she said. "A lot of people know where I am. Father Gaston, Brian Ward—"

He looked at her. "What do you think I'm going to do to you?"

"Nothing." She held the weapon across her chest, hating the feel of it against her, knowing she could never use it. "But if I'm forced to go back to Nairobi before I find a site, I will raise such a stink—"

"That's certainly got me quivering in my boots—"

She raised her voice over his. "Then try this. The minute I'm forced back to Nairobi against my will, I'll make a telephone call to a friend. He's a combat reporter for *World*. You've heard of *World?* This is right up his alley. He'll be here on the next plane. Whatever it is you're doing will be plastered all over the international press. And he knows I'm here—"

He held up a hand to stop the flow of words. "What is it you want?"

"What you agreed to. I want to follow the exact route my brother followed. I want a hotel site I can use. And then I'll leave. What you do is your business, as much as I hate it."

He turned without speaking, staring toward the grove of trees that sheltered the camp. Tom was a small figure, barely discernible.

"People do know where I am and who I'm with," she said.

He pulled open the passenger door of her Land Rover. "Get in."

"I'll follow you." With the gun, she motioned him toward his own vehicle.

He shook his head in disbelief, then got behind the wheel, turned on the engine.

Cat waited until he started to move before she racked the rifle, slipped into her seat. She placed both hands on the wheel, rested her head on them, trying to control the shaking as the adrenaline drained from her body. Then she followed him back to camp.

Fourteen

Campbell and Tom exchanged a few sentences in Swahili, then Campbell took off again across the grassland. Tom motioned Cat to his Land Rover, and she got into her usual place.

"Where are we going?"

"There's a Maasai village close by. We're going to talk to them."

"What's this about?" She was careful not to accuse, not to sound threatening. Even to her, her voice sounded strained.

"An old elephant named Ahmed."

"You give elephants names?"

"Only this one."

"And you are going to shoot him, an elephant who has a name?" she asked.

"I hope not," Tom said.

"Then what's going on?"

"Well, we hope to find out at the *engang*."

This was going nowhere, she thought. She tried another tack. "Why do you do this, Tom? Hunting."

"Hunting's illegal, you know that."

"Yes, I do. Do you?"

He didn't answer, and Cat glanced at the gun rack behind his seat. She could not push harder. Tom was charming and cultivated, but for all she knew, charm or not, if she got in their way, he—or Campbell—would shoot her without hesitation.

A thornbrush stockade gradually took shape through the wavering heat, and a few minutes later Cat could see the Maasai village, fifteen or twenty round huts built against the encircling brush. To the west, jackals ran back and forth along the edge of the herd of migrating wildebeest, waiting for an easy kill.

Campbell's Land Rover was parked outside.

Tom threaded carefully through tall, rust-colored spires of anthills, hardened and complex, like castles in a fairy story, and stopped beside Campbell's vehicle.

Cat could hear the sound of voices and the excited laughter of children from inside the stockade. She stood in the door of the Land Rover, hanging on to the top so that she could see better, amazed at what she saw.

Campbell was surrounded by children, and behind them, their bare-breasted mothers, wrapped in sarong-like red skirts, their necks and arms decorated with ornate beadwork, were laughing and touching him in greeting. Cat watched as the women hushed their children and made a path to allow an old man, red cloak fastened on one shoulder, tall spear in hand, to walk slowly toward Campbell. An air of ceremony surrounded him. A retinue of elders, almost as tall and clothed as he was, followed him.

The old man, taller than Campbell by at least six inches, greeted him, resting both hands on Campbell's bent head. Then he gripped Campbell's shoulders and held him away, inspecting him, nodding and speaking vehemently. Campbell listened respectfully without answering.

"He's giving Campbell a tongue-lashing," Cat said to Tom. "What's he saying?"

"The short version is that he is the son of the old man's heart, so why has he allowed so long to pass between visits?"

The old man was looking at Tom now, beckoning, the women waving at him to come inside the stockade.

"They look as if they're glad to see you."

Tom was grinning. "We lived here once."

"Here?" The huts looked as if they were built of a mixture of dried mud and cow dung and straw. "What were you doing here?"

She didn't really expect him to say they were hunting, but his answer surprised her.

"We were searching for someone who was lost." His smile had disappeared.

Before she could respond—who? when?—he excused himself, striding away to join Campbell. He bent his head to the old man's touch, received his own rebuke until the cackle of an ancient voice rose above sudden shouts of laughter. The crowd parted to allow an old woman to greet the two men. Campbell picked her up, swung her around in his arms, laughing while she beat on his shoulders and yelled at him.

As he set her down, Campbell caught Cat's eye over the top of the old woman's head. In spite of herself, Cat felt the hard knot of fear and suspicion soften in the seduction of the moment—the laughter of children, the women arguing with him in loud teasing voices. Thornbrush barricades and round huts thatched with grass, black against a crimson-streaked sky. In the smoke from cooking fires mixed with the pungency of cattle and the smell of the grassland.

The women waved to Cat in the Land Rover, stepping up

their clamor, beckoning to her. The old woman slapped Campbell, and raising both hands in surrender, he came through the
brushwood gate.

"They don't see strangers here much," he said. "They'd like to
see your hair."

"My hair?"

Campbell spread his hands and shrugged—who can understand the minds of women? apparent in every motion. Cat waved
at the women, pulled the ends of the green scarf tying her hair back
and shook her head to allow her hair to spring free.

"It looks good, what you do to it," Campbell said. "Tribe up in
the Sudan does something similar, but yours smells better. They
rub fat into theirs to make it stand out like that, and it gets a bit
ripe after a time."

In spite of herself, Cat had to laugh. He took her hand and drew
her forward, into the village and the crowd of women.

They were narrow-boned, and Cat was surprised to see that in
spite of the great height of the men, the women were no taller than
she was. Their eyes were almond-shaped, and the lobes of their
ears had been pierced and plugs inserted, stretching the lobes until
they hung almost to the shoulder. No one seemed as shy as she felt.
They laughed a lot, showing widely spaced, irregular white teeth.

Cat smiled while they fingered her hair and commented to
each other. The old woman gazed with yellow-tinged dark eyes
into hers, placed a hand on Cat's stomach, touched her hipbones,
then spoke long and fervently to Campbell. The women looked at
him sidelong and shrieked with laughter at his protests.

"What are they saying?"

"Not much. Just chat—"

"They think I'm a skinny American, don't they? Is that what
they're saying?"

"No. Not exactly. They say you will be the mother of young bulls. That you will give me fine sons." He grinned, held her eyes.

Cat felt her heart lurch, and she grappled with her reaction. He was dangerous—a killer—and in this moment, suddenly, unexpectedly appealing. She tried to think of something to say. Nothing came. Then the old woman touched Cat's face with a callused hand, and glad of the touch, Cat covered the bony hand with her own, trying to hide her confusion by laughing and looking into the old face.

"Dan!" Tom called from where he stood among the elders. The urgency in his voice stilled the laughter. Tom pointed through the gate to a distant speck. Slowly it emerged into a human figure, a young man loping at a steady pace across the yellow grassland, a spear balanced easily in one hand. As he came closer, he shook the weapon toward the north.

A buzz of excitement ran through the women. Campbell, his face hard, threaded his way toward the old men. Cat pushed to Tom's side.

"What's happening?"

"He's found Ahmed in the hills."

"Tom, you can't do this. Please. Campbell has agreed you're going to go on with my work."

"When this is over. You insisted on being here, Cat. You should have left when you had the chance. Excuse me."

He went to join the men, and she hurried after him, hovering outside the circle. The elders hunkered down, their long skinny legs folding easily, bony knees pointed to the sky, heavily callused bare feet covered in dust, the skin pale and cracked where it touched the ground. She studied the wrinkled faces, the folded angular forms, the colors of the earth and sky and surrounding grassland, and wished she had a sketchbook.

Flanked by Tom and the chief, Campbell sat on his heels and

drew lines in the dust with a stick. Each line was discussed by the group before the chief nodded approval. Then the old men were smiling huge gap-toothed smiles and Campbell was laughing.

Tom stood up, joined Cat and grinned at her. "They rarely get a chance like this anymore. They can hardly wait. Life's too civilized for them now."

"What are you going to do?"

Tom held up one hand. The old men creaked to their feet, and the chief was speaking to Campbell at length.

"Ah," Tom said, "An invitation to dinner."

Cat shot a look at the round huts made of cow dung. "I can't drink blood from the veins of cattle." She couldn't even imagine how it was done. Through a straw? Or was it caught in some kind of calabash? Her stomach churned.

"No, no, you won't be expected to do that," Tom said. "Women don't drink blood, or milk, or eat anything from the cattle. That's kept strictly for the men."

Cat looked around for an escape.

"You'll get goat." Tom pointed to an old nanny goat on the end of a woven grass rope, udders slack, teats dragging in the dust, shambling along behind the child leading her. "That old girl looks past her prime. She's probably on her way to the cookpot."

"Oh my God!"

"You'll enjoy her, cooked over an open fire. Smoky. Very delicious." Tom's black eyes were wide, innocent. Behind him, Campbell and the old man were still talking.

Cat caught the look, the amusement in Tom's voice, and shook her head. "Tom, that's not funny—"

Holding up his hand for silence, Tom made a show of listening. "Dan's explaining that we have to meet our men, says we have plans to make for an early start. Ah, too bad, he's giving our apologies."

Cat joined in the goodbyes, threw smiles toward everyone as she made her way through the crowd of women. She stood by Campbell's Land Rover, listening to the calls of farewell, the bursts of laughter. The Maasai seemed loath to let the two men go, walking with them through the gate, crowding around the Land Rovers.

Cat touched Campbell's arm to get his attention. Above the clamor of voices, she said, "You can't do this. You're breaking your word. You said you would continue with my safari, not do whatever it is you've just planned with these people."

"Well, you're stuck now. I canceled the plane that was coming to take you back to Nairobi." He got behind the wheel, turned on the engine. "Tom's waiting. You can get in, or you can stay here until this is over." He nodded toward the smiling women crowding around his vehicle. "They'd be glad to give you a bed." He gunned the engine gently, moving forward through the throng. Then the Land Rover stopped, and Campbell leaned out of the window and called to her.

"It's the men we're going after. If we get to them in time, Ahmed will keep his tusks."

"And if you don't?"

"Then we'll have to go after Ahmed. But we'll get them."

My God, she thought, she was caught in an African range war between poachers. Is this what had happened to Joel?

She slid in beside Tom. The *engang* dropped into a blue distance. Ahead, the round hills deepened into purple. Cat wondered why Campbell had bothered to reassure her. It wasn't like him.

Fifteen

"You have to keep up. You understand?" Campbell looked up briefly from the weapon he was loading by the light of a lantern, then slammed home the clip with the heel of his hand and set it down on the camp table.

"I've always kept up," Cat said. "Don't worry about it."

"I won't. I'll park you in a Land Rover and lock you in if I have to." He turned toward the men loading their vehicle. "'Twalla," he called. "Check the ammunition. Take extra clips."

"*N'dio, bwana.*"

"I still think we should leave her here with Thomas." Tom's skin merged with the blackness of the predawn hour. "It would be safer—"

"Christ, Tom, we've been through all that. You're like an old *bibi* with one goat," Campbell said impatiently.

"I don't like it."

"You'd like it a bloody sight less if Reitholder manages to get through. He knows she's here."

Cat looked from face to face. "Who's Reitholder?"

After a moment's silence, Tom said, "The man we're after. Deals in ivory. Rhino horn, if he can find any. Skins."

"Oh. The competition."

Neither man answered. Tom reached for an ugly, snub-nosed weapon. Cat turned away, walked to the Land Rover. Excitement undulated through her empty stomach. All she'd had this morning was coffee, and Thomas for once had been too busy to stand over her and insist that she eat more, as he'd taken to doing lately.

She clenched her teeth to prevent them from chattering, wishing she had brought her ski thermals. Jess had told her to, but she just hadn't believed it could be this cold in East Africa. Cat looked at her watch. In Malibu about now, Jess would be bathing Rosie, settling down with her for a story before Mike got home. A born wife and mother, Jess. If only Joel could have seen how good she would have been for him.

Cat held her arms across her chest, trying not to think of the hours ahead. Around her the men worked with a spare discipline, their voices punctuated by laughter.

Finally, Campbell walked toward her. "Right, *memsahib*. Get in." He waved to the men. "Let's go. And keep that engine quiet."

He settled behind the wheel. Cat slid in beside him, Tom crowded against her. Engines turned over, and they drove into the darkness. Behind them, the dawn sky lightened.

Cat pulled her dark heavy sweater closer. She was pressed against Campbell. Each time he changed gear—every other minute it seemed as the Land Rover ground up a dry watercourse—his hand brushed her thigh. She found herself waiting nervously for the next contact and inched toward Tom.

"Besides, I can't let her out of my sight." Campbell spoke into the silence as if continuing a conversation already under way. "You know that, *n'duga*."

"Yes,"Tom said. "I know that."

Cat didn't look at them. Their words cloaked so much, but they wouldn't tell her anything if she asked. An hour passed with only monosyllables exchanged. The sky brightened, the passing terrain took form. Trees and rock formations appeared. They were in the hills they'd seen from the village the day before.

On a downslope, Campbell thrust his arm out of the window, drew his clenched fist down sharply, then cut the engine. Behind them, the second Land Rover cut out, and the vehicles coasted silently, drifting to a stop.

The heights above were wreathed in mist. The men made no noise as they took weapons from the gun racks. Cat crossed her arms, fists tucked into her armpits, and leaned against the warm hood of the Land Rover, waiting to be told what to do.

Campbell took off his jacket and threw it into the back of the vehicle, then reached behind his seat, emerged with a long coiled leather whip. He thrust an arm and shoulder through the coils, then looked up to see her eyes on him. He grinned, and suddenly she found it difficult to breathe and looked away.

Campbell motioned to the men and led the way onto a narrow game trail. In single file, they worked their way upward. Cat felt dwarfed by Sambeke and Olentwalla in front of her, Moses behind, then Thomas and Tom at the rear. It was like being out for a hike with a basketball team, except that their silence was eerie. Almost the only sound she heard was the strike of her own boots on stone.

They kept up a sharp pace, and when they stopped below an outcropping, she was sweating in the cold air, glad of a breather. Campbell hunkered down, the men around him.

Campbell spoke softly. "The *moran* will be in position by now—"

"What's that, the *moran?*" Cat interrupted in a whisper.

Campbell glanced at her impatiently. "The young warriors of the village. Tom'll explain later." He looked at the intent faces of the men. "So let's go over it again. The *moran* will form two columns. They'll swing down from above, close from the east and west. Moses, Sambeke, 'Twalla, we'll press up the middle and herd them into the horns, and the horns will close. It's the old Zulu flanking movement we've used in the past. I know we're a bit short on men, but it should work. Now, I want Reitholder alive. Understand?" He looked at each man in turn, waiting until he received a murmur of agreement. "Right. Tom, be ready in case any of them get through."

Tom protested. "Dan, we're outgunned. I'd feel better if I were on the hill—"

"No, you and Thomas stay down. We've already agreed on that. If Reitholder slips through, he'll come for her. Don't attempt to take him alive at that point. Just kill him."

Tom nodded.

"The two white men the Maasai say are with him are unknown to us. Don't take chances with them. Shoot to kill."

Cat swiveled her eyes from face to face. She felt almost numb. *Shoot to kill.* They were talking about men. Killing men.

She jumped her eyes back to Campbell. "Why would this man Reitholder want to kill me?"

"There's no time for that, now," Campbell said shortly. "If Tom or Thomas gives you an order, don't argue. Just do as you're told immediately—"

"Is the elephant here? The one you're after. Ahmed? Is he here?"

Campbell shook his head impatiently. "Listen to what I'm saying to you. Do what Tom or Thomas tells you. If either of them gets hit, no heroics from you. Your job is to stay under cover. You understand?"

"Yes, don't worry."

The men rose to their feet. Campbell looked at the gold-streaked sky. He grinned and struck Tom's shoulder. "Great morning for it, Tom."

Above them, gray peaks stood against an apple-green sky and the morning was filled with birdsong.

Reitholder nudged his boot against the prone form of Peter Stone. "They're coming," he said. "Get on your feet. Get Watson awake."

He went over to the men's fire and kicked at the first sleeping body. "Get up, you bastards." The man rolled and was on his feet, weapon leveled, before he had a chance to kick again. The rest of the men sat up, rubbing their eyes, grabbing weapons.

The goddamn *kaffirs* had dozed off while keeping watch. When he'd got up to piss, he'd swept the glasses over the area as he did out of habit every chance he got. In the shadow of some rocks two miles away, he'd picked up a Land Rover. No way of knowing how long it had been there, but he stayed alive by not taking chances.

"Get up." Reitholder ground the words out, keeping his voice low. He didn't want to give Campbell a sound he could pick up. "The men who've been tailing us are halfway up the bloody hill. If you want to be paid, you'll kill them before they get to the ivory."

He looked around the hunting camp. Tusks and skins, loaded drying racks. Four months' work threatened because the fucking *kaffirs* couldn't keep awake.

"Wait a minute, Reity." Bobby Watson stamped into his boots, grabbed his bush hat from the branch he'd hung it on before turning in. "Got to pee first and have a cup of tea. Round our way, it's not civilized to ask a bloke to kill anyone before breakfast, without even a cup of tea first. Right, Peter?"

"Tea? What do you mean, tea?" Reitholder exploded. "Fuck tea."

"Careful, mate," Watson said. "That's our national beverage you're talking about."

Stone laughed. "Come on, Bobby. It's a bit early for old Reity here. Poor bugger hasn't got a sense of humor at the best of times, let alone before breakfast."

"Well, tell the truth, I'm not too keen on killing some bloke I don't even know," Watson said.

"He doesn't know you, either," Reitholder said. "And I assure you, it won't stop him from putting a bullet in you."

"Well, if you put it that way." Watson picked up his AK-47. "We'd better get going. You got a plan of action?"

"Keep them downhill, away from the ivory, kill them before they kill us."

Frowning, Watson pondered the words, then nodded. "I like it, Reity. It's got class." He grinned. "Simple plans for simple folk, always the best way to go, mate."

"Can't we just sort of run 'em off?" Stone asked. "Wing a couple of 'em, maybe?"

"Campbell has five seasoned men, we've got twelve *kaffirs* who can't even keep awake on watch. No, he will not be run off, my friend. Fortunately, he's handicapped by the Stanton woman."

"Ah, Jesus, don't count on me to shoot any women, mate," Stone said.

"Well, you better think about that, mister." Reitholder gestured around the camp at the skins and tusks. "We've got almost a million dollars here. Four months' work, and you get equal share for a couple weeks." Yes, and a good man gets through the eye of the needle, he thought.

Watson said, "What do you want to do?"

"Get downhill as far and as fast as you can. Spread out and take cover. Just make sure there are no survivors to tell the tale."

He saw the glances the Australians exchanged and grinned. After this they'd be in too deep to get out. "Come on, you've killed enough," Reitholder said. "Animals, men, what's the difference? You've got the balls for it. Them or us. It's the only way. Let's go."

Sixteen

Campbell and the three Maasai climbed silently. The hillside gave plenty of cover—with luck they'd catch Reitholder with his pants down. Campbell scanned the heights above. The *moran* was up there somewhere, but no one would know it. Not a leaf moved.

A shrike called from his right. Sambeke's call. He nodded at the Maasai, then stared upward to where Sambeke pointed, realizing this would be no surprise visit. Reitholder not only had his pants on; it looked as if he had his men deployed below a small escarpment. Campbell nodded, signaled to Olentwalla and Moses, then picked up a large rock in each hand. He waited until the Maasai had each found rocks, then raised his hand, gave a silent count of three. Together they loosed a shower of rocks far to the right.

Gunfire crashed across the mountain, rolled from rock to rock.

Reitholder waved his AK, yelled at his men to hold their fire. Bastards. None of them had a target. They were giving away their positions, just what Campbell wanted.

"Do you see anything, Bobby?" Stone called.

"No, mate. Just a lot of bloody rock being blown apart," Watson replied. "You?"

"Nah—"

From above them, a series of shrieks tore through the silence, then faded to a gurgle.

"Christ!" Watson called. "What the hell's that?"

A clamor of voices shouting in half a dozen dialects fought to be heard. Reitholder roared at his panicked men for silence. Ignoring him, men broke from cover, firing as they ran. A barrage from below cut through them. Three men fell. Again, unholy challenging screams came from above.

"What the hell's going on?" Stone searched the hillside. "Who the hell's up there?"

"Reitholder!" A voice reverberated, thrown back from the rocks. "Can you hear me?"

"Fuck you, *kaffir* lover." Reitholder stood, sprayed a wide arc of bullets in the direction of Campbell's voice, then dropped back into cover.

"Who are you?" Stone shouted.

"You are surrounded—"

"Bullshit," Reitholder yelled. He jumped from the cover of the tree, rolled, threw himself under the protection of a rock, closer to the voice.

"Look above you," the voice shouted.

The two Australians searched the terrain above them. "I can't see anything, Bobby, can you?"

"Nothing, mate. Bloke's got us on." Watson stood, fired toward the voice.

A rain of spears thudded into the earth. Shrieks resounded over the hillside. Both Australians whirled, fired upward toward the unseen target. The voice shouted again, this time in Swahili.

"Reity, what's this bloke saying?" Stone shouted.

"I'm telling them to throw down their weapons," the voice shouted back. "You haven't got a chance."

"Yeah, and what happens then?" Stone yelled.

"Nothing. You go home."

"Without a dollar in our pocket," Watson called to Stone. "That's no offer." He eased his AK over the edge of the boulder, squeezed off a few rounds.

Reitholder could see Campbell now, climbing toward them, his men spread out behind him. More men were pressing down from the trees above, men he couldn't see, couldn't pinpoint, men killing with spears. *Kaffirs,* coming after the ivory he'd endured four months of hardship to gather in this hellhole of a camp.

Rage, hot and powerful, poured through his body like magma. He welcomed it, welcomed the strength and power rampaging through him. He half stood, crouched against protecting rock, peering upward.

"They have a woman with them," he shouted to his men. "Do you hear me, *kaffirs?* A woman. She's yours. You want her? Come on, take her."

"Now wait a minute," Stone shouted. "We won't go along with anything like that—"

"Shut up! What does it matter? We need these bastards to fight."

Reitholder fired at Campbell, then raced forward. Half a dozen of his men emerged from cover and started to follow.

"This is going to be bad, Bobby," Stone yelled. He stood. Bullets struck the trees and bushes, the ledge behind him. He staggered, looked down at the blood spreading across his belly. Slowly he leaned back against the rock, sliding down until he sat.

"Peter!" Watson hurled himself across the few yards of sun-drenched hillside. He threw down his gun, dropped to his knees. "Christ, mate——"

Stone looked at him. "I'm shot, Bobby." He touched the blood oozing from above his belt. "I'm bloody shot."

Watson wrestled with the buckle, then yanked the blood-soaked jeans apart. He tore off his shirt, wadded it against the exposed intestines, gobs of flesh. "It'll be all right, Petey," he said. "We'll get you out of here."

Reitholder clambered toward the two men. "Leave him," he shouted. "He's gut shot. Finished."

"No, he's not. No. He's hurt——"

"Get on your feet. They're coming for the tusks." Reitholder grabbed Watson's shoulder, tried to pull him to his feet.

Watson fought him off. He pulled Stone against him, cradling his body. "Hey!" he shouted. "Hey, down there. Don't shoot. We're finished."

"Get on your fucking feet," Reitholder shrieked.

Watson seemed unaware of the tears pouring down his face. He held Stone's head against his chest. "It's okay, mate," he whispered. "Don't worry, Petey. I'll see you okay, mate."

Reitholder turned his AK-47 toward the Australian. A red film of rage obscured his vision. "Leave him. I need you."

"Fuck you."

Reitholder pulled a 9mm Glock from his belt, held it against Stone's left eye. He squeezed the trigger. A spray of white bone fragments, gray brain matter, blood spewed over the red rock, coating the lichen, dripping like vomit down the rock face.

Bobby Watson screamed. He lunged for his AK. Reitholder turned the Glock toward him. The bullet crashed into Watson's chest, blowing it apart. Reitholder thrust the Glock back into his belt. He heard a sound from above and looked up.

Campbell dropped from the ledge the Australians had used for cover, thudding into him. The spongy rock gave way, gathered momentum, tumbling them together to ride the avalanche down the hillside, grappling in the rising red dust. Reitholder labored for breath, knocked from his lungs when Campbell landed on him. He fought to stay conscious, resisting the blackness clouding his brain, scrabbled for the AK as it slipped from his grasp.

Campbell felt him weakening. He dragged Reitholder to his feet, pulled the broad back against his chest. He slipped his hands under Reitholder's arms, linked his fingers together behind the bull neck. Slowly, he increased the pressure of the full nelson, felt the bones begin to give. Reitholder sagged to his knees, and Campbell felt his own muscles bunching for the kill. Another inch and it would be over. His breath steadied, he eased the pressure, dragged Reitholder upright.

"Tell them to throw down their weapons," he said against Reitholder's ear.

"Fuck you, *kaffir* lover."

"Christ, you're limited," he grunted.

Campbell shouted in Swahili. One by one, the surviving men stopped running. They stood still, holding their weapons above their heads. Sambeke and Olentwalla circulated among them, driving them into a small group. Campbell counted heads. Six were still alive. Moses was checking the rest. A shot rang out. There would be no wounded. He shoved the stumbling Reitholder in front of him, back toward the hunting camp.

* * *

Cat heard voices floating in the thin air, the sound of metal hitting rock. Tom and Thomas eased their fingers from the triggers of their Uzis. Standing on the edge of an escarpment above them, Campbell raised the gun in his hand, jerking it up and down in two sharp movements.

"Stay behind me, Cat," Tom said. "Thomas, watch the *memsahib*."

They started to climb. Her boots slipped on the rocks. The going was harder than Campbell and the Maasai had made it seem. A bush she grabbed to pull herself upward gave way, a nail broke and she swore. The sun was higher now. She stopped to breathe, remove her sweater. Thomas took it from her, tucked it into the coil of rope over his shoulder. Cat blinked the sweat out of her eyes and fished a tissue from her pocket. She nodded. "Okay."

They climbed on. She kept her eyes straight ahead, at the next step, the next boulder over which she had to clamber, fearful of stumbling over bodies. There had to be bodies. The gunfire had been deafening. Then Tom turned and yanked her over a final lip of rock. They were on a plateau, forty feet deep, a lichen-furred cliff striated in broad red and gray bands towering at the rear. Enclosing the plateau were falls of red-pitted boulders, dotted with brush.

The stink of putrefaction in the air was an almost palpable presence of death.

Zebra skins were stacked high. Antelope horns tangled in piles, sorted by type. She recognized the tiny horns of the Tommies, the little deer who bounced like rubber balls. Worse were the pathetically small pelts of lion cubs stretched over a drying frame. Below the frame was a pile of tiny bodies not yet skinned—leopard, cheetah, eyes crawling with maggots. Beside them stretched a lion, the black mane stiff with the arterial blood that drenched it. The muzzle had drawn back in his death agony, exposing white teeth. He'd been in his prime.

And, lashed in twos with gaily colored plastic rope, were the elephant tusks. Tusks too small to rope had been tossed into woven carrying baskets.

Belly quivering with horror, Cat managed to get to a small tumble of rocks, found a flat surface on which to collapse before her legs gave way.

What if Joel had seen something like this?

"Tom," Campbell called. He walked to the far side of the plateau. "Get the *moran* down. We're ready here."

Hands on hips, Campbell studied the bound men in front of him. Dressed in the oddments of a variety of military uniforms mixed with T-shirts and jeans, sockless feet thrust into athletic shoes and sneakers, they squatted on their heels, their wrists lashed together. Beside them, a white man was on his knees but upright, and unbound. The three armed Maasai stood over the group, their weapons trained on them.

Cat looked away without sympathy. *Her father had been like them, killing as casually. Sick seals beached in front of the house in Malibu used for target practice. Stray dogs crippled while scavenging for scraps in the sand. Seagulls exploding into clouds of bloody feathers. She could hear his voice taunting their mother. "You're soft, Karen. And you've made your children as weak as you are."*

She thought of Joel, his eyes filled with murder, mirroring her own.

On an order from Campbell, Moses dragged the kneeling man to his feet. Twisting one arm behind his back, Moses frog-marched him to the pile of tusks and forced him back down onto his knees.

Sjambok in hand, Campbell walked to where she sat at the edge of the plateau, as far away as she could get from the skins, the smell of putrefying flesh.

He stopped in front of her. "Thomas will take you down to the Land Rovers," he said.

Cat felt drained of strength. It was almost too much of an effort to tilt her head up to look at him. "I can't, I'm sorry. You'll have to give me a few minutes."

"We haven't got a few minutes. You'll have to try. This is no place for you."

"Who is he, that man? You know him, don't you?"

"His name's Reitholder," Campbell answered shortly. "Come on."

She ignored the hand he held out. "Yes, but who is he? You know him—"

He cut her off, dropped his hand to his side. "Go down to the Land Rovers, Cat. Thomas will help you."

She did not move.

"Are Olentwalla and the rest okay?" she asked.

"Yes, they're all right."

"Why did you make me climb up in the first place if now I have to leave?" My God, she thought, panicked. Maybe they don't want a witness.

His lips tightened. "I needed Thomas. I didn't know we'd find all this." He looked away. "I'm sorry."

"How many men are dead?"

"We'll count them as we bury them and I'll let you know. Now go on down the hill, Cat. When we're finished here we'll get you a site for your hotel that suits you."

She looked at him, aghast. "That's not what... My God, Campbell, men are dead..." She stopped.

Campbell's patience seemed suddenly exhausted. "Just get down off this bloody hill." He walked away.

Cat followed his retreating figure with her eyes. Then, on the hillside, a flash of sun on metal caught her attention. She looked up, drew in a sharp breath.

Tall, long-limbed men, their hair braided into cornrows and

plastered with red clay, stood silently on the pitted boulders flanking the plateau. She had heard no sound. They were suddenly just there. Sun polished their skins, deepened the red of the cloth they wore around their waists and shoulders into the color of old blood, touched the points of their spears.

The poachers stared up at them. Terror creased their faces.

Alarmed, she called after Campbell. "What are you going to do?"

Campbell looked up at the hillside. "Whatever they decide," he said over his shoulder. He walked over to the frightened poachers. Reitholder had scrambled to his feet again and was waiting, erect, chin raised.

"Come on, Miss Cat." Thomas was at her shoulder. "Better you do as he say."

"Thomas, who are they? What are they going to do?"

"The young men from the village, Miss Cat. The *moran*."

Before she could press for a reply to the question he had not answered, Campbell's voice rang out, speaking to the men on the hillside in Maa. Her neck prickled at the full-throated roar that answered him. Cat shook her head. Nothing could drag her away from the wild scene that was unfolding in front of her eyes.

The coiled *sjambok* in one hand, Campbell faced the gathered *moran,* his back to the gray and red rockface. The sun struck the bloody stumps of white elephant tusks, shone on fat iridescent green blowflies massed in the blood-encrusted mane of the lion.

The sun was high now, the air too hot to breathe, too filled with the reek of death. Cat moved into the shade of a tree that was miraculously clinging to life, its roots climbing over a pile of boulders. The tree gave off a faint, sweet resinous scent that cut the stench of rotting flesh, and she leaned closer to the trunk.

On the hill, the *moran* had started to drum their spears against the boulders on which they stood. The sound of wood smacking rock bounced from the cliff, building in volume until it almost drowned out Campbell's voice. A turbulent silence fell. Then Tom struck the pile of skins with an AK, shouting to the Maasai as he did so. They murmured angrily, drummed their spears, the sound resonating among the hills. Red dust rose around long thin legs already coated the color of rust.

Among the bound poachers, only Reitholder was still on his feet. The glare was relentless, heat undulating in ripples. The stench was a noxious blanket, pressing down. Cat opened her mouth to breathe, gasping at the rush of dry air that robbed her lips and mouth of moisture.

Accompanied by a young Maasai, Tom went to the body of the lion. Tom stood back, and ceremoniously the young man stood astride the dead animal, buried both hands in the black mane, pulled up the heavy head. The tawny bullet-shattered neck was a mass of shredded flesh, coagulated blood, white bone.

The drumming ceased, the sudden silence of the Maasai unnerving. The young man lowered the head to the ground.

"Thomas," Cat whispered. "Is that lion special in some way?"

"In old time, Maasai warrior go alone to kill *simba* with spear. No wives till then. No cattle. No manhood. Now all change. Government law say no one kill *simba*. If Maasai not kill *simba, memsahib,* no man kill *simba.*"

Campbell walked to the bound men cowering on the ground. He pulled the nearest man to his feet, motioned the rest to get up.

Raising his voice, Campbell thrust the poacher forward. The *moran* jerked their spears back and forth as if measuring the distance before throwing.

Reitholder shouted, trying to drown Campbell's words. Suddenly everyone was shouting, poachers screaming, the Maasai roaring and stamping, menacing the bound men with their spears.

Campbell cracked the *sjambok* and raised his voice above the hubbub. The turmoil faded. Reitholder's shouts alone continued.

"Moses!" Campbell roared.

Moses leaped forward, the butt of his gun raised to slam into Reitholder's face. Reitholder jerked his head back, and Moses stopped the butt an inch short of the white man's teeth. He grinned, then tapped it almost gently at Reitholder's mouth. Still grinning, Moses stepped back.

At a gesture from Campbell, Sambeke dragged the poachers into a cowering, ragged line facing the Maasai, then moved away to a safe distance. The tall Maasai who'd displayed the lion's shattered neck shouted a command. The men on the hill raised their spears.

Cat started from the shade of the tree toward the bound men, but felt Thomas's hand dragging her back.

"Let me go." She struggled against Thomas's grasp, her nostrils filled with the smell of sweat from his body and the stink of the plateau. "Campbell!" she shouted. "Stop it. Stop it—"

Thomas crammed his hand over her mouth, and she sank her teeth into the callused palm. Then she heard the thud of the spears and sagged against him, waiting for the shrieks of pain. What came to her ears was laughter. A storm of high-pitched male laughter. Thomas took his hand from her mouth and she looked up. A forest of spears bristled inches away from the feet of the prostrate poachers. On the hillside, the Maasai roared with laughter.

Thomas released his hold. Weak with relief, Cat rested her head against his chest.

A joke. It was all a sick, primitive joke. She looked up to apologize for biting him, but Thomas had his eyes fixed on what was happening behind her.

Cat turned to see Campbell slashing through the rope binding Reitholder's ankles. At a nod, Sambeke and Moses dragged the struggling Reitholder to a pile of zebra skins, threw him face downward. Campbell raised the *sjambok*. The Maasai on the hill were silent.

The thud of whip on flesh immobilized her with a sick horror. Reitholder flinched as the whip curled around him, but he made no sound. Campbell's arm rose and fell, the white shirt on Reitholder's back shredded, reddened. Then his silence broke into a scream.

Cat crouched against the tree, hands muffling her ears, trying vainly to shut out the terrible sounds of the whip, the screams. But they seemed to go on and on. The muscles in her empty stomach clenched. She took her hands from her ears to press them against her belly and realized that what she was hearing now was the absence of all sound. Then somewhere a lone bird called and gradually others took up song. She lifted her head.

Reitholder was on all fours, shirt hanging in bloody shreds. Blood coursed through the curled yellow hair on his arms, dripped onto the stony ground. Standing over him, Campbell recoiled the whip.

The young Maasai who'd given the earlier order shouted. Silently, the men on the hill turned and started to climb. In seconds they were gone.

"Thomas!" Campbell shouted.

"Bwana!"

"Get this man doctored before the blowflies get to him."

"You all right, Miss Cat?" Thomas asked anxiously.

Cat nodded, too numb to speak. She lowered herself to the ground, wrapped her arms around her knees and rested her head, careless of the large insects scurrying around her on the rocky ground. She felt violated, the savagery stamped indelibly into her brain. What she had just witnessed would be there forever, taking its place among the other scenes she tried so hard to blot out. The animals their father mortally wounded, so that he could watch their death agony. Joel's eyes, his finger tightening on the trigger—strange how that image stayed with her, the small finger curling around the metal. And the blood.

Campbell saw her slumped figure and beckoned Tom. "Get something into her, Tom, coffee or something, before she passes out," he said. "Did Thomas bring a thermos?"

Tom nodded. "She shouldn't have seen this. She should have gone down—"

"Well, I tried, but she's as arrogant as her bloody brother. She won't listen, either."

Around them the plateau had erupted into action. Drying racks crashed to the ground. Moses bent over the tusks, sorting them by size. Most were small, taken from adolescents killed before maturity—the last of their line. There would not be another generation.

"Did you round up the rest of them?" Campbell asked abruptly.

"Yes. Four were dead, Moses put a couple of them out of their misery. Two are still alive."

"How bad are they?"

Tom shook his head.

"Any papers?"

"No."

"Well, maybe they know something N'toya can use. See what you can get from them. But get that coffee into her first. She looks as if she's going to collapse."

Cat sensed someone standing in front of her and looked up.

"I've brought you some coffee." Tom unscrewed the plastic cup from the top of the thermos, filled it and handed it to her.

"Tom. God, Tom." She held the cup in both hands to steady it. The coffee was strong and sweet, and she felt better as the caffeine hit her system. Tom towered over her. She felt diminished, crouched at his feet, and she rose on shaky legs. "You knew, didn't you? You knew what he was going to do?"

Tom shrugged.

"What a life you lead," she said. "Killing. Brutalizing human beings. Did my brother find out what you were up to?"

"There was nothing to find out."

She handed back the empty cup. "You two are going to get a bullet in the back one of these days. You should quit while you're ahead."

He screwed the cup back in place. "I'll leave this with you. We'll be going down the hill as soon as we clean up here."

When he left, she found a small boulder on which to sit, poured more coffee, drank it slowly. Across the plateau Thomas had moved the group of poachers into the shade. She drained the mug, then walked over to the men, sitting on their heels, puffing on the cigarettes Thomas had handed out. Reitholder was crouched as far from his men as he could manage and still remain in the shade.

She held the thermos out to the man nearest her. Smiling uncertainly, he took it, then filled the cup with coffee, took a mouthful before handing it to the man next to him. The men passed the mug from hand to hand. When it came to Reitholder, the man next to him hesitated, then leaned over to offer it to him. With an expression of disgust, Reitholder dashed it from the man's hand. Thomas picked up the cup, refilled it and gave it to the man closest to him.

"Don't waste your coffee and sympathy, missy," Reitholder said to Cat. His English was guttural and ugly. "*Kaffirs* don't feel much. They're not like us, you and me. White people. They're animals."

He stared at her through faded blue eyes, bloodshot eyes rimmed with lashes so pale that, like his eyebrows, they appeared nonexistent. Cat could see scaly reddened patches on his face where the sun had damaged his skin, but except for the sheen of sweat, the pinched lines of pain around his mouth, he looked hard and fit.

Before she could speak to him, Thomas pushed a tightly woven basket containing a gray paste into her hand. "You doctor him, Miss Cat. He not let me."

Cat put the basket on the ground. "Then let the flies get to him."

"Bwana Dan say fix him." Thomas picked up her hand, put the basket firmly into it. "We fix him. Turn, you," he said to Reitholder. "You let the *memsahib* help."

Reitholder turned so that she could see his back, watching over his shoulder to see her reaction. He managed to bare his teeth in a smile when he saw her face.

His back was a mass of brutalized flesh. The man needed hospital dressings and antibiotics, Cat thought, not this dubious mixture of native medicine—God only knew what was in it. It smelled vaguely earthy. She scooped the paste from the basket with fingers that were grimy from her climb. She started to feel ill again, sick from balancing the past and the present, unable to speak.

Reitholder's broken skin was slick under her fingers. Panic started to rise in her chest. The paste wouldn't hold. It slipped across the wet flesh like the Vaseline she had used to try to plug the wound in her father's chest the day Joel shot him, trying to fill a hole that wouldn't stop bleeding.

"Campbell brings his woman with him into the bush now, does he?" Reitholder said over his shoulder. His breath was foul, the corners of his mouth crusted with dried saliva, lips chewed raw where he'd tried to stop himself from screaming. "Blood excite you, missy? Turn you on? Good for the sex, later, eh?"

He laughed, the glottal sound ending in a gasp as she continued to smooth on the paste—blocking out his voice, blocking out Joel and their father by concentrating on each small section of the ooz-

ing meat on which she worked. Finally, she was finished. God, she
thought, what a mess. She took a crumpled tissue from her pocket,
wiped her hands.

"You want to be careful, missy. You're a babe in the woods here."
His bloodshot blue eyes moved slowly as if they were glued in place
by pain. "Do you think your *bwana* Campbell will protect you?"
He forced a laugh, a strangled sound that ended in a gasp. But he
went on. "You will get eaten up, little missy, just like your brother."

"What do you know about my brother?"

"Aah! So now the dirty elephant killer has your attention.
Not too superior to talk now, eh? Not so much the delicate-fin-
gered lady—"

"What do you know about my brother?"

"He was a babe in the woods." Reitholder gave another strangled grunt of forced laughter. "So he got eaten up."

"What do you know?"

He regarded her silently, then said, "What are you trading?"

"What do you want?"

"My freedom."

Cat looked around to make sure Thomas could not overhear and
leaned closer, lowering her voice. "I can't do that. I don't know
how—"

"Find a way."

"Memsahib!" Thomas called. "You finish here now."

Under the guise of checking his back, she put her lips close to
Reitholder's ear. "I'll try to get you untied, but first—"

"Memsahib!" Thomas came toward them.

"So, tell her, *kaffir,*" Reitholder sneered. "She wants to know
about her brother—"

"What the hell's going on here?" Campbell had approached on
silent feet.

Reitholder laughed. Campbell struck him across the mouth with the back of his hand. Blood spurted from Reitholder's already damaged lips.

The brutality sickened her—the man was already beaten and disarmed. She pushed down her revulsion. "He knew Joel's name—"

"Christ, everyone in Kenya heard about your brother's accident."

"How did he know Joel was my brother?"

"You're as alike as two peas in a pod. Of course he knows." He turned to Thomas. "Get these men on their feet. They can dig the graves."

Cat dropped to her knees in front of Reitholder. "Tell me. What do you know about my brother?"

Campbell pulled her to her feet. Over her head he spoke harshly to Reitholder in a language she didn't understand. She thought it had to be Afrikaans.

"Reitholder," she said again. "What about my brother? Why are you after me?"

Blood still trickling from his lips, he stared at her out of stone eyes. He ran his hand across his damaged mouth and spat out a tooth at her feet. Then he laughed.

Seventeen

"Moses," Campbell shouted.

Moses trotted across the plateau.

"Don't take your eyes off this bastard," Campbell said. "If he moves, shoot him." He took Cat's arm. "You come with me." He stopped close to a clump of trees on the other side of the plateau, at the base of an animal track leading up onto the hillside. "Now, look. Reitholder's a psychopathic bastard. Keep away from him. He wouldn't know the truth if he fell over it."

"And you would, I suppose? Who is he?"

"Keep away from Reitholder," he repeated.

"Or what?"

"Or I'll tie you to a bloody tree. I don't want to do that, but you're giving me no choice. Thomas has other things to do here, I can't have him wasting his time guarding you."

She gestured toward the piles of small pathetic tusks. "What's going to happen to all this?"

"It will probably end up in a government warehouse in Nairobi."

"You're not keeping it, of course."

"No," Campbell said. "We are not keeping it."

She wanted to answer, to challenge him, but kept silent. Over his shoulder she caught sight of Moses and Sambeke maneuvering a body down the rocky hillside, toward a clump of trees. Dark curly hair hung over Sambeke's arm, a bush hat still hung by its strap from an exposed throat. There was a massive bloody wound where his chest should be.

"Wait! Moses, wait!"

"Cat." Campbell made a grab for her but she shook him off and rushed after the two Maasai through the small patch of scrubby trees. She stopped, shocked.

Two rows of bodies were lined up, too many to count at first glance. The two Maasai had lowered their burden at the end of the first row, and Cat dropped to her knees beside him.

"I know this man!" Campbell had followed her and she looked up at him. "My God! I know him. His name's Bobby Watson. He comes from Adelaide." Two weeks ago, less than that, she'd laughed with him, flirted a little. Now his chest was a gaping hole, and his dancing brown eyes were filmed with dust. She put out a hand to close them. He was still warm. She looked at the body lying next to him and gagged. Most of the head was missing. Blowflies had already found him.

"And this is Peter Stone. I think he comes from Adelaide, too." Suddenly she felt as if she could smell evil in the very air she breathed. In the stink of blood from the men stretched in rows in front of her, in the rotting flesh of animal carcasses. "Who will tell their families?" As she had been told about Joel. A spurt of terror chilled her blood. She rose to her feet.

"We'll let the authorities know about them," Campbell said.

Cat heard the strike of metal on rock, glanced over at the group of poachers digging graves, every movement watched by Olentwalla, an AK held across his chest.

A sob broke from her control, and another. She put a hand to her mouth. Incredibly, Campbell put an arm around her, his touch gentle. Reitholder's ugly words resonated in her head—sex and blood and killing—and she moved away from him.

Campbell let his arm drop. "Don't waste your tears on them, Cat," he said. "Africa's full of men like this, black and white. Mercenaries, poachers, murderers. They take their chances. Today these two lost. They knew the risks."

She wondered where he fit on that grim list. She said, "I don't want to know anymore."

A low moan came from one of several men lying separate from the others. "Can you do anything for them?"

He shook his head. "Not much. They'll survive or they'll die."

She nodded, turned away, then made her way on shaky legs through the trees to the resinous little refuge at the edge of the plateau, as far from the charnel pit as it was possible to get.

For the next hour she sat, leaning against the trunk of her tree, listening to the captive poachers digging graves with the tools used at the hunting camp for digging latrines. She looked for a chance to speak again to Reitholder, but Moses lounged against a rock only a few yards from him, his Uzi in one hand, his eyes locked on his prisoner. Someone had provided cover for the wounds Campbell had inflicted—a T-shirt taken from a body, by the look of the bloodstained holes in it, but it protected the damaged flesh from most of the flies.

Thomas came by to offer another thermos of coffee, a sandwich crumpled from hours in his backpack. Cat shook her head at the food but took the coffee gratefully. She noticed that Reitholder was offered nothing and found she didn't care.

Gradually the heat went out of the day, small creatures appeared, tiny vervet faces peering from the branches above her head. But the little green monkeys, usually so friendly, refused to leave the safety of the tree, probably fearful of the activity on the plateau, the smell of blood that attracted predators.

The entire camp was dismantled. Blackened hearthstones used for cooking were dispersed, wood from the drying racks carefully stacked—Thomas said the Maasai women from the *engang* would pick it up later and use it for fuel. Sometime during the afternoon, the *moran* had appeared as silently as before. They did no work, but squatted on their haunches, watching Campbell and Tom sort through the tusks, pile them by size.

Crimson streaks appeared high in the sky, birds squabbled as they started to settle for the night. Tom stood in front of her.

"We're ready to leave."

Cat stood, sent a glance toward Reitholder. Moses had not left his post. She looked back over the plateau, said a silent goodbye to the two young men who'd once been so filled with life and laughter. Would the authorities really be informed? Their people in Australia? Would she herself live to tell them?

A shot echoed across the plateau, followed by another. Birds rose screaming into the air. She felt rooted to the spot.

"Someone just shot the wounded men," she said. She was empty of emotion and didn't really care about it. Too much had happened. It just seemed necessary to keep straight with what was happening here. "You just killed two men as if they meant nothing."

"They didn't," Tom said.

Cat bent to pick up her sweater, stood to find Campbell had joined them. She stared at him, and he said, "Cat, this is Africa, not some Hollywood set with tailored grass and toothless animals."

His voice softened. "It's better this way, believe me. They would not have survived the night."

"What about Reitholder? Are you going to kill him?"

"We'd have done it by now if we were going to do that, don't you think?"

"What will happen to him?"

"He's going to Nairobi."

The *moran* were leaving by the same route they had used earlier, tall black figures climbing the hill, silhouetted briefly against the reddening sky, each man carrying a pair of tusks across his shoulders. They disappeared over the brow of the hill, in the direction of the *engang*.

Cat turned without comment, allowing Tom to help her over the lip of the plateau, too tired, too dispirited to insist that she did not need help. She did, and desperately. But there was no one to ask.

Eighteen

Cat opened her eyes, the image of Reitholder's face, the ugly voice, the poisonous words, echoing in her brain. She fumbled on the camp table for her watch: 2:00 a.m. Inside the enclosure of the mosquito net, the smell of crushed grass mingled with the dry dust and a faint trace of soap. Outside the tent, the watch fire flared as one of the men replenished it.

Faroff sounds reached her—the cry of an animal suddenly silenced, the ululation of the triumphant predator. Jess had suggested she bring sleeping pills. She wished she hadn't been so stubborn. Every time she closed her eyes, the scene on the plateau—dead men, tusks, small bodies of cubs, the whip rising and falling on a reddened back—played and replayed against her eyelids.

Drained when she and Tom got back to camp with Thomas, she'd longed for the oblivion of sleep. But she'd forced herself to eat a sandwich in her tent, then use the hot water Thomas brought her for a sponge bath before turning in, only to drift in and out of uneasy sleep.

About midnight, Campbell had returned, and she'd heard the murmur of voices. An hour later a Land Rover left.

Suddenly cold, she pulled the brown blanket up around her chin. In daylight she'd have a clearer head. There had to be a way to get to Reitholder if he was still alive. Maybe in Nairobi—Stephen would know his name, or even Father Gaston, or Brian Ward, or the police.

She closed her eyes, confused images playing in her mind: Peter Stone with half of his head missing, Bobby as she'd seen him in Nairobi, dancing brown eyes, bush hat on the back of dark curls, laughing when she tried to tell him that he had a hole in his chest. Reitholder, Campbell, *sjambok* in hand, Tom leaning over wounded men, carefully shooting each one and toppling them into the graves Moses was digging.

And then she was running across the savannah, stumbling over tussocks of grass…trying to reach Joel, shouting at him…warning him…Joel turned, waved…oblivious to the buffalo bearing down on him…massive horns lowered…their father behind them, firing above their heads, driving them faster and faster…she could hear herself shrieking at Joel, warning him…struggling to reach him…then he went down, under the hooves…and she was screaming…screaming…

"Shh, shh. It's all right. Shh."

A voice pulled her free from the horror. Instinctively, she wrapped her arms around the solid comfort of human contact.

"Shh. It's all right." Campbell stroked her back. "You're having a nightmare. You're all right."

Her panting breath was labored. Dread hovered over her. He was warm and alive, smelling of moist night air, the sweet reality of wood smoke. She pushed her face against his chest, her eyes still clenched tight against the dream.

Campbell murmured wordlessly, lifting the hair from her damp neck, tugging at the strands clinging to her throat. "That must have been some nightmare. Are you all right?"

His hand on her back was soothing. Cat nodded without releasing him. Her panic was receding, the harsh gasping breath had started to ease, but she was unable to open her eyes. She was so tired, she thought. Tired down to the bone. Tired with the weight of years behind it.

"What was it?" Campbell put a hand on the back of her head, holding her against his shoulder. "Tell me about it."

"It's Joel."

Campbell bent his head closer.

"I should have been with him. I could have stopped him. Now it's too late."

"You couldn't have done anything, Cat."

"You don't understand." She was alive and he was dead. She was always the only one who could stop him taking risks, stop him proving over and over that he was more than his father said he was. She could have stopped him, and she hadn't. She'd wanted him to do it, she'd wanted him to kill their father. So he'd pulled the trigger. And he'd borne the guilt for them both.

"I do understand. I was there," Campbell said. "I know you could have done nothing. You must believe me."

If only she could. Cat opened her eyes to search his face. She felt the thump in his chest as he stared back at her, then a change in the steady rhythm of his heart.

He tightened his arms around her, and suddenly she was aware of her bare legs, the thin T-shirt only just covering her, the fire outside glowing through canvas walls and throwing diffused golden light onto the white mosquito net enclosing them.

Campbell's breathing deepened. Her own heart started to beat with a heaviness to match his. She raised her lips, drew his head toward her, opened her mouth to his tongue. For a brief moment, she welcomed passion that would mask the pain and grief and loss.

Gradually Cat became aware of a skittering on the roof of the tent, the rustle of breeze in the thorn trees, the distant high-pitched call of an animal sounding like the cry of a lost soul.

A cool draft of air touched her damp skin, and she shivered and opened her eyes, looking over Campbell's shoulder into the mosquito netting above them.

What was the matter with her? she thought. She could not believe what she had just done. And there was a woman waiting for him in Nairobi. She felt sick with guilt. "Campbell. Come on. You've got to leave."

He lifted his head. "Wait a minute. Give me a minute to catch my breath, for God's sake."

"No. You've got to leave."

She shoved at his shoulder, and he shifted his body, rolling to the edge of the narrow camp bed.

"Are you always this tough?"

"Come on, please."

Campbell raised himself on one elbow, tugged at the sheet covering her, touched his tongue to her nipple. She jumped again at the shock of it. She felt him begin to harden, and she pushed a hand into his hair, pulling his head away from her breast.

He looked into her eyes. "Is this the same trembling, frightened woman who clung to me such a short time ago?"

"Next time you hear me having that nightmare, walk away. I don't want a repeat performance."

"Correct me if I'm wrong, but you sounded to me as if you rather liked it."

"The earth moved, I liked it. Thank you. Good night."

"I'll be damned." He started to laugh, then swung his feet to the ground. He walked with an easy grace to pick up his clothes, pulled on his pants.

"Campbell?

He turned, looked at her inquiringly.

"Don't let's speak of this again," she said. "Not a look. Not a hint. Nothing. This never happened. Okay?"

He kept his eyes on her while he buttoned his shirt, his eyebrows raised, as if considering her words. He tucked the shirt into his pants, buckled his belt, then walked over to the camp bed and separated the white netting. He bent over her, kissed her, dropped the mosquito net back into place and was gone.

Nineteen

The heavy wooden door of the church swung open, allowing a dim arrow of light onto cracked paving stones. A stout Kikuyu woman, head bound in brightly patterned cotton, hands clasped piously in front of her, stepped across the threshold. The door closed behind her, and she made her way down the path through the churchyard, passing within feet of where he stood.

Stephen N'toya melted deeper into the shadow of the large angel weeping over an ornate tomb. When the door opened, he'd managed to catch a glimpse of the interior, parishioners still waiting to make their confession. He settled down for a long wait. Gaston was the only priest serving the church, and in this neighborhood, the amount of sin to confess would be considerable.

The raucous noise of a bar blasted from just outside the very British lych-gate. Music, heavy on the beat, women squealing as men slapped at their rumps, laughter at the ribald shouted comments of patrons lounging around tables made from giant wooden cable spools. Hurricane lanterns swung in the breeze, throwing a moving pattern of light and shadow over the scene. The scent of the roses edging the churchyard was overwhelmed by cigarette smoke and the deep sweet smell of reefer.

Interesting neighbors for a fancy old English church down on its luck. N'toya grinned to himself, imagining the reactions of the original parishioners to the African tide lapping hard against their once-exclusive fences.

An hour passed. One by one, a parade of absolved sinners left the church. Mostly women—women seemed to care more about the state of their souls. When the latest penitent opened the door to leave, he saw no others waiting inside. He let fifteen more minutes pass, then dropped the cigarette he'd kept carefully cupped in his hand, ground it under his heel, stepped onto the path.

He pushed open the door to the church, and for a second stood riveted, staring down the nave toward the enormous figure of the crucified Christ behind the altar. The figure was black, the distinctly African features illuminated by a soft yellow light mounted from a high cross beam, the crown of thorns rammed down over tight, kinky hair. The only other source of light came from two banks of lighted candles, one on either side of the church. The place was heady with the smell of incense.

A rustle from the confessional broke the spell. N'toya shook his head, clearing the hypnotic image. The Belgian had an admirable sense of drama. He'd provided some great theater for poor black Africans. N'toya crossed the stone floor, his rubber heels soundless, and slipped inside the confessional, pulling the door behind him, but careful not to close it completely.

Behind the screen he could see a white face. The silver mane of hair told him he was speaking to the right man.

"You were almost too late, my son. I was about to leave." Father Gaston kissed the stole he had just removed and replaced it across the back of his neck, allowing each end to lie flat against the front of his cassock.

N'toya said nothing, listening to the silence in the church to make sure the place was empty. All he could hear was the sound of the priest breathing. The faint sour smell of tobacco-laden breath came from the other side of the screen.

Father Gaston raised his head. "How long since your last confession?"

"I am not here to confess my sins," N'toya said.

"Are you a Catholic?"

"I have no religion."

"Ah. You are in trouble, perhaps."

N'toya gave a short laugh. "No more than any other man."

"Then how can I help you?"

"You can get some information into the right hands."

Father Gaston leaned closer to the screen. "Who are you?"

N'toya put his hand onto the slatted wood, blocking the priest's eyes. "If I wanted you to know my identity, priest, I would have called first, asked for an appointment. Perhaps you would have invited me to talk over tea."

Father Gaston sat back. "You have my attention. Please continue."

"Reitholder has been brought to Nairobi—"

"Should this mean something to me? Who is this man, Reitholder?"

"Don't play games with me, Father Gaston. I am talking about the Afrikaner, Dieter Reitholder—"

"What makes you think I am interested in someone named Dieter Reitholder?"

"I want you to listen carefully, priest. I know you can get the information I am giving you to the right people. Do you understand?" N'toya nudged the door of the confessional open. "Or would you prefer me to leave?"

"Well, I suppose if this man Reitholder is in trouble, it may be that I can be of some small help. What information do you have?"

"Reitholder was taken two days ago at a hunting camp stacked with illegal ivory. He has been brought to Nairobi. He is being held in a warehouse." N'toya gave the address, a run-down area on the edge of the city. He waited for the priest to ask about the ivory, but he didn't. "For the next two nights, I will make sure the guards there will be minimal."

"Is he being held by the army?" Father Gaston asked.

N'toya laughed. "No."

"What am I to do with this information?"

"Father Gaston, in your position you have connections to many people," N'toya said. "Through the confessional, through your parishioners, through your order. Who knows? Just make sure what I have told you gets into the right hands."

"My son, you overestimate my influence——"

Suddenly impatient, N'toya cut him off. "Two nights, tomorrow night and the following night. That's all. I am leaving now. Stay where you are for ten minutes. I do not wish my identity to be revealed." He held his PPK automatic flat against the screen. "Do not be foolhardy. Do you understand me, Father?"

"I think I do, my son."

N'toya kept the automatic in his hand as he pushed open the door of the confessional and stepped out into the church. He looked at the black Christ, but the light on the cross beam had been turned off. Only candlelight remained. The crucified figure was nowhere near as dramatic.

Twenty

The morning following what Cat thought of as "the episode," she emerged from her tent to find the camp empty except for Thomas. Campbell returned an hour later, called a normal good morning as if nothing had happened between them, casually informed her they'd be getting a late start, then got back into his Land Rover and disappeared in the direction of the *engang*. He did not ask her to go with him, and Cat stared after him, not sure whether to be relieved or disappointed.

Tom rolled into camp just after lunch, apologized briefly for the delay. Camp was struck, and the two Land Rovers packed. They did not see Campbell or the Maasai again until nightfall.

But she was alive and no one seemed interested in threatening her life.

Gradually her fear, at least, started to abate. Several times in the next few days, Cat made tentative attempts to speak of what had happened on that nightmare hill, but each time, Campbell or Tom directed the conversation back to the events of the day just past, the plans for the one ahead.

And Campbell remained as remote as if what had happened between them had been a part of her dreams, a figment of a fevered imagination. Cat found herself watching for a suggestion that he thought about her, that he was seeking her out. But he was as hard as he'd ever been, wrapped in that strange solitude he seemed able to draw around him at will.

Finally, they got to Mount Elgon, and she found that Campbell had been right. There was nothing there for her. None of the sites Campbell suggested were even remotely like Joel's sketches, and it was clear that the forests of Mount Elgon could not survive for long.

A generation ago, it must have seemed impenetrable, inhabited only by wild creatures. Now the trees were gone, cleared for small farms, *shambas* Tom called them, and only on higher slopes did the huge cedars with strangely twisted trunks still withstand the march of agriculture. A few colobus monkeys, with their long, silky black and white fur, managed to hang on in spite of the pressure from human expansion.

She was no closer to the truth surrounding Joel's death. Maybe there was no truth, Cat thought. Then why the note? "Something odd's going on here, nothing's what it seems to be." Why this continuing queasy emptiness in the pit of her stomach? And why had Joel's route taken in so many borders? Mount Elgon itself straddled the border with Uganda.

The two men were patient, Tom, as usual, the one to accompany her on her explorations so she had no time alone with Campbell. After two days, she suggested they leave, braced herself for some "I told you so's." But Campbell simply nodded without comment, and the next day, they turned south.

The going was torturous as they traveled heavily rutted roads that were axle deep in red dust for mile after agonizing mile.

They resupplied at Kericho, a small market town, refilled the auxiliary gas tanks and the extra cans each of the three Land Rovers carried. Cat mailed postcards—to Rosie and Jess, the office and John Rifken. And Paul Neville. As a way of reminding herself that he existed, that they had a relationship worked out that suited them both, she'd been writing a message to Paul every night on postcards she had brought with her from Nairobi, pictures of baby animals meant for Rosie. In Kericho she wrote on the last of them—an appealing group of tiny baboons, "Love the guy on the right. Got a decidedly Nevillish glint in his eye. Miss you." But she didn't, and that, too, made her uneasy. The safari seemed to have taken on a life of its own, sufficient to the day, and she was sleeping soundly now at night, the first time since Joel died.

Once on the Mara, the game tracks made traveling easier, and they made better time. The Maasai still ranged out of sight, but Cat no longer questioned it. Somehow they managed to rendez-vous at the end of the day, seemingly in the middle of nowhere, and Thomas produced enough hot water for tea and a sponge bath. Life was reduced to its simplest elements.

Their first full day on the Mara, Cat leaned out of the window and filled her lungs. Even the air felt different. The morning was bright, the Land Rovers dwarfed by rolling golden savannah stretching toward the horizon. Red termite hills like dry skeletal fingers pointed at a deep blue bowl of sky decorated with a few light clouds. Campbell and Tom had been talking about the coming rains, but today, at least, rain seemed a distant possibility. The clouds, certainly, held no moisture. The air smelled sweetly of dry grass.

"In Los Angeles we say at least we get to see the air we breathe," she said to Tom.

Tom took his eyes from the game track. "What?"

"It's a sort of joke. Smog, you know."

"Why do you live in such a place?"

"Be it ever so smoggy, there's no place like home. What about you? Where's your home?"

"Nairobi."

"Your people are from the city?" She thought of the old photographs of generations of M'Balas and Campbells hunting together.

"No. My mother comes from the Cameroons. She was fourteen when she became my father's fourth wife. My father's people, though, are Maasai. Sooner or later they usually return to the old life, adding cattle to their herds, becoming respected elders." He grinned. "Buy a new young wife to warm them in their old age."

"Bet you can't wait to do that," she teased.

He frowned, considering her question. "It has a certain appeal." He shook his head. "But I don't think I could get Miriam to roam from waterhole to waterhole with a load of cattle. We'd have to take the kids out of school for one thing, and, anyway, she prefers to practice medicine in Nairobi." He grinned, pretending to flinch as Cat punched his arm playfully. "Besides that, she'd kill me if I even looked at another woman."

For a moment Cat watched a dozen vultures in a drought-stricken tree, their unblinking naked eyes tracking Campbell's Land Rover as it passed. Bare, wrinkled pink skin covered their heads in place of feathers. They looked like characters in a horror movie. But at least on the Mara Reserve they hadn't been feasting on elephants slaughtered for their tusks.

"Reitholder knew my brother." Suddenly she was tired of being careful, waiting for the right moment to broach the subject of her brother. Since they'd been on the Mara, she had felt Joel's presence more and more. He had died somewhere on these grasslands; she was sure of it. "Reitholder said Joel was a babe in the woods who got eaten up. Did you know that?"

"Reitholder didn't know your brother."

"Then how did he know we were as alike as peas in a pod? Campbell said that's how he recognized me. But that doesn't add up if he didn't know my brother. Does it, Tom?"

"He didn't know your brother," Tom said again.

"Stonewalling. A word for your list." Tom had been teaching her a little Swahili, names of animals, some simple phrases, and she'd been teaching him American slang. It was hard to stay aloof, locked as she and Tom were for hours alone together in the Land Rover. He was charming, a good companion, easygoing and humorous, full of information. She had to keep reminding herself he was probably also a poacher, and certainly a killer.

"What does it mean, stonewalling?"

"Think about it. Or ask Campbell. He's an expert at it."

Tom spun the wheel to avoid a large rock. The breeze changed direction, bringing a strong bovine smell from the great black stream of wildebeest thirty yards away, coming north from the Serengeti in Tanzania in search of grass.

"Why did my brother and Campbell dislike each other?"

"They liked each other—"

"Oh, please! Campbell makes no secret of it. Why should you? Campbell told me Joel got out of the Land Rover to take pictures. I don't believe that. I'd like to know why there was bad blood between them. What did Campbell do to him?"

Tom glanced at her face, then leaned out the window. He signaled to Campbell, shouted a few words in Swahili. Campbell waved and went on. "I told him to go on, we'd be just a few minutes."

He eased the Land Rover into the shade of a baobab tree. Vervets scattered, disappearing into the intricate root system. Tom groped in his pocket for a cheroot, lit it.

Suddenly the sun on her neck lost its warmth. Tom never smoked during the day.

"Joel wasn't an easy man to deal with," Tom said. "He took too many risks."

She knew he was looking at her, waiting for her agreement, and she refused to meet his eyes. "What risks? You were searching for a hotel site. What's the risk in that?"

"Did you know your brother?" The expression on his face was difficult to read.

"No one knew him as I did," Cat said.

"You are lucky, indeed." Tom puffed on the cheroot. Blue smoke wreathed his head. "Then you know why he had to prove himself. All we knew was that he refused to listen. Refused to be warned. That he seemed to think it would be cowardly to show caution. He was foolhardy."

"So, that's it? That's why Campbell disliked him? Because he was difficult. I'm difficult—a lot of people are difficult. I know you're a killer, Tom, but it doesn't stop me from liking you."

For a moment he stared at her, his mouth slightly open, the cheroot motionless in his hand. Then he said, "If you knew your brother as well as you think, then perhaps you can tell me why he lost all control when Dan had to shoot a lioness."

Cat's breath left her body. She couldn't speak. Her eyes felt fixed on Tom's face. *Zuma Canyon. With their father in the Jeep.*

"And why," Tom continued, "after that, Joel never let an opportunity pass to rub our faces in his anger. Sadistic savages. Barbarians. Digs about men who killed to prove their masculinity."

* * *

They were supposed to be shooting rabbits. Somehow they always man-
aged to miss. Their father knew how much they hated it. He'd excused her—
all she'd had to do was handle the small dead bodies, endure the feel of
the blood her father rubbed on her face. Blooding her, he'd called it. They
did it in England, he said, fox hunting. But not Joel. Joel was forced to han-
dle a rifle. To make a man of him, their father said...

"Why did he kill the lioness?" Cat demanded. "How could that be
necessary? You're not supposed to, Thomas told me—" She broke off.

"He had to."

"Oh, for God's sake, Tom! You're supposed to be experts or
something. What's a good enough reason for killing a lioness? He's
a butcher, Tom."

Tom looked at the end of his cheroot. "Then you're saying that
I, too, am a butcher. And that may or may not be true, but it was
not true that day. I'll tell you what happened, but you're not going
to like it." He looked at her, expecting an answer, but she kept her
eyes on him without speaking, so he went on. "We'd come on a couple of lionesses dragging a kill, a zebra. Joel wanted pictures. Dan
warned him they were dangerous, but he said he knew what he was
doing. He got out of the Land Rover, and he got closer and closer."

The mountain lion was one of the few left in the Santa Monica Moun-
tains. They saw it at the same moment; their eyes met, immediately agree-
ing without words not to speak. Their father was looking in the other
direction. Then he'd turned, caught sight of it. He'd wheeled the Jeep, gun-
ning the engine, trying to run it down. Two cubs ran from cover. Whooping
and laughing, their father twisted and turned, trying to cut them off. He
never stopped shouting and laughing. Making a game of their deaths. The
mountain lion loped along, running just hard enough to allow her cubs
to keep pace with her.

* * *

"Joel refused to return to the Land Rover. He got to within a few feet of them, and his presence, the scent of him, forced them to drop their kill. Dan called to him to back up slowly. But he kept clicking away. Then they started toward him. Dan fired over their heads. One turned off, but the other kept coming."

The mountain lion stopped finally and turned, managing to keep her cubs behind her. Derek Stanton picked up the rifle. He shot her. Point-blank. In his excitement it was a messy shot. She screamed once, tried to keep on her feet, get at the Jeep before she collapsed.

"The next shot killed her. There was no choice. And then Joel lost control. He threw himself at Dan. I went after him, and Moses. It took us both to drag him off. If he'd been armed, he'd have killed Dan. But finally we got him quieted. Then we found out why she wouldn't stop. She was lactating—there must have been cubs close by. He went insane. Four men had difficulty holding him. He was truly a madman."

Their father pushed the rifle into Joel's hands. "Get them! Get the cubs!" Their father was wild with excitement. Joel lifted the rifle. Cat watched his finger curl around the trigger, tighten. He glanced at her. The moment was suspended in time... Joel's finger tightening on the trigger. Herself staring at his finger, then raising her eyes, looking straight into his. Their father grabbed for the rifle. "I'll do it, you little coward. I can get them both." And then Joel lowered the rifle until it aimed at their father's chest and he pulled the trigger.

Cat fumbled with the door of the Land Rover, wrenched it open, almost fell from the vehicle. She leaned against it, trying to get air into her lungs...

* * *

Their father stared down at the front of his shirt, slowly soaking in blood, then up at Joel, who was stone-faced, still aiming at his father's chest. Then he fell across the steering wheel. Cat struggled to pull him back. She tore open his bloody shirt, hands shaking, trying to plug the wound with great gobs of Vaseline from a jar kept in the glove compartment. No one spoke. Then Joel put down the rifle, helped her push their father into the passenger seat. She held him steady while Joel drove down the canyon, his feet barely able to reach the accelerator and brake.

Tom climbed out, came around to her. "Cat, it's what happened. You wanted to know."

"It's okay, Tom." She dragged at her collar, opening it wider. "I'm glad you did. I just need some air. Give me a minute." She walked closer to the baobab tree.

A hunting accident. That's what they'd said. The police accepted their story without question. They'd been only ten——who would doubt them? They went out the next day, searched for the cubs, but they had disappeared without trace, too young to survive alone. Coyotes probably. Their father survived. Hours of surgery, months of recuperation. But he didn't die.

He didn't die, but they had thought that they would be free of him. Such innocents. They had never been free of him.
Either of them.

Twenty-One

The drumming on the canvas roof stopped as suddenly as it had started. At four that morning it had sounded as if the sky had tipped like an overfull barrel. Since then, sleep, already fitful after what Tom had told her, had been impossible.

"*Jambo,* Miss Cat." Thomas banged on the canvas door of Cat's tent. "*Kawaha.*" He unzipped the bottom of the door, slid through a tray.

"*Jambo,* Thomas. *Asante.*" Since that day on the mountain, her relationship with Thomas had moved to a different level. He fussed over her, brought coffee to her tent, saw to it that she ate what he considered to be enough. "What's going on out there?"

"*Mvua.* Rainy season going on, Miss Cat. We pack up fast."

Cat splashed cold water on her face, pulled on jeans and a sweater, shoved her feet into boots and picked up her coffee. She stepped out into a chill morning filled with the scents of grass and wet earth, coffee and frying bacon. From horizon to horizon, the sky billowed with clouds, five separate storms clearly discernible.

Miles away rain fell like brush strokes in a watercolor, and the sky was torn by lightning. The whole storm system was moving south in waves, every shade of gray she could imagine was visible, tinted with violet and pink and a heavy sulfurous yellow.

The men not on watch had slept under canvas last night for the first time, and a mess tent had been erected. She slipped on a green slicker, sloshed her way through the mud.

Tom was finishing as she arrived, and Campbell, avoiding her as usual, was already supervising the men. She ate alone, not inclined to linger over breakfast in a mess tent enclosed on three sides and open to the elements on the fourth. Half an hour later they left the men to finish loading their Land Rover and headed south.

Overnight, game trails that had been axle deep in dust had become racing streams. On a parallel course, the wet black bodies of wildebeest glistened as they made their own relentless way across the rain-soaked grassland.

Inside the Land Rover, the air was heavy with moisture. Rain pounding the roof made conversation difficult, and Cat stared out at the drenched landscape, her mind on what Tom had told her—pondering how similar it was to what Campbell had said was the way Joel died. The camera, the refusal to be warned. All his life Joel had needed to prove himself. He'd been courageous. Rash. Foolhardy, even. But he would never have taken the same risk twice, as these men claimed he had.

The vehicle slid through mud. The ground was more deeply rutted, and the Land Rover ground its way over limbs of downed trees, churned through water-filled depressions.

"This looks like a battlefield," she said. She had to raise her voice to be heard. Everywhere trees were shattered, entire root systems upended, mud dripping from them like clots of blood.

"Looks worse than it is. Elephants lean on the trees, knock

them over and eat the roots. Actually it creates water catchment and new grazing." He slowed. "There's a few of the culprits."

Enormous gray shapes appeared eerily through the rain, showing no fear of the Land Rover. Cat wound down her window. Just a few feet away, its outline softened by the mist of rain, a single elephant fanned huge ears. Cat looked into a large, long-lashed eye that seemed filled with an ancient knowledge, a window on a remote past. Time stilled. Then Tom pressed gently on the gas, and the elephants faded, blending with the gray mist, then disappeared, shrouded by rain.

"There used to be millions, once," Tom said.

"Then why do you still hunt?"

"Why did you Americans kill sixty million buffalo?"

"To subdue the Indian nations. Why have you Africans killed ten million elephants?"

After a moment's silence, he said, "We didn't go after Ahmed, did we?"

"Not this time. You wiped out your competition, instead."

He looked as if he wanted to answer her and was biting back words. Thunder rolled and crashed. Rain sheeted across the windshield, the wiper terthunking back and forth, useless against the deluge. Impossibly, the rain grew heavier, hammering the roof. Lightning flashed. The herd of wildebeest veered, surrounding the Land Rover. Among them, zebra and impala were carried along by the press of bodies. The wildebeest broke into a trot, changed course, then milled around without purpose.

Ahead of them, Campbell signaled with a circling arm out of his window. Tom drew alongside.

"They're getting a bit spooked," Campbell shouted. "They're thinner toward the southwest. We'll go around them and swing southeast."

Tom nodded.

"Keep up close, Tom."

Campbell's Land Rover moved slowly forward. A crack of lightning tore through the rain.

"What is it?" Cat asked anxiously.

"Nothing to worry about. *Nyumbu* are giddy creatures at best. In these numbers—"Tom shook his head. He put his fingers to the front of his shirt. "Panic can spread through the whole herd. It's best to go around them. Don't worry."

"Don't keep saying that. You're making me nervous." Only recently had she realized that when he was worried or uncomfortable, Tom fingered the intricately beaded antelope-skin medicine pouch he wore under his shirt. Tom often surprised her. He was an educated man, but his roots went deep into a primitive culture.

The long faces of the wildebeest seemed suddenly sinister; they were no longer simply lovable clowns with silly little beards and cute rumps, prone to kicking up their heels and prancing about out of sheer *joie de vivre*. Now the beards were matted, dripping with water, and she couldn't see the skinny rear ends. All she could see was the spread of curved horns as long as the span of Texas longhorns.

The terrain was dropping noticeably, and Cat reached for the map. "I don't think we'll be able to use that streambed," she said. "Not now." The streambed was marked on the map as a dry watercourse. Their plan had been to follow it south for several miles, then cross and turn east toward Maasai Springs. They had expected to be across by midmorning. It was already long past that.

Tom slammed a foot on the brake. The ground had fallen away abruptly, and the western bank of the watercourse was almost under the wheels. In one night it had become a raging, debris-clogged torrent filled from bank to bank with wild, silt-laden water.

Wildebeest slipped over the edge, the press of their numbers on the steep mud slope forcing them into the stream. They waded toward the eastern bank, the smaller animals fighting to keep to their feet, the old and weak swept downstream by the rush of water.

A few yards downstream Campbell had come to a stop at the water's edge and was out of his vehicle. He pushed his way through the crush of wildebeest and leaned in the window, handing Tom his binoculars.

"Take a look. About ten o'clock."

Tom stood in the doorway, trained the glasses and swore.

Cat took out her own glasses, peered through the rain-slashed windshield, seeing nothing but gray. Then slowly, on the other side of the torrent, a dim red-clad figure wavered into view. Two or three figures, surrounded by moving animals.

"They look like women. Who are they?"

"I'll have to go across and ask them," Campbell said.

"That stream's running too high," Tom said.

"Well, we can't just leave them there."

Campbell pushed his way back to his Land Rover. Axle deep in mud, the vehicle ground down the deep bank, edged slowly into the water and rocked toward the middle of the stream. Water frothed like detergent as it eddied around the Land Rover. A drowning wildebeest slammed again and again into the chassis. The vehicle rocked drunkenly. The animal swirled away. Campbell was in the middle of the stream, the rush of water obliterating the sound of the laboring engine. The Land Rover stopped. An age passed. It jolted forward. Cat let out her breath.

"He's got them," Tom said after a moment. He wiped the rain from the binoculars, put them back to his eyes. "He's bringing them across."

The wildebeest, packing more densely on both banks, reluctantly gave way to Campbell's Land Rover, then closed in behind it. Cat turned in her seat and felt the blood drain from her face. A solid mass of animals was pressing in, a sea of horns in every direction.

Campbell ground back across the stream, leaning from his window as he drew alongside. Water dripped from the heads of the three Maasai crushed together in the front seat—an old woman, a much younger heavily pregnant woman and a small girl. They leaned forward, peering around Campbell to stare with friendly interest at Cat. She smiled and waved. They broke into wide answering smiles and waved back.

"They're on their way to their home place for the birth," Campbell shouted. "Time's near so they decided on a shortcut to beat the rain. You'll have to take them, Tom, we can't let them travel alone. You know their place, over by Fig Tree. Take you a day or two in this weather. Better hurry, though, or you'll find yourself acting as midwife."

Tom swore in Swahili and Campbell laughed, then climbed out of his Land Rover. He reached back for the little girl. The two women clambered out and followed close as he opened a path through the crush of animals, carefully holding the child high against his chest. Tom opened the door, and the two men used their bodies as a barrier against the pressure of wildebeest while the women crowded into Tom's Land Rover.

Campbell forced his way around the vehicle, opened Cat's door. "Your turn. Come on."

Her mouth was dry. Outside the safety of the Land Rover, the world seemed full of horns. Not longhorns, she told herself.

Not longhorns. Wildebeest. She'd been about the age of the child now grinning happily at her from behind the gun rack. God, she prayed silently, don't let me pee my pants. She took Campbell's hand, climbed out into the maelstrom.

Rain slashed her face. She turned to pull out the portfolio from behind her seat—it was filled with photographs she had taken of possible sites, but more importantly, it contained the sketches Joel had sent her. She struggled to keep the door open.

"For God's sake, Cat." Campbell grabbed her shoulders. "Come on!"

"My portfolio," she yelled against the noise of the rain and rushing stream.

"We can't get at it now. It's safe with Tom."

"No!" The Land Rover was beginning to move. Suddenly she could hear Raul Guitterrez's amused comments about women, their place in the world, the laughter about what they did best, cute asses, great tits. She couldn't lose that portfolio. Rain beat against her face, blurred her vision. She pounded the roof.

Campbell pulled her away from the door. She turned to beat at him. "I've got to get my portfolio!"

He slammed the door, bent to wave Tom on, then shoved her behind him. "Hold on to my jacket."

Cat grabbed at the door but the Land Rover was gathering speed, breaking from her grasp. Frustrated, she turned back to Campbell. He shouldered his way through the herd, and she held his belt, fearing to be separated from him. Steam rose from the backs of the wildebeest pressing against them. Every minute she expected to be crushed by the heavy, moving bodies. The powerful bovine smell, the cacophony of bleating grunts hammered against her. A thirty-inch span of horns fanned her cheek. She closed her eyes, pressed her head into Campbell's back. Then he was forcing open a door, shoving her into a seat. The floor of the Land Rover was black with mud. The whole interior smelled of river water, but after the chaos outside it was sanctuary.

The stream, filled now with swimming animals, was higher. Another piece of bank gave way, melting into the torrent. The Land Rover tilted.

Cat held on to her seat. "We're going in!"

Campbell pressed gently on the gas. The wheels spun, then grabbed. He backed up. "We'll find a place to cross downstream."

They turned southwest, away from the river, stopping frequently to search for a path through the gathering herds. The sky was darker. Large bulls turned to face the Land Rover as it passed, and she remembered Tom telling her they were courageous in defense, often fending off young lions.

Thunder cracked across the darkening plain. The animals broke into a trot, jostling each other nervously, disoriented, aimless. Lightning forked and cracked, again and again. Thunderclaps shook the earth. Lowering clouds seemed to empty. The rush of water was impenetrable. Directly overhead now, the storm was deafening.

"We'll have to wait it out," Campbell shouted. "I'll find a—"

The rest was lost. A hundred feet away, lightning struck the earth, a double jagged strike, snaking blue flame. As one body, the herd moved. Inside the Land Rover, Cat felt the vibration of thousands of pounding hooves streak through the earth like a seismic wave as the terror-stricken animals fought to get away, gathering speed, galloping, colliding. Panic spread like wind-driven floodwater. Animals stumbled, struggling to regain their footing, then disappeared. The Land Rover rocked under the onslaught of terrified beasts banging against the sides. Icy sweat beaded Cat's face. Her own panic was rising.

Wrestling the wheel, Campbell brought the vehicle parallel with the racing herd. He was calm, his movements sure, and her panic receded. She ached with the effort of keeping away from the door, from being thrown out, crushed. Like Joel, crushed beneath relentless hooves.

She wanted to close her eyes, shut out the sight of tossing heads. The straining corded necks. The ropes of foaming saliva dropping from open mouths. The tangle of massive horns in wild jerking motion only inches away on the other side of the door. But she was riveted, compelled to watch. She thought she screamed, but it could have been in her mind. Nothing could be heard above the storm and pounding hooves.

Suddenly the terrified creatures wheeled. The herd thinned, no longer buffeting the Land Rover.

Campbell stamped on the clutch, twisted the wheel hard. "Christ! Tom's going to get caught from the side." He fought the wheel and the Land Rover bounced and skidded. "They'll tip him over like a toy. We'll have to turn them."

Her first thought was the portfolio, a stab of shame hard on its heels as she remembered the women and the child. "How can we? There must be thousands."

Campbell glanced at her. "Scared?" he shouted.

"Sure!" she shouted back. "You think I'm crazy?"

He laughed. "It's all right. Trust me."

Cat snorted in derision, amused this time not caustic, but the sound was lost in the turmoil. He hit the gas, eased the Land Rover back into the stream of panicked, charging beasts. The vehicle bucked, but matched the pace of the wildebeest galloping at full stretch, then gradually the Land Rover began to overtake them.

Cat clung to the metal frame. The Land Rover slammed again and again against the earth. She couldn't look down, fearing that she would see the floor buckling, giving way, exposing the ground racing beneath them. Clumps of mud encrusted the windscreen, obscured the light from the doors. Suddenly she was filled with a wild excitement. She wanted to whoop and shout, scream at the storm.

Campbell braked hard, changed down, then slammed to a stop

under the upturned roots of an elephant-ravaged tree. Wildebeest hurled themselves blindly, thunderously, across the fallen trunk. He turned, wrenched a rifle from the rack behind him. "Stay here! You'll be all right. Just stay with the Land Rover. D'you hear me? Stay put."

"What are you going to do?" She grabbed his arm. "You can't go out there!"

"Do as I say. Stay here."

She tried to hold him. He looked at her face, then bent and kissed her. His lips moved against hers—he was saying something but she couldn't hear him. She put her arms around his neck, trying to hold him, but he tore loose and opened the door against the muddy dripping roots. In an instant the storm had swallowed him.

Cat clambered across the seat, fumbled at the gun rack.

"Come on. Goddamn it, come on." She sobbed the words. A rifle jerked loose. She threw herself out of the Land Rover, rolled into a mud-filled pocket of space between the wheels and the towering roots. She struggled to her feet, sliding in red gelatinous mud. Wind tore at her. She couldn't think. Couldn't feel.

"Campbell!" she shrieked into the madness of storm and stampede.

Rifle shots answered her. She struggled toward the sound, somehow managing to keep hold of the rifle. Clods of mud from the roots matted her hair. She wiped a hand over her face, across her eyes. Dimly she made him out, his back against the downed trunk of the tree, firing high, over the herd. Animals buffeted him in their wild, leaping gallop—but they were turning away from the gunshots.

A huge bull loomed behind him through the rain.

"Campbell!" She shrieked his name again, slammed the butt of the rifle against her shoulder and fired.

The bull veered. Madness and noise surrounded her. She felt a blow from a heavy body. Consciousness slipped away as she fell.

Twenty-Two

Her eyes opened to a dome of canvas. No mosquito net. She was on the floor of her tent, lying on the thin foam pad from her bed. No bed. Under the sheet and blanket she was naked.

Her body felt as if it had just been taken out of a cement mixer. Cat turned her head. The portfolio leaned against the wall, her bag next to it. Apart from that, the tent was empty. No sound came from outside. No rattle of cooking utensils, no voices. Just the hum of deep silence.

A large tanned hand held open the canvas door. "I was waiting until I heard you stir," Campbell said.

"Hi."

She watched him walk toward her, allowing herself to see the natural grace of his movements. Very soon she would be gone, she thought. Raul Guitterrez would do John's work here, and she would never see Campbell again.

He sat on his heels by her side. "How do you feel?"

"Terrific."

He grinned. "I didn't realize you knew your way around fire-arms." He picked up her hand. "If I'd known, I'd have been more concerned last time you turned a gun on me. Who taught you?"

"My father. Years ago, when I was a child. I didn't know I even remembered how. Did I kill that poor animal?"

Campbell laughed. "Well, you scared it half to death, but you bloody near killed me."

Cat looked at him in horror. "I didn't!"

"I heard that bullet whistle past my ear and almost died of fright."

She curled her fingers around his and laughed.

"I told you to stay in the Land Rover," he said. "Do you ever do as you're told?"

"Not if I can help it. What happened?"

"A bloody great beast gave you a thump, tossed you like a sack of mealies into the mud. It was just luck you were thrown under the roots. Knocked you out cold."

"I see my portfolio arrived. Are Tom and the women okay?"

"The main herd turned before it got to them. They're all right." He grinned. "Tom's relieved that baby's still where it was last time you saw it."

Cat laughed, glad to be with him, close to him, holding his hand. She pushed the thought of Joel into the back of her mind.

"How did we get here? Where are we, anyway?"

"Maasai Springs. The men got here as we did, and got a fire going. We're a Land Rover short with Tom gone, so they had to go back for the rest of the gear."

"I remember some of it." Campbell holding her against him while he drove. His voice speaking her name, talking to her, forcing her to answer him. She rolled her shoulders. The sheet slipped, leaving the pink edge of one areola bare. One small movement, and her nipple would be exposed. She left the sheet where it was. "I'm going to be very stiff, I think." She didn't look at him.

Campbell rose to his feet, pulled her robe out of her bag, dropped it on the end of the bed. "You won't even have a bruise if we move fast enough. A soak in the springs and you'll be fighting fit. Your old self, in other words." He dropped the canvas door in place behind him.

Gingerly, Cat stood upright. She examined her body. No marks that she could see, but her head felt filled with cotton batting. Her hair was damp, curling in tendrils around her face as it did when allowed to dry naturally, and a strange, rather pleasant medicinal smell clung to it.

More was coming back to her. Her protests when Campbell stripped her to examine her for broken bones. His gentleness when he sponged off the mud before tucking her under the blanket. She slipped on her robe and went outside.

Turbulence was still apparent in clouds that frothed like meringue, but the storm had passed. The air was crisp and smelled green and washed, with the same dry undertone that clung to her hair. Around her was a scene that on a travel poster would be thought an exaggeration. From the palest jade to deepest emerald, tiny jewel-like pools shimmered under canopies of steam. Towering gray rocks etched by weather, washed to yellow and pink and copper by minerals. Weaverbird nests hung like basketware Christmas ornaments from the thorn trees. The vast drenched plain stretching to distant purple hills was filled with browsing animals. And elephants were close—the downed trees were evidence of that. About a mile away was a waterhole, so their continued presence was ensured. They'd always come to drink.

The site was perfect. Raul Guitterrez would be stopped in his tracks.

Campbell placed the rifle he was cleaning on the camp table in front of him. "Well, what do you think?"

"It's wonderful."

"I thought you'd like it. It's the place I wanted to bring you to begin with. The perfect spot for a hotel for the gouty rich."

"Did Joel see this place?"

"Yes," he said shortly.

"Well, this is the most marvelous place I've seen." Later, she would check Joel's sketches. There was nothing even remotely like the wonderful pools among them, but something in the contour of the distant hills seemed familiar. "Can we get in touch with Los Angeles?" she asked. "I'd like to tell my client that we've got his site, then start the preliminary studies."

"It will have to wait until tomorrow. The radio's waterlogged, so we're out of touch until the men arrive. Let's hope they managed to keep everything dry. Anyway, right now, you should soak in one of the pools before the stiffness sets."

"You can soak in them?"

"Come on."

He led the way over a narrow game trail threading through the rocks and stopped beside a deep green pool. Its stone outline wavered through steam, bubbles rose from a rocky bottom, the surface fizzed with action.

"How lovely. It looks pretty deep."

"No. When you sit, the water will come to your shoulders." He stood behind her, slipped her robe from her shoulders.

She was nude, shaking slightly—from the cool air, from waiting to feel his hands on her.

"Just inch your way down."

He might have been talking to a child. He didn't touch her.

Cat sat on the edge of the pool, then lowered herself into its depths. The water was warm, nudging and bubbling against her skin like the butt of tiny noses. She sat on the bottom, stretched her legs. The water was buoyant.

"Campbell?" The pool was large enough for two.

"I'm here."

She turned to look for him. Only the back of his head was visible. He was immersed in a pool about ten feet away. She slid deeper.

"It's like bathing in hot champagne."

"The Maasai believe it cures everything from broken bones to broken spirits."

His voice held the strange sad note she'd heard before.

"And does it?"

"If you believe it will, I suppose it does." He changed the subject. "It's a favorite with baboons, too. I've even seen hyenas in these pools. Any number of animals use them."

"This one I'm in?"

"Certainly."

"Oh."

"Don't worry. These pools are also used by a U.N. agricultural outfit when they're in the area and they run tests. They say the water's quite safe."

Gently Cat pulsed her arms up and down, watching pale green bubbles rise through emerald water and break against her skin. She pillowed her head on the smooth rock edge and stared at the sky. Nairobi was far distant, Los Angeles no longer even existed. Languor spread through her, every limb felt heavy. Minerals always smelled terrible, but not here. The air was moist and green. The place was magic.

A strange heat penetrated her bones. Her mind drifted. No minutes, no hours, no days. No past. No future. Only limitless time and space in which anything was possible.

"That's enough," Campbell said. "By morning you won't even have a bruise to show for your little misadventure."

Feeling insubstantial, she opened her eyes and had to make an effort to focus. He was fully dressed and crouched beside her.

"Mmm."

"Come on, time to get out. You can get too much of this." He moved behind her, put his hands under her arms and hauled her out of the water.

She let him drape the robe over her. He pushed first one arm then the other into the sleeves. Her heart beat in slow, heavy thuds. Blood moved thickly through her body. Nerves close to the surface of her skin made her aware of the roughness of the terry cloth on her nipples, the catch of it on her pubic hair, its movement against her thighs. She wanted to lean against him, but his touch was efficient and impersonal.

She followed him along the game trail. It was almost dark. A great bite of time had been swallowed while they were soaking, and she hadn't noticed. Tufts of grass quivered in a light breeze and the thorn trees were black silhouettes against a purple sky. The first bats of evening fluttered.

"Put on something dry, Cat. Your things are there."

She nodded. Inside the tent, she stood for a moment in front of the portfolio of sketches, then turned away. Not tonight, she thought. Whatever she had to find out, it could wait. She opened her bag, dragged out a crumpled skirt and a loose white sweater. Every movement she made felt significant, complete in itself. She smoothed lotion onto her breasts and thighs, lingering over the softness of her skin, the feel of her hands on her body. She put on the sweater and skirt, ran a brush through her hair, glad, after all, she hadn't had it cut off before leaving Los Angeles.

"Drink, Cat?" Campbell called.

"Great. Scotch?"

"Water, no soda. Okay?"

"Sure."

Cat stepped outside and took the drink he held out to her, then sat and watched him coax a fire into life. The deft movement of his hands, the muscles in his forearms moving as he tore apart fallen branches. She noticed the silver in his hair, and she studied his face, the level eyebrows and strong bones, the hard mouth. Desire for him was moist and heavy, but without urgency. She wanted to savor it all, every feeling in her body, the nearness of him.

He broiled steaks from the cooler. They shared a Tusker, talked very little.

The night rustled with small sounds: the metallic clink of guinea fowl as they moved toward the water, the breath of the wind through leaves, the creaking swing of the weaverbird nests. It was bittersweet, she thought, a lonely place on the verge of change.

Cat slipped her feet out of her sandals, pressed them into damp grass. Darkness the color of blue-black velvet had fallen and clouds drifted across the face of the moon. Lightning still flickered in the south. She sat on a boulder close to the fire, staring into the flames. Her breath was shallow, and she wondered if he could hear the thud of her heart——he had the hearing of a wild animal.

Campbell got up to replenish the fire. As he passed her, Cat caught at his hand. She looked up at him. He held her eyes for a heart-stopping minute. Slowly he drew her to her feet. A hand on each side of her head, he tipped her face to him and kissed her. She welcomed his tongue. Then she had a brief flash of sanity and turned her head.

"Campbell, this is madness. I don't have room in my life for a man like you." And there was the woman in Nairobi. And Paul...

"Too late," he said. "I'm already in your life." He put his lips to her neck, slipped his hands beneath her sweater, caressing her back.

Cat shivered. He was right, it was too late. She didn't resist when he drew her into the dim cocoon of the tent, lowered her onto the pad from the camp bed. He knelt beside her. Slowly, savoring each moment of discovery, he removed her sweater and skirt—she was naked beneath—then pressed his lips to her belly.

From outside, the dim fire glow wavered against the canvas walls. She put her hands in his hair, pulled his head up. "What are you doing to me?" Her voice was shaky.

He moved up to kiss her. "If you have to ask, I must be doing it wrong."

"No. You're not doing it wrong." She put her arms around his neck. "You're doing it exactly right."

"Mmm." He nuzzled her neck then shifted his weight onto her, encircled her wrists, pinned her arms above her head. He looked into her eyes, murmured softly to her in Maa.

"What?" she whispered. "What are you saying?"

"You bewitch me, beloved. With the golden eyes of the lioness, you hold me in thrall."

Gradually the night sounds pressed in. The fire had burned down, the light inside the tent was low. Campbell had one arm around her, the other under his head. He looked down at her.

"Welcome back," he said.

"Mmm." She moved her body languorously against him. Directly below her ear was the strong, steady beat of his heart. She was replete, but knew it wouldn't last. The hunger for him hovered still. Perhaps it would always be there. A frisson of fear touched her. He had led her into unfamiliar territory, opened her to a depth of passion that was new. There was no way back from what she felt for him. She didn't want to love this man. Too much was between them. Too many questions.

"Cat?"

"Mmm." She pushed her face deeper into his chest. "Thank you for this."

He grinned down at her. "Well, I aim to please, *memsahib*. Give me a few minutes, and I'm again at your disposal—"

She poked him. "No, I meant Maasai Springs."

"Oh, I thought you were overwhelmed by my charms."

"Well, that, too. But, Campbell, I want you to know I'll be careful with this place. Joel and I were looking into what can be done with rammed earth structures. No wood is used, so you save natural resources. It's an ancient method of building, and I think it's perfect for here. I'll design something that will blend perfectly with the site. You won't even know it's here."

"Well, if it has to be developed, better you than the other chap. What's his name? Guitterrez?"

She looked up at him, surprised. "You know about him?"

"I made it my business to find out a bit about the kind of work he did."

"You amaze me. I didn't think you'd be interested in architecture."

"Well, I can't say that I am, generally. But this place needs a delicate hand. I spoke to John Rifken when I was trying to head you off. He said it was you or the other feller. Even without this rammed earth business, you're better."

"Thanks." A great rent seemed to open in her chest. "We should have come here first. It would have avoided so much trouble."

Campbell tugged her arm to release her hold on his neck. "If I don't feed that fire, I might lose you to a hungry lion."

She clung tighter. "Not to bloodthirsty poachers?"

"No."

"How can you be so sure?"

"If someone's out there who shouldn't be, I'll know it."

"How?"

He hesitated. "There are men watching."

"You mean Moses and Sambeke and the others? Dear old Thomas?"

"Dear old Thomas?" he repeated, laughing.

Cat tucked her hand deeper behind his neck, took a breath.

"Campbell, your father said the place Joel died was close to Tanzania. I looked at the map. Maasai Springs is very close to Tanzania."

"It's a long border."

"Yes, but the map shows Maasai Springs to be close to the Mara River. That's where he was killed, isn't it?" She waited for him to say he would take her there. He didn't. "I want to go there." When he still didn't reply, she said, "Will you take me?"

"All right."

"When?" she pressed.

"When the men get here. Tomorrow if you like."

"I don't want a circus, the men watching."

He looked down at her, stroked the hair back from her face. "Yes, sweetheart, I promise. I know what you want. Now, let me up. I must get to that fire."

She released him and turned on her side to watch him cross the tent, trying to imagine him in Beverly Hills. The whole thing was mad. She couldn't enter his world and he was completely alien to hers. The tent brightened, then he was silhouetted in the doorway, the flames behind him, a bottle in one hand, plastic glasses in the other.

"This should be champagne," he said. "But it's the last of the Tusker."

"Who needs champagne?" She plumped the pillow, bent it in half and leaned back.

His eyes roamed over her. She lifted her hair off her neck with both hands, let it drift through her fingers. The years of sweaty early-morning workouts had not been wasted. Her muscles were firm and sleek, her breasts high. A woman's body, and none the worse for that. She crossed one ankle over the other and grinned at him.

"You're a wanton," he said softly.

She raised her eyebrows. "And you're priapic."

Laughing, she held him at arm's length, reaching for the Tusker. "First some sustenance, then we'll see."

He discarded the bottle, pulled her toward him. Cat put her hands on his shoulders, pushed him onto his back on the narrow bed, then knelt across him. She guided him into her, rocked her hips slowly. Then somehow she was beneath him and she heard his deep rumbling moans, his words in a language she did not understand.

Twenty-Three

Cat put out a hand, but he was gone. Drowsily, she burrowed into the pillow, reluctant to open her eyes and look at the time. They had made love all night, and talked. It had been after four when they finally slept. She had sunk into the deepest sleep she'd had since Joel's death.

Outside she could hear voices. The men must have arrived. There would be no more time alone, at least until they got back to Nairobi. Unwillingly, she opened her eyes—a dark dawn had broken. She got up and put on her robe, then knelt in front of her portfolio, quickly unzipping it and spreading it open on the floor. One by one she studied Joel's sketches. She was right. The contour of the land was familiar, but the only thing she could be sure of was that they had not been done from the perspective of Maasai Springs. It was time to show them to Campbell. She had to trust him—she did trust him. She smiled to herself, thinking about the hours just past. Rain pattered lightly on the roof, thunder rumbled. She looked at her watch and strained to hear Campbell's voice.

"*Jambo,* Miss Cat. *Kawaha,*"Thomas called.

"*Jambo,* Thomas." She opened the door.

Thomas's startled eyes took in the chaos of the tent, the riot of tangled blankets and scattered pillows. An empty Tusker bottle. Plastic glasses tipped on their sides. Laughter rippled silently through her as a blank, well-bred curtain fell over his face. Thomas placed the coffee on the camp table.

"You get big push from mad *nyumbu,* eh, Miss Cat? Maasai Spring fix you good, though."

Cat thought she caught a glimpse of amusement in his black eyes, gone before she was sure. "Yes, it was a young bull, I think." She kept her voice neutral. That was what the Maasai called their virile young warriors. Young bulls. "I tried to shoot it, but it got me instead. I'm fine now, though."

"Ah,"Thomas said, nodding seriously.

Cat stepped outside into an unfamiliar landscape. Gone were the bright pools of water. Instead, the world was clothed in drifting, eerie wetness. The site was still phenomenal, but this kind of weather would be a handicap. She'd have to find out how often this happened. Please God, she thought, only in the rainy season and then only occasionally. She sipped coffee and looked around, waving to Moses and Olentwalla, dim figures wreathed in mist. Sambeke was nowhere to be seen. Neither was Campbell. She glanced at the sketches in her hand.

"Where's Campbell?"

"He gone, Miss Cat. Gone to Nairobi."

Cat was not sure whether the thunder was in her head or rolling across the country. The coffee cup tilted and the hot liquid splashed on her bare feet.

"Nairobi? When?"

Thomas took the tilting cup from her fingers and turned to re-fill it. Rain sputtered against the canvas sheet above their heads.

"He leave soon as he hear. Early. We come at five, tell him message on radio from *Bwana* Jock. He gone in quarter hour."

Cat waited for an explanation, wanting to shake him as he clattered with dried milk and sugar. "Why did he go to Nairobi?"

"Miss Morag gone."

Pain opened like a chasm in her chest. "Jock Campbell called you on the shortwave?"

"Say boss not answer his radio call. He call us, say drive like hell, tell boss Miss Morag gone."

Thomas fiddled with the coffeepot, checked its contents. Every word he said was acid dripped into her heart.

"He try raise *Bwana* Jock when we get here, but now our radio flooded. He swear big, the boss. Swahili. Maa. Kiingereza." Thomas shook his head in admiration.

She remembered the portrait over the fireplace in Nairobi, the snapshots stuck in the frames of old pictures in Campbell's office, the young woman storming out of the house. "Did he leave a message for me?"

"He call you on radio."

"That's all?"

"No one talk much. Keep head down, Miss Cat. Talk soft. *Bwana* Dan bad when he get angry like that. No one talk."

How could he have gone without a word? She looked at the sketches still clutched in her hand, glad she hadn't shown them to him.

"Well, you'd better take it easy today, Thomas. You must be tired after driving all night." She was pleased to hear that her tone was easy. Nothing wrong here, Thomas, old buddy. "*Bwana* Tom should be back in a couple of days. He took some women to their village."

"We stay close with you until he get here."

Cat put the coffee down and turned to enter the tent. Her stomach writhed with disgust. The place reeked of stale sex and spilled beer and looked like the scene of a debauch.

"Get this place cleaned up, please, Thomas. If you brought the rest of the gear with you, put some furniture in place."

He had entered the tent behind her and picked up the empty Tusker bottle and the plastic glasses.

"You eat breakfast, Miss Cat, and this all be neat and set up."

"Keep something for me. I'm going to soak in one of the pools first."

As she walked into the mist, she stumbled over tussocks of dried grass where she remembered only a soft green smoothness underfoot. Nothing was as it seemed. Exactly what Joel had said. Color had been drained from the landscape, everything now was in shades of gray.

Campbell's guard had been down, and she'd missed an opportunity that would never come again because she had wanted the time with him for herself, to feel there was no one in the world but the two of them. She had never asked about Joel's death.

Astringent water bubbled against her skin, heat seemed to melt her flesh. The truth was Morag had done her a favor—given her the chance to step back and reclaim herself. Unlike her mother who had surrendered herself body and soul. She and Joel had never had anyone to stand between them and the harsh reality of life—and never needed it. Illusion was dangerous.

But in the light of a dreary morning, the passion of the night before had left her defenseless, and pain was bleeding through the membrane between past and present. Her mother slipped into her mind only in dreams, but suddenly she couldn't escape the sun-filled kitchen in Malibu, the sound of the Pacific Ocean sparkling outside the window, her own young accusatory voice breaking the unwritten rule of silence.

"You never even try to protect us. We're pawns in some terrible game he plays with you, and you let him torture us."

"How can you say that?" Karen Stanton said. "What does he do to you that's so bad? He just wants you to grow up strong. He's your father. He loves you. Children need their father——"

"We tried to kill him when we were ten. Didn't that tell you anything?"

"You did no such thing! That's a terrible thing to say! It was an accident——"

"It wasn't an accident, Mother. You know that, you've always known it. We tried to kill him. And he knows it, too, and that's when he started on Joel, calling him a little sissy-boy, the little homo because he wouldn't kill those poor cubs. All those jokes about me being weak. Don't you care what he does to us?"

"They're just his jokes——"

"They are not jokes," Cat shouted.

"What do you want me to do? He's your father——"

"God, you're pathetic. He's destroyed you and you've helped him do it. Bit by bit. Year by year. You were a real person once. You had a career, you taught history. You could leave him, go back to it. Other women have."

"Why would I leave him? He loves me, and I love him. More than——" Karen Stanton stopped.

"Go on, Mother. More than me and Joel. Is that what you were going to say? We don't even exist for you, do we? We never have."

Her mother turned to look out of the kitchen window at the pelicans diving for fish just beyond the breaking surf.

"As long as he keeps fucking you, that's all you care about, isn't that right, Mother? It doesn't matter how he treats your children." Cat felt incandescent with rage. "Nothing matters, as long as he keeps fucking you——"

* * *

Cat felt again the pain of her mother's hand striking her face, first one cheek then the other, the rain of fists on her shoulders and chest.

Cat's face was wet, not only from the moisture-laden air. Her breath caught in her chest, then sobs wrenched her body. She pressed the heels of her hands hard into her eyes to blot out the image of her mother's poor drained body, the slashed wrists, the photographs of Derek Stanton in bed with different women floating on top of the water like poisonous flowers. She and Joel guessed their father had sent them to her himself, another knife turned in their mother's heart. She'd left a note thinking he would find her body. The ultimate move in their terrible game. Instead, it was Cat who'd come home to try to patch up their quarrel.

It wasn't her fault, she knew that. It wasn't her fault. But sometimes...

"Goddammit," she said aloud. "Goddammit." She hated crying, hated being out of control. Hated being sodden with self-pity. Hated being weak. But she couldn't stop it. She wept like an abandoned child. The sobs deepened, reaching into the well of grief she had kept contained for so long it had neither name nor form. Grief for the lost woman whose desperate need for love at any cost had ultimately destroyed her. For the children they had been. For Joel, who had never been free of his father's shadow. For herself, a tough little girl who had survived yet had still to find her own way out of that same shadow.

The sobs slowed. Cat splashed her eyes. Her fear had been that if she ever started, she would cry forever—she hadn't even been able to cry for Joel. But it was over now. It would not be repeated.

She hauled herself out of the pool, slipped on her robe and made her way over the tussocks without stumbling.

* * *

The mist turned to drizzle. Sambeke appeared and for the next
several hours, the three heavily armed Maasai kept up separate patrols, appearing through the rain every thirty or forty minutes,
then, just as mysteriously, vanishing. Cat spent the morning walking the site, making notes about the terrain, with Thomas dogging
her every footstep. She kept Joel's sketches in her hand, compared
them to a distant escarpment, but the mist made it difficult to be
sure of what she was seeing.

"Thomas, I'd like to get a bit farther afield."

Thomas shook his head. "You wait. *Bwana* Tom here soon."

"I don't think so, Thomas. He's going to be a couple of days at
least. I think we could just try that escarpment up there. The
views must be sensational."

Thomas shook his head, turned to look out at the wet landscape,
making it clear that he did not intend to answer questions.

As the day wore on, the drizzle stopped. Emerging from the
mess tent after lunch, Cat checked the location of the men—
Thomas at the kitchen fire, smoking and drinking tea, Sambeke
and Olentwalla hunkered down beside him, still eating. Moses was
somewhere out of sight—she'd have to take a chance on him.

Casually, she made her way to the lone Land Rover, slid behind
the wheel and turned the key. The noise was deafening in the silence. Thomas appeared in the rearview mirror, Uzi in one hand,
alarm written clear on his face. Olentwalla and Sambeke, similarly
armed, were hard on his heels. Moses came into view from behind the towering cluster of gray rock.

"Back in an hour, guys," she yelled. "Don't worry. I'll be fine."

Quickly she slipped the clutch into gear, and pressed a foot on
the gas. The mist had lifted, and the ridge of the escarpment was
now clearly visible.

The Land Rover skidded through pockets of mud, jounced

heavily over half-exposed rock. Just being free of watching eyes was a relief. Since leaving Nairobi, she hadn't made a single move without being told what to do, when to do it. She had felt like a prisoner in the middle of nowhere.

The escarpment was much farther away than it appeared, and it was well over an hour before she reached it. At the approach to the cliff, she hit a game trail. Each time it branched, she took the fork to the right, closer to the hills. When she returned, it would be simple to reverse the process—getting lost in the African bush was not part of her plan. At least she had nothing to fear from the mysterious Reitholder.

Brush was now scraping against the sides of the Land Rover. The path wound gently uphill, then switchbacked. She made the turn, then another. The path became a series of tighter and tighter switchbacks, the gradient steeper. She stopped and looked behind. The back wheels of the Land Rover were dangerously close to the edge. The drop was dizzying. There was no way to make a turn, impossible to reverse back down the trail. She was locked into going on.

The grind of the engine seemed lost in the great silence. No birds swooped across the sky, no animals darted from the underbrush causing her to brake, not even the ever-present vervets.

The higher she climbed, the more breathtaking the view over the plains. The sun had broken through, throwing distinct paths of light across the golden grassland, picking out the striped backs of zebra among the black bodies of migrating wildebeest and the soft brown counterpoint of impala. Far below, the pools of Maasai Springs sparkled like jewels—green, turquoise, blue, set among silvery towering rocks.

Cat halted on the next switchback, picked up the folder of Joel's sketches from the seat beside her. She checked the terrain against the drawing in her hand.

He had been here.

Her brother had seen what she was seeing now. But for some reason, he'd left out the identifying pools and rocks of Maasai Springs on the plains below—almost as if he didn't want anyone to know exactly where he was.

For a moment she listened to the silence, and she was suddenly aware of how alone she was. Gently she let in the clutch.

Ten minutes of rough driving later, the game trail switchbacked again, then funneled into a giant bowl. A hundred yards across, she calculated. Three hundred from end to end. The size of two football fields. Cat brought the Land Rover to a halt. Nothing stirred. White birds skittered across the packed earth, as if blown by the wind. Then, incredibly, the white birds morphed into scraps of paper. Up here, as far from human habitation as she had ever been, scraps of paper lifted into the breeze, settled, lifted again to dance across the packed earth.

Packed earth. The huge flat area was an anomaly, carved out of the brush surrounding it. Deliberately cleared and flattened.

Cat kept her eyes on the scene in front of her and leaned over to feel beneath the dash—all of the safari Land Rovers had a specially built compartment tucked away, fitted to hold binoculars and a pistol. She found the catch and pressed it. The compartment sprang open at her touch. She took the pistol, placed it on the seat next to her, then reached for the binoculars. She raised them to her eyes, swept the glasses over the enclosing brush, went back and focused steadily on the far end.

What had appeared to the naked eye to be brush now became mud colored walls, roofs of thatch.

Cat put the binoculars on the seat with the pistol, let in the clutch and drove slowly around the perimeter. The ground was dry and hard, baked in the sun, as if the storm had never passed this way—quite possible, the way she had seen the storm system move. As she got closer, the small thatched huts became clearer, and behind them, against the hillside, was a larger building.

It looked as if she had come across an abandoned village, larger than she had first thought, with rows of houses built around some kind of community center, or communal kitchen.

But why had Joel sent her sketches of the surrounding country, and not a single drawing of the place itself? And what use would a village have for such an enormous piece of open ground? A place for dancing? She shook her head. This was not the *National Geographic*. There had been nothing of that sort in the *engang,* no "meeting hall," no "dancing ground." Certainly nothing this large. A small army could be paraded here.

She drove closer to the group of huts. Out of the corner of her eye she caught a flash of movement and her heart stopped, then raced. She was not alone. And whoever shared the village with her did not want to be seen.

Twenty-Four

Cat eased her foot off the gas, made sure the pistol was on the seat beside her, then turned, lifting an AK-47 from the gun rack behind her, and held it across her lap. Slowly, she drove closer to the cluster of round thatched huts, then allowed the Land Rover to coast to a stop in front of the large building, although with a closer view she could see it was merely four large posts support-ing a shaggy thatched roof.

Engine idling, foot ready to jam, she studied the rows of huts. Nothing moved in the silence, but she felt the pressure of eyes on her. She slipped off the AK's safety. Warily, she got out of the Land Rover, alert for the slightest movement among the huts. She moved to the hut nearest, bent to look inside.

Light streamed through cracks in walls woven from branches and leaves. The hut was empty.

Sound erupted behind her—someone moving on the other side of the meeting hall. She whirled around but saw nothing.

"I'm armed," she shouted. Her voice was shaky. "Come on out."

She started to walk toward the sound. This was crazy, she thought. She was crazy. Joel wouldn't expect her to hang around here. Even he wouldn't be this stupid—

Suddenly, she was surrounded by noise. Heavy bodies crashed from dwellings all around her. She brought up the AK. Before she could fire, a large brown baboon burst from the hut to her right. The animal leaped by her, and she caught a glimpse of the wide eyes of the baby clinging to its back. Then the troop was gone, the sound fading as they disappeared into the brush on the hillside.

Cat withdrew her finger from the trigger, took several noisy panting breaths. She'd damn near killed a mother baboon and her child! Shakily, she went back to the Land Rover, took a moment to lean against it, waiting for her heartbeat to return to normal. Then she ducked under the overhanging thatch of the meeting hall. Papers littered a long rough trestle table left in place at the far end. Holding the AK across her chest, she walked cautiously to the table, picked up what looked like a page out of a book.

It was covered in what appeared to be Chinese lettering. Puzzled, she turned it over. On the other side was a drawing of a gun with arrows pointing to different parts and more Chinese lettering.

She was looking at instructions on how to field-strip a semi-automatic weapon. She picked up another page. The drawing was the same. These instructions were in Swahili.

Joel had found this place. And he had died because of it.

Her breath caught in her chest—she could hardly hear over the pounding of her heart. Nothing was what it seems, he'd said in his note. Will call you. Then he'd been killed. By buffalo, they said.

She had to get away from here, Cat thought. Weapon in hand, she ran to the Land Rover, remembering to slip the safety back on the AK before she put it on the seat beside the pistol. The engine roared to life. Her foot was pressed so heavily on the gas the vehicle lurched forward, skidded as she swerved to avoid a clump of thatch knocked from one of the huts by the fleeing baboons. Somehow she managed to catch at her panic, and she eased up on the accelerator. An accident up here would be disastrous.

Now that she knew what she was looking at, it was clear the breaks in the heavy brush she had first taken for game trails were man-made. She slowed, peered through a large opening. It led into another clearing. Nowhere near as large as two football fields, it was filled with rows of drying racks like those in the hunting camp Campbell had dismantled. Scraps of red and blue nylon rope— the same rope used to bind the tusks of the slaughtered elephants—hung from the racks and littered the ground. About halfway down on the left, a track opened up. It seemed heavily rutted, by wheels, not by human feet.

Another way off this escarpment. She wasn't even tempted to look.

It took half an hour to get down the hillside. Although it was plain the training camp was abandoned—that's what it was, she was sure, a combination terrorist training camp and poachers' camp—every minute she expected shouts demanding she stop, the crash of gunfire backing up the demand.

She reached the grassland, turned in the direction she thought would bring her to Maasai Springs. As long as she kept the escarpment directly behind her, she thought, she should end up somewhere in the general vicinity. To make certain, earlier she had made a mental note of a number of landmarks—a tree with broken limbs, an outcropping of rock, a large baobab tree—that would guide her back.

Half an hour later, she realized she was lost. The escarpment was still behind her but in front on every side was nothing but open plain. The Land Rover carried no water, no supplies. And the sun was distinctly lower in the sky. Campbell and Tom made it seem so easy, driving from place to place without landmarks, always knowing exactly where they were even without the use of a compass, heading unerringly for the campsite set up by Thomas and the Maasai.

The thought of the Maasai seemed to conjure them up out of nowhere. They appeared, rising out of a declivity in the terrain. Cat slowed, reached for the binoculars, and saw that Moses, distinctive because he was taller than the others, was in the lead, Olentwalla and Sambeke in single file behind him. The three men were eating up the ground in a long, loping stride.

Cat lowered the glasses. Who were these men? she wondered. Were they friends? Foes? Right now, they were a search party, and without them she would never find her way back to Maasai Springs.

She stopped the Land Rover, got out, replaced the AK in the rack. The pistol she slipped into her bag. Then she drove toward them.

Twenty-Five

By four they were back at Maasai Springs. She had been away for only four hours. Thomas brought tea to her tent, but greeted her thanks with an impassive stare.

Cat lay on her bed, staring up into the white net. The Maasai had been silent on the way back. Moses had taken the wheel, and no comment had been made about her absence. But Moses made it clear that she would not have another chance to leave Maasai Springs alone. As soon as they arrived in camp, he had removed the keys from the ignition, dropped them into the pocket of his crumpled khakis. Since then, Olentwalla had been hunkered down outside her door. They answered no questions, but there was no mistaking they considered her a prisoner.

As evening came on, the mist closed in and rain pattered lightly on the canvas roof. She had no desire to get up, turn on the lantern. The grayness matched her mood. All she could think of was Joel, the terrorist camp, who she could tell. How. When. Whether she should say anything at all, to anyone. Or just get home to the

United States, let it all go. Forget it. Joel might have been killed because he'd seen too much. Should she take the same risk? Certainly, she wasn't about to mention what she'd seen to anyone until she got back to Nairobi, and even then—

The low hum of an engine disturbed her reverie. Cat propped herself on one elbow. A Land Rover engine. Her heartbeat missed, then picked up uncomfortably. Tom couldn't possibly be back so soon. Campbell said it would take him a couple of days at least to get to the home village with the Maasai women and back again.

It had to be Campbell. Should she go to meet him? Let him come to her? She grabbed her slicker, opened the door of her tent. Olentwalla unwound his six-foot-nine-inch frame.

"*Bwana* Tom come," he said.

Cat responded gratefully to the friendly word, the gap-toothed grin he gave her. "I don't think so, 'Twalla," she said. "They said it would take at least two days for him to get back."

"That *Bwana* Tom," Olentwalla insisted.

It had to be Campbell, Cat thought, and he would not find her languishing in her tent. With Olentwalla almost literally on her heels, she forced herself to saunter to where the keyless Land Rover was parked and peered into the rain. A vehicle became clear. A black arm waved from the window, and she waved back.

"*Jambo,* Cat," Tom called. "Didn't expect me today, I bet. Everything quiet?" He climbed stiffly from the mud-encrusted vehicle. He spoke to Olentwalla in Maa. Olentwalla answered. Tom's eyes flickered, but he gave no other sign that what he was hearing disturbed him. He gave a few short commands and Olentwalla turned, faded into the rain.

"How did you manage to make such good time?" Cat asked pleasantly.

"Dan said to get here without delay." Hands on his hips, Tom flexed his spine. "I'm famished. Any food about?"

"Thomas can rustle up something, I'm sure. So you know he's gone to Nairobi. Where did you see him?" She hated asking, but couldn't stop herself.

"I didn't. He met a U.N. party. He must have driven like a maniac to get to them in the time he did. They were on their way to the Fig Tree area, anyway, so they intercepted us, took the women on, and I turned back."

They entered the mess tent. Cat leaned back in one of the canvas chairs.

"Thomas is going to bring you some tea, but would you prefer a drink?" Tom asked. "You look exhausted. Are you all right?"

Cat straightened in her chair. "Why shouldn't I be?" She heard the sharpness in her voice and smiled to take the edge off the words. "Just bushed. I got knocked out by a wildebeest."

She told him about it, putting an amusing spin on the story. They chatted about the stampede. Like Campbell, he'd managed to tuck the Land Rover under an uprooted tree, but in any case, the herd had veered off before reaching them.

It was almost surreal, chatting about events that now seemed so far in the past and completely unimportant. Did Tom know that the hills they could see in the west held a terrorist camp? Buildings made of fronds and branches deteriorated rapidly—had Joel discovered it after it had been abandoned, or had it been abandoned because he'd discovered it? Had he been killed to ensure his silence? Surely they had to know about that camp; they were supposed to know everything about the bush.

Thomas placed a pot of tea in front of her, a sandwich and a Tusker before Tom.

"So, what do you think of Maasai Springs?"Tom asked. "I don't think we can show you anything better."

"Yes, I think you're right." She sipped the tea. "I really have to get back to Nairobi now, but before we leave the area, I'd like to see the place where my brother died." She studied him. He had to be even more exhausted than she was—he'd been driving two days nonstop over horrendous terrain. "I know you're tired, Tom, but I'd like to do that. Then we can go on to Nairobi."

Tom lowered the Tusker to the table. "You must wait until Dan gets back for that."

"But we don't know when that will be."And Campbell would not find her waiting breathlessly for his explanations. "There is nothing more to do here, but there's a lot I still have to do in Nairobi. And you, too. I suppose the land is in trust for a particular tribe, so that will have to be sorted out. That's part of your contract, I believe. Then I have to get back to Los Angeles. I've been out of touch for too long because of the damn radio being damaged."

Tom was shaking his head doubtfully. "The weather's very unstable, Cat. A lot more rain is on the way. It would be wiser to wait here until Dan gets back."

"Who knows how long he will be? Just take me to see where Joel died, then we'll start back to Nairobi."

Tom shook his head. "I'm sorry, Cat. I can't undertake a journey like that with you."

"It's not a major undertaking. Campbell was going to take me this morning but something more important came up."

"He said that?"

"He didn't have to. He just left."

"No. That he would take you to see where your brother died."

"Well, I'm not making it up, Tom. That's what he said. The plan was to leave as soon as the men got here so that we could be back in Maasai Springs before you arrived tomorrow or the next day. I just want to see the place, we don't need to stay long."

Tom picked up his Tusker, put it down without drinking. "I cannot take you into Tanzania, Cat. I'm sorry."

She stared at him, feeling as if she had been struck. When she recovered her voice, she said, "Joel died in Tanzania?"

Tom looked up. "You just said you knew that."

"No. I didn't."

Tom stared at her. "Cat, you just said that Dan was taking you there."

"I didn't say Tanzania. No one has said that." She stared at him. "No one has ever mentioned Tanzania. Joel would not have been looking for a hotel site in Tanzania. What were you doing there?"

Tom passed a hand over his eyes and forehead. He let out his breath and spoke without looking at her. "We'd just wandered over the border by accident."

"You people are experts, Tom. You'd never just wander over—" She stopped speaking. Wait a minute, she thought. They were searching for smuggling routes to take ivory out of the country using Joel's safari as cover.

She stood, pushed her chair tidily back in place. "Okay, if you won't take me there, we'll leave for Nairobi tomorrow, instead. Will you alert the men?"

"Cat, let's at least wait until we know what the weather is going to do." As if to emphasize his words, rain gusted against the canvas. "I can't risk trouble with you along. We have only two Land Rovers."

"If you want to wait here for Campbell, that's up to you. But tomorrow morning, I am going to start back to Nairobi. Moses can drive my Land Rover—he's tough enough." She thought of the pistol tucked away in her purse. "You keep the other Land Rover and wait for Campbell." She waited for him to tell her she would not be allowed to leave. They'd traveled closely together, talked for hours, but she realized she did not know him at all. "Or am I going to be held here, whether I like it or not?"

Tom's dark, curved lips pressed tightly together, his skin took on a slight gray tone. He touched his fingers to the leather pouch under his shirt. "If you feel that strongly, we can start for Nairobi in the morning."

"Thanks. Don't wait dinner for me. I've got work to do."

The atmosphere in the Land Rover was as heavy as the soaked landscape. Maasai Springs was far behind them, still wreathed in mist, pools steaming, guinea fowl clanking their strange, metallic call. Her rapport with Tom was shattered, and Cat was too deadened to attempt to retrieve it. She fumbled in her bag for her calculator and notebook.

The Land Rover tipped, the engine sputtered and died. Cat looked up. Tom cursed in Swahili and threw the gear into four-wheel drive. Slowly they ground out of the mud-hole into which they had sunk up to the axle. Cat turned back to her notes. Rain slashed at the windshield. The mood in the vehicle spiraled downward.

If she had kept her mouth shut, something might have been reclaimed from yesterday, Cat thought. Enough goodwill to make the journey bearable, at least on the surface. Instead, this morning she had hammered the final nail into her relationship with Tom.

"The men are quiet," she'd said.

"Yes," Tom answered shortly. "This is not good weather for traveling."

The day had dawned with heavy rain. Not the diaphanous curtains of water that had been intermittently sweeping the plains, but a sullen, steady downpour.

She attempted a little of their old friendly banter. "You keep touching that pouch under your shirt. Is the weather that dangerous?"

"Africans are superstitious, if that's what you mean," he said stiffly. "If I thought the weather was dangerous, I would not allow you to leave here. But it's not good. We're too small a party traveling with only two Land Rovers."

"People travel in small parties all the time. Keep both Land Rovers together. No one rides point, or whatever it is that you have the men do usually." She glanced at him. "Tom, I have to get back. I need to be in touch with my office." When they had tried to use the radio earlier, there had been nothing but static. The knot of fear in her diaphragm was tightening. She had to get back to the city, talk to Stephen N'toya, maybe get Father Gaston to make some inquiries. "Look, if we get to Nairobi in two days instead of four, let the men know there will be a bonus in it for them."

The instant the words left her mouth she wanted to recall them. But the damage was done. The man she knew as Tom seemed to simply walk back into his skull and disappear. She was staring into total blankness instead of his eyes. And it seemed interminable before those eyes came back into focus.

"You think because we are African, we can be bought? We do not take *bukshi, memsahib.* I will get you to Nairobi in the shortest possible time. I will not insult the men with this remark. They cannot be corrupted."

"Tom, I'm sorry. That was stupid." Cat suppressed a flash of irritation. She had offered a tip, not a bribe. At worst stupid, certainly not an enticement to corruption. It seemed to her that this group was corrupt enough. Clearly, tender scar tissue had been bumped by her words.

Tom had turned and left the mess tent. Those were the last words that had passed between them. Five hours of silence.

Cat looked out at the rain. Wildebeest still plodded north on their migration, but the herd was widespread, posing no threat. A small group of giraffe rocked in their unique stately fashion, unconcerned among the soaking antelope. A few days ago, Tom would have pointed them out, made her repeat the name in Swahili. *Twiga,* she said to herself.

At noon, Tom signaled a stop. Thomas brought coffee and food. Tom climbed out into the rain, ate while pacing between the two Land Rovers as if unable to tolerate her presence in the close confines of the vehicle.

The sandwiches were cotton in her mouth. She threw them to the vervets scampering from nowhere, their greenish-brown coats impervious to rain.

Fifteen minutes later, Tom got back into the Land Rover, water dripping from his small tight ears.

The afternoon dragged on. Twice they had to stop and wait for Olentwalla driving the second vehicle. Each time, Tom jumped out and blistered the air with a mixture of Swahili and Maa.

"Ease up a bit, Tom," she said after the last episode.

"You want to get to Nairobi. This is the way to do it."

"Tom, I said I was sorry."

He slammed the gears.

Late in the afternoon they drove close to a herd of elephants. They were knee deep in swamp, green plants hanging from their backs, caught there when they had wallowed in sedge and water hyacinth. Calves about as large as Shetland ponies held up little trunks, fanned translucent ears and watched them curiously through the gray misting rain. Once Tom would have stopped so that she could watch them for a while—groups like this were increasingly rare now. But today they drove on without slowing.

When they stopped for the night, they tried again to patch

through to Nairobi. Still nothing but static. The men did not linger around the fire gossiping. They threw the tents up, posted watch and turned in.

Sleep was intermittent. Cat kept jolting awake. In the early hours, she looked out of her mesh "window." Sambeke hunched close to a sullen fire, weapon across his knees, wrapped in a red Maasai cloak that completely obscured his khaki bush clothes. The sounds of the night were muted by rain. Even the lions were quiet.

The first light of dawn filtered through the mesh as she dressed. Her head felt brittle, with that strange light-headed clarity that came from lack of sleep. Outside, steam misted the wet grassland, but the sun was rising in a day that was clear.

Her spirits rose. Today had to be better. It could hardly get worse.

Twenty-Six

The inside of Campbell's eyelids felt as if they were made of sandpaper, and he could smell his own sweat. His shortwave unit had been flooded when he'd crossed the river to pick up the Maasai women, so he still knew only what he'd gathered from the message Jock had left with the men. Morag was gone.

He hit tarmac, stopped at the first phone he saw—in a small Indian grocery at the center of a village—and phoned Jock in Nairobi.

"She's safe," Jock said. "She was with Dougie Maxwell."

"Let me talk to her."

"She's got her door locked, won't speak to anyone."

"All right. Take her up to the farm. I'll see to Dougie Maxwell."

"Good." Jock's voice was grim. "There's a dance at the club tonight. Try there first."

Campbell drove across Nairobi without stopping, got on to the Thika Road, pushing the Land Rover to its limit. He skidded into the turn onto Muranga, slowing only when he drove into the driveway of the Muthaiga Club. He slammed to a halt, climbed out and threw the keys to the doorman.

"How're things, Matiba? Are you well?"

"*Bwana* Campbell! Good to see you, sir. We keep well, praise be to Allah. And you, *bwana?* You are well?"

"Yes, well, thanks, Matiba."

The rule in colonial times had been "white only," but that had changed with independence. Campbell glanced through the open door of the ballroom as he passed. A light-skinned young man with a voice that could pass for a young Sinatra fronted an eight-piece band, and the dance floor was crowded with a mix of races, the women in cocktail dresses, the men in dinner jackets.

His own appearance, unshaven and dirty, bush clothes travel-stained, wouldn't raise an eyebrow. The old Muthaiga, the most venerable club in East Africa, had been the scene of many a wild gin-soaked debauch in its time. Nothing shocked its membership. He went into the "men only" lounge, ran his eye over the stag line propping up the long dark bar. Most of the men were in black tie. One of them detached himself, came toward Campbell, beaming a welcoming smile.

"Well, look who's back from the wars. How are you, old son?"

"Not complaining, Ben." Campbell looked around the bar, nodding briefly in response to an expansive wave from Brian Ward. Cigar smoke rose in blue wreaths, moving lazily as the broad arms of the ancient wooden ceiling fans slowly rotated.

"Come and have a drink," Ben Masters said. "Clive's here. We've just been reliving some of your greatest glories. Wales's Whoppers." He laughed, waved at a large blonde at the end of the bar, his face buried in a pint mug of beer. "Clive, look who's turned up. Speak of the bloody devil, eh?" Masters's jovial voice carried across the room.

Clive van der Moot roared a greeting. "Where've you been? You're too much the stranger in these parts." He ambled over, threw an arm around Campbell's shoulder, then wrinkled his nose. "Whew! Well, a drink first, then you better clean up. Bit of a dance going on. You can't go in smelling like that."

"Can't stay, I'm afraid." At any other time, Campbell would be glad to see him. As boys, he and Clive had played rugby for the Prince of Wales Academy in Nairobi. Jointly, they'd been known as Wales's Whoppers. Whenever their old schoolmates got together, talk eventually turned to those long-ago exploits on the rugby field. "I'd like to rescue your poor wife, Clive, but Ben'll just have to give her my sympathy." He grinned at Ben. "Tell her I've seen those size fourteens of his in action."

"Just jealous, old boy," Clive said loftily, "because you don't have my sense of rhythm."

"Dougie Maxwell here?" Campbell asked.

Clive made a show of looking around. "No. Haven't seen him. You, Ben?"

Ben Masters opened his light green eyes as if he had difficulty recalling the name. "No. Can't say I have, old son."

Campbell looked from one to the other, then shook his head. "You're a couple of piss-poor liars. Where is he?"

Masters put a restraining hand on Campbell's arm. "Now, Dan, don't do this. Just get him in here and talk—"

Campbell turned his full attention on him, challenging him to continue. Blood rose in Masters's ruddy cheeks. He looked away.

"I'll find him myself," Campbell said. He clapped Masters on the shoulder. "Good try, Ben."

Campbell exchanged greetings with a number of men as he moved toward the end of the bar and the door to the terrace beyond, shaking his head to the shouted invitations to have a drink.

Just in front of the open French doors, Brian Ward planted himself in Campbell's path, making his immense bulk impossible to avoid.

"Good to see you, Campbell. How's that young woman? The Stanton girl I mean, of course, not the other...er, your other—" He grinned, letting the words hang, malice sparkling in the small hard eyes. "Heard you've had a bit of trouble again in that quarter."

Campbell stopped. If this man even mentioned Morag's name, he thought, he'd hit him. In spite of the difference in age and physical condition, he'd put this soft sack of blubber right on his arse. "Trouble, Ward?" He shook his head. "You must be listening at the wrong keyholes."

Ward used his belly as a battering ram, moved even closer. "I don't think so." He looked around at the crowding men, intent on their own boozy conversations, and leaned forward until Campbell could smell the sour, whiskey-laden breath. Ward lowered his voice. "Heard about the other matter, too. The Australians. Keep it all under wraps, that's what I say. Not good for business, not good at all."

Campbell kept his face expressionless. There was a leak in N'toya's organization, he thought, stunned. The two bodies had been brought back to Nairobi with Reitholder——N'toya was keeping all three, the quick and the dead, secure until the ivory was in their own hands. Then the old man would have to decide what to do with the Australians. He would figure something out.

"You've got me at a disadvantage, Ward," he said. "I haven't heard of any trouble with Australians in the bush."

"Yes, you have. Couple of Australian boys. Killed in a raid on a poaching camp, according to my sources." Ward put his mouth to Campbell's ear. "Don't worry. Mum's the word, of course." He tapped the side of his nose. "Mum's the word, Campbell. Old bush hands like us have to stick together, don't y'know. What? What?"

"What are you drinking, Ward? Scotch?" Campbell turned to the bartender. "Kauna. Couple of doubles here, please." He took Ward's arm. "Let's find a table, I'd like to know more about this poaching camp—"

A voice from the terrace cut through his words. "If he's looking for me, here I am." The pale curtain, floating in the breeze from the open door, was thrust aside. A tall, well-muscled figure stood in the doorway. He was in black tie, his waist encircled by a wine-red cummerbund. "There you are, Campbell. I hear you want to talk to me."

"Well, Campbell," Ward said softly. "Just like the old days. *Cherchez la femme,* eh?"

Campbell barely heard him. He stood, shouldered through the suddenly quiet crowd of men, then stopped in front of Dougie Maxwell.

Maxwell started to speak, and Campbell slammed an open hand against his shoulder. Maxwell staggered backward, through the door, Campbell following. Light from the open doors to the ballroom spilled in golden pools onto the flagstone terrace, curtains blew gently in the jasmine-scented breeze. Dance music came to a crashing finale, a burst of clapping following a riffle of drums, a few high-spirited bellows of appreciation.

"Now wait a minute, Campbell. Let's talk about this—"

"You were warned, Dougie," Campbell said.

"It was only one night. I swear. I won't see her again. I don't want to fight you—"

"Too fucking late." With one hand, Campbell caught a handful of Maxwell's dark hair, jerked his head down to meet an upswinging fist. Blood spurted and dripped onto Maxwell's tucked dress shirt. He broke loose, brought up his hands, dropped a shoulder, turned his body, threw a hard punch at Campbell's face. Campbell landed two short blows to the kidneys, then a right deep into Maxwell's diaphragm. The man doubled over, fighting for breath.

Campbell stepped in. The beating was businesslike and system-
atic, without passion, finished in minutes. Then he held up the half-
conscious Maxwell, pushed him into Clive van der Moot's arms.
"Get him a vet."

As he left, no one tried to stop him.

In his office, Campbell took a healthy swig of the scotch in his
glass, leaned back gratefully in his old swivel chair. Maxwell had
connected enough to make him ache. He took in the trophies
covering the walls, wondering whether he would ever again enter
this room without seeing them, as he'd done for so many years.
Before Cat Stanton. She had got to him, and he couldn't afford it.
He needed the hard shell he'd cultivated. He propped his feet on
his desk, closed his eyes. Exhaustion ran like rods of hot iron
down the back of his neck, into his spine.

He jerked awake, reached for the hunting knife at the same moment he brought his feet softly to the floor. The scratch at the door
sounded again. He crossed to the door, opened it.

Stephen N'toya slipped into the room. As usual, he was dressed
entirely in black. Cautious man, N'toya, Campbell thought. He
should live a long time, die surrounded by his grandchildren. He
closed the door, dropped the knife on the desk.

"You making a habit of home visits?"

"It's not wise to trust the phone." N'toya took in the bruise just
beginning to blossom on Campbell's cheekbone. "I heard there was
trouble with Morag. You should have let me know. I would have
had Maxwell dealt with."

"I handle my own affairs, thanks."

"Yes, but your affairs get to be mine when they interfere with
what's on hand. We've got too much at risk, here, Dan." He took
the glass Campbell held out to him. "Where's Morag now?"

"Jock took her upcountry this morning," Campbell said shortly.

"To Erukenya?"

Campbell grunted an assent.

"How long is she going to be there?"

Campbell frowned. "Why the sudden interest?"

"Just friendly concern, *n'duga.*"

"Save your concern for your own business, Stephen. Brian Ward was drooling all over me at the Muthaiga Club tonight, couldn't wait to tell me about dead Australians."

"How did he get hold of that information?"

"Pays the same eyes and ears you do, I suppose. You are going to have to stop it somehow. My men take enough risks without that."

"I'll see what I can find out, but you know how it is. Rumor takes on a life of its own."

"I don't care how you do it, just do it. And there's something else. Talk to the old man and get a decision on what to do with this new load once we get it. If it's as much as you say, we can't take it to the farm." Campbell got up, went to look through the shutters at the main house, empty now with everyone upcountry. Maybe, before she left for Los Angeles, Cat could.... He stopped the thought, mentally shook himself. He had to keep his mind focused. Too much was at stake. "Reitholder secure at the warehouse?"

"That's why I'm here. He's out."

Campbell turned. *"He's what?"*

"Two nights ago. He bribed a guard."

"Jesus Christ! Again? Again? Don't you ever learn?"

"Bribery is endemic. What is there to learn from that?"

"I'll have to get back to Maasai Springs," Campbell said. "He's going to go straight for her."

"I don't think so, not now. Moving the ivory is his priority, he won't have time for Cat Stanton. Anyway, how would he know she was there?"

"He'll find out. If that psychotic bastard thinks her brother told her anything at all, he'll send men to kill her."

"Tom will get her back to Nairobi—"

"Tom has no bloody idea Reitholder's broken loose."

"Cat Stanton has become important to you, *n'duga*—"

Campbell cut him off. "I am not your brother. I never was. And keep out of my private life."

"In our business, personal feelings are a complication. Don't get soft on me, Campbell."

"Do I sound soft to you?" Campbell asked.

Stephen shrugged without answering.

Campbell checked his watch. "It'll be daylight in about five hours. I'll fly back to Maasai Springs. If anything happens to her, Stephen, I'm going to hold you responsible. You'd better start praying I find them there."

Twenty-Seven

He should never have agreed to meet in the fucking bush just so this fool could put on his fatigues. Reitholder tuned out General Francis's voice and listened to the hyenas skulking just beyond the ring of light thrown by the lantern. He was tired and in pain, but he was still under orders from the Afrikaner Broederhood, and he knew his duty as his father had before him. He brought his attention back.

"The rhino horn will be sent out by diplomatic courier," General Francis was saying. "The same embassy, but the ambassador has increased his price. We have to agree to it, but we'll find someone else for the next load."

Reitholder nodded. "And the trucks?"

"The same trucking company and the same drivers. Half now, half when the trucks have delivered their load safely. No pay if they are apprehended."

"Who the fuck is going to—" Reitholder put a sarcastic twist to the word "—*apprehend* them? The police are paid off and the army is in our pocket, man."

Reitholder threw a couple of pills into his mouth, washed them down with a weak scotch and water.

"You want to be more careful with those things, my friend," General Francis said. "A mixture of codeine and alcohol can be deadly."

"When I need advice on my health, General, I will get a doctor." Reitholder reached for the bottle of scotch on the center of the camp table Francis's men had set up beneath the canvas lean-to before he'd arrived and deliberately poured another two fingers of whiskey into his glass. He leaned back without flinching. The wounds had started to scab, but still every movement caused them to bleed. "Let's move on, man. I don't want to spend the whole night here. I got a couple of girls waiting for me in Nairobi." He laughed, watching Francis's face. "Virgins, twelve years old. Twins. I bought them from their father, guaranteed clean, and I don't want them fucked by someone else before I get there."

Francis looked at him with distaste. "The tusks are in Nairobi, being sorted for quality and size," he said. "When that has been done, they'll be moved to Mombasa and loaded onto the freighter. The Broederhood will have a representative on board, and I will have two—"

Reitholder grunted. "You must be going cross-eyed, man, watching your watchers."

General Francis went on, "The tusks will be counted again while in transit, then transferred to the Chinese dhows lying off Macau. They will be counted for the final time after landing in Macau and turned over to the buyers from Hong Kong in the usual way. All that is now in place. You and I will not meet in person again after tonight. However. . ." Francis paused dramatically, lit a cigarette, blew out the match, broke it in two and placed it on the table.

"You must have been a Boy Scout once, General. I didn't know that." Reitholder grinned, careful not to resplit his damaged lips. "We've both traveled a long bloody trail since those quiet days, eh?"

Their paths had crossed and recrossed, from Angola to Mozambique, Francis part of the Communist struggle, while he himself had orders from Johannesburg to fish in troubled waters. Francis was a Marxist in the old Stalinist mode, unleashing wholesale terror, burning villages, ordering executions to maintain discipline, rape to bring husbands and fathers out of the forests, starvation to subdue civilian populations. They were two sides of the same bloody coin, he and Francis, Reitholder thought, both using destabilization to achieve their goals. Too bad Francis was such a moralistic prick.

Francis ignored his comment. "However," he went on firmly, "word has come to me of a large cache upcountry. Few men guarding it, easy to take. My informant was the same man who had a hand in your release. I don't know him, but he knows of me. I have already put some noses to work on that, sniffing the air. But since we have everything in place, I propose we act on this tip and add these tusks to what we are already sending to Hong Kong."

"So, why tell me?" Reitholder said. "My men live in the bush. We take the tusks, the horns and skins. And we take the risks. You do the rest."

"Colonel, the herds are severely diminished, and a new man has been appointed to clean up the Wildlife Department—"

Reitholder broke in. "Ach, reform movements, they come, they go. Nothing changes, man. *Kaffirs* can always be bribed. And while there is a beast left standing, I'll bring it down."

"Of course," General Francis said smoothly. "But consider this. We take this ivory at very little risk, and at the same time we send a very large message to the people involved to go into another line of work."

Thunder rumbled in the southwest and lightning forked. The rains had started. Reitholder took a moment to think.

"I have some business to take care of first," he said finally. "My *kaffirs* are already on their way to Maasai Springs."

"What for? What can be more urgent than ivory?"

"Survival."

"Whose?"

Reitholder grinned at him. "Mine. Who else you think I give a shit about?"

"What has that got to do with Maasai Springs?"

"The Stanton woman is there."

"You are sure?"

"I got people tracking rhino in that area."

"This is a mistake." Francis shook his head. "If she's a problem, I will take care of her myself in Nairobi. You have my word. I can have her followed. I'll use our contacts in the army, or I can arrange a traffic accident in the street. Anything is possible. She can be stopped. The ivory, Colonel. Keep your mind on the ivory. This is a one-time opportunity. The woman is nothing. What damage can she do?"

"I don't want her back in Nairobi," Reitholder said stubbornly. "Her brother knew my face. He was always taking pictures. Maybe he got mine. He could have sent her letters. Who the fuck knows. If she gets back to Nairobi she will keep asking her questions." He grinned, winced at the stretch of healing skin. "Besides, she's Campbell's woman. Eh? Eh? I know that old story. Snatching another woman from under his nose will be like snatching his balls." He laughed. "Worse than killing him."

"Another accident in the bush, and to Stanton's sister, is foolhardy. Imagine the shock waves. The new man heading the Wildlife Department won't let it go. He's serious and he's incorruptible. Romantic fools in the international press already call him Richard the Lionheart. You'll have the Americans asking questions, the government forced to respond. And Campbell will come after you, personally. Make no mistake about that."

"Sure. Gets even better, eh?" Reitholder took a gulp of the stronger drink, felt it jolt his nervous system. "Two dead Americans not so easy to cover up as one. He'll have to answer some hard fucking questions, Mr. Fucking Campbell. So, I take care of this first, then we talk about the other. *Ja.* Sounds good. But this we take for ourselves, General. What you think, man? Who would know? A little retirement fund, just in case you decide you'd rather retire to Florida than be Kenya's Fidel Castro."

He thought he'd choke on his own laughter.

Twenty-Eight

The sun blazed straight overhead, and noise seemed to crush the nerves in Cat's brain with each grinding change of gear. She fumbled for aspirin, pressed her fingers against her throbbing temples and closed her eyes behind her dark glasses.

She had thought the second day of driving would be easier. She was wrong. The sun shone brightly, but the drying surface of the land was deceptive, firm only until the weight of the Land Rovers broke through into sludge-filled holes. Olentwalla, driving the second Land Rover, couldn't keep up the pace Tom set. They lost sight of him four times before noon. Not one of the three Maasai was a good driver, and Thomas was no better.

Once they were in Nairobi, Cat thought wearily, she would make sure they were well rewarded for the extra effort. If cash was an insult—which she doubted, Tom was riding his own pony with that one—then an apology before she got on the plane home would take care of it. Or they could refuse to take the money, it was all the same to her. She was too dispirited to care. Tom was driving the men hard, and she was the goad behind him. She could live with that, and so could they.

But she missed the old camaraderie, and that amazed her. For all she knew, these men could kill her without missing a beat. For all she knew, that's exactly what had happened to Joel.

Tom stopped on the bank of a fast-running stream and climbed out to wait for the men.

"Can you see them?" Cat asked.

"No. We'll wait for them on the other side."

Cat nodded. They were the first words he had spoken to her all day.

They inched into the stream, ground across, then parked in the shade of a thorn tree. Cat closed her eyes, slid down in her seat, allowing relief from the pounding engine to wash over her.

The second Land Rover roared into earshot. Without slackening speed, it hurtled down the bank, water surging around it. The engine died, then growled like a tormented beast as Olentwalla repeatedly turned the key and pressed on the gas.

On the bank, Tom yelled in a mixture of languages, English, Swahili, Maa. Moses thrust his head out of the passenger window, started to reply. Tom shouted an order. Moses stopped in midsentence, took a moment to stare haughtily at Tom, then withdrew his head. The engine caught. They jolted forward. Tom had the men change places, put Thomas at the wheel. Silently he slid back into his own Land Rover and turned on the engine.

"We're all tired, Tom," Cat said.

"They are not tired. They are Maasai, and they are too arrogant for their own good. Every Maasai I've ever known thinks he knows best about everything."

Cat wondered if he included himself in that assessment—he was Maasai on his father's side.

Tom wrenched the wheel, swerving around the half-eaten car-cass of a giraffe, scattering a group of jackals. As the jackals ran, vultures hopped forward awkwardly, wings outstretched, crops bulging obscenely. Cat looked away.

Two more streams were navigated successfully. Thomas had taken the wheel and, hard-faced, Tom got out to watch him cross each stream before driving on. Gullies, marked on the map across Cat's knees as dry, were now filled with dirty foaming water. The sun had disappeared. Clouds hung just above their heads. Visibil-ity dropped.

At midafternoon, they turned onto a game trail, running with water but well-defined, and followed it for several miles. Now that they were no longer lurching from tussock to tussock, traveling was easier. They picked up speed through thickets of thorn and brush, then stopped at what was marked on the map as a stream. Only now it was a storm-tossed river laden with debris. The men were nowhere in sight.

"We can't cross here," Tom said. "We'll wait for the men and try to ford—"

The scream of a protesting engine cut through his words. The second Land Rover tore past them through the screen of rain, hur-tling toward the river at full speed.

Tom threw himself out of the vehicle, raced down the bank after it, waving his arms and shouting furiously. The vehicle hit the river. Water broke over the hood. Too late, Thomas slammed on the brake. The Land Rover slid sideways, rocked drunkenly and took the full force of water running like a bore through flood-deepened banks. A door burst open. Olentwalla, in the passenger's seat, struggled to close it, his body half out of the vehicle, buffeted mercilessly by its wild swinging. He clung to the door as Thomas brought the Land Rover around, still miraculously upright. Then the engine died. Slowly the vehicle moved backward, pushed by the force of the racing water.

"We'll have to get a rope to them,"Tom shouted to Cat over the noise of rushing water. "Take the wheel."

He mimed his intention to the men. They waved and nodded. Tom attached a rope to the rear bumper, then signaled to Cat. She slammed the engine into reverse, slowly backed down the slope, feeling the wheels being grabbed by the soft mud. Tom tossed the end of the rope to the men in midstream. Thomas leaned out to catch it and missed. Tom pulled the rope back, rewound it, threw again. The rope grazed Thomas's outstretched fingers, then fell uselessly into the water. Thomas climbed through the window onto the hood, then slid into the water. The running force of the torrent pinned his back awkwardly against the bumper. Once more Tom threw the rope. Thomas reached for it. Suddenly he was shoulder deep, struggling to keep his footing. Olentwalla insinuated his body out of the window across the hood, reached a long arm toward him. Thomas grabbed for it. He slipped, floundered briefly, then disappeared beneath the surface of the racing stream.

"Tom," Cat screamed. "Crocodiles! Are there crocodiles?"

"No!" Tom was already sprinting back toward the Land Rover. "No! Not here!"

He reached behind her seat, brought out a *panga* in a worn leather sheath and withdrew the blade. He waved at the watching men, then pointed it downstream. Thin shouts of response rose above the sound of the roaring water. Cat grabbed her slicker, jumped out into the rain.

Tom chopped at the heavy brush lining the river, working his way downstream, his progress maddeningly slow. Behind him, feverish with anxiety, Cat pushed through the branches, trying to keep them from whipping back at her face, her eyes searching the river, praying for the sight of a head.

"There he is!" Tom shouted, pointing with the *panga*.

A khaki-clad body was caught against the trunk of a tree brought down in the storm. Precarious roots still held. Thomas, entangled in the drowning branches, swung up and down, disappearing beneath the water with each downward swing as the current tore at the remaining shreds of earthbound roots.

"Is he alive?" Cat shouted.

"I don't know."

If he was, it wouldn't be for long. No one could take that punishment. At each downward pull, the roots gave a little more, and the weight of his body kept him below the surface for seconds longer. Thomas was drowning, inches at a time. Cat stumbled against Tom's back as he slashed at the brush with wide heavy swings of the *panga,* clearing a path to the edge of the roaring water.

"I can get at him from here," he shouted.

Tom shoved the *panga* into Cat's hand. Keeping one arm over the fallen trunk, he edged into the river, cautiously placing each hand, fighting not to be swept away by red-tinged water being hurled like pale foaming blood at the tree. A branch moved as Tom grabbed for it, then slithered into the water. Cat choked back a scream as the undulating body of the snake brushed against Thomas, hesitated. Then, triangular head held high, it writhed across Thomas's back, melding with the brown and green of the foundering tree.

Tearing through the entwining branches, Tom stretched to grab the back of Thomas's tunic. The tree began its downward swing, the inexorable movement pulling Thomas from his grasp. Tom lurched forward, thrust a shoulder beneath the trunk, reached for Thomas's hair, only just managing to keep his head above the surface. Then the weight of the tree bore them both down.

Cat threw down the *panga,* tore off her slicker and waded into the water. The stream wrenched at her thighs, then her waist. She threw an arm over the trunk of the tree as Tom had, inched her way toward them. The streambed moved treacherously under her feet, reluctantly releasing her at each step. It seemed to take forever to reach the struggling men, freed now for the upward swing. A portion of the bank gave way, the tree sagged deeper into the river.

"I can hold it," Tom yelled. "Get the vines off him."

Cat tore at the thick fibrous ropes snaking around Thomas's body, fastening him to the drowning tree. She thought of going back for the *panga*—she couldn't tell vine from snake—but knew there was no time. The bank was collapsing, and with every downward swing, Tom, with Thomas and the weight of the tree on his back, was sinking deeper.

The tree began to vibrate even more heavily in the racing water. It was going down. She pushed a shoulder under Thomas's body. The trunk submerged, and her knees bent under the pressure as she braced herself against it, feeling the strain across her back, in her belly and legs. She couldn't hold. She was going down with it. Her face was submerging in the silt-laden water.

Then the tree hesitated, the pressure eased, and the tree started its upward swing. She tore at the vines and the last of them parted. Tom lifted Thomas's body free. Cat pressed her back against the trunk, grabbed at Thomas's legs. With the unconscious man suspended between them, their backs scraping the trunk, they forced through branches she feared would become live as she touched them. Then the water was shallower, and they were on the bank. Unable to lift her head, Cat dropped to her knees in the mud. Tom lowered Thomas beside her. For a long moment, she couldn't move. Then she put out a hand to touch Thomas's face. He felt dead.

"We've got to get him warm—"

"Turn his head."

Tom placed the heels of his hands on Thomas's chest and pushed. Cat watched his face for signs of life. Water trickled from his mouth and nose. Tom pushed again. Nothing. Then the eyelids fluttered. Tom increased his effort. River water gushed from Thomas's mouth. He retched, his groans mingling with the sound of vomiting. Cat put her hands on each side of his head, steadying him, thinking it was the most wonderful sound she had heard. Gradually the flow of water ceased, and Tom propped Thomas against his chest, murmuring in Swahili. Thomas answered weakly.

"He thinks his leg is broken," Tom said.

"He's going to go into shock unless we get him warm. Can you carry him?"

Tom nodded, then thrust a shoulder under Thomas's body and stood, Thomas draped across his back. Cat threw her slicker over them both. Tom's shirt was torn, exposing the decorated amulet pouch plastered against his chest. Water dripped from his eyebrows, ran down his face. His clothes squelched at every step. Her own were as bad.

She grabbed the *panga,* held it in both hands to slash at the brush in their path. Slowly they worked their way back to the Land Rover.

Tom lowered Thomas into the passenger seat. Cat found a blanket in the back and wrapped it around him.

"Okay, Thomas?"

"Okay, Miss Cat."

He smiled, and his gray metal dental work had never looked so beautiful. It seemed she hadn't seen him smile in days. She pressed his hand. Already it felt warmer.

"You'll feel better as soon as we get you under cover and a fire going."

"We have to get that Land Rover free before we light a fire. They've got the tents and blankets," Tom said.

He signaled to the men in the middle of the stream. Moses crawled through the window of the Land Rover and carefully moved around to the front. Tom wound the rope and threw it. Moses grabbed and missed. Tom dragged the rope back, rewound it, threw again. Moses caught it. Within minutes, he had it attached to the tie bar. Tom got into his own Land Rover, turned on the engine, pressed gently on the accelerator. Slowly, the rope tightened and the stranded vehicle jerked, then started to roll forward.

Two men were injured. Thomas and Olentwalla, whose ribs were probably broken. Both radios had again been soaked, and one Land Rover was out of commission entirely. Tom and Moses straightened Thomas's leg and bound it with splints Tom slashed from a tree. Throughout, Thomas was impassive while Cat held his hand and flinched for him. She prevailed upon Olentwalla to remove his shirt and let her look at his ribs. The flesh on the right side of his chest was puffy, his breath was shallow, and sweat beaded his face. Cat found a wide crepe bandage in the first-aid box and wound it around him, more to show her concern for him than any good it would do. He, too, needed more care than they could give him.

By five the fire was alight and tents were in place. With everything soaked from river water, an uncomfortable night was ahead of them, and Cat felt like cheering when Tom unearthed the brandy. She made tea, added plenty of sugar and generous amounts of brandy and handed mugs out to the men. She put her head inside the tent where Thomas slept. He was breathing heavily, his mouth open. He looked unconscious rather than asleep. Pain had etched the lines on his face even deeper, and his black skin had an unhealthy grayish tinge.

Cat took a mug to Tom, where he was working on one of the soaked radios by the light of a lantern. "We've got to get Thomas to a hospital. I think you should plan on taking him and Olentwalla back to Nairobi in the Land Rover that's working. I'll stay here with Moses and Sambeke."

"That's out of the question. Tomorrow, I'll take you on to Nairobi, and come back for the men."

Tom's face was a blur. She looked around. The darkness was relieved by the light from one lantern and the fire being fed, one soaked twig at a time, by Moses. The sound of rushing water filled the muddy clearing. Trees dripped. The smell of rotting vegetation underlay the acrid tang of wet, burning wood.

"Thomas doesn't look good, Tom. God knows what bugs he swallowed." She refused to think of the gallons of filthy river water she had taken in. When Tom didn't answer, she said, "Well, we'll see what he's like in the morning and talk about it then." She hesitated, then added, "I'm sorry about what I said to you in Maasai Springs, about... I don't know what came over me."

Tom looked into his mug, then up at her. "You are a brave woman. Many men would be unwilling to do what you did. Share a tree with a mamba."

"Well, I was too worried about bugs to even think about snakes," she lied, glad to see Tom shake his head. And smile.

Later, she lay fully clothed and sleepless, shrouded in the limp white cocoon of the mosquito net Sambeke had insisted on hanging. She listened to the night, the murmur of voices as the men changed the watch, missed the sound of Olentwalla's drum. These men were poachers, she thought, implicated in some way in Joel's death. They were not friends or comrades. How could she allow herself to feel affection for them?

Twenty-Nine

When she awoke at four, she couldn't remember closing her eyes.

The rain had stopped. Only a fitful pattering from the dripping trees remained. That and the sweet, musical song of hoopoes and nightjars, the first birdsong she had heard since the night she had spent with Campbell.

A dawn like those in the early days of the safari broke at last. Gold-edged clouds billowed in a pale blue-washed sky, and the rising sun blushed the grasslands with pink. Tom had made coffee, and Cat picked up a tray, took it to Thomas's tent, knocked on the canvas door before putting her head inside.

Thomas was muttering in his sleep, his eyes half-open, a rim of white showing above his lower eyelids. Cat put a hand on his forehead. He was burning. She left the coffee tray by his side and made her way to where Tom was working on the engine of the Land Rover.

"Thomas is in a bad way," she told him.

"Yes, I know." He stared at the small pile of engine parts on the hood of the crippled Land Rover. "If Dan were here, he'd have this done in no time. His fingers have a knowledge of engines in them."

"How's the radio?"

Tom shook his head.

"Well, we've got to get Thomas to a hospital," Cat said. "Why don't I take the Land Rover that's still working. I'll drive and Moses can watch for trouble." During the night she had considered all angles of being alone among these men. Finally, she had pushed everything aside. If they were going to harm her they'd have done it already. Life was chancy anywhere. In Los Angeles these days, sometimes it seemed just leaving the house in the morning was dicing with death. "We'll take Olentwalla as well, his ribs need attention. You stay with Sambeke and we'll send help as soon as we can. How would that be?"

"Impossible."

Exasperated, she said, "Tom, for God's sake—"

"There is no point in arguing. Anyway, I think I can get this engine working in a few hours."

"We can't wait too long. Thomas is in bad shape," she repeated.

"He's tougher than you think."

Cat looked at her watch. "It's eight now. If we leave by noon, we can still get some miles behind us before dark. That's it, Tom. By noon, one of us has to be driving out of here." She spoke with more confidence than she felt, with no idea how she was going to enforce her wishes. Certainly not by threatening five armed men with the gun she'd hidden.

She retrieved her portfolio and tried to work. Every thirty minutes or so she checked on Thomas. The hours crawled by. At eleven she went to her tent and started to throw a few things into a small bag. The Land Rover would be crowded. Thomas's leg would somehow have to be kept immobile.

"Miss Cat," Moses called softly from outside. "Boss here."

She did not answer.

"Miss Cat," he repeated.

"Yes, I hear you."

She went outside. The runoff had fallen dramatically in the night, and over the gurgle of the stream she could hear only hornbills, tapping like small drums played in syncopated rhythm, and the tiny shrieks of hyrax, the little rock rabbits that Tom said were the closest relative of the elephant. No Land Rover engine.

"Are you sure?"

"Yes, I hear it."

Cat shaded her eyes and looked across the empty distance. A light breeze rippled through grass that seemed to have sprung up overnight. She could see nothing but grazing animals and the bones of slain elephants. Then a faint drone reached her. A speck in the sky grew larger, becoming a small plane swinging in a circle, preparing to land.

Tom ran toward it.

"Good thing we waited," he yelled over his shoulder.

The Piper Cub touched down and rolled to a stop. Cat turned and walked to Thomas's tent without waiting to see Campbell climb out. He knew the country, guessed which way they would go. Or he'd followed their tire tracks. What didn't he know? Certainly, enough never to stray across a border without knowing about it.

"You're on your way, Thomas." His forehead was still hot, but he was conscious. "Superman just dropped in."

She fiddled with the blanket, tucking it more securely around him, and Thomas smiled his thanks. A shadow fell across them, the sunlight cut off by a figure in the doorway.

"Cat," Campbell said.

"Hi." She stood. "Good trip?"

"Not bad." Campbell entered, sat on his heels beside Thomas, spoke to him in Swahili. Thomas answered and Campbell laughed and patted his shoulder. "We'll have you in Nairobi in a couple of hours," he said in English.

Cat moved toward the doorway. "I'll get my bag."

Campbell followed her. "Can I come in?" He stood in the doorway of the tent. "We have a few minutes to talk. The men are unloading supplies."

"Yes. Come in." She swung the bag off the bed, dropped it to the floor. "We've got time, I'm sure, for you to tell me why you lied to me."

"What are you talking about? How have I lied to you?" He gave her no time to answer. "If it comes to that, why don't you tell me why you insisted on leaving Maasai Springs against my instructions—"

She cut him off. "My brother died in Tanzania. And you lied about it. That's all I'm interested in."

"I see." He picked up a jar of moisturizer from the camp table and held it to his nose. Cat noticed his hands. The skin on the knuckles was broken and bloody.

"There's no mystery." He replaced the jar on the table. "We'd strayed across the border, that's all. It's easy to do. We brought your brother back and didn't mention it. If we had, the whole thing could have been blown out of proportion. With the drought and the refugees pouring into the country from all directions, there's a lot of political unrest. The region's a tinderbox."

"Don't talk to me about politics." He was so glib, Cat thought. Made it sound so plausible. "You don't *stray* across borders, Campbell. You know every stream, every village, every inch of this country. You could have told me—" She stopped before she mentioned the night they'd spent, the opportunities he'd had to tell her. Suddenly, she couldn't wait to leave this country, get back to her work. That was all she had ever cared about. Joel and work and Rosie. And Paul Neville, she reminded herself. She cared about Paul Neville. "Who was to know? You think I was going to run to the police and tell them?"

"Dan!" Tom's voice came from outside. He banged on the canvas wall. "We're ready to leave."

"Be right there," Campbell said.

Cat grabbed her bag, started across the tent.

"There is no room for you this trip," Campbell said. "Tom can take only two."

"What do you mean, Tom?"

"Tom's flying. The plane takes two passengers. Thomas and Olentwalla must go."

She turned away without answering, threw her bag on the camp bed.

"Listen, Cat. This will give us some time to talk—"

Not trusting herself to speak, Cat pushed past him. She drummed her fingers on the men's tent before she ducked inside.

"Hey, I hear you two will be resting between clean sheets tonight."

Moses and Sambeke carried Thomas between them to the plane, Olentwalla walked behind, insisting that he was well enough, that he should wait until tomorrow. Cat looked at his face and knew each breath he took was agony—he had to get to a hospital. The two Maasai maneuvered the injured men into the small plane, and Cat looked around to say goodbye to Tom, found that he and Campbell were deep in conversation a few yards away. Then Tom nodded, and walked to the plane.

"Tom," Cat started. He looked at her, and a lump rose in her throat. How could he have been involved in Joel's death? She said, "Thanks, Tom. Take care."

"*Memsahib,*" he said. But he smiled and put up a hand in salute before swinging aboard. The little plane turned, headed toward Nairobi.

For the rest of the afternoon, she kept close to her tent, concentrated on some sketches she had started in the first days of the safari. A smiling Thomas holding a teapot. The three Maasai wrapped in their traditional red cloaks, their AKs held at port arms, a herd of elephant in the background. At five, Sambeke brought her a can of hot water. She had a sponge bath and changed into wrinkled clothes that had been dried in the sun but still smelled of river water. The evening yawned in front of her like a chasm to be crossed. What was the point of questions when she knew she would get no answers? She'd get back to Nairobi, talk to people there.

"Cat." Campbell was a dark shadow against the canvas wall of her tent. "Dinner."

"I'll eat here, thanks."

"Don't make me come in there after you."

She thought of the scene that would make and unzipped her door. A deep golden light hung over the grassland, trees outlined in black against the huge red disk of the sun. A few zebra had come to drink at the edge of the now-quiet stream. Long mournful cries of birds echoed from tree to tree. The evening was hushed and waiting.

Campbell handed her a drink. "Thank God for good whiskey," he said pleasantly.

"Thanks." She matched his tone. "Where is everybody?"

Campbell had brought another Maasai with him, introduced him briefly. Cat didn't quite get his name, and she didn't insist on knowing. The camp was quiet, Moses and Sambeke and the new man nowhere to be seen.

"They're around. Dinner's going to be sketchy without Thomas, I'm afraid." Campbell went back to his own chair.

So the patrols were out as usual. "A sandwich will do."

"That's what I thought, too. Did you get my message?"

"Yes. Thomas gave it to me. Thank you. Campbell, if a long discussion is on your mind, forget it. I don't want to go into it. I know you are going to continue to lie to me about my brother and, really, that's all I care about. For the rest, well, we had a couple of nights together. They don't mean anything. Not to me."

He looked at her in silence, then said, "Christ! What sort of attitude is that?"

"My attitude," she said sharply. "I'm not interested in explanations—"

"Well, I am. Why did you insist on leaving Maasai Springs before I got back?"

"As you said from the beginning, Maasai Springs is perfect for my purpose. So now I have to get back home." She put her glass down on the table and got to her feet. "I'm not very hungry. I think I'll turn in."

"No. Not before we talk this out—"

"Listen, you don't seem to get it. I don't want to talk. I'm tired. Good night."

She turned to walk to her tent, a few yards. Far away she heard the laughing cry of a hyena and shivered. A strange sound. Campbell grabbed her arm, spun her around to face him.

She tried to wrench free. "What the hell are you doing? Take your hands off me."

He pulled her toward him. Cat struck at his face, then jammed a shoulder into his chest, twisting her head away from him. He searched for her mouth, ignoring the blows on her shoulders. Cat brought up a knee, trying to slam it into his groin—not sure who she was fighting, herself or him. Campbell bore her backward, toward the tent. She wrapped her arms around his neck, clinging to him, mouthing the skin on his neck, using her teeth. Her body was on fire. Wanting him. Hating him because she did.

The canvas floor scraped her back. The musky smell of leaves and mud and sex inflamed her senses. In a fever, she tore at his shirt, thrust her tongue against his, tasting the blood on his mouth where she'd hit him. She pulled at his shoulders and neck with her teeth as she helped him tear off the barriers of cloth separating them, raising her hips to slam against him as he entered her. She locked her legs around him, forcing him deeper. Rage and desire entangled, and every thrust was a contest. Groans seemed forced from his chest, and his hands gripping her buttocks clenched convulsively. Then fire exploded deep within her.

For a few seconds, she lay quiet. Sickened. It was over. She pushed at his shoulders, trying to move him. Every vertebra seemed scraped raw by the hard, canvas-covered ground under her. When he didn't move, she twisted from beneath him and got to her feet. Sweat was cooling on her skin, and she picked up her terry-cloth robe from the camp chair, clutched it around her while she groped for the lantern. The harsh glare filled the tent.

"You can get out now." She threw the words over her shoulder. "You've had your triumph."

"And sweet it was," he said. "But a triumph for both, I thought. Unless, of course, you're a better actress than I gave you credit for."

Cat turned. He bent to pick up his shirt from the floor. Long scratches streaked across his back, and in the thin blue light she saw red blotches on his shoulders, the marks of her teeth. Or maybe Morag's. She looked away.

"You really are low," she said.

"Can't argue with that." He buttoned his shirt, tucked it into his pants. "But I don't think either one of us is much to brag about right now. Do you?"

Cat reached for the bottled mineral water, pouring with shaky hands. She wrapped both hands around the plastic glass to prevent it from smacking against her bruised mouth.

"Spare me the preaching. Just leave." Cat turned her back, walked the two paces to sweep back the mosquito netting over the camp bed.

"Well, memories for a lifetime," he said. "You've been quite an experience, Miss Stanton."

She heard him drop the canvas door into place behind him.

Tom arrived in the Cub soon after dawn. Fifteen minutes later, the plane was bumping over the uneven ground, scattering zebra and antelope, causing birds to burst from the cover of deep grass. The plane rose and Tom turned toward Nairobi.

Cat shaded her eyes with one hand and looked out the window. Below, Moses and Sambeke were stick figures walking back to the tents on the bank of the river. Campbell stood alone watching the plane. She had not said goodbye. She kept her eyes on him until he fell into the distance and she could no longer see him clearly.

Thirty

Cat tucked the telephone against her shoulder and leaned against the open doorway of the balcony, watching the traffic in the square below her hotel window as she listened to the ringing tone. She imagined the sound traveling through empty drafting rooms, into her office where the sun filtered through the leaves of the coral trees on San Vicente Boulevard and splashed across the ebony partner's desk she and Joel had shared. In Los Angeles it was 9:00 p.m. yesterday, too late even for Mave to be working. She'd dialed the number simply to make contact with her life.

While listening, she studied the postcard in her hand. It had been among her mail, a picture of a magnificent building in downtown Jeddah designed by Skidmore, Owings and Merrill. On the back Paul had written:

Too bad you'll never get to see this. Saudi Arabia's an interesting place. Leaving for Johannesburg tonight. Miss you.

Suddenly Mave Chen's voice was in her ear. "Okay, okay, hold your fire. I found him. He's on his way."

"Mave. It's me," Cat said, surprised. "Who's going where?"

"Cat! Is this timing or what? I got here a minute ago. All hell's breaking loose."

"What's happening?"

"They've hit water on the Spring Street job."

"Much?"

"Sounds like it."

"Where?" Cat walked over to the desk, picked up a legal-size yellow pad and a ballpoint, hooked a chair into place with her foot and sat.

"Murphy says it's the southwest corner, under column B4."

"Okay." The drawings of the subterranean garage of the twenty-five-story building in downtown Los Angeles started to unroll in her mind. "How deep are they?"

"Sixty feet."

Sixty feet below grade, getting ready to pour concrete for the pilings to support five stories underground.

"The drill riggers are putting in double shifts," Mave was saying. "Murphy went back to check everything was going okay and happened to be there when water started to flood. He called Doug at home, got no answer, so he called me to find out where he is. I thought you were Murph checking in again."

"Okay." Doug Jones, her design chief, was running the office while she was away. "I'll call the job now and get back to you."

Quickly she dialed the job number, drumming her fingers while she listened to the phone ring in the construction trailer.

"Yeah," Murphy yelled in her ear. "Spring Street Plaza."

"Murph? Cat Stanton. What's going on?"

In the background she could hear a buzz of voices and the heavy grind of machinery. She could almost smell the cement dust and diesel exhaust, the stale smoke from Murphy's chewed-up cigar. She was struck by longing for a cup of his coffee, the same bitter brew she'd had on a hundred job sites. Construction bosses seemed to specialize in it—their secret ingredient was probably iron filings.

"We've hit water at ten feet under the B4 caisson," Murph was yelling in her ear. "How did you know? You're supposed to be in Africa or someplace."

"Yes, well, good news travels fast." She heard him laugh, and her heart lightened just to be in touch with her own world, dealing with problems she could handle. "You got it pumping yet?"

"I got the Hercules on its way, Cat, but your office will have to authorize it in writing for me. Hold a minute." Cat heard a muffled roar. "Chrissake, hold it down, you guys. I'm on a call from goddamn Africa here. Yeah, okay, Cat, what d'y'say?"

"Murph, when the well-point system's going, make sure to keep pumping until we get the footings in."

"Yo."

"It'll take time, but don't skimp on this, it will cost a lot more if we don't get good bearing. Okay?" Murph was a professional, with years of experience as a construction boss. Cat felt her work reaching out to her, stabilizing the ground under her feet.

"Yo."

"Did Doug get there yet?"

"Yeah, he's here."

"Let me talk to him."

"Hold on." The phone banged in her ear as he put it down. She heard him yelling Doug's name.

"Hey, Cat," Doug's voice said.

"How bad is it, Doug?"

"Well, it's not good. We've hit an underground stream."

"That's what I thought. Same thing happened on the Mount Sinai job. There's no way those streams can be tracked on a survey. Any danger of collapse?"

"Can't be sure."

"Well, better keep the men out of the hole until it's dried out." She brought him up to date on the instructions she had given to Murphy. "Did you get hold of Armstrong?"

"Not yet."

"Well, when you do, tell him I want a composite pad to sit on a cluster of triple columns to replace the one we've lost. And Doug, keep on him. Authorize what you have to and we'll go over it when I get home. Delay costs the client money, and you know Armstrong. He's a good structural engineer, but you have to be a squeaky wheel with him."

"I'll take a sleeping bag over to his office if I have to."

She laughed, then briefly told him about Maasai Springs. "A joint venture, the government of Kenya and Bluebonnet, leased land, no outright purchase possible. A lot of palms will have to be greased but payoffs are part of the cost of doing business here."

"So what else is new? Here we call it campaign contributions."

Cat laughed again, feeling reconnected to her work and all that mattered to her. She hung up, then redialed the office. Mave brought her up to date on the rest of the jobs in progress. As they spoke, Cat made notes as she usually did of telephone conversations. When she got back, she would load them into the computer.

That done, she dialed Stephen N'toya's number. After a dozen rings, she hung up and checked the telephone book. No listing, no address. She called the operator.

"I have the telephone number of a friend in Nairobi," she said. "But I have mislaid the address. Could you give that to me?"

"*Memsahib,* that is a problem. I cannot be knowing the addresses of all who own telephones."

"No, of course not, but couldn't you look it up on a computer?" As she spoke, she wondered if the telephone company had computers. Kenya was too poor even to keep the roads passable.

"Even if such were possible, *memsahib,* it would not be correct, you see, for this information to be given to any person just for the asking."The voice conveyed shock, as if what she had asked him to do was entirely improper. "If the subscriber was wanting his address known to all who fancied it, he would be publishing same in the phone book, do you see."

"Is there any way you could make an exception? I'm only in the country for a few days."

"Ah, well, most unfortunate, *memsahib.* No way, you see."

"Okay.Thanks. *Asante.*" She hung up. It had been a long shot at best.

By ten she was crossing City Square. The turn-of-the-century building that housed the State Law Office was on Harampe Avenue, across the street from a lively produce market.After the heat and raucousness of the streets, the lobby was cool, the measured pace of the men coming and going heavy with authority.The few women among them stood out brightly in saris, one or two in tribal dress, the rest fashionably western. Everyone carried dark, bulky briefcases. The place smelled as if the floors above were filled with moldering paper.

She walked over to the information desk. "Could you tell me where I can find Mr. Stephen N'toya, please."

The uniformed guard ran insolent eyes over her. He didn't answer. Holding her gaze, he picked up a telephone and murmured into it. He lounged in his chair, watching her. Suddenly his spine snapped straight. Jumping to his feet, he stood at attention, barked a single-word reply. Carefully, he replaced the phone, then spoke to her in Swahili.

Cat smiled. "I'm sorry, I don't speak Swahili."

Everywhere else in Nairobi, English was spoken. In the State Law Office, a government department, she had assumed this would also be the case. She took her Day-Timer from her bag, printed Stephen's name in block capitals, tore out the page and pushed it across the desk. "Stephen N'toya."

The guard glanced at the page, pushed it back to her with another torrent of words.

Cat put a finger on the printed word. "Stephen N'toya," she said again, speaking slowly, careful to keep her smile in place.

The guard stared at her. He got to his feet and came around the desk. Standing too close, he loomed over her. Six foot four, she thought, two hundred and seventy-five pounds easy, solid muscle. Could play tackle for the Rams. And smelled as if he just had. She stepped back. He followed, pushing his face into hers and speaking as slowly as she had, and a lot more ominously. He did not smile. Her heart was tripping over itself. Only the thought of the policemen Stephen was supposed to be finding, the knowledge that Joel died in Tanzania, the cover-up of that, kept her from turning and walking out. She stared up into the man's yellow-tinged dark eyes.

"Are you sick? Your eyes look terrible and your breath smells worse. I think you should see a doctor."

He blinked and straightened.

Cat raised her eyebrows. "I knew you could speak English," she said pleasantly. "You really shouldn't keep it to yourself like that." She looked around. "Well, thanks for your help."

She headed for the directory of names by the side of the elevator. The guard came after her, grabbed her arm. Cat pulled free.

"Now, wait a minute—"

Then, without knowing where they had come from, she was surrounded by armed soldiers in combat fatigues and the camouflage baseball hats that seemed part of the uniform of modern armies. Their heavy black boots clattered on the tile floor of the lobby.

"*Memsahib.*" The officer in charge blocked her way. "Your name, please."

"Cat Stanton. I'm an American——"

"Your passport, please."

Cat rummaged in her bag, handed over her passport. The officer studied it, several times looking from her photograph to her face.

"You must leave this office."

"I'm here to see a friend. Stephen N'toya. He works here."

"No Stephen N'toya."

"You must be mistaken. He works here."

"*Memsahib,* you have been informed there is no one of that name here. If you refuse to leave, you will be placed under arrest."

"What for? I have legitimate business——"

"You are disturbing the peace of this government office."

"That's ridiculous. All I've done is ask to see Stephen N'toya. He's an attorney. He works here."

The officer barked an order. Her arms were grabbed. Cat stood very still. They could throw her in jail and no one would even know she was there. The hands grasping her were not gentle. Fingers dug deliberately into her flesh. She restrained a grimace of pain, refusing to let them know what she felt.

"Well, I guess you hold all the cards," she said. "So, if you'll just give me back my passport, I'll be on my way."

The officer motioned to his men to release her. Cat held out her hand for her passport. The officer gestured toward the door. She walked to the exit, a soldier on either side, another marching behind her. In the crowded vestibule, the men of affairs continued about their business, eyes carefully averted. A couple of the women slid sympathetic glances her way. But no one stopped. The officer held open the door. Cat put out her hand for her passport. Without moving, he held her eyes. With an effort, she kept her own steady. Then he handed the passport to her, and she walked through the door into the sun. Her legs felt weak.

She had a feeling she had just been very lucky. Her name had been known. Someone with a long arm was making sure she would not find Stephen N'toya. Or his policemen.

Cat glanced over her shoulder. Her follower was still there, thirty feet back, sauntering along. She forced herself not to hurry, to pace herself in the heat, careful not to trip on the broken sidewalk.

She had shown Stephen's business card to her self-appointed guardian, the friendly doorman outside her hotel, mentally cursing Stephen for giving only his name in the center of the card, a telephone number in the right-hand lower corner. The doorman had taken out a map of Nairobi and shown her the general area served by that number. Residences, he'd said. Very nice. Very safe. Then he'd called a *teksi* for her and given the driver instructions in Swahili.

The cabbie had dropped her off at a corner. In each direction, mature, broad-leaved trees lined pockmarked streets. As she paid him, a car had stopped a few yards behind in the shade of a tree. Normally she wouldn't have noticed, but after the scare at the State Law Office she found herself checking her surroundings.

A burly young man climbed out of the car, locked it, lifted the trunk lid and leaned inside as if searching for something. She'd watched her cab drive away, not quite sure what to do next. She had a ridiculous picture of herself standing at the intersection, yelling Stephen's name, waiting for him to shout a response. Or knocking on doors, trying to explain what she wanted in a language no one understood.

People began eyeing her with curiosity as they passed——a white woman far from the tourist centers of Nairobi. She glanced at the half-seen figure still buried in the trunk of the car, then started to walk, choosing a street at random. The young man slammed the lid of his trunk, looked nonchalantly——too nonchalantly?——in each direction and started after her.

The sun was blinding, and she was glad of sunglasses and a wide-brimmed straw hat. It was well after the noon hour, most people were sensibly inside, out of the heat, so her tail was easy to spot. She turned right, onto a street much like the one she had left, and glanced behind her. He had picked up his pace to keep her in sight.

In spite of her fear, she found the streetscape interesting. Small houses, close to the street and to each other. Well-kept front gardens the size of pocket handkerchiefs. An old neighborhood, modestly prosperous, probably built by the British in colonial days for minor civil servants, clerks, shopkeepers, and taken over since independence by their African counterparts.

The houses gave way to a line of small stores, older by several generations and more solid than the cheesy minimalls now appearing on every other street corner in Los Angeles. Cat averted her eyes from a chipped white enamel shelf fronting a small shop, the dried puddles of brownish blood that had drained from lumps of raw, unrefrigerated meat, the green flies buzzing happily as they fed on sun-warmed flesh. She ducked into the next dark doorway, waited to see what her follower on the other side of the street would do. He slowed his steps, turning his head, obviously searching for her, and she retreated deeper into the store.

Swags of fabric decorated the walls, bolts of cloth stood upright, crowding the linoleum-covered floor.

"Jambo, memsahib." The turbaned Indian shopkeeper, appearing

from the dark recesses of the shop, was not quite successful in hiding his surprise at his unlikely customer. "You are looking for a nice piece of material for a dress. We have the best, *memsahib*. Look no further." He started to unroll a bolt. "Genuine polyester, *memsahib*, top quality." With a flourish, he displayed a length of dazzling blue, green and purple fabric, rippling it gently to show off the play of colors.

"It's very lovely. No, I was wondering if perhaps you know a friend of mine, Stephen N'toya." Looking confused, the storekeeper stared at her. Cat felt her face begin to color, and she stumbled on. "He lives in this neighborhood."

"Stephen N'toya? He said I was knowing him?"

"No, he just lives around here, and I wondered if perhaps you did know him." Oh, God, she thought.

The man kept his smile. "I deal with ladies, you see, *memsahib*. Husbands rarely." His head wobbled in a strange side-to-side motion. "But I will ask all the ladies when they come in. Stephen N'toya. Yes, I will ask." Expertly, he rerolled the fabric. His smile was losing its brilliance, and Cat thanked him and turned to go.

From the sanctuary of the dark doorway, she searched the street in both directions. To her relief, her follower was nowhere in sight. She wanted to laugh at her fears. Poor guy was probably an ordinary young man on his way to see his girl. Her encounter with the military had made her jumpy, suspicious of everyone. She stepped out into the sunlight.

A few minutes later, she picked him up again, sauntering along on the other side of the street, pacing her, sometimes slower, occasionally faster, never more than ten yards behind. Her heart pounded. Sweat dampened her skin, ran stickily down her chest into her bra, but in spite of the heat, she felt suddenly cold. As long as she stayed where people were, she told herself, she would be all right. But in the heat of the day, few people were about. Well, even so, what could he do? she asked herself. Snatch her off the street? Sure, a small voice answered. He could do that. Easy.

She started to look for a cab, but the streets were empty of traffic. Taking refuge now as much as seeking information, she entered the more likely stores she passed—the newspaper and ice cream and sundries shops, with stale air smelling of chocolate and sugar. The wooden-floored groceries with open bins of coffee beans, crushed wheat, dried roots she couldn't imagine a use for. The drowsy storekeepers were invariably Indian, speaking the same singsong English as the desk clerks at the hotel. After a Coke, a few words about Nairobi—yes, very interesting, and Kenya, certainly, very beautiful, many animals—she asked if perhaps Stephen N'toya was known to them. Heads wobbled from side to side. An exchange similar to that with the fabric man ensued. "Excuse me, *memsahib*. Stephen N'toya? Sorry, *memsahib*."

Around four, she exited a shop and almost ran over the man from the car. A young tough with skin as dark as Tom's, thick neck, one eyebrow scarred. He looked like a fighter, in the ring or the street, impossible to tell.

She broke into a half run, praying for a *teksi*. He was bolder now, no longer making any attempt to disguise his presence.

Her flight had taken her to a treeless market area. On the broken sidewalks, carts displayed their goods, plastic bowls, wooden pegs, dingy vegetables. But at least people were about now, mostly heavy-bodied women, gossiping, balancing woven baskets on their heads, shopping for the evening meal. Children ran in and out of the crowd, paying no attention to the calls of their mothers.

Cat began to have a glimmer of understanding of what it might feel like to be black in a white neighborhood. Hers was the only white face, and she felt every eye sliding over her while refusing to make contact. The man behind her was close now, obviously fearing to lose her among the women.

Panicky, she entered into a small grocery shop. Even without air-conditioning it was mercifully cool after the heat outside. Her legs were shaky from tension and anxiety, from the hours of pounding the streets. And she had to pee. The endless cans of Coke she had consumed as an excuse to linger and ask questions were making their presence known.

Over the heads of the women waiting to be served, the shop-keeper looked at her expectantly. Cat pointed to the old refrig-erator case, then opened its door, extracted yet another Coke and took her place in line to pay.

At the counter, she counted out the money for the soda, asked the same questions it seemed of the same shopkeeper with the same result. "No, *memsahib.* Stephen N'toya? Very sorry, *memsahib.* This is a friend you have lost, perhaps?"

"I guess so. I wonder if you could do me a great favor?" Cat said. "Could you call a cab for me? I have to get back to my hotel and I don't see any cabs on the street." She pushed a few pound notes across the counter, too tired to care how many. "I'd be very grate-ful." She wouldn't dare ask to use the john. It would likely turn out to be Eastern style, a hole in the floor with a depression ei-ther side for the feet. She couldn't cope with that.

The shopkeeper palmed the notes and smiled at her. "You are in good fortune to choose this poor shop, *memsahib.* My brother-in-law has a car, do you know. He would be most pleased to do this small service." He called a name, and a skinny young boy, large horn-rims almost obscuring his narrow face, appeared from be-hind a beaded curtain. The shopkeeper seemed to grow two inches in height, his chest swelling. "My son," he said, obviously waiting for her comment.

Cat smiled. "Congratulations. A very brainy boy, one can see. A credit to you." She glanced toward the door.

The man nodded, satisfied. The child stared at her while his father spoke to him in Hindi, then he disappeared behind the curtain again.

"You wait, *memsahib*. Not long at all. In no time. Very efficient."

"Thank you."

"A pleasure to be of service, *memsahib*." He raised his hands, then clasped them in front of his little round belly. "Just the cost of the petrol, you understand." He named a figure three times more than the cabdriver had received earlier. "We are poor people, you see."

Cat nodded. "Of course."

She went to the door, looked out. Her shadow lingered on the sidewalk across the street.

She withdrew, but he had started to cross toward the shop, his stride purposeful.

Cat glanced at the shopkeeper, chatting now to the crowd of customers in front of the counter. A small, frail man, out of condition. No help to be had there. The rest were women.

She couldn't wait for the young thug to make the next move. She had to do something.

She moved casually toward the back of the shop, waited until the shopkeeper was distracted and slipped behind the beaded curtain. Heart pounding, she paused, listening for the sound of protest, but no one had noticed. Several doors faced her. Then on the other side of the bead curtain, a loud male voice started to ask questions in Swahili, and she heard the hurried nervous answer of the shopkeeper. She opened the door that seemed the most likely to lead toward the outside rather than the living quarters, and pulled it closed behind her.

After the shop, the darkness was impenetrable, the room filled with unfamiliar smells. It seemed to be a storeroom. As silently as she could, she groped her way toward the back wall. A tower of boxes swayed as she bumped them. She steadied them, fearful she would bring not only the boxes down on her head, but also the man looking for her.

She stopped to listen. The male voices still sparred, one demanding entry, the other denying it. Or so she hoped.

As her eyes adjusted to the darkness, she saw a faint line of daylight. The bottom of a door. Her eyes fixed upon it as if on the Holy Grail, she inched forward, her hands outstretched in front of her.

Then the door was flung open. A bulky figure blocked the sudden dazzle of sunlight. Cat reached into the bag slung over her shoulder, glad she had kept the gun she'd stolen from the Land Rover.

"My dear young lady," a voice boomed. "I thought I'd find you here." Brian Ward, Trackers, Ltd., stepped into the storeroom.

Her hand curled around the butt of the automatic. "In the storeroom of an Indian grocery?" With an effort, she kept her voice steady. She could hardly hear herself speak over the thunder in her ears—the sound of her racing blood. "Why would you think that, Mr. Ward." She slipped her finger through the trigger guard.

"I saw you enter in the front, of course. Seemed a strange sort of shop for a gel like you to be frequenting. What? What?" He barked his stupid laugh. "So I followed you. But the Indian wallah out there said you were not about. I knew he was lying—they all do, you know. But you hadn't come out the front door, so I nipped behind, into the alley. All these places are built alike, know them like the back of my hand. Now then. Something's got you spooked. Eh? Eh?"

Cat removed her hand from inside the shoulder bag, dropping it to her side, allowing him to see the weapon.

"Do you shop in this neighborhood often, Mr. Ward?" She felt like Alice down the rabbit hole, involved in a conversation with the Mad Hatter.

"As a matter of fact, my tailor has his place of business a few doors away. Good man. Trained in Saville Row, so he says. Lying of course, but he's not bad for all that." He glanced at the gun in her hand. "Saw the johnny following you, thought it might have something to do with the two Australian chaps that bought it. You were there, of course, with Campbell. Strange old business, eh? Coming on the heels of your brother's death? What? What?"

Her head was reeling. *Who the hell was he? The bumbling colonial act was too broad brush to be genuine.*

"Come on," Ward urged, "my car's down the alley. This is not a neighborhood for tourists. As soon as it gets dark, they'll pinch the clothes off your back. And you won't want to use that cannon in a crowded street, my dear. The police don't take kindly to that sort of thing at all. Not at all, I can assure you."

She looked at the gun in her hand. "Yes, this could take a man's head off. Thank you, but I'm not going back to my hotel."

"Well, where do you want to go? I'll drop you—"

He was moving toward her, all two hundred and fifty pounds of him. She backed away, fumbling with the door behind her.

"No, thank you."

She opened the door. She dared not take her eyes from Ward, still advancing.

"Ah, *memsahib*. I was looking for you." The little Indian shop-keeper stepped into the room. Then his voice rose in alarm. "What is this? Who is this? Sir, this is my storeroom. Nothing valuable here, sir. Nothing." He waved at the stacked crates. "Just Tusker, you see."

"Is my cab here?" Cat asked.

"Yes. My brother-in-law. Yes."

"Thanks." Cat backed up.

"Miss Stanton! What's the matter? No need to be frightened of me, m'dear. I think you need a friend—"

"Thank you, Mr. Ward. I have a friend." She kept her hand on the weapon she slipped back in her bag. "I'll see you at the hotel, perhaps."

She followed the little shopkeeper through the beaded curtain, into the crowded shop, Brian Ward, still talking, close behind them. Out of the corner of her eye, she saw her shadow trying to fold his large frame into a small space behind the old upright refrigerator case.

Outside, an elderly gray Honda stood at the curb, a turbaned man holding open the back door. She got in, gave him the name of the hotel. As they left, Cat looked out the back window. The young thug was on the street. Behind him, Brian Ward stood in the doorway. Then the car eased around a corner, and both men were lost from sight.

Thirty-One

Cat leaned back in the car, allowing her heartbeat to return to normal. The scent of patchouli wafting from the front seat was cloying and powerful, catching in the back of her throat, but the narrow-shouldered, turbaned figure behind the wheel was her knight in shining armor, at least for the moment.

Brian Ward was right. She needed a friend. She was scared and alone, and in these circumstances a Beretta lacked a certain human warmth. In all of Nairobi, there wasn't one person she could turn to. Her eyes opened. She sat up.

Not quite.

"Excuse me." Braving the patchouli, she leaned forward to tap the owner of the Honda on the shoulder. "I've changed my mind about the hotel. Could you take me to Saint Francis Xavier Church, instead? Do you know it?"

"Yes, *memsahib*. I know this church." He shook his head doubtfully, clucked his tongue. "Much farther than the hotel, you see."

"Of course, I'll pay for the additional petrol." She felt a flutter of amusement. Her knight's armor had a few rusty spots.

He was no Arthurian knight, she discovered. Under that small, humble exterior beat the heart of a kamikaze. Hunched over the wheel, he leaned on the horn for the entire journey across the city, changed lanes without warning, turned corners as suddenly and finally stood on his brakes triumphantly in front of Father Gaston's church.

Exhausted, Cat counted out the new figure they had agreed upon, thought about Brian Ward and her grim-looking follower possibly still hanging around his brother-in-law's store and added a generous tip. Her rescuer jumped out, opened the door for her, hand pressed together as he salaamed his thanks.

Cat paused under the lych-gate. The churchyard was empty, roses nodding peacefully along the fence. Music floating from an open-air bar across the road was muted, a background to the twittering of birds wheeling from tree to tree as they settled.

The church door opened and Father Gaston, dressed in a black cassock, a wilted bunch of flowers in one hand, came out, starting toward the long building where they'd had tea last time she'd been here.

Cat opened the gate. "Father Gaston."

He stopped, astonishment clear upon his face. "Miss Stanton." He looked over her shoulder, then back at her. "What are you doing here at this hour? Are you alone?" The sky was beginning to show streaks of crimson. So close to the equator, there would be little twilight. Evening was close.

"I need a cup of tea, I think." Tears of relief misted her eyes. She smiled. Her lips were trembling and she pressed them together before he noticed. "I was wondering if you had a few minutes."

"My dear! Of course. Come, I'll call my houseman."

He waited until she reached him, then turned toward the house.

The stems of the flowers in his hand were green with slime from being too long in dirty water and gave off a powerful stench of decay.

"Was your journey into the bush successful? Did you get the site you wanted for the hotel?"

"Yes, I did, I think. A place called Maasai Springs. Very lovely. Have you heard of it?"

"I wouldn't know about the bush country. I'm very much an urban priest, I'm afraid. But good, good. I am glad you found what you wanted. Joel talked to me so much about the plans he had, what he hoped to accomplish. Fine young man. Very fine."

When they reached the veranda, Father Gaston looked at the dead flowers he carried. "Excuse me, *mademoiselle*. I will order tea and at the same time rid myself of this unpleasant little burden. We have a small altar society, but I'm afraid some of these duties are overlooked."

Cat sat at the table where they'd had tea before she left Nairobi and drank in the peace, the scent of the roses, feeling calm returning to her. Outside the surrounding fence, lights came on in the bar, twinkled eerily behind the statues of winged angels guarding the graves. Father Gaston was gone a long time, and she hoped he wasn't planning anything more than just a cup of tea.

He appeared finally along the darkening veranda. "Now, my dear Cat. Come." He opened a door, turned on a light in a book-lined study carpeted in beige sisal. Behind the desk directly across the room, drab brownish chintz framed a long window. A couple of battered old armchairs with a table between them were illuminated by large standing lamps that looked as if they had stood in exactly that place for generations of priests. Clearly an intellectual's retreat and well used.

"Sit, please."

Books were piled on the floor by one of the armchairs and Cat took the other. When she was settled, he sat back in what was obviously his favorite spot. They took a few minutes to talk about the room, about the comfort of books when far from the company of one's own kind, the difficulty of keeping them from being eaten by termites in a hot climate. About the problems he'd had obtaining reading material in the Belgian Congo and the many other places he'd served in Africa.

A knock at the door brought Father Gaston to his feet. He took a tray from a tall thin shadowy figure outside. Cat thought it was the same man she'd seen before, weeding in the churchyard. The priest busied himself for a moment with the tea, handed her a cup, then took his own and resumed his seat.

"Now, my dear. I think you have come for more than tea. Is this so?"

"Yes." She was grateful to him for giving her an opening. "I had some frightening experiences today. I don't know what they mean. I remembered what you said about being a friend and just came over here."

She poured out the events of the day, the soldiers at the judicial building, the young man who'd followed her, the sudden appearance of Brian Ward in the storeroom.

"Who is he, Brian Ward? Do you know him, Father?" The word slipped easily off her tongue. She never used that word to her own father. She and Joel never called him anything at all. Not Father, or Daddy, or Pops, as Jess referred to her own adored father. Nothing. "He knew about the Australians who were killed. How could he have known that?"

"Australians? What Australians?" Father Gaston looked startled.

"Their names were Bobby Watson and Peter Stone. They were from Adelaide. I don't really know who killed them. Campbell or someone else. Reitholder, maybe."

The priest confirmed her suspicion she wasn't making too much sense. "Cat, I think it would be clearer if you start from the beginning."

"While we were out there in the bush, we came across a lot of murdered elephants." With anyone else, she would not have used that word, but the sympathy on Father Gaston's face told her that he would understand exactly how she felt. "Dan Campbell decided we had to go after the poachers. He said he wanted to protect an elephant called Ahmed, a national treasure because he is so old and large. But I think he wanted to go after the poachers because he's in the same business."

"But Ahmed is well known, Cat," Father Gaston said. "He really is under the protection of the president of the country. Even I know of him."

"Yes, all right, but I still think Campbell is a poacher. He wanted to eliminate his competition. Why else would he go after poachers when he had a safari client with him? It was a real risk."

Father Gaston shook his head sadly. "Who knows what motivates such men as these?"

She told him about the Maasai village and the beating of Reitholder and what Reitholder had said about Joel. The priest got to his feet, went to his desk, rooted around in a drawer. "Go on, my dear. I am listening. This is a terrible story, too much for you to carry around alone." He produced a pack of Gauloise and held them up. "Do you mind?"

Cat shook her head.

"I shouldn't, I know," the priest said. "It's a bad habit. Ruining my lungs." He lit up, settled himself back in his chair. "These Australians. Who exactly were they?"

"I don't know. Just Australians. Hunters. Funnily enough, I'd met them in the hotel in Nairobi before I left. It turned out they were working with this man Reitholder, killing elephants." The enormity of what had happened in the last few weeks seemed suddenly too much for her. She put a hand to her eyes. Snatches of overhead conversations come flooding back, bits of dialogue that had stopped when Campbell and Tom noticed her approach. "I think Campbell has a lot of ivory already hidden somewhere, but Campbell and Tom M'Bala are going after some more that is being sent down to the coast by some general. I don't know who he is. The authorities have to be informed. But who? After what happened today, who can I tell? Where can I go?"

Father Gaston leaned across the table, put a comforting hand over hers. She noticed the nicotine-stained fingers. He was so human and warm. And a priest. She found herself saying, "I saw a strange place just above Maasai Springs." She told him about the camp, the training manuals in Chinese and Swahili. "I think it was a terrorist camp."

"Terrorists? Surely not. Not here in Kenya."

She restrained her impatience. He'd lived all over Africa. How had he managed to remain so naive? "Why not? Joel had certainly seen this place before he was killed. He sent sketches to me."

"My dear! That sounds very dangerous."

"Father Gaston, I didn't really come to Kenya for a hotel site—I came to find out about Joel's death. And I found out that he was killed in Tanzania. His body was brought back to Kenya. I think they were using his safari to scout smuggling routes. I know there was a cover-up. I know about this terrorist camp, and the poachers are probably the same people. They kill for the ivory and sell it to finance their activities. What I need to do now is get this information to the right people. The police must have investigated—a foreigner can't be killed without an investigation. I have to talk to them and find out what they know. Stephen N'toya is the only one who can help me do that, but I can't find him. He doesn't answer his telephone."

"My dear, I don't think you should do anything more about this. You are dabbling in dangerous affairs. Powerful men are involved in ivory smuggling, it goes higher than you would believe. It is well known in Nairobi. Even I've heard the rumors."

She looked down at the forgotten cup in her hand. The tea was cold, unappetizing. She returned it to the saucer.

"I know Brian Ward," Father Gaston said. "Strange man. I'll make some inquiries, if you wish."

"I'd rather you made some inquiries about Stephen N'toya," she said. "Do you know him?"

"No, the name is not familiar. But I will ask around, my dear. People give information to priests they wouldn't give to others. But you must be careful. Don't talk to anyone else."

"You be careful, too, Father Gaston," Cat said. "If it's dangerous for me, it could be dangerous for you, as well. I don't believe that Joel's death was an accident."

Father Gaston smiled reassuringly. "Who would harm an old priest?"

Cat looked at him. Her idea of an old priest was Barry Fitzgerald in the vintage movies she loved so much on video. Not this handsome, silver-maned man sitting across from her.

"Who knows you came here today?" he asked.

"No one. Oh, Mr. Gupta, the man who brought me. No one else. If you would try to find out where I can reach Stephen N'toya, I'd be grateful. I'll write his name down for you." She picked up her bag, took out the Beretta, put it in her lap so that she could more easily find her Day-Timer. She printed Stephen's name and looked up to hand it to the priest. His eyes were on the Beretta. Embarrassed, she shoved the gun back into her bag. "I stole it from one of the Land Rovers," she said.

"Do you carry it with you all the time?"

"I'm never without it now."

"Do you know how to use it?"

"Yes."

"And would you?"

Part of her mind disengaged from the moment. She was with Joel in Zuma Canyon, and their father, looking down at the blood spreading across his chest. She looked at Father Gaston.

"Yes," she said. "If I had to."

"Well, that is good. If you are threatened, you must defend yourself." He went to the telephone on the desk and dialed a number. "I am calling a *teksi*. You look exhausted. I think you should go straight back to your hotel and get a good night's sleep. Tomorrow, go and see something of Nairobi. Forget all this. Buy some gifts for your friends, see the City Market. I will call you when I have some word. But if you need me, come here immediately. Do not hesitate."

He opened the door. They stepped onto the veranda. After the smoke-laden fug of his study, she filled her lungs with sweet-smelling air. She threw her bag over her shoulder, feeling the comfortable weight of the Beretta. "Thank you."

They strolled down toward the lych-gate. The *teksi* was waiting. Father Gaston opened the door. "A shared burden is always easier to carry, Cat. Remember that."

She felt as if an enormous hole had opened up in her chest and all the pain and anxiety of the last few weeks had poured out and she could breathe again. Who would have believed, she thought, that talking to a Catholic priest she didn't really know could be such a catharsis?

When she got back to the hotel, she called Paul Neville in Washington, D.C., on the chance he might have returned to the United States. She listened to his voice repeating the familiar message—

"Paul Neville. On assignment. If it's urgent, call the bureau. They usually know how to contact me."

She felt nothing. No love or excitement. Not even reassurance.

The following morning, she awoke just as color was staining the eastern sky, the hour that Thomas would rap on the canvas wall of her tent and call, *"Habari ya asubuhi,* Miss Cat. *Kahawa."*

After a long, hot shower, she wrapped herself in Joel's robe, fresh from the laundry, ordered strong coffee and warm crois-sants from room service and made her calls to the United States. The Spring Street job was under control. Doug was riding Arm-strong, the structural engineer. Mave had nothing to add to what she had already reported about the rest of the work in the office. But just to be in contact restored Cat's spirits. She put off her call to John Rifken to tell him she'd found a site. She'd have to talk to him about Campbell, and she wasn't sure she could do that.

Stephen N'toya's phone remained unanswered. Impatiently, Cat hung up, then called Mave again in Los Angeles.

"I want you to search everything on the computer, Joel's files, his address book, his Christmas-card list, the notes he made be-fore he left for Kenya, see if you can find Stephen N'toya's address and telephone number. Call me back."

For an hour, she tried to concentrate on some ideas for Maasai Springs—an earthen structure would save precious timber. Fiber bags pumped full of earth amended with a small amount of cement and some barbed wire, then laid in place. A cement pump could be used, or if Bluebonnet Development wanted to provide jobs for the local people, the bags could be filled by hand. In the modern world it was still experimental, but rammed earth construction was a new take on an ancient idea—and ideal for this site. She checked her watch every five minutes. When the phone rang, she grabbed it.

"Cat, I found an address and telephone number," Mave said. "Got a pen?"

Cat felt a surge of triumph. "I knew it had to be somewhere. Shoot."

"Sheria House, Harampe Avenue." Slowly Mave read the address and Cat's heart sank. Mave was repeating the address of the building from which she had already been expelled.

"What about a phone number?" she asked without much hope. Her spirits lifted slightly. The number was unfamiliar. Thanking Mave, she hung up and redialed. The number had been disconnected.

The rest of the morning she played with ideas for the site, working until the walls of the room seemed to be closing in on her, and she had to have a breath of fresh air. Before leaving the hotel, she hovered in the doorway, searched the streets. Her friendly doorman was off duty, and the unfamiliar man in his place did not question her strange behavior.

She walked purposefully toward Patel Brothers, the surveyors Joel had lined up, weaving through the crowds, keeping a wary eye on her surroundings. She saw nothing suspicious. No young thug. As far as she could see, no one was tailing her.

Patel Brothers agreed to make a Land Office search, fly new aerials of the site and have a report delivered to the hotel. Satisfied, Cat wrote a retainer check, the rest to be paid upon delivery of the report within three days.

"Three days. Oh, yes, most certain. Three days." Mr. Patel the Elder bowed her out of his office. Then as she was leaving, he murmured, "At the outside, *memsahib*, five days."

She didn't know whether to laugh or fight, and finally took the line of least resistance. Africa wins again, Campbell would have said.

Some time, she would have to be in contact with Campbell Safaris about the work they were contracted to do—liaison with tribal authority and government agencies. Poachers or not, they were well connected to high places in the government, another reason Rifken insisted on using them. But right now she was too raw, literally as well as figuratively. She still hurt from that last bruising encounter with Campbell. Later, she would contact Tom, tell him what she required, let him pass the message on to Campbell.

After lunch in the hotel coffee shop—the only place she felt really safe was in the hotel—she crawled back into bed and sank instantly into dreamless sleep.

When she awoke at four, she dialed Stephen N'toya, without success. She was no longer even disappointed.

Father Gaston did not call.

The rest of the afternoon stretched ahead of her. She showered again, dressed in gray linen trousers and jacket, then ventured out to buy gifts to take home, as Father Gaston had suggested. She looked up the City Market in the guidebook. From the pictures it looked well lighted, crowded. Safe.

For once, a guidebook did not do justice to its subject. Light from high clerestory windows flooded the immense building. Tiny open-fronted shops crammed together under the great canopy of roof offered wood carvings, many showing great skill and artistry. Handwoven sisal baskets, mats, rugs. Gourd dishes. Flowers, fruit, vegetables. Market women shouted back and forth, everyone haggled over price, a lot of body language, a lot of laughter. Cat wandered from shop to shop, buoyed by the vitality.

On the second-floor gallery, a seller of tribal drums pushed padded drumsticks into her hand. She tapped a zebra-skin drum softly. The man took the sticks from her.

"No, no, *memsahib*. Like this." He thumped loudly. The sound reverberated, and she thought of Moses and Olentwalla and the nights she had listened to them weaving their complex rhythms. He thrust the sticks back into her hand.

"How much?" She pointed to a couple of three-legged drums as large as tables. One for herself—God knows where it would fit in her high-rise condo overlooking the Pacific—the other for Rosie.

"Ah, you have a good eye, *memsahib*. My very best drums. Good zebra skin. First quality." He named a price in Kenya shillings.

Cat shook her head.

"What you pay, *memsahib?*"

Cat offered a third of what he asked. He jumped back as if she had stabbed him to the heart, hands clenched to his chest, eyes rolled back in horror.

"*Jambo,* Cat."

She looked around. "Tom!"

He smiled, a trace of reserve in his face.

"How are Thomas and Olentwalla?" she asked.

"Better. Going back to their villages so their wives can wait on them. They don't trust hospitals. Can't say I blame them. I don't, either."

"How many wives do they have?" The conversation was strange and stilted.

"Enough to keep them busy." He looked around at the drums. "You are thinking of buying one of these for yourself?"

"A couple of them. One for me, another for my goddaughter."

"They're not zebra skin, you know. They're cow."

"Oh, thank God. Zebra skin would just make me feel guilty." Tom snorted in derision.

"We're at a ticklish part of the negotiation," she said. "Only separated by about sixty-six percent."

"Don't worry. I'll do it for you."

He took over the haggling in Swahili. The drum man looked as if Tom were extracting the gold from his teeth, but finally she was the owner of the drums at about a third of what she had been prepared to pay. The drum seller bowed happily, golden teeth still shining, so it looked as if he, too, had gotten a good deal. Everyone came out a winner. Everything in life should be so simple, Cat thought.

While Tom filled in the custom forms for her, she looked around, her skin rippling with a strange disquiet. Someone was watching.

"Is Miriam with you, Tom?"

"No, she's taken our boys upcountry to her father's *shamba*." He leaned over the wooden railing of the gallery. "Dan's down there somewhere."

Surprised, she said, "I thought it would take him days to get back to Nairobi."

"I flew back and picked him up. Moses and Sambeke are driving back."

"They're traveling alone?"

"I took a couple more of our men to join them." He waved. "There they are."

The hall was a mosaic of color. Great purple mounds of eggplant, golden pawpaw, bins overflowing with yams and ears of unshucked pale green corn. Red and yellow gladioli, gerbera daisies the dusty red of Kenyan earth, delphinium from pale blue to almost navy. Shoppers in tribal cottons, saris, turbans, western suits and light summer dresses.

Campbell was easy to spot—the bright blond hair of the young woman beside him stood out like a beacon. She held a cantaloupe to her nose with both hands. Her light eyes were fixed on Cat.

For a long moment their eyes locked, then the girl turned and nodded to the stall keeper, handing the melon to him. She spoke to Campbell.

He looked up. Unsmiling, he raised a hand in greeting. He looked tired.

"Why don't you have dinner with us, Cat?" Tom said. He leaned over the railing, mimed eating, pointed at Cat.

"Thanks, Tom, but I can't. I have work to do."

"Come on, you have to eat. Leave early. It's just us, we're cooking for ourselves. Mary's upcountry with Jock at the farm."

Cat glanced below. Morag was discussing gladioli with a flower seller now, carefully examining each stem before placing it in Campbell's arms. Cat shook her head. "No, thanks. I have too much to do."

Morag was laughing with the flower seller, counting rumpled notes into his outstretched hand. Campbell's arms were piled with blossoms. They looked good together, she as fair as he was dark. It was a sweet domestic scene.

"I'll call you, Tom. We still have some business to discuss. Thanks for your help with the drums."

Suddenly she'd had enough of the City Market, the color and noise, the exotic smells, the crush of humanity. Enough of watching Campbell trail after the lovely, laughing girl.

The following day dragged. Cat felt caught in a nightmare, unsafe on the streets surrounded by people, any one of whom could be a threat.

One more day that Stephen N'toya did not answer his telephone.

Another twenty-four hours waiting for Father Gaston to contact her.

She completed her own calls by noon. Patel Brothers were working hard, they said. When she pressed them for a time commitment, Mr. Patel the Elder had been soothing. Four days, *memsahib*. No longer. Frustrated, she'd hung up.

Later, in the Nairobi Museum, she thought she'd picked up another follower, this time a well-dressed young man, meandering from room to room as she did, keeping her in sight. In front of the glass case of skulls recovered from the Rift, he'd engaged her in conversation, then asked her if she would like some tea. She had fled, leaving him staring after her. A *teksi* brought her back to the hotel. She spent the rest of the day in her room, working, close to the telephone.

It didn't ring.

She took another shower, the third that day, wrapped her hair in a towel and inspected the contents of the tiny hotel refrigerator. The usual giant bottles of Tusker, several cans of apricot nectar. The ubiquitous Coca-Cola. A couple of bottles of wine. She poured a glass from a bottle of wine with a picture of Mount Kilimanjaro on the label and turned on the television. A rhinoceros appeared on the screen, the picture flipped unsteadily and she fiddled with the knobs. When the maid rapped on the door, she called, "Bed's already turned down. Good night, see you tomorrow."

"This ancient animal," the voice-over said, "less than two hundred left in the wild—"

The picture steadied. She stood back. The screen turned green. The maid rapped louder. Cat turned off the set and, rubbing her damp hair with the towel, crossed the room and opened the door.

She stared unbelieving at the figure in front of her.

Thirty-Two

Automatically Cat registered details. Eyes the pale gray of glacial ice, not blue as she'd thought. Skin finely textured, a light golden tan. Hair colored to give that silvery sheen, but it was over a natural blond. And up close it was clear she was much younger than she had appeared. Seventeen, no more. Self-possessed. Beautiful. The portrait above the fireplace in Campbell's gun room, vibrant and alive.

"I would have called first, but I thought you might find you had another appointment." Morag's voice was light, sweet, English. Her eyes flickered over Cat's shabby terry-cloth robe. "You didn't wait to say hello yesterday in the market."

"No, I had to run. Morag, isn't it?"

"Yes. Can I come in?"

"I'm sorry. You're right. You should have called first. I'm just getting ready to go out to dinner."

"For a minute. I won't keep you."

"I'm sorry. This is not a good time——"

"Please." Morag's throat jerked. The large gray eyes filled. She looked down, the tip of her tongue moved over her lips. "I did want to talk to you. I won't stay long."

A master manipulator, Cat thought. Feeling like a prize fool, she opened the door wider and stood back. "Okay. A few minutes then."

Morag moved past her in a cloud of Opium. She wore a scarlet jacket cut close to her body, deep vee neck showing a hint of golden cleavage, short narrow white skirt, high-heeled white sandals, bare legs. Her body was slender but mature. Cat closed the door behind her, tossed the damp towel through the open door of the bathroom. The truth was, the girl's body was fabulous. And she'd probably never seen the inside of a gym in her life.

As she followed Morag into the room, Cat scooped up a crumpled chocolate-bar wrapper from the floor, dropped it on top of the detritus of a day's work overflowing the wastepaper basket.

"What can I do for you, Morag?"

"May I sit down?"

Cat walked to a green velvet chair, swept the drawings covering it into a pile, dumped them on the desk. "Please."

"Is this your work?" Morag picked up several sketches, the paper rustled in her hand. She was shaking. "They're very nice." Cat let her eyes drop to the girl's left hand. No rings.

"Thanks." Cat perched on the edge of the desk and folded her arms. "Look, I don't wish to be inhospitable, but perhaps you'd better get to the point."

Morag eyed the open bottle of wine. "May I have a glass of wine?"

Cat opened the tiny refrigerator. "Apricot nectar. Coke." She turned, waiting.

"Coke, then, please."

Cat filled a glass with ice, poured the soda, handed it to her. She popped the top on a can of apricot nectar for herself, filled a glass with the bright, cloudy liquid and resumed her perch on the edge of the desk.

"Okay," Cat said. "Now let's cut the bullshit. What's going on here?"

"It's Dan. He's terribly upset."

Cat shrugged. "I'm sorry. But that's hardly my business."

"Well, yes, it is. You've been sleeping with him."

Cat felt the blood rush to her face. She stood, put down the glass of nectar. "Now wait a minute. I'm not going to listen to this."

"No, you don't understand. I didn't mean... You're old enough to do what you like...I mean——"

"I know what you mean. Let me explain something to you. I'm an architect here to do work that's important to me and to a number of other people. Campbell Safaris was employed to facilitate that work. That is the extent of my interest. Come on. Time's up."

"Wait. Just a minute. He wrote you a letter. It was propped up on his desk this morning. It wasn't sealed and... It wasn't a letter to a safari client——"

"You read other people's mail? Well, any correspondence with me should be addressed to my office. Now, please do not drag me into your love affairs."

A horn in the square below seemed to be stuck, bellowing on and on. Morag's face crumpled. "You know about that? Dan came back and almost killed poor Dougie Maxwell——"

"Don't tell me all this. I really don't want to know. I'm a stranger in Nairobi, and I don't give a damn who you sleep with. Who Campbell sleeps with——"

"This is all my fault. All of it. I don't know what to do now."

"Just smile and say you're sorry," Cat said dryly. "You'll think of what to do next."

The noise of the car horn filled the room. Cat slammed the balcony door closed, shutting off the sound. The air was too hot to breathe. Cat turned down the thermostat to sixty-eight degrees, and the air conditioner kicked in with a crash.

Morag stared into her glass, sloshing the liquid back and forth, rattling the ice cubes. "Poor Dougie can't speak or anything. He has to eat through a straw. His jaw's broken. And some ribs. I'll never get another boyfriend. Every man in Kenya will be afraid to come near me after this."

Confused, Cat stared at her. A light was beginning to dawn. "My God," she said. "I don't believe it. You're his daughter."

"No. I'm not." Morag raised a hand to her hair, lifted it from her neck. Her breasts moved, she tossed her head, a deliberate attempt to look provocative. Except that her lips were trembling and she was on the point of tears. "Do I look like his daughter?"

"No, I can't say that you do. If you're not his daughter, who are you?"

"I'm my mother's daughter. So I'm told. Go and ask him. He's at home now, mean as an old hippo."

"Don't play games with me, Morag. You came here, remember?"

"I'm not playing games. You could drop me off on the way. I'll have dinner at my friend Jane Terry's house. I called, so Mrs. Terry's expecting me. He won't mind that." She smiled, showing small white teeth. "I'm not supposed to be out, but he won't mind when you tell him where I am. Mrs. Terry hates poor old Dougie, too."

"I can't go anywhere. I'm having an early night."

"I thought you were going out to dinner."

"I lied."

"Then you do have the time. Please. You have to go and talk to him now. I counted on that. If you don't, I'm really going to catch it. I'm already in trouble for causing all this. If you don't go, it'll be worse—"

"You should have thought of that."

"But I did. I was just trying to put it right for him. I thought you'd want to see him, too." Tears welled in the large gray eyes. "I think he's in love with you."

Stunned, Cat stared into Morag's eyes.

What did she really know of Campbell? What proof did she have that he was a poacher? What she did know was that he would drive hundreds of miles of trackless, rain-soaked country when he thought his daughter—or whoever she was—needed him. Her own father had never cared about her or Joel. Never. Not even enough to acknowledge the letter she'd sent him, telling him of Joel's death.

Beloved, Campbell had called her that night. She could see the golden light of the fire outside the tent, hear the sounds of the night. Feel him against her skin.

"Please," Morag was saying.

It was an opportunity that might not come again, a chance to talk to him, find out... And Morag would know she was there. Nothing could possibly happen to her.

The cab drove slowly along a tree-lined road as quiet as it had been the first time Cat saw it, but much darker now. The sun had completely disappeared, and the leaves of the blue gums rustled in a breeze that cooled the air. Cat peered at the tall hedges guarding the privacy of the houses beyond, hoping she would recognize Campbell's.

"Stop here." Cat leaned forward to speak to the cabdriver. They had already dropped Morag at the Terrys' house on a similar tree-lined road. "And wait, please." The cabdriver nodded, slid down in his seat, tipping his battered chauffeur's cap over his eyes.

The tunnel of Nandi flame trees lining Campbell's driveway was dark. Cat started toward it. Somewhere out of sight, she heard a car engine whine, catch, increase in volume. A small car, headlights dimmed, tore out of a secondary, smaller driveway without stopping, narrowly missing her. Cat jumped closer to the hedge of scarlet hibiscus. The car tore past.

The driver was Stephen N'toya.

Her heart thumped like an ancient generator. She raced back to the cab, threw herself in.

"That car," she yelled. "Follow it."

The cabdriver struggled upright. He turned to stare at her. Cat banged on the back of his seat in frustration.

"Follow that car." In a fever of impatience, she stabbed a finger at the retreating taillights. "Hurry. Hurry. It's getting away."

The driver, a delighted grin splitting his face, switched on the ignition. Cat stared out the rear window. The red dots of the car's lights were fading into the distance. The cabbie put his rheumy old Chevrolet into a wild three-point turn in the narrow road, then jammed his foot on the gas, laying down a patch of rubber. At the next crossroad, he paused, dramatically racing the engine while Cat searched in every direction.

"Turn off that engine," she said urgently. "I can't hear anything."

"He has left us," the cabbie said, but he turned the key.

Only the sound of insects—cicadas, grasshoppers, or whatever their African cousins were called—came through the open window. Not even the murmur of a distant engine.

"Yes, I guess he has." She sat back in a cloud of exhaust fumes. "Thanks for trying, anyway. You'd better take me back to the house."

"Just like Rambo," the driver said happily.

In the pitch black, the tree-enclosed main driveway seemed longer than on her first visit. Underfoot, petals dropped from the flower-laden trees muffled the sound of her footsteps. As she crossed the veranda, crimson bougainvillea drifted around her feet. From the road at the end of the driveway she heard the cab draw away, and her heart hit her sandals. The cabbie must have misunderstood her request. God, she thought, she was stranded here. There was no going back.

To reassure herself, Cat put her hand in her bag, touched the butt of the friendly Beretta. Then she seized the heavy metal knob of the front door and turned it. This time, at least there would be no announcement of her presence. The door gave. She stepped across the threshold into the hall.

The silent house smelled of floor polish and roses and had a natural coolness that owed nothing to air-conditioning. Her heels clattered on the polished wooden floor, and she restrained the urge to slip off her sandals. The only light came from an open double doorway along the hall.

"Morag!" Campbell's voice was deep, cold and ominous. "Come in here, please. You, miss, are in a lot of bloody trouble."

Cat walked toward the door, relieved to step silently onto the zebra skin just inside the room.

A large wing-back chair concealed its occupant. Light from a floor lamp pooled on a green baize-covered table covered in pieces of a dismantled rifle and cleaning rags. The corners of the room were in shadow. Along one wall, rifles were racked in glass-fronted gun cabinets that gave back a splintered reflection of the portrait of Morag over the fireplace. She couldn't see him, but his presence filled the room.

She shouldn't have come here.

"I just saw Stephen N'toya leave this house," she said.

Campbell rose to his feet. He replaced the gun rod on the table, then turned to face her, wiping oil from his hands with a piece of cotton waste. He showed no surprise at her presence. "I don't know any Stephen N'toya." He dropped the cotton waste on the table. "The man you saw was Isaac Mwega, field rep for a Dutch film company. They want to do a documentary on rhinos." He went on, giving her no time to comment. "What are you doing here?"

Could she have been mistaken? She'd seen Stephen N'toya only once since college, and that, too, had been at night, in the park across from the hotel. "It was Stephen N'toya," she insisted.

Campbell shrugged. "And I say I don't know a Stephen N'toya. If you want to come to my office, I'll show you the paperwork on the rhino documentary Mwega came here to discuss."

"Morag came to my hotel tonight," she said.

"Oh. So you've met." He shook his head. "Jesus. My back was turned for five minutes and she skipped out. What did she want?"

"Well, for one thing, she wants you to know she isn't out with Dougie Maxwell."

"She didn't need you to deliver that message. Maxwell's in the hospital." He gestured to the corner of the chesterfield in front of the fireplace. "Come in, for God's sake. You're hovering in the doorway like a bloody servant. What else did she want?"

"She said you had a letter for me." Cat moved into the room until she stood behind the end of the chesterfield. All thought of Stephen N'toya had fled.

Her words seemed to take him by surprise. "So you just decided to make a courtesy call, is that it? Emphasis on courtesy, I hope. I'm tired of fighting."

"Then why do it? Most people manage to settle their differences without using their fists."

He grunted. "But nothing's as satisfying as beating the shit out of a man who deserves it." He looked at her. "Except maybe loving a woman who needs it."

"Love? That wasn't love. I doubt you know the meaning of the word."

"And you do, of course. But you're probably right. It's a bit outside my line of country."

He went over to a table by the window, selected a bottle from among half a dozen others and picked up a glass. "Scotch?"

"Yes. All right. Thanks."

He came toward her, his masculinity hitting her like a shock wave. As she reached to take the drink he held out, her eyes dropped to his hands. The grazed knuckles were beginning to scab.

He followed her gaze. "Don't look so bloody prim. Maybe men don't take a personal sort of action in your part of the world, but here it's not exactly unknown. Sit down, Cat. You're making yourself nervous, standing there ready to run."

"Do you work at being a bastard, Campbell, or does it come naturally to you?" She sat in the corner of the chesterfield, leaning forward to put her drink down on the table in front of the fireplace.

"Morag was everything you expected, no doubt. The classic femme fatale."

"I never for one moment thought—"

"Of course you did. You thought I was sleeping with her. Naturally you didn't check the facts with me first. That would have been too bloody reasonable."

"Your word has been so trustworthy, of course. Have you ever once told me the truth?" When he didn't answer, she said, "Why would I expect this time to be any different?"

"If you'd waited for me at Maasai Springs, I would have told you what you wanted to know."

"I seem to remember a promise to take me to see where Joel died. You didn't mention it was in Tanzania. Tom M'Bala did."

"I planned to take you across the border without anyone knowing."

"Why? What was the point? Secrecy for its own sake?" She made a dismissive gesture. "I came back to talk to the policemen who wrote the report about my brother's death. There was a report, I suppose?"

"Yes. But you know everything there is to know about it. We brought his body back, Cat. That's all. It seemed at the time the best thing to do. It still seems to me the best thing. If you think that's sinister—" he shrugged "—I'm sorry."

"I'm still going to talk to them. Joel sent me sketches," she said abruptly. "They arrived after he'd been buried. How did they get to me? You were in the middle of nowhere."

"Is it important?"

"It is to me."

Campbell frowned "He probably gave them to Lynnie Masterson, one of the Flying Doctors. She was in the same area we were and dropped in for a meal. Lynnie was likely delayed getting back to Nairobi and posted them after the accident." He glanced at her face, gave a grunt of impatience. "Why are you determined to find a conspiracy of some kind? He didn't mention it to anyone because there was no need to."

"Those sketches arrived seven weeks after Joel died."

"I'm not surprised. Our postal system is hardly the model of efficiency. Bloody wonder anything gets where it's supposed to at the best of times."

"Would it be possible to meet Lynnie Masterson?"

"Last I heard, she was up around Turkana, working in the refugee camps there. People are pouring over the borders. She's a dedicated doctor, it's not likely she'd make too much effort to take time away from starving babies to talk about a letter she posted in Nairobi for a stranger."

Cat's fingers tightened on the glass, and she looked away from him. He made her suspicions seem so ridiculous. She was beginning to think they were. But she'd wait to hear from Father Gaston before telling him about the camp above Maasai Springs. She looked up at the portrait above the fireplace.

"Is Morag your daughter?"

"What do you think?"

Irritated, she said, "I think that no one answers a straight question. When I asked Morag, she went into some sort of movie-star pose and said she was her mother's daughter."

Campbell crossed the room, swung back the drapes. He opened the French doors, looked out into the garden. A fresh breeze stirred the branches of the jacaranda trees.

"I don't know what gets into her sometimes. Sheer bloody-mindedness, I think."

"Campbell. Is she?"

"Of course she's my daughter." Campbell turned back into the room. He switched on the portrait light above the gilded frame. "This is her mother."

Had he hesitated? Or had she imagined it? Cat studied him for a moment before she turned her attention to the portrait. Light flooded the canvas. Morag, but not Morag. The girl was riveting, on the brink of womanhood, fourteen, maybe fifteen. Pale hair lifted by a breeze, wide blue eyes focused on something only she could see. She'd been painted against a wide African background—sun-drenched plains dotted with flat-topped thorn trees and grazing animals, mist drifting among three distant jagged peaks. There was challenge in the tilt of her head, the smile touching her lips. The artist had caught a wild, untamed quality.

"She's breathtaking."

"Yes. She was," Campbell said. "She was my cousin. Fiona Sinclair. She was killed just after this was finished."

Cat tried not to show her shock. She took a beat before looking at him. He was staring at the portrait. The air around him seemed dense with pain.

"She was sixteen when she died. Morag was two months old. I know what you're thinking. And you're right. She was a child. I wasn't."

"That's not what I was thinking, Campbell." But she was. "What happened?"

"She was killed in the bush. Lions. Wild dogs. I don't know. By the time I got there, the tracks had been obliterated. Her body was never found."

Cat looked at him, speechless with horror.

"I was away when it happened. At the university in Edinburgh."

"Then you must have been very young, too."

"No. I wasn't. I was eighteen. But I was a seasoned hunter and experienced." He glanced at her. "There were always plenty of women, usually in love with some romantic bullshit about 'great white hunters.' Anyway, I wasn't a boy."

He began to prowl the room. Only zebra skins were scattered on the dark polished wood, but he made no sound. Tom told her that he seemed to think like an animal, moved through the bush like one. It was a rare gift, Tom said.

"I'd like to know about it, Campbell."

"Satisfy your curiosity?"

She made no effort to hide the pain his remark caused.

He looked away. "I was old enough to know she was too young. It didn't make any difference." He hesitated. "Listen, I don't talk about this kind of thing. Not even to Tom. So I'll just tell you that I wanted her more than I'd wanted anything in my life."

Cat remembered her own first love. Jim Banks. She hadn't thought of him for years. A golden surfer in Malibu.

"Fiona's mother and Jock were brother and sister. Penny and

her husband were killed on the way back to their farm in Tanzania when Fiona was eleven, and she came to live with us. She was a gawky kid, I didn't really take much notice of her. Then I went away to the university in Edinburgh, and when I came back from my first year, she was different. All sidelong glances and tossing hair. Unpredictable. Moody. She knocked me over."

Campbell sat on his heels, held a lighted match to the logs in the fireplace. Flames curled around the wood, caught and flared into sap-filled color. "Ancient history."

"Not to me. Please. Go on. What about your mother? You don't talk about her."

He stared into the flames. "My mother was killed in the Mau Mau Rebellion, when I was young. Our housekeeper Mary, took care of me after that. Anyway, Jock never even noticed what was going on. He was out in the bush most of the time then, only got back to the farm occasionally. He adored Fiona. Never questioned why I didn't want to go out with him. He'd never wanted me to be a professional hunter and thought I was coming around to his point of view. He knew it was coming to an end, anyway. We had endless discussions about adapting to the new Kenya. Land was being turned over to Africans for farming and that meant hunting as a way of life was at an end. He was right. There was no pretense of sport anymore. It had already started, the dregs of armies after what they could get. No permits, but it didn't matter. Everyone was paid off. It was find the herds, get the machine guns, hack the ivory." He got up, replenished his drink. "I never even knew she'd had a child until she was dead. She never wrote."

"No one else told you? Your father? Tom?"

He shook his head. "I thought she was angry because I'd refused to defy Jock. I'd told him I didn't want to go back to Scotland, that I wanted to start hunting full time. He wouldn't hear of it. I didn't want to leave her, but I thought we had plenty of time, and I couldn't defy Jock. I just thought we'd marry as soon as I got home for good. We quarreled about it before I left. She wouldn't even come to Nairobi to see me off."

Cat could see the sheen of perspiration on his face and realized how hard this was for him. He probably never had spoken about it before. He went from the fire to the open French doors. Curtains billowed in the cool, jasmine-scented breeze. He looked into the garden, his back to her.

"What happened to her?"

"After I'd left, Jock was off with a safari client. Mary could not stop her from going on some half-baked expedition with a neighbor upcountry and a friend of his. A lawyer from Italy. No cooks, no trackers. No one. It seems they fought over her, and the bastard slammed off in a jealous rage, left her alone in the bush with this Italian office *wallah* from Rome who knew nothing about the bush. No weapons even if he'd known how to use them. The Maasai brought in what was left of him. We never found Fiona's body."

He filled the doorway into the night, one arm braced against the frame, his solitude shared with a phantom. He'd shut her out, and Cat wanted to touch him, call to him, "I'm here. Alive."

"They sent for me, and the Maasai helped us search. Tom was with me. There wasn't any point. They all knew it, but they helped, anyway. They tried. Anyway, that's it. That's the story of Morag."

Cat wondered why Morag said she was not his daughter, but it was a question she'd ask Morag directly. She went over to him, put a hand on his arm. "Campbell."

He turned and pulled her to him. He held her as if he wanted to absorb her into his own body.

I love you. The words formed in her mind but she didn't speak.

Campbell held her away from him. He said, "Cat, I think you should leave—"

"No, you don't," she said.

"You should have seen Thomas's face when he saw the interior of that tent." Cat grinned. "He asked how I felt after the mad *nyumbu*. I told him a large bull had got me and I felt pretty good. I thought he was going to laugh out loud, but he managed not to."

A jug of delphinium and shasta daisies stood in the center of the plain wooden table in the kitchen. With a soft plop, a stem of delphinium showered dark blue petals onto the well-picked steak bone on her empty dinner plate.

Campbell raised her hand to his mouth, speaking against her palm. "I'd told him to let you sleep. You weren't embarrassed that he knew?"

"No. I did wonder what Tom was going to say, though."

"When I got back and found you gone, I damn near had a fit."

"I couldn't wait, Campbell." She stroked his upper lip, enjoying the grate of stubble against her fingers. "I didn't want you to know that I cared that much."

He hadn't said he loved her. Not in English, anyway. It would not change anything. In a week, she would be back in Los Angeles. Less than a week if Patel Brothers came through. Their lives could never converge.

"You haven't shown me the letter Morag said you'd written me," she said, smiling.

"I chucked it." Campbell divided the last of the wine between them. "You were not the only one mad as hell."

"Then tell me."

"About being mad as hell?"

"No." She let the petals drift from her fingers. "Are you always this closed about what you feel?"

"Am I?"

Cat forced herself to match his lighthearted tone. "You're a hard man, Dan Campbell."

He didn't reply, and she started to tell him about the phone conversation she'd had with the telephone operator, the visit to the State Law Office and the young thug who'd followed her, trying to make it sound funnier than it had been. "I've been trying to reach Stephen N'toya for days, so I guess everyone, including your Isaac Mwega, is beginning to look like him."

Campbell listened without comment, crumbling bread between his fingers.

"Then I ducked into the storeroom of this little Indian grocery, and who do you think I ran into? Brian Ward! That's one spooky guy, Campbell. I told Father Gaston about it. He's trying to find out something about him."

"You've seen him since you've been back?"

"I went over to his church. I'm laughing now, but at the time, I was scared to death. I needed to talk to someone and he knew Joel."

"What did you tell him?"

"I told him I thought you were a poacher. And a killer. And an ivory smuggler. And possibly a terrorist in your spare time."

Campbell laughed. "Well, you pretty well covered everything except bank robbery. What did he say to all that?"

"Not much. I guess he thought I was a bit overwrought. He humored me, though. He's looking into Brian Ward—and your poaching and smuggling activities."

"I bet he is."

"He told me to be careful." She was suddenly serious, watching his reaction. "He thinks that maybe I'm in danger."

"Then I'll just have to keep you under close guard until you leave." He got up, opened a cupboard door, produced a canister. "Why don't you make us some coffee while I make a few calls?"

"Sure you can free up some time for me?" she teased. "I've got a few days."

Campbell dropped a kiss on the top of her head. "For you, sweetheart, I'd move heaven and earth."

As he left the kitchen, Campbell glanced back at her. She was filling the kettle at the sink, dressed in one of his shirts, her long legs barely covered.

It was time she left. Past time.

In the gun room, he picked up the telephone and dialed a number, listened to the ring at the other end, then hung up. A few minutes later, the phone rang. He picked it up.

"Did she see me?" Stephen N'toya asked in Swahili.

Campbell answered in the same language. "She certainly did. Went tearing after you, in fact."

Stephen swore. "What did you tell her?"

"That you were Isaac Mwega, representative of a Dutch film company."

"Did she believe you?"

"I don't know. I think so. She's certainly not convinced she's had the whole story about Stanton's death. She's still determined to talk to the men you're supposed to be producing." He dropped his bombshell. "Did you know she went to see our old chum, Gaston?"

"What!"

"You heard me. Gaston."

"I knew she was being followed, but he lost her when she jumped into that car."

"Gaston says he's making some inquiries for her about Brian Ward." Briefly, he repeated what Cat had told him.

There was a pause, then N'toya said, "Maybe we should let the thugs take care of this..." His voice trailed off.

"You're a cold-blooded bastard, N'toya. I thought she was an old school friend."

"That was then. This is now. Priorities change."

"Be careful, Stephen," Campbell said softly. "Nothing is going to happen to this woman. You understand me? Random mayhem to Joel Stanton's sister would really get the old man asking questions. Do you want to risk that?"

"I can produce a story that would satisfy him."

"She's no threat. She never has been. But I'll find a way to put her mind at rest, stop her questions. I'm taking her upcountry—"

"What about the job at hand?"

"Tom can get the men mobilized, and I can be back within hours."

"Don't fall in love. We can't afford the distraction."

"Fuck you, N'toya," Campbell said pleasantly. He dropped the phone into the cradle.

Thirty-Three

A pink haze moved in the silvery mist of early morning, undulating in a wave of changing color along the shore.

"Flamingos, about half a million of them," Campbell called over the sound of the engine. He put the Cessna into a low sweep over the lake. "Lake Nakuru."

Below them, green, algae-rich water blushed as the birds rose, long legs trailing, necks outstretched, their wings spread into a pink and coral cloak that almost hid the lake from view.

The moment was magical. Cat laid her hand over his, and he smiled at her without speaking, then put the plane into a banking turn to follow the shoreline. Cat turned to watch the birds drop peacefully back into the water as the shadow of the plane passed over them. The lake fell away, the engine of the small plane roared as Campbell climbed to skirt a ridge rising to the west.

Last night she'd protested weakly she couldn't leave Nairobi before hearing from N'toya. He'd had an answer for everything. Tom would make a few calls, see if he could find someone who knew

Stephen. The minute Tom got in touch, they'd come back. She'd wanted to be won over. So much time had already been lost to suspicion and mistrust. For a few encapsulated days she wanted to allow herself to love this man. Without waiting for her to agree, he'd arranged for Morag to remain with the Terrys until Jock came down from the farm.

So she'd stayed the night, slept curled into his body, his arms wrapped around her. This morning they'd laughed a lot, scrambled eggs and burned toast together, then left before Jock arrived.

For most of the journey, Campbell kept the plane low, flying over cultivated fields and small round-roofed villages, open forest and grassland rippling with grazing animals. Brown streams trembled with gold as sunlight caught the silt-laden water. The hours ran together, passing mostly in silence. Occasionally Campbell pointed out a herd of galloping giraffe, or the thin strands of a waterfall tumbling into a ravine. Cat gazed, entranced at the changing scenes, lulled by the drone of the engine, wishing the journey could last forever, the two of them alone in a magic box of space and time, floating, no demands, no pressure, no unanswered questions. No other world outside themselves, now, in this place of blue sky and forest and grassland below the wings.

The engine whined, changed its pattern, the plane banked sharply. Cat sat up, her reverie shattered.

"Here we are. Kitale." Campbell looked down at the small runway rushing to meet them. "We're going to drive up to Elgon from here."

"Elgon! You told me there was nothing worth seeing up there."

"The situation has changed quite a bit since then." He threw her a grin. "Hold on, the airstrip's a bit pitted."

Cat clutched her seat to steady herself as the plane lurched in and out of deep potholes. They came to rest in front of a Land

Rover with extra fuel tanks attached to the rear bumper, parked outside a small shed on the edge of the airstrip.

"The airport crew keeps an eye on it for me. I come up as often as I can."

"Alone?"

"Until now."

Cat smiled at him over the top of the vehicle. He stowed their gear, slotted two rifles into the empty rack behind the driver's seat and nodded to the passenger's side. "Hop in."

The Land Rover lurched over rutted red earth, and they turned west, a different route to Mount Elgon from the one they had taken previously. Two hours later they were climbing a series of rough, narrow tracks. The air thinned. Their silence was companionable, easy. Cat found herself unable to stop touching him—a hand on his thigh as he drove, or resting lightly on his shoulder. She wondered whether it was safe to allow herself to feel this way.

"Campbell, could this be that you are breaking your ironclad rule?"

He glanced at her quizzically.

"You know, the famous grade-B movie line about never taking women into the bush."

He laughed, then braked hard as a troop of baboons broke from the brush ahead of them. A huge male, his upper lip raised to show great yellow incisors, stopped in the middle of the track, forcing the Land Rover to a halt. Campbell shouted at him to move. The baboon snarled back defiantly. Campbell thrust his head and shoulder through the open window and yelled at him, banging the side panel of the door. The baboon held his ground, and Cat started to giggle. Finally the animal turned, taking his time to swagger off, disappearing among the twisted limbs of enormous cedars.

"Cheeky bugger!" Campbell said, voice filled with outrage.

Laughing, Cat grabbed his head, pulled him toward her, planted a kiss on his cheek. "Maybe he didn't understand Swahili."

The forest was deep now, the air sweet with resin, giant vines curled around tree trunks and hung from huge branching limbs. They stopped to eat in an open sun-filled glade Campbell said had been created by grazing antelope. Cat spread a blanket and opened the cooler they had brought from Nairobi.

Campbell reached for her, slipping a hand inside her shirt, cupping her breast. "First things first."

"I can be had for a Tusker," she said, laughing. He removed his hand to reach for a bottle. Cat dragged the shirt over her head and wriggled out of her pants. "On second thoughts, the hell with it."

They made love leisurely, afterward spending an hour feeding each other shreds of roast francolin. Juice from cold slices of tomatoes dripped onto their bare skin. They shared a couple of bottles of Tusker, and Cat knew she had never been so happy.

While she enticed bright-eyed vervets with the remains of their lunch, Campbell called Tom on the shortwave. Before leaving that morning, Cat had spoken to Mave and arranged for Doug to relay news of any emergency through Tom in Nairobi, telling Mave she would be out of touch for a few days.

"No news from Los Angeles," Campbell called.

"Wonderful," Cat said with relief. Today, construction shacks with their girlie calendars on the walls, bitter coffee and stale cigar smoke seemed a distant echo from another life. One that belonged to some other Cat Stanton.

The afternoon wore on. Gradually the game track disappeared, and they were traveling over open heath. Campbell swung the Land Rover around a stand of rock, maneuvered the vehicle carefully in descent.

"Hold on. It gets easier in a couple of minutes."

The slope was covered with vegetation, russet where the sun touched, black in the shadow. The decline became more gentle, full of small crevices and ravines. The air was sharp and resinous, like needles of pure oxygen.

He stopped in a tiny box canyon no more than fifteen feet across, sixty at the deepest point. A small spring bubbled out of the earth into a catchment it had hollowed out of rock. The sun was dropping and the air had cooled noticeably. While Campbell unloaded the Land Rover, Cat picked up scattered fragments of wood, trying to remember how he'd built the fire at Maasai Springs. After a few sputtering tries, she gave up.

"I think you're going to have to give me that lesson in wood-craft," she called out to him.

"No time for that now, sweetheart. If we're going to be at the caves before dark, we have to move fast."

"We're going to caves? Tonight? It's going to be freezing. Why don't we wait until morning?"

"Here." He tossed her a down jacket. "Morag's. And get these warmer pants on."

As she balanced on one leg then the other, changing into the heavy cords he'd brought for her, he caught her around the waist.

"On the other hand, they'll still be there tomorrow night."

Cat thrust an elbow into his chest. "No dice, cowboy. You just put a leash on those hormones until we get back. But, I warn you, this better be good."

"Trust me." He nuzzled her neck.

"Never trust a man who says trust me," she said, laughing, "and never eat at a coffee shop called Mom's. Old American folk saying. Let me go."

When they left finally, he kept the lights off on the Land Rover. He didn't need them. Clearly he knew every rut, every stone, every opening in the brush. Fifteen minutes passed. In spite of her cajoling, he refused to give her a clue about the caves—what they were, why they had to go there at night. Fleetingly, Cat thought about the Beretta in the bag at her feet, then, ashamed, dismissed it. Something was tickling the back of her mind—she seemed to have got into the habit of disquiet. But for the next few days—all she would have of him unless a miracle occurred, and she didn't believe in miracles—she would do as he asked. She would trust him.

He stopped under a large boulder, discernible to Cat by that time only as a denser black against the night sky. Darkness had fallen with the suddenness of a curtain closing.

"We'll walk from here." Campbell pulled the rifle from the rack behind his seat. "Not far. Stay close."

Deliberately, she dropped her bag, and the Beretta it contained, onto the floor of the Land Rover. "Don't worry. That's me breathing down your neck."

A three-quarter moon was rising. Every shadow seemed threatening, dancing in the breeze rustling through the brush. There was no path, but Campbell moved silently, without hesitation, and she followed closely, noticing that her breath was becoming heavier. They were climbing steadily.

An indefinable noise drifted through the night—a strange, soft gurgle. Mouth dry, Cat grabbed the back of Campbell's jacket. He stopped, put an arm around her, motioned silence. Twenty feet away, an enormous boulder moved. Cat thought her heartbeat would be heard in Nairobi. The moon broke from the cover of trees, flooding silver light over a game track slightly below where they stood on a brush-covered cascade of rock. The track was as clear of vegetation as if it had just been weeded by a giant hand. On the other side of the track, the shadow moved again.

"Elephants," Campbell said softly against her ear. "Mountain elephants."

The great shape was pewter in the moonlight, trunk raised, testing the air. Another elephant appeared. The two stood together as if conferring, trunks weaving from side to side. Satisfied, they moved ponderously over the rim of the path and started to climb.

Cat caught her breath. Behind them, elephants of all sizes appeared on the ridge and swung into single file. Their feet made no sound.

Over a hundred, she thought. And babies.

"We're looking at the last of them," Campbell said. "Only a few years ago there were ten million. At last count there are about five hundred thousand. Only half that number will be protected."

"What about the rest?"

He shook his head. "They take their chances."

The elephants paced to the speed of the smallest calf. The smack of their ears against their heads as they walked was clearly audible, as well as the strange sound she had heard earlier.

"What's that gurgling noise?"

"Their stomachs rumbling." He laughed softly at her delight. "Come on."

In spite of the cold air, she was damp from effort and excitement, her lungs laboring. Campbell stopped on a stone ledge above the track. Across a small ravine was the black entrance to a series of caves. The open ground in front was filled with great moving beasts, dappled with silver moonlight. Cat hardly breathed, riveted by the gray shapes, the strange mixture of sound—stomachs rumbling, rock ground beneath huge feet, grunts of welcome, tiny squeals. The smell of dust and dung and moisture, the green scent of crushed vegetation. It was a scene from the morning of the world.

"How many do you think are there?"

"Three or four hundred. A number of family groups. You don't

find single herds that size now. Once there were herds of five thousand and more."

Trunks were raised in greeting, ears and eyes explored gently.
Every adult seemed aware of the fragility of the babies and young
calves. Above them, black shapes against the moon, bats and flying foxes fluttered from the dark mouths of the caves.

"These are the elephant caves of Kitum." Campbell's breath
stirred the hair just above her ear, and she shivered. "Dug out by
countless generations of tuskers bringing down rock to get at the
mineral salts. Watch. When the matriarch gives the signal, the whole
group will sort themselves out. They communicate by sound, even
over long distances, a sort of rumbling below our hearing."

The herds were separating, one group starting the trudge back
into the bush, another climbing into the caves. The rest continued to mingle.

Campbell pointed. Cat dragged her eyes away from the elephants to see a leopard springing fluidly from rock to rock, slipping into the cave. Below, a few jackals followed. She looked closer.
The rocks leading to the cave were alive with moving shapes.

"The tuskers bring down the minerals, the rest benefit,"
Campbell said.

"Can you get inside?"

"Well, it's best to be in position before the trek begins at night.
I'd hate to find myself arguing with a female that size. I know when
I'm outmatched."

"Let's do it tomorrow."

"It's far too dangerous." He touched her cheek. "You're freezing. We should go back, get a fire going, warm you up."

She was shaking, but it was not with cold. "Not yet. It's wonderful, this place."

He pulled her back against his chest, wrapped his arms around her to give her his warmth. "I'm glad you're here, sweetheart," he said against her ear.

Not even Tom came up here with him, Cat thought. But he'd wanted to share this with her, something of his world for her to take back to her own. She leaned against him. Automatically, she found herself studying the terrain, checking the site, the slope of the land. Guitterrez would sell his soul for a site like this, she thought.

Any architect would.

Thirty-Four

"There it is," Campbell said. "Erukenya. It's Maa for Misty Mountain. The ancestral home." He put the plane into a sliding turn. "Let's give them a buzz."

The low, rambling house was shaded by trees and set in a sea of green lawn. Behind it, the jagged sun-touched peaks of Mount Kenya were wreathed in boas of feather-gray mist.

Two days on Elgon had flashed by in a dream of sex and sun and laughter. Now, below the wings of the Cessna, scarlet canna lilies and yellow hibiscus bent in the slipstream, and purple bougainvillea lifted like a cloud of confetti.

"That's some farmhouse," Cat said. If Father Gaston had been right about the Campbells having been wiped out by rinderpest, their financial recovery was impressive.

A tennis court was tucked away behind a stand of trees, the ruffled water of a swimming pool sparkled aquamarine in the sun. Horses galloped around white-fenced paddocks, spooked by the circling plane. In the distance was a small cluster of outbuildings, then a village of round thatched houses. Great squares of irrigated green faded into undulating yellow grassland.

It was beautiful. It was real. And being here meant sharing him with Jock and Morag and the ghost of Fiona. To please him, this morning she'd hidden her reluctance to leave Mount Elgon and return to the world of questions and doubts.

Already the thought of losing him was more than she could bear.

In a few days from now, what they'd had together would degenerate into juggling an eleven-hour time difference, patched-in, static-filled conversations, she in Los Angeles, Campbell in the bush somewhere, their exchanges becoming more and more stilted until finally they'd both be grateful to let them fade into memory.

And who knew what he was, really? Her fears were already pressing in again. Cat looked down at the ground racing below, remembering the raid on the poachers carried out so professionally. The sound of bullets striking rock, the deadly fountains of dust thrown up around him. The savagery he'd shown.

Yet the thought of leaving him was a cold, dense pain in the center of her being.

Campbell flew to the end of the small airstrip, checked the windsock and put the plane into a slow descent. A herd of zebra wheeled, kicking their heels like circus ponies, tossing their heads in the cloud of red dust that arose as the Cessna touched down. Cat reached for the gold and enamel Cartier powder compact that Paul Neville had given her when they'd first become lovers and peered into the mirror.

"Don't tell me you're nervous," Campbell said.

Cat snapped closed the lid of the compact and slipped it back into her bag, hearing it click against the Beretta. "Nah." She held up one trouser-clad leg, inspected a scabbed knee through a gaping

L-shaped tear. "What's to be nervous? I've spent the last two days with twigs in my hair, wrestling naked with you on bare ground—"

"Not entirely bare," he protested. "I remember a bit of grass here and there—"

"Bare ground," she said firmly. "I am about to meet your father for the first time, unexpectedly, I might add, and renew acquaintance with a rebellious daughter. But I'm on top of it, Campbell. Never fear. I am on top of it."

"Well, N'kosi will get the pants patched up. The twigs, though..." He shook his head doubtfully. "I think you're on your own with that."

She laughed, pushed her hair back with both hands. Campbell taxied toward a small corrugated hangar at the end of the strip, scattering a dozen marabou storks who strutted regally off the tarmac just ahead of them, feathers ruffling in the passing breeze, too dignified to hurry.

Inside the dark building, he parked next to another small plane, jumped out and went around the front of the aircraft to swing Cat down before she could open the door herself.

Cat linked her hands around his neck and leaned back against his encircling arms. "You're right. I am nervous. Don't throw me to the wolves."

A discreet clearing of the throat echoed in the enclosed space of the small hangar. In the doorway, two dark figures were silhouetted against the brilliance outside.

"Jock!" Morag said in a loud stage whisper. "Don't! They're so sweet."

Cat rolled her eyes. Campbell grinned, held her around the waist and walked toward them. With each step, Cat felt the tear in her pants flap against her knee.

"'Afternoon, Jock. So you're out of school, Mogs. How did you manage it this time?"

"The nuns are having a teachers' conference. Honestly. Isn't that true, Jock?"

"True enough, puss. Welcome to Erukenya, Miss Stanton." Jock Campbell greeted Cat with an outstretched hand, covering hers in a warm grasp. He looked at his son. "How are you, lad?"

"Fine, Jock, thanks." Campbell put his arm around Morag and kissed her. "I never managed to get out of school as often as you do."

"Not what Jock says. He says he used to have to run you down on a horse and throw a rope over you."

Campbell laughed. "Tall tales."

Cat greeted Morag, then turned her attention to Jock, studying him as frankly as he studied her. Campbell had said his father was sixty. He looked ten years younger. Over six feet, he carried more weight than his son, but was muscular and fit. Weathered skin, thick, close-cut iron-gray hair with the same tendency to curl. Eyes a shade lighter than Campbell's navy blue. A thin white scar, running from the corner of his left eye to his mouth, looked as it had been carved by a blade.

A man who has paid his dues, Cat thought. Powerful and aware of it. Attractive to women still. But she was one woman who viewed him with reserve. Underneath that charm and good looks, he was ruthless. Why had he not told his son that a pregnant Fiona needed him? And he had managed to put her off about the police report and make it plausible.

Jock Campbell tucked her hand into the crook of his elbow and turned to the open doors of the hangar. "I'm glad to have a chance to extend my sympathies personally," he said softly. "The accident must have been a terrible shock to you."

For a second, Cat looked at him. "Thank you. And for the arrangements you made. You were very kind." And very glib, she thought silently.

Jock nodded, patted her hand. He led her to an open Land Rover parked in the shade of the building.

"You'll stay a few days, I hope. Should think you'd be needing a bit of a rest by now."

Cat felt herself flush with embarrassment.

"Yes, it's been quite an arduous trip," she said coolly.

"No joke that, a run-in with a wildebeest," Jock went on. He opened the door of the Land Rover. "They can be frightening beasts, en masse."

Cat breathed again and climbed into the back seat. Campbell slid in beside her, Jock settled himself in the front passenger seat. Morag got behind the wheel and crashed the gears. Tires screamed, dust and rock flew and Cat's back slammed against hot leather. She struggled to regain her balance. Campbell grinned and pushed her upright. Jock twisted in the front seat, one arm braced on the frame of the windshield, and pointed out landmarks on the way: cattle barns and stables, an orchard of experimental trees, the cemetery where four generations of Campbells were buried. Cat nodded numbly, vainly trying to keep hair out of her eyes. The journey was a blur of blinding sun and shade.

At last she saw a gravel drive, an avenue of trees, and the Land Rover swept up to the house. Morag jammed on the brakes, her passengers lurched forward.

"Good show, Mogs," Campbell said. "Your driving is improving, I see."

Morag tossed her head, jumped out and slid Cat a sly grin. Cat smiled back.

Close-up the house looked as if it had grown as a family had grown, a generation at a time. Architecturally, it wasn't much, but the long, meandering structure had weathered well, and it had been loved into beauty.

"This is N'kosi." Jock introduced the short, stout man waiting for them. "Couldn't run this place without him. And Mary takes care of everything else. I think you met in Nairobi."

Cat murmured a greeting to each in turn.

"Jambo, memsahib." A smiling N'kosi reached for a bag. Clad in a parrot-green dress, her feet bare, Mary nodded, as serious as she'd been in Nairobi, then turned her smile toward Campbell, who put his arms around her and kissed her. Cat remembered that he'd told her that Mary had been the only mother he'd known after his own mother had been killed.

As N'kosi turned to greet Campbell, Cat had to struggle to keep her face neutral. One side of his head was completely naked, the shiny black skin criss-crossed with horrendous scars. At some time in his life, someone had made a hacking attempt to scalp him.

After the almost painful brilliance of the sun and the vivid flowers surrounding the house, the interior was restful. A large hall— from the layout it looked as if it had once been the entire house—opened into a room whose windows framed Mount Kenya. It was filled with hand-loomed rugs, couches the color of old ivory, large deep chairs, hammered-copper bowls filled with roses. No trophies or animal skins. The walls were decorated with African art that would grace a museum. The air was sweet with the roses and the cedar logs in the stone fireplace.

"How beautiful!" Cat exclaimed.

"Dan's mother loved this place," Jock said. "Always thought of Erukenya as home. We keep it as she left it. Well, I know you'll want to rest for an hour. Morag, show Cat to her room." He turned to Campbell. "You should take a look at the farm, lad. You'll be pleased."

Campbell nodded. "See you at dinner, Cat."

The two men left, their heads together, talking in an undertone. Cat watched him, but Campbell didn't look back.

Morag led the way through the house, then threw open a door. A vase filled with bird of paradise, their exotic orange and purple blossoms looking exactly like their name, were on a low table. In the hearth, a fire was just beginning to flame.

Morag opened French doors leading into a small enclosed garden still dappled with the last of the sun. Blue plumbago spilled over a rear wall, and the sound of trickling water came from a mossy stone catch basin in one corner.

"You'll have to be a bit careful of cobras, but a mongoose lives in those bushes, so you should be all right."

Cat nodded. "Snakes don't bother me. We see a lot of rattlers around Los Angeles. I just shake out my boots every morning."

Morag caught her eye, and they both laughed. The girl peeked into the bathroom, then nodded toward a connecting door.

"That's Dan's room." She grinned. "Mary wanted to put you in the other wing—she's Presbyterian—but N'kosi and I wouldn't let her. You've got time to rest, if you want, but we usually have dinner early at the farm. We don't dress up or anything." She eyed Cat's pants. "Just as well, really."

She disappeared through the door, then thrust her head back into the room. "Dinner's at seven. You'll hear the gong."

"Ah!" Jock looked approvingly at the dishes N'kosi deposited upon the table. "Seven-boy curry." He turned to Cat. "That's pretty mild. Mary's going easy on you, Cat." Jock pushed a tiered stand across the dark refectory table. Mango chutney, pale green watermelon rind coated with a thin syrup, peach chutney, peanuts, raisins, shredded coconut, spears of banana, a sticky yellow fruit Cat didn't recognize. "In India under the Raj, each condiment was carried around the table by a young boy. It was usually their first job and they took it very seriously. You knew what you were in for by the number of youngsters marching around. Eight condiments, an eight-boy curry, nine condiments, a nine-boy—"

"Oh, Grandpa, everyone knows that," Morag said.

"No, they don't, Mogs. You think that because you do—"

"Grandpa, you've got to get into the modern era, really you do. No one cares about all that colonial stuff anymore. You've got to get more up to date."

"What do you mean, up to date? I think I'm very up to date."

"What, just because you wear those terrible old jeans?"

Campbell winked at Cat, and she looked down at her plate, suppressing the urge to giggle at the wrangling between Jock and the young girl so plainly the apple of his eye. The flames of thick beeswax candles flanking the bowl of roses trembled in the cool breeze from the open doors to the terrace.

Dessert was a raspberry tart with rich yellow cream, produced on the farm, Jock said. He turned to listen as N'kosi reentered the room and bent to murmur in his ear.

"There's a call for you from California, Cat," Jock told her a moment later. "Why don't you take it in the office? N'kosi will show you the way."

"Thank you. Excuse me."

Following N'kosi, she kept her eyes fixed on a point between his shoulders, avoiding the terrible crosshatch of scars on his head. Earlier, Campbell told her that N'kosi had remained loyal to the Campbells during what the British regarded as the Mau Mau Rebellion—and the Kenyans regarded as the war of independence—the long brutal fight to end colonial rule spearheaded by Jomo Kenyatta and the Kikuyus. Jock had got back to the farm one night in time to fight off attackers, but N'kosi had already been half scalped. Thousands of Africans died in that war, Campbell said, not many Europeans, but his mother had been one of them.

Cat thought of the woman, younger than she was now, smiling into the sun in the photograph on the piano in Nairobi, the two children, Tom and Campbell, clinging to her skirt.

N'kosi led the way across the hall, opened the door to the office and stood back to allow her to enter. Cat crossed the room, noticing the deep chairs flanking the dying fire, the photographs and bookcases lining the walls, the blank computer screen.

She leaned across the green leather-topped desk and picked up the phone. "Hello?"

"How are you doing, honey?" John Rifken's usually booming voice was tinny in her ear.

"John! How did you know I was here?"

"Lucky guess. Tried the hotel first, then Campbell Safaris in Nairobi. Spoke to Tom M'Bala. Nice boy, but couldn't tell me a goddamn thing. Jock loves to show off that farm of his, so I took a chance. Doug Jones called me, told me about the site you've found. Thought I'd better give you a call since you don't seem inclined to keep me informed about how you're spending my money."

"Now, John, it's all covered by the fee we negotiated—"

"Just kidding, honey. How's it going?"

"Fine, John. Never better."

A burst of laughter penetrated the room, and Cat found herself smiling. Holding the telephone to her ear, the extended cord trailing behind her, she crossed the room and opened the door. On the far side of the hall, an archway framed the dining room, the two men and the young girl around the table. Campbell had a knife balanced on the tips of his fingers and was slowly moving it through the air, demonstrating God knows what. Morag leaned forward, eyes sparkling, lips parted ready to laugh, and Jock watched her, smiling. Cat thought of the silent mealtimes when she was growing up—her mother never seemed to be around—herself and

Joel, and whoever was the current live-in help. Juanita, Consuela, Ynez—a parade of women eager to get back to their own children. They never stayed long.

"Did you get on okay with Campbell? Giving you good service?" John was asking.

Cat grinned. "Very good, John, thanks. Why didn't you tell me they would not deal with a woman?"

"Honey, you want to play in the big leagues, you gotta deal with the curveballs. I figured you had to win that battle without my help."

"I almost didn't. You should have warned me what to expect."

John snorted. "I'm not breaking into a man's world, kiddo. You are. Toughen up. So, you got any paperwork? Anything I can show the board yet?"

Leaving the door open so that she could watch the scene in the dining room, Cat returned to the desk, picked up a pen. She thought more clearly with a pen in her hand. "Some sketches. I'm having new aerials flown and the land records are being searched. I can fax what I have, if you like."

"No, you'll be home in a couple of days, right? Any idea when?"

"I want to get the aerials at least before I leave. Patel Brothers are not the most reliable outfit going. But the site will knock your socks off, John. I guarantee it."

"That's fine, honey. But it's going to depend on the cost, no matter how sensational the site."

"Sure. But I know what should be done there. Is there any trouble with the banks, John?" She looked for some paper on which to make notes of the conversation for the file. There was nothing on the desk, and she pulled out the top drawer. Rubber bands, extra pens, paper clips. Not a scrap of paper.

"Some carping. Nothing I can't handle."

"Anything more you want me to do before I leave?"

"No. Just get back here so that we can go over the figures together before the next board meeting."

"Okay."

"Anything about the other business? Joel's accident?"

She hesitated. "No. I'll fill you in when I get back. Your buddy Jock is right across the hall. Do you want to talk to him?"

"No, I'll talk to him later. Enjoy the time you've got there, honey. That's some spread they've got, the Campbells."

There was another burst of laughter from the dining room.

"Very impressive," Cat agreed. "Particularly since I heard they've had some pretty bad times." A picture flashed across her mind: Maasai climbing the hill after the raid on Reitholder's camp, carrying tusks Campbell had told her would be left under guard for the government. "They went broke, I understand."

"Yeah, had it tough for a few years. Don't let that Limey charm fool you. Jock'll fight like a pit bull to keep that place going." Rifken laughed. "Guarantee he'll have you on the back of a horse before you leave, showing off his eland project."

"That sounds like a fun afternoon."

Opening a lower drawer, she renewed her search for paper, lifting out a buff-colored folder to look beneath it. Photographs spilled out. She started to shuffle them back into the folder, then picked one up to look at it more closely.

What at first glance seemed to be an expanse of empty golden grass, on closer examination was a pride of lionesses, bellies low to the ground, the dark tips of their ears betraying their presence, menace in every line. She looked at another—a rhinoceros knee deep in swamp, both horns removed—no doubt by game wardens in a desperate attempt to make him useless to the poachers destroying a species for horns worth more than gold when ground up and sold in the bazaars of the Orient as a useless aphrodisiac.

Joel had captured him perfectly: mutilated, alone in the world, the last of his line.

John's voice was in her ear. She made appropriate noises, agreement, dissent, sorting almost frantically through the photographs. A herd of Thomson's gazelle like arrows in flight. A close-up of a bird, brilliant, beautiful and lethal, a small frog in its death throes speared by the curved beak.

"...so okay then, honey, I'll see you in a few days."

She said goodbye, put down the phone, sat staring at the photographs in her hand.

"Cat?" Campbell stood in the doorway. "Is everything all right in Los Angeles?"

She looked up. "These are Joel's photographs."

Campbell entered the room, closed the door behind him, shutting out the sound of Morag's teasing laughter, Jock's admonishing tone. "I was waiting for the right moment to give them to you."

For a second she was stunned. "And when would be the right moment? You told me they were lost."

"Yes. I'm sorry."

"You're sorry!"

"Cat, I didn't know what was on that film—"

"Why did you need to? They are not yours!"

"No." He looked at the open drawer. "You were searching the desk?"

She slammed the drawer shut. "Don't try to put me on the defensive. I was looking for scrap paper to make notes of a conversation for my files. Have you *ever* told me the truth about anything? Ever, from the beginning?"

He crossed the room to the fireplace, picked up a poker and stirred the embers.

"Campbell, answer me. What is going on?"

He replaced the poker in its stand. "Nothing I can tell you about. All I can do is ask you to trust me."

"Why? Why should I? *These are my brother's photographs.* You told me his film had been lost in the bureaucracy. You lied to me."

"In some things I have no choice, Cat."

She stared at him, willing him to go on, thinking the pain in her chest must be her heart breaking. "What is that supposed to mean?"

"Cat. Darling. I know you have a lot of reason to doubt me, but believe me in this. Please. If I could tell you more, I would. I can't."

Cat gathered the photographs together into the folder.

For a moment, they were silent. Then Campbell crossed to where she stood. He turned her toward him and put his arms around her. For a second she resisted, then melted into him. They had two days, a couple of nights, and then she would return to Nairobi for a flight to Los Angeles. Would she ever feel about anyone, she wondered, as she felt about this man she did not know. And definitely should not trust?

Dressed in the Princeton T-shirt she wore at night, Cat sat on her heels in the middle of her bed, half listening to the sound of Campbell showering. Joel's photographs were spread around her. She studied each in turn. When she got home she'd organize the best of his wildlife photography over the years into a book, a memorial of sorts, something for his friends to keep. Closure, perhaps, for her. The book would end with the pictures taken in the last weeks of his life.

Then she realized that she was looking at only twenty-four photographs. If Joel had followed his normal practice, in the two weeks on safari before he died he would have taken hundreds.

Where were the rest?

Thirty-Five

The lion yawned, showing his pink tongue, his powerful white incisors. Rays of morning sun pierced the trees, throwing bars of light across the full black mane. Tail low and motionless, the lion moved slowly through the mist-wreathed reeds. Suddenly he stopped.

"He's caught our scent," Campbell said softly. "He'll ignore us, they're lazy devils. But no sudden moves."

Standing in the open door of the Land Rover, Cat slowly lifted the binoculars, adjusting them until she was looking into golden-green eyes on the far side of the pool. "He's beautiful!"

"He's hoping she thinks so." Campbell nodded toward the underbrush.

A lioness, her body melding with the background of trees and yellow grass, strolled toward the water. As she came close, the lion turned his massive head and gave a soft cough of greeting. She ignored him, stopping at a small inlet among the reeds. She picked up one huge paw, shook it delicately like a great domestic tabby, then lowered her body and put her mouth to the water. Coughing gently, the lion moved toward her. She went on drinking, her only movement in her tail and the lapping pink tongue. His shadow fell on her. The lapping ceased. Eyes wide, she was as still as the water.

"Do you think they're going to mate?" Cat asked softly.

Campbell shook his head.

The lion touched his nose to her shoulder, then rubbed his face against hers. She remained motionless. Encouraged, he put a tentative paw on her flank. The lioness looked up, nose wrinkled, teeth bared. He held his ground. She slashed at him, claws unsheathed, and he jumped back, coughing a protest.

"Wow! She means business!" Cat said.

The lion hovered just out of reach while the lioness leisurely drank her fill. She stood, shook each forepaw, then slowly sauntered back toward the cover of the bush.

Cat looked down at Campbell, seated behind the wheel of the Land Rover.

"What happens now?"

"Nothing."

She raised the glasses for another look at the lion. He was gone.

Campbell turned on the ignition, twisted in his seat and backed the Land Rover through the trees onto a track.

Cat collapsed into her seat. "Campbell! What's going to happen?"

"Oh, he'll fight to keep other lions away from her until she's ready to mate. Maybe he can. He looks strong, but nothing's certain in his life. A younger male could kill him, take over the pride. The new male would then kill all the cubs to bring the lionesses into season again.

"God! How awful!"

"He is driven by instinct to perpetuate his own seed. And she's unpredictable. This is probably her first time to mate."

"How do you know that?"

"The look of her. Tight in the belly for one thing. She's never had cubs."

Through the thin open forest, Cat watched the mist-shrouded peaks of Mount Kenya appear, disappear, appear. Elusive. Like Campbell himself. She hadn't asked about Joel's pictures. They had to get back to Nairobi soon and there would be time enough to deal with her questions then. "Where are we going?"

"I have something to show you."

The sound of a galloping horse came from behind them. Barely touching the tiny saddle, Morag crouched over the neck of a bay hunter. She wound through the trees, parallel with the Land Rover.

"Beat you to the compound," she yelled.

Campbell laughed, eased his foot off the accelerator. "You want to break your bloody neck, you're on your own," he shouted back.

Morag waved a crop, crouched lower, disappeared in the trees. Campbell followed until a heavy-log stockade became visible through the trees, the horse standing with reins thrown over a hitching rail. Campbell drew to a stop beside the tethered horse. A short dark block of a man wearing khaki raised a hand in a sharp, military salute.

"*Jambo, bwana.*"

"*Jambo,* Zama. This is Miss Stanton."

Zama snapped a salute in Cat's direction. "*Memsahib.*"

"Tembo ready?" Campbell asked.

"*N'dio, bwana.* She ready."

"Good. Open up."

Zama pushed against solid wooden gates. Campbell took Cat by the arm, guided her into a stockade. A buffalo calf, several gazelles, a tiny giraffe wandered freely. Enclosures built against the inside of the stockade housed antelope, baboons and odd-looking catlike animals—a litter of young hyenas only slightly more appealing than they would be when adults. Activity among the khaki-clad men working—cleaning cages, feeding, replenishing water troughs—picked up noticeably as Campbell entered.

Morag was trying to hold a plastic bucket of alfalfa pellets away from the inquisitive trunk of a small elephant.

"This is Tembo," Campbell said.

Morag wiped a wet green hand on the seat of her jeans. "Ugh! Elephant slobber. I wish we could keep her."

"She's not a pet," Campbell said.

"What is this?" Cat looked around. "Not a zoo."

"Christ! No!" Campbell said. "We only keep them until they get back on their feet, then out they go. Costs a bloody fortune as it is."

Cat touched the head of the small elephant. What was Campbell, really? If not a poacher, then a thief who stole from poachers? She thought again of the Maasai, old friends from the village that had cared for him, carrying tusks.

"Here." Morag handed Cat the bucket. "You feed her. She was orphaned by poachers. We've had her three years."

Cat thought of the tiny elephant trying to nurse on a mutilated mother. She looked at Campbell. "Why didn't you try to save that calf?" She did not have to explain which calf she meant.

"It was too dehydrated to have survived the journey. It had another hour or two at the most. I put it out of its misery."

"Then why didn't you tell me that?"

He shook his head. "I don't know. I should have."

Tembo's small gray ears moved gently, stirring the air. Cat held out a palm filled with alfalfa pellets. The moist tip of the little trunk searched delicately for each morsel, lifting it expertly to her mouth.

"Where's she going?"

"Well, she came from Tsavo—"

"You can't take her back there!" Morag interrupted. "It's terrible down there. The poachers have wiped almost everything out."

"Zama will stay until she joins up with a herd—"

"What herd? Jane Terry's brother was down there last month. He says Tsavo's been shot out. The elephants left are so panicked they barely stop to feed or to drink anymore. We should keep her here."

"Morag, she's going back where she belongs. We can't keep her. You've always known that."

"We could if *you* wanted to. But you never change your mind about anything, do you? God, you're impossible." Morag turned, ran across the kraal and disappeared behind a long thatched building.

Campbell stared after her. "Now, what do you think of that? I never know what's going to set her off."

Cat took his hand. "What's that building?"

"An infirmary of sorts. Come on, I'll show you to the rest of the place, give madam a chance to cool down."

Like a giant dog out for a stroll, Tembo accompanied them around the enclosure. The young elephant waited patiently when Campbell stopped to talk to the men, then tried to push her way through the door of the infirmary as soon as Campbell opened it. Laughing, he held her back while Cat eased through, then shut it before the little elephant could follow her inside. The latch rattled.

"It's been Tembo-proofed, but she doesn't believe it. She'll be busy for a while."

The large rectangular room was filled with small pens, most containing sleeping young animals. At the far end was a row of doors. Storage, Campbell said, and a small isolation room for those animals too sick to be in with the general population.

Morag was on her knees, holding a bottle to the mouth of a tiny gazelle with a leg bound in a splint.

"Dan, look," Morag said. "Teddy Cavellini brought this little fellow over yesterday."

Cat felt his sudden stillness.

"Keep away from the Cavellini boy, Morag. I don't want him here."

"Oh, he's all right. Nice boy, really." Morag didn't look up. "I rather like him. He took the trouble to bring this little fellow. Didn't he?" she cooed to the gazelle. "Drove thirty miles to do it. A lot of people wouldn't have bothered, they'd just have killed him. Wouldn't they, little thing?" she said to the gazelle. "I said I'd go and have tea at their place on Sunday." She smiled up at Campbell. "He's the right age for me."

"As soon as you get back to the house, call them and cancel. I've told you before, keep away from the Cavellinis."

Morag turned her head and looked up at him. She stood, her face tight. "I thought you'd be pleased. But no. Always you—never what I want. What's the matter with you? Why do I have to keep away from every boy you don't like? Poor old Dougie—"

"That's your idea of a boy? Doug Maxwell's damn near as old as I am—"

"Well, Teddy Cavellini isn't! I've known him forever—"

"No, you haven't. I've made bloody sure of that."

"Why? What's he done to you? Why are you like this with everyone—"

"Because you make some pretty rash choices. Now, cancel those plans for Sunday and keep away from the Cavellinis."

"Why should I? You can't make me. You don't like anybody. Not anybody." Morag's voice was rising. There was a flurry of anxious movement from the penned animals. "You can't stop me from seeing everyone. I'm not a child."

Cat looked from one angry face to the other, unable to intervene.

"Then stop behaving like one for a change. If I say I don't want you consorting with the Cavellinis, assume I have a good reason—"

"I didn't consort," Morag shouted. Behind her a young baboon grabbed the bars of his cage and shrieked. "He brought a bloody gazelle here, that's all. You can't control everything. I'll do as I bloody want."

"Morag!"

Campbell started to move toward her, and Cat put a restraining hand on his arm.

"Get away from me!" Morag shouted. "It was just tea, but I'll fuck him if I want to. That's what you're afraid of, isn't it? That I'll fuck him? You think I'm like my mother, don't you? Well, I am. I want to be like her." Her face was suffused with blood. "I know all about it. You can't beat up everybody in the world."

She raced across the room, heels drumming on the wooden floor. She struggled with the door. Cat held Campbell's arm with both hands, but he made no attempt to go after her. The door slammed back against the wall, shaking the building. At the end of the room, one of the storage doors bounced open with the impact.

Startled, Campbell looked toward it.

The little elephant put a triumphant head inside the room, and Cat hurried to shoo her out before she wedged herself in the doorway, then turned back into the nursery to ask Campbell what Morag meant about her mother.

Beyond him, she could see into the room whose door had just burst open.

It was an armory. Shoulder-held rocket launchers she recognized from television news programs, other weapons whose purpose she didn't know. Ammunition. Cases of it.

Campbell slammed the door. "I don't know what she's learning in that bloody expensive convent school," he said over his shoulder. "If the nuns knew what their senior girls get up to, it would wither their wimples."

"What is all that stuff for? All those guns?"

"The farm's pretty isolated. You never know when weapons are needed. We have licenses for them." He snapped the padlock in place.

Questions she wanted to ask whirled through Cat's mind. Suddenly none of her questions seemed safe. This was a complicated puzzle she didn't understand.

But her instincts couldn't be that wrong, she told herself. How could she be mistaken about loving him?

"What did she mean about her mother?"

"Who the hell knows what Morag means? She doesn't know, herself, I shouldn't think." He went to the outside door, opened it, holding Tembo aside. "Aaron," he shouted. One of the khaki-clad men came on the double, snapped to attention in front of him.

Campbell switched to Swahili.

Aaron's eyes strayed to the door.

Campbell continued in Swahili.

Aaron stayed silent while Campbell blistered the air. Finally he stopped, and Aaron saluted and turned, marched away, back rigid.

Campbell came back into the infirmary, his face grim. Cat said, "He looks like an ex-military man."

Campbell took Cat's arm. "I'm starving," he said in English. "Let's get some lunch."

"Now, these are eland," Jock Campbell said. "Resistant, easy to raise." He rode with the ease of a man used to long hours in the saddle.

Cat let the chestnut mare she was riding dance a little, enjoying the creak of the leather, the restrained power of the animal. She studied the herd of enormous antelope on the other side of the fence.

"Six feet at the shoulder," Jock said. "They'll thrive in areas where rinderpest makes it impossible to graze cattle."

"Don't encourage him. He'll tell you more about rinderpest than you ever knew existed," Campbell said.

"That wouldn't be difficult," Cat said. Jock had been delivering snippets of information since the inspection of the farm started just after lunch. A paramyxovirus, fiercely contagious, that caused high fever, skin lesions, diarrhea—he'd spared none of the details.

"You can't know too much about rinderpest. It's the curse of East Africa," Jock said. "I've seen it kill the cattle in an entire section practically overnight." He laughed. "I can be a bit of a bore about it, I suppose. Terrifies me. Damn near wiped us out more than once."

Close-up, the farm looked as prosperous as it had from the air. Cat had already admired the thoroughbred mares, the trophies won by Campbell Farms at the course in Nairobi over the last five decades. Bloodstock that had taken years to perfect had been sold off to raise cash, but they'd been lucky enough to buy back offspring from some of their own mares, Jock said, so they had hopes of reestablishing a breeding program.

All this regained prosperity from raising eland instead of beef? Cat wondered.

Campbell looked at his watch. "I have to get back. Tom's calling in half an hour. See you at teatime, Cat. And, Jock, please, easy on the rinderpest. She's from Los Angeles, remember." Laughing, he put his gelding into an easy canter.

"Ask Tom if he found out anything about Stephen N'toya," she called after him, and he waved without turning.

Campbell took the gelding back to the stable to be unsaddled by the groom, then drove the mile or so back to the house instead of taking the forest path on foot as he usually did.

A telephone was ringing as he walked into the office. He picked it up.

"Campbell."

"I was about to hang up," Stephen N'toya said. "I'm at a public phone and people are lined up waiting for me to finish."

"Sorry, I was out on the farm. Where are you?"

"Main post office in Nairobi. Everything all right?"

"Yes. The tusks we took from Reitholder have been brought in, and I've increased the security around the barn, but we've got to get rid of it, and soon. Jock's getting jumpy. What have you found out?"

"The largest collection of ivory moved through this country in years is now on dhows riding just outside our territorial waters, waiting for the rust bucket that will take it to Macau and Hong Kong."

"You mean it has slipped through our fingers?" Campbell said incredulously.

"What do you expect? When you grabbed Reitholder, you sent a clear signal to Francis that he'd never get a chance like this again. Like the good general he is, Francis jumped on it. He moved the ivory while Reitholder was locked up in Nairobi, and while there was no one from Johannesburg to monitor exactly how many tusks he was moving. You want to guess how many were skimmed off the top? He had a meeting with Reitholder and let him believe the stuff was still held in Nairobi, so Reitholder went on a two-day binge. Let him explain that to his masters in Johannesburg."

Campbell swore. "The dhows can be taken from the sea."

"I'm working on it. But we can't lose sight of the original objective, which is to take Francis and Reitholder together and break them. I've got some things going, and I need to discuss them with you. I'm coming up to Erukenya tonight."

"You can't do that. Cat Stanton is here. It's too big a risk."

"Then make sure she's in bed. You should be good at that by now. Tom's flying me up around eleven."

"Don't be a fool," Campbell said. But N'toya had hung up.

Cat watched Campbell cantering back toward the stable, admiring the grace of his body moving as if part of the gelding. She felt Jock's eyes on her and looked away quickly. Her feelings must be right there, printed on her face for all to see.

"Started to ride as soon as he could walk," Jock said. "His mother was a fine horsewoman." He turned his mare toward rows of cultivated trees, pausing until Cat fell in beside him. She was quiet, hoping he'd say more about Campbell's mother, but he didn't. They entered one of the long verdant tunnels.

"Macadamia trees. Got them from Hawaii," Jock said. "Best macadamia nuts in the world come from Hawaii." He stopped, pulled one of the branches toward him and examined it. Far down the row of trees, Cat caught a glimpse of deer cropping grass, and flocks of tiny green birds swooped and landed, chattering in the trees. Apparently satisfied, Jock let the branch spring back, then led the way onto a wide rocky roadway.

Around them, men went about their work, moving from barns to sheds to kraals built in the shade of the magnificent cedars that dominated the area.

"This is the working heart of the farm," Jock said. "The barns contain feed, equipment, that kind of thing." Cat wondered about rocket launchers but remained silent.

They skirted the farm buildings. A number of men squatted on their heels in the shade of a structure standing away from the rest in the center of a large cleared area.

Cat tipped her hat away from her eyes. "There's Moses. And

Sambeke!" She stood in the stirrups and waved. "They were with us on safari."

Jock made a show of looking, shading his eyes with his hand. "I don't think so. Dan's people are not here. They're all on leave before the next safari client arrives. Dutch film company doing a documentary on what's left of the rhinos. Let's get out of this sun." He pressed a heel against his mare's flank, and she broke into a slow canter.

Her own mare picked up pace. Cat reined her in. "But I'm sure that's Moses. He's a lot heavier than most Maasai." Cat narrowed her eyes against the sun, squinting at the row of men.

Moses and Sambeke had disappeared. But it was clear the rest of the men were armed. She couldn't be mistaken about that.

She gave the mare her head, catching up with Jock ahead of her. "What is that building?"

"A quarantine barn," Jock said. "I don't take any chances now. When I get new breeding stock, they're quarantined. Any suspect animal is shot and the carcass burned."

They had entered the trees and the barns were behind them. Like his son, Jock Campbell was fast on his feet, Cat thought. But the sun had been blinding. Maybe she had been wrong about Moses and Sambeke.

She found herself saying that a lot, lately. She could have been wrong about this. About that. Compromises. Silences. Nothing was as it seemed. Or was it? She no longer knew. She did know those men were armed. Lately, she had become more familiar with assault weapons than she had thought possible.

Underfoot the path was rocky. The only sound now was the ring of iron-shod feet striking stone, the snorting breath of the horses as they climbed, the call of birds. Barns and paddocks and cultivated farmland fell behind them as they moved into an open forest of mixed trees, broadleaf and cedar.

Jock certainly wasn't intending to show her farming methods up here. He had something in mind, though. She had the feeling Jock Campbell never did anything without purpose.

At the edge of an escarpment, he stopped. "We'll let them breathe a minute." He leaned forward to run his hand over the mare's damp neck. "Look down there. That's the Boran cattle of the Maasai. They're rather like the Brahmas you used to breed in the American South." He pointed out the humped-back cattle mingling with grazing zebra and gazelle on the plain below.

Cat nodded, but at this distance one large animal looked very much like another.

"Dan spent the better part of a year living with the Maasai, did he tell you that?" Jock asked.

"When he and Tom were searching for Fiona's body. Yes, he told me, but I didn't realize it was for that long."

Jock grunted. He swung out of the saddle, threw the reins over his arm. Cat dismounted, and they turned to walk slowly along the edge of the escarpment.

"Did he tell you about Fiona's death?"

"Yes. It was tragic."

"He was pretty torn up. The Maasai were good with him. And I knew Tom M'Bala would stick like glue. They've been insepara-ble since boyhood." He stopped to check a girth. "What do you think of my granddaughter?"

The question surprised her. Morag had been missing at lunch. Mary had taken a tray to the girl's room. The scene in the infir-mary had been mentioned only briefly.

"She's a lovely girl, young and feeling her way," Cat said. "I also think she's spoiled and confused."

"Mmm. Possibly. Dan's too hard on her and I indulge her. Is that what you mean?"

"Something like that."

"How much do you know about her mother?"

"Not much. Young. Spirited. In love with your son. I saw her portrait in Nairobi. She was very beautiful."

"Yes. I still miss her. The light went out for a long time after she died. For all of us. Morag's very much like her in a lot of ways."

"So she says."

"Dan is not Morag's father, you know."

Cat stopped walking. The mare reached for a choice clump of grass, nudging her with a heavy shoulder, and Cat swayed. Her body felt like rubber. Did he lie about everything? Why? Why? *Why?* The word reverberated.

"Then how can you be her grandfather?" Her confusion was complete.

"Strictly speaking, I'm her granduncle. I worry about that child," Jock said. "I worry she's going to turn out like her mother."

Cat caught hold of herself. "I thought you adored her mother."

"I did. That doesn't mean Fiona was perfect. My God. Far from it."

"Jock, as I understand it, two kids had an affair when they were too young. No big deal. Even eighteen years ago, an affair between two youngsters couldn't have been that scandalous. Especially what I've read about Kenya."

"No, of course not. If that's all there was, an isolated affair with Dan, no, far from it. I didn't realize what was happening myself until it was too late. Then what could I have done? Brought him home? No. I had some ridiculous idea of sparing him. He was just turned nineteen, for God's sake."

"Sparing him from what?"

"I thought from a life of misery. But he's never forgiven himself, anyway. Nor me, I think, sometimes."

"Fiona sounds like a kid who needed a strong hand and didn't get it—"

"Fiona was not an innocent child."

"Jock, what was she, fifteen, sixteen? She was a kid—"

"After he left for Edinburgh—" Jock's voice caught and he cleared his throat "—she became different from the sweet creature I knew. She had every man within fifty miles mad for her. And I mean *mad* for her. I think it amused her to keep them stirred up. She was one of those women." He glanced at her. "Oh, yes. I know what you think, but she was a woman, the sort of woman men kill for. Not an exaggeration. Women like that are a blessing and a curse. I was afraid Dan would end up killing someone if they spent a life together."

He started walking and Cat kept up, side by side now as the track broadened.

"After she died it was mere luck he didn't kill the man who took her on that damn safari. God knows, he tried to. Guido Cavellini. Not that I blame Dan. I wanted to kill the bastard myself." Jock looked out over the plain below, but gave the impression of a man staring into the past, not liking what he saw. "I didn't bring him home when she got pregnant. I didn't want him to know until we sorted out what we were going to do. In any case, I thought she ought to have time to settle down. For the situation to cool off. But she didn't settle down. A lot of men walked very carefully around Dan when he did get home. He claimed Morag as his, and no one dare even look as if they doubted his word. He took his fists or that whip to any man who even mentioned Fiona's name."

"What happened to Cavellini?"

"He left the country. He was distraught over Fiona's death, I'll give him that. Morag is probably his child. The only thing I'm sure of is that Dan is not her father. He'd been gone too long when Fiona got pregnant." He sighed. "Anyway, Cavellini was married, had a couple of kids—young Teddy was about four then. As soon as he got out of hospital, he took his family off to Italy. They stayed away several years."

"This boy Teddy Cavellini is Morag's half brother?"

"Very likely."

"She has to be told. The way he's going, Dan's going to drive Morag right into his bed."

"Yes, I know."

"Why are you telling me all this, Jock?"

"I thought it would be better coming from me instead of you hearing the old gossip."

"I'm leaving in a couple of days. Not much time to hear gossip."

"But you'll be back?"

"Only if I'm commissioned to do the hotel. And that's looking doubtful. These things often don't go ahead."

"My son loves you. You must know that."

Cat didn't answer.

"Apart from the boyhood passion for Fiona, he's never cared for anyone. Never brought a woman to Erukenya. I was rather hoping... I think you would be good for him, Cat."

"I've got a life of my own going on in Los Angeles, Jock. A career that means as much to me as your son's career does to him." Whatever that might be, she thought silently. "Los Angeles is a long way away. I don't think there's much future for us."

They paced without speaking, then Jock said, "This farm means everything to me. This farm and Morag. And my son. If anything happens to him, it'll be the end of Erukenya. Morag will be about her own life. The farm will go to strangers."

"Why should anything happen to him? Conducting film companies around, putting radio collars on animals. What's so dangerous about that? Or does he do something else I don't know about?"

"No, of course not. You're right." Jock looked at the sun. "Well, we'd better start back if we want any tea."

Cat remounted, watched him climb into the saddle with the agility of a man twenty years younger. "Jock, wait a minute."

He looked at her.

"I do love him," she said. "What is he involved in?"

Jock stared at her without expression. Then he wrenched the mare's head around, put his heel to its flank.

Cat stared after him. Jock Campbell was really afraid.

Thirty-Six

"We thought you two were going to miss tea," Morag called. "We're on our second cup." Smiling, pretty in a sundress that made her gray eyes look blue and showing no trace of the earlier storm, she raised a teapot.

They were sitting at a white wicker table set under a tree in an expanse of green lawn, laden with silverware, tiny sandwiches, scones and a Victoria sponge cake oozing raspberry jam and cream, dusted with powdered sugar that made Cat think of her god-daughter, Rosie—the cake was her favorite, reserved for special tea on Sunday. Maribou storks and peacocks hovered around the table like a family of dogs waiting for scraps.

"And Dan's on his third scone. You'd better grab one before he scoffs the lot."

Campbell put the last of his buttered scone in his mouth and stood to pull out a chair.

"Good ride?"

"Lovely. Learned a lot."

"All you never wanted to know about rinderpest, I bet."

Cat laughed. "And more."

"Indian or China, Cat?" Morag asked.

"China," Cat said, unaware of the difference.

"Grandpa? Indian or China?"

"Morag, I've had two cups of Indian tea every afternoon at this time for the past forty years. I think I'm going to continue the habit."

"Just thought I'd ask. Maybe you'd changed your mind and decided on something adventurous, like China." She offered him a plate of small sandwiches. "You're getting set in your ways, Jock. You worry me."

"Well, that's a switch."

Behind the house lay Mount Kenya, teased the eye with glints of snow that disappeared behind drifting mist as if in a mirage. Red and yellow canna lilies and beds of roses bordered the tree-dotted lawn, and under the scent of the roses was the green smell of newly cut grass and the dry dustiness that came up from the plains. A white peacock fanned his great tail feathers, shimmering the pale chocolate-colored eyes as he turned slowly in a circle. Morag threw a morsel of bread to him, laughing as a drab little peahen bullied him aside to snatch at it.

Cat sipped tea, only half listening to the exchange. Campbell was silent, staring out over the lawn. "Cat," she fantasized him saying, "there are some things about my life I want you to know." And, "I love you, we'll meet halfway in London every couple of months. We can make it work." But of course they couldn't.

N'kosi walked from the house.

"*Memsahib.* A telephone call for you from Los Angeles."

Cat put down her cup and murmured her excuses, trailing her fingers across Campbell's back, secretly, out of sight of the others as she passed him to follow N'kosi into the house.

* * *

Campbell turned to watch her cross the lawn.

"Lovely young woman," Jock said.

"Mmm." Campbell glanced at Morag, busily feeding the peacock and his mate, laughing at their eagerness.

"It's time to let the past go, Dan," Jock said softly.

"And the present?" Campbell asked. "Can I embroil her in all this?"

"You can get out of it——"

"No. I can't. It's the life I've chosen, Jock. A woman can't share it. And, anyway, she's got a career in America. She'd never give that up."

"Maybe she'd surprise you."

"I like her a lot." Morag looked over at them. "I'd like to be an architect, you know."

"Good idea. Maybe you could start by doing better at your math." Grinning, Campbell checked his watch and rose to his feet. "I'm going down to the compound. Tell Cat, will you, Mogs? See you at dinner."

In the office, Cat picked up the phone.

"Cat, honey, sorry to drag you back to business," John Rifken's voice said.

"You're up early, John." In Los Angeles, it was before 6:00 a.m. She wondered if there was a touch of asperity in John's comment— he was used to seeing her in a rush of perpetual motion, nothing but business, and here she was having a vacation. "What's up?"

A legal-size yellow pad was by the phone. She walked around the desk, sat down and reached for a pen.

"A board meeting's been called. If you want this job, I think you'd better be there."

"When?"

"They want it in four days, but I'm going to stall until you get here. That bastard Guitterrez is going behind my back on this one, and I don't like it." The heavy Texas humor was gone from his voice. "He wants this job, and he's lining up support to get it. Looks like he's done some research—he's suggesting we bypass East Africa altogether. If we do go for another location, you'd be out."

"You mean build elsewhere?"

"Yeah. Political situation all over Africa is a bitch, no one can disagree with that. But the little son of a bitch is politicking behind my back and I don't like that. He's going to have to find out who, exactly, he's taking on."

"John, I'm going to need time to prepare a professional presentation to the board—"

"You get home right away, you'll have time for a preliminary report. That's good enough. If this Maasai Springs deal looks promising, I'll get you the time you need for professional presentations. Just get your ass home. Now, okay, kid? Don't linger."

"All right."

"Good. See you in a couple of days, then. Have a good flight."

Cat put the phone down. It was over, she thought. Time had run out. Finish.

She sat back in the chair, breathing deeply. If her idyll was over, so was her search for the truth about Joel's death. And what had she learned? Not much. All she had was a new set questions. If she wanted answers, she had to have them now. Not in Nairobi. She couldn't wait for Father Gaston, or N'toya, or anyone else.

Her eyes dropped to the drawer in which she had discovered Joel's photographs. On impulse, she tugged at the knob. The drawer was locked.

Cat reached across the desk for the paper knife, pushed the tip into the space between the drawer and the desk, sliding it along to tap against the lock. Nothing. Quickly, she straightened a paper clip, inserted the wire into the lock. One eye on the door, she jiggled the paper clip—this worked on her desk at home. But not here.

Frustrated, she picked up the paper knife again, slid it harder against the lock. Nothing happened. She knelt in front of the drawer, concentrating. The wood creaked ominously under the knife, and she stopped before it splintered, considering for a moment what it was she was doing. She was jimmying open a private desk! A desk in her lover's home.

The hell with it. Where were the rest of Joel's photographs?

She ran her hand under the desk, feeling for a taped key.

And found it.

Heart pounding, she went to the door, cracked it. The house was quiet. Everyone was still outside having tea. Quickly, she returned to the desk, inserted the key. The drawer slid open. She reached into the deep space, sorting through the folders, lifting the thickest onto the floor, crouching beside it. The file was bulky with photographs.

A record of slaughter, mostly elephants, great hacking wounds where tusks had once been. But they were Joel's work, she was sure of it. Sickened, she started to shuffle them back into the file. Then suddenly, she was staring at a snapshot of five men, grim-faced, armed, unposed. But Joel had not taken this. He was in the foreground, half turned to the camera. The others were Campbell, Tom M'Bala, another man she didn't recognize but who looked enough like Tom M'Bala to be his brother. And Stephen N'toya.

Stephen N'toya, the man Campbell had repeatedly denied he knew. Stunned, she sat back on her heels, oblivious to her surroundings.

Voices in the hall grabbed her attention. Morag's high laughter, Jock's lower tone. Hands shaking, Cat folded the picture, shoved it inside her pants, flat against her belly. She closed the file, pushed it back into the drawer, eased the drawer closed. Then she got up and sat in the chair.

Not a moment too soon. After a tap at the door, Morag opened it, poked her head into the room.

"Dan said to tell you he'll be back in a couple of hours. Gone off to do some farm thing or other." She started to withdraw her head, then changed her mind. She came into the room. "Did you have bad news, Cat? You look all white and shaky."

"A bit tired, I guess. It was a long ride, I haven't been on a horse for a while."

"Old Jock can really wear you down, can't he? All that about cattle with runny sores and the squits. Ugh! You better take a rest before dinner. Unless you fancy a nice quiet game of Scrabble?" She sounded doubtful, a dutiful hostess doing her best.

Cat shook her head. "A rest, I think."

And time alone to think this through, she thought. Morag nodded and closed the door.

Campbell had lied about knowing Stephen N'toya. Every other lie he'd told faded next to that. Trust me, he'd said. And like a fool, she had. All her doubts about Joel's death came roaring back. Joel was right. Nothing was as it seemed. That was the only thing she could trust.

Why was an armory of sophisticated weapons housed in an animal infirmary? Why did Moses and Sambeke disappear when she waved to them? Why would a simple quarantine barn be guarded by heavily armed men?

Why would Joel send her sketches of a terrorist camp and yet never mention it to Campbell?

She felt as if she had entered a maze from which there was no return. She could only see the path ahead. And she had no choice but to take it.

* * *

Somehow, the evening passed. Around nine, Cat started to yawn. With a small, apologetic laugh, she replaced her coffee cup in the saucer. "Sorry. I can hardly keep my eyes open. It must be the altitude. I'm going to have to turn in." She rose to her feet.

"I'll walk you to your door." Campbell put his own cup down and stood.

Morag slid a knowing smile in Jock's direction, then sang out, "Good night, you two."

"I'll be right back, Mogs," Campbell said, grinning at her. "I've got to go down to the compound. Zama's taking Tembo out in the morning."

"To Tsavo?" Morag brought her chin up, ready for battle.

Jock intervened. "No. She's going to a private reserve near Meru to join a herd made up of orphans. She'll be safe there. We finished the arrangements today."

"Oh, that's brilliant!" Morag looked at Campbell with shining eyes. "I'll come with you."

"No, not tonight, Mogsie," Campbell said. "You'd be in the way. Turn in early, and you can go with Zama tomorrow to get Tembo settled at the reserve."

A chorus of thanks and good-nights followed them. As soon as they were alone, Campbell said, "There's been something wrong all evening. What is it?"

Cat had managed to avoid him before dinner, unsure she'd be able to carry off being alone with him. In spite of the holes, the things unsaid, what had been between them had been sweet beyond belief.

"I have to leave in the morning, too," she said. "I have to see Patel Brothers in Nairobi, and then get the flight to London tomorrow night."

His face settled into heavy lines. "I thought we had more time."

"The call this afternoon was from John Rifken," Cat said. "I'm needed in Los Angeles."

"Cat. I—" He stopped.

She put her arms around him, her head against his shoulder, waiting for him to tell her what she wanted to hear. She felt as if her veins were open, her love, hope, trust draining out, pooling around their feet.

"I'll be late tonight," he said.

"I'll be awake."

She slipped out of his arms, opened her door before he could see her tears. Inside, she leaned her back against the door, listening for his receding footsteps, hearing nothing. But she knew he had gone.

She crossed the room, swung the curtains wide and opened the French door to the enclosed garden. Cold air rushed in. The night was peaceful in the silver wash of moonlight. No roar of hunting lions, or screams of dying prey. No maniacal laughter of hyena that always caused the hair on the back of her neck to ripple. Just the breeze whispering through the long, errant strands of plumbago spilling over the walls of the garden. She wondered if the resident mongoose was sleeping, or whether the hours of darkness was when it dragged torpid snakes from their slumber.

Half an hour passed, then she heard the engine of a Land Rover start up, fade into the night. Campbell going down to the compound. She turned back into the room, cracked the door into the hall. Voices floated from the sitting room. Jock and Morag saying good-night. It had been sheer luck Campbell had to go down to the compound, saving her from pleading her period had started and she needed to sleep alone. He'd have thought her crazy, but it was all she could think up at such short notice.

Cat eased the door closed and returned to her place looking out into the garden, waiting. The house had that indefinable feeling of settling for the night. Somewhere a door banged. Then nothing but the gentle breath of silence.

Quickly she changed into the dark cord pants and the boots Campbell had insisted she take with her to Mount Elgon. She dragged a dark sweatshirt over her head, checking to see that the Beretta was loaded before shoving it into her belt. She looked at her watch, decided to give it until ten-thirty—five more minutes. She vibrated with tension. If only she hadn't pried open that drawer, she could have spent the night unaware, safely wrapped in Campbell's arms. Instead, she would be skulking about his home like an armed bandit.

At ten-thirty, she pushed a flashlight into the pouch of the sweatshirt, followed it with a couple of apples from the bowl of fruit Mary kept replenished, then opened the door to the hallway. Moonlight flooded through the windows in the corridor connecting Campbell's quarters to the main part of the house. She closed the door gently behind her, sped as quietly as she could on booted feet to the entry hall, glancing into the sitting room as she passed. The fire was low, the room as peaceful and lovely as his mother had left it.

Opening the front door, she slipped through, pulling it closed behind her, then took a minute to listen, hearing nothing but the sound of her own blood thumping in her ears. So far so good.

The driveway was a rocky white stream vanishing into the darkness. Without giving herself another minute to think what might be out there—her imagination had already been doing overtime—Cat plunged into the night. Above her head the wind soughed through creaking branches. Just before the curve of the driveway hid it from view, she turned to look at the sleeping house.

She still had a choice, she thought. She could go back, forget all this. Wait for Campbell to return. Make love. Go back to Nairobi tomorrow, then home to Los Angeles.

And then what? Ask herself questions for the rest of her life? Or try to live with the knowledge she had been lied to and manipulated, her time here managed? Wonder about the camp Joel had sketched, and whether he'd been killed because of it? And if a man she loved had been a party to his death?

She put her hand in her pocket, touched the Beretta. It was warm from her body. She turned back into the darkness.

Halfway down the driveway she found the break in the trees Jock had pointed out to her when they'd passed it that afternoon in the Land Rover on the way to the stable. In brilliant afternoon sunshine, the track had looked well used. But tonight, within half a dozen steps, she was lost in what felt like deep forest. All she had was a general idea of the direction she had to take. For a moment she stood still, examining the surrounding bush, reluctant to ruin her night vision by using the flashlight. Slowly, tree by tree, the forest began to take form. Not as thick as she'd imagined.

Carefully feeling her way, she moved forward, following what she thought was the track. Every other step, it seemed, enormous exposed roots caught at her feet. Occasionally, a glimpse of the moon penetrated the canopy of trees, and she watched it when she could, more for comfort than for the thin silvery light. Far off to her right, she thought she heard the rustle of a heavy body. Stalking her. She took the Beretta out of her pocket, slipped off the safety. Hands shaking, she switched on the flashlight. Like ghosts, the trunks of trees gleamed white in the beam. Nothing moved. She could hardly breathe, let alone aim and fire at whatever was there. The waterhole Campbell had shown her was miles from here. Miles. But lions, Tom had told her, traveled great distances.

She stopped, ears straining to hear every sound. All she heard was the sigh of wind high in the trees. If she was going to do what she intended, her night vision was all important, so she switched off the flashlight, waited for her eyes to adjust to the blackness around her before she continued, the gun clutched in one hand.

Then the forest ended as suddenly as it began, and she could see the stable yard and the barn where the riding horses were kept at night, separate from the bloodstock, but as safe from predators. Jock had been delighted to give her a tour of inspection when she had admired the stable before riding out early that afternoon.

Briefly, she lingered in the shadow of the trees, watching for a guard—Jock had said the area was patrolled regularly. No one seemed to be about. She slipped the safety back on the Beretta, pushed it into her pocket. It took only seconds to race across the exposed yard, slip into the barn. She left the door open to allow light from the moon to enter, hoping no one would check during the few minutes she would be inside.

Equine heads peered at her curiously from over the half doors. She made her way quickly along a line of looseboxes, stopping in front of the mare she had ridden earlier. The animal whickered gently with pleasure at the unexpected company, and Cat offered her an apple, rubbing her nose, murmuring softly. Then she lifted the mare's bridle from its peg outside the door, slipped it over her head, led her out. It took a minute to pick up the saddle she had used earlier, resting now on the saddletree by the half door, and throw it over the horse's back.

Three stalls down, she found Campbell's gelding and offered him the other apple. While he mouthed it gently, she reached for his bridle, finding only a rope halter on the peg. Alarmed, she looked at the saddletree. No saddle. This afternoon, she had re-marked on the immaculate condition of the tack. Cleaned and oiled after every use, Jock had said, replaced only when the groom finished with it. So it was bareback, she thought grimly. There was nothing else for it. She slipped on the halter, snapped on a lead rope, opened the door. The gelding followed willingly.

In the dark open doorway of the barn, she waited, listening. Satisfied the patrol was nowhere about, she led the two horses out, closed the barn door behind her, then mounted the mare. Leading the gelding, within seconds she had gained the safety of the trees.

Murmuring encouragement to the mare, she turned toward the collection of farm buildings, the roped gelding firmly in hand. The moon was high, pooling in open glades, deepening the shadows. She could sense the disquiet of the horses.

The distance seemed interminable. She was tempted to turn on the flashlight, look at her watch, but she dared not chance it. She had gone too far to risk discovery now. Then an enormous cedar loomed ahead, and she knew where she was.

At the edge of a patch of grass, she dismounted. She pressed her face against the gelding's neck, stroking him, offering up a brief plea to whoever watched over horses that the powerful smell of him would not attract the lioness she and Campbell had admired that morning. Only that morning. It seemed hardly possible. Then she tethered him to a tree.

"If all goes well, I won't be gone long," she murmured against the satin hide. "Fifteen minutes, I promise. I'll be back for you."

Quickly she remounted the mare, pulled her head around, urged her past the giant cedars into the remaining belt of trees.

A few minutes later, she was looking at the building Jock claimed was the quarantine barn.

Thirty-Seven

The building was in darkness. She could see nothing, but the men were there. She was sure of it. Suddenly at the base of the building, a red dot flowered and faded. On the periphery of her vision several more red blossoms flowered.

Cigarettes.

She remained motionless in the darkness of the trees. The soft murmur of voices reached her. A man stepped into the moonlight, an AK over one shoulder. He strolled toward the end of the barn, casually, expecting no trouble.

Now or never, Cat thought. Do it. Breathing an apology, she slammed her heels hard into the mare's flanks, simultaneously jerking back on the bit. Startled, the mare reared, fighting the conflicting signals. Cat loosened the reins, pulling the horse's head around, slamming her heels repeatedly into the animal's flanks. The mare raised her voice in protest. Unnerved, she reared and plunged, squealing in outrage.

The noise carried through the silence. The men called to each other in alarm. Cat couldn't understand the language, but hoped the message she intended was being received. *Simba.* Lions. Attacking one of Jock's straying, prized, blooded broodmares. To ram the message home, she fought the mare, causing her to wheel and plunge, creating enough noise to convince the men a major disaster was in progress right under their noses.

Calling back and forth, men ran to investigate. Cat waited until they were well clear of the barn, then jumped free from the kicking animal and threw the reins securely over the limb of a tree to prevent the mare from actually escaping into the maw of a lion.

Avoiding the men running toward her, their voices raised in anxious questions and answers, weapons at the ready, Cat raced through the trees. Any moment, she expected to hear the crash of gunfire, feel the impact of a bullet. She kept to the trees until she was as close to the barn as she was going to get, then dashed across the open clearing in front of the great double doors. Hands stiff and shaking, she fumbled to open them. They were locked. Panicked, she ran her hands over the door. She knew there was a way—she had seen it earlier. A small judas gate cut into one of the doors. She found it, wrenched it open, stepped inside the barn.

She dared stay only seconds. Swiftly she took out the flashlight, switched it on, played the beam across the interior. Elephant tusks. Rows and rows of tusks piled tidily on each other like corpses, disappearing into the deep gloom of the barn. She was looking at the madness of human greed, the reason for the insane slaughter of a species. Ivory. Hundreds of elephants had been killed for this cache alone. Maybe thousands. She couldn't tell. Didn't want to know. The place smelled like a charnel house. But perhaps that was in her mind?

Vomit caught in her throat, and she swallowed, praying for control. Later, she could throw up. Now there was no time. She switched off the flashlight, stepped back through the judas gate into the night, gulped great breaths of sweet air.

Fear gave her legs strength. She could hear the men——it sounded as if they had found the tethered mare and were fanning through the woods. She tore back to the refuge of the trees, making her way toward where she had left the gelding, too frightened to think about what else might be hunting in the darkness. The men behind her were the predators to worry about.

The gelding was where she had left him, dancing about nervously, pulling at the head rope. Forcing herself to be calm, she spoke soothingly as she untethered him, then, praying he would stand still for it, she jumped onto his bare back. He snorted and tossed his head, then settled down, taking comfort from his human burden. Cat turned his head toward the stable. The gelding needed no urging. He knew he was going home, back to his safe stall, out of the dangerous darkness.

Cat gripped the horse with her knees, keeping low to avoid being swept off by the limbs of trees. Branches tore at her clothes, caught in the band holding her hair in a ponytail, tearing it free. Hair whipped around her eyes. They reached an open area, and the gelding stretched into a gallop. The voices had faded, but still she was unsure whether her trail had been picked up. From experience, she knew Moses and Sambeke could keep up a tireless, silent pace through the bush.

By the time she reached the stable yard her heart had steadied. A grim exhilaration fizzed in her blood. At least one of the questions had been answered. Again, she lingered warily in the trees to watch for a patrol before riding into the open. She dismounted, led the gelding inside to his stall.

With the occasional flick of the carefully shielded flashlight to pick out the way, the return to the house seemed shorter than the journey out. The house still slumbered, no lights, no alarm raised.

When the front door closed behind her, she had been gone less than an hour.

On the other side of the hall, light seeped from beneath the door of the office. She crossed to it, listened, ear pressed against the wood. Hearing nothing, she turned the knob.

The computer screen was dark, but the desk lamp was on, picking up the gold tooling around the edge of the green leather desktop, reflecting off decanters and glasses on a table. The fire had been made up and was blazing merrily. The room was warm and inviting. Waiting for someone.

Quickly, Cat tiptoed to her own room, retrieved the photograph of Joel and N'toya, Campbell and Tom M'Bala looking into the camera, Tom's arm across the shoulder of the stranger, and returned to the office. She smoothed the picture flat on the desk, studying Joel's face. He wore a smile, but it looked as if it took effort to keep it in place. Perhaps, though, she was reading more into that than there was. Arms folded, she perched on the edge of the desk and prepared to wait.

Not for long. She heard a Land Rover stop outside. A moment later the door of the office opened. Stephen N'toya entered, his head turned away, speaking softly to Campbell behind him.

In shock, Campbell stared at her over N'toya's shoulder. It felt like a moment stretching forever—N'toya's mouth moving, Cat's wide eyes blazing in a dirt-streaked face, her glorious hair unbound, carelessly pushed back.

He recovered quickly. "Cat! What the devil are you doing here?"

"Hi," she said. "How are you doing, Stephen? I'm glad I waited up. I would have hated to miss you. You are one hell of a difficult man to reach. Even your friends don't seem to know you."

Campbell crossed the room, looked down at the desk drawer.

She followed his gaze. "I didn't have to jimmy it open. I found the key. And I've seen the photographs." She turned her eyes to the door. "How are you, Tom?"

"Cat." Tom M'Bala closed the door behind him. Arms folded, he leaned against a wall.

"Well, the gang's all here, so I guess it's a good time for a chat. Correction. The gang's not quite all here." She reached behind her, picked up the photograph, pretended to study it. "You three are here. Joel, of course, is dead. That leaves one unaccounted for." She looked up. "Looks like a relative of yours, Tom. A brother?"

She held the picture out to him, but Tom did not look at it, or make a move to take it from her.

In the silence, the peal of the phone seemed inordinately loud. Campbell picked it up. "Campbell."

"*Bwana,* a horse has been found in front of the ivory barn," Moses's voice said.

"A horse?" Campbell said, incredulous.

"I had a little moonlight ride," Cat said. "Over to the barn where the ivory is stored." Quickly, she added, "I called Father Gaston to tell him about it. He knows I'm here. He's going to the authorities."

"I think not, Cat," Stephen N'toya said gently.

"Don't bank on it, Stephen. If anything happens to me, if I don't return to Nairobi tomorrow, Father Gaston will be paying a visit to the American embassy."

N'toya showed perfect white teeth in what passed for a smile and shrugged. "Well, if you insist."

Campbell hung up the phone. "Christ, Cat! Couldn't you let well enough alone?"

"Is the mare okay?"

"Yes. The men thought she was being attacked by a lion."

Cat just stared at him.

"Very clever," Campbell said, and she shrugged. "So now you know more than you should," he said. "I wish you had taken my word——"

"Oh, Campbell, please! Enough bullshit. I saw the ivory. I've heard the lies." She kept her eyes on him. "Now it's time for a little truth, don't you think?"

"Now is the time to keep silent," N'toya said in Swahili. "To tell her anything will jeopardize all that we've done——"

In English, Campbell said, "Stephen, this has to stop. She has to be told the truth."

Stephen answered in Swahili. "Too much is at stake."

Campbell answered in the same language. "What? In a few days, she will be back in Los Angeles where she belongs. Nothing's at stake." Nothing for N'toya, anyway. Tom had already paid his price. And his own, Campbell thought, would be paid bit by bit for the rest of his life without her.

"She can still be dangerous," Stephen insisted.

"Christ, Stephen," Campbell said wearily. "What the hell is the risk? Your political future if it comes out we've been stealing ivory? That's no worry. The end will justify the means, just as it always does in politics."

"What if she does go to the Americans? They will demand we reopen an investigation. It's been done in the past—you remember the English? The girl killed by game wardens? They didn't let it rest."

"Hardly the same thing. She will not go to the authorities."

"No, *n'duga,* I'll make sure of that." N'toya switched to English and said to Cat, "Joel killed two men. He was responsible for the deaths of several others——"

Cat reached behind her, felt for the desk to steady herself. "I don't believe you——"

Stephen's voice rode over her protest. "...and for the escape of Reitholder from custody. That is the truth you have been seeking."

"Stephen, for Christ's sake!" Campbell said. He picked up a decanter, splashed brandy into a glass, put an arm around her and held it to her lips. Over her head, he looked at N'toya. "You sorry bastard. What was the point of that?"

Cat pushed the glass away. *"What is he talking about?"*

"The night Joel died," Campbell answered.

"Not quite," N'toya said. "You want her to know. Do it, or I will."

Campbell hesitated, glanced briefly at Tom, then said, "All right. The ivory in the barn was taken initially by poachers. Then my men and I took it from them. Tom, Moses, Sambeke, Thomas, Olentwalla, others you don't know. Zama, some of the people at the compound." He stopped her from interrupting. "It's true, we do operate outside the law, but not entirely without an official brief. We're a commando, to use the old Boer term. We're highly mobile and our job is to go after poachers, engage them whenever and wherever we can. The ivory trade is worth millions. It's like the drug trade—ministers paid off by poachers, the army corrupted." Campbell paused, looked again at Tom. Tom's face showed nothing of what he was feeling, and Campbell went on. "You won't find our names on any government payroll. We answer to only one man, the head of the Kenya Wildlife Service, and through him, to the president of Kenya. Stephen here is the liaison between us."

"I don't care about all that," Cat said. "Tell me what you mean about my brother."

"Cat, if you understand the framework—"

Stephen N'toya interrupted impatiently. "You wanted to know, so listen. We know the South African military is deeply implicated in the poaching of ivory and skins in East Africa. The Afrikaners fuel corruption, destroy our resources, funnel the cash from the sale of the ivory to political organizations—right or left, they don't discriminate as long as they destabilize the chosen country. What we

need is proof that will hold up. Proof that links the Afrikaner Broederhood with the political underground working to destabilize *this*
country. When we get it, we will take it to a court of law."

Cat held his eyes. "None of this makes my brother a murderer.
How could you say that? He was never involved in anything like
that. What would he know of Afrikaners?"

N'toya started to answer but Campbell raised a hand to silence
him. Then he said flatly, "We involved Joel by using his safari as a
cover to track smuggling routes."

The crackle of the fire was suddenly the only sound in the room.

"Did Joel know that?" Cat asked finally.

"No. I planned the route to take us where we needed to go. I
showed him sites on the way."

She stared at him. "What are you saying?" She spoke slowly.
"You're telling me that you really were responsible for his death."
She looked at Tom, leaning motionless against the wall by the
door. "And you, Tom. You, too. Why don't you say something?"

Campbell picked up the decanter, poured brandy into a glass,
put the glass down without drinking. He could not bear to look
at Tom's face again. This was getting too close. . . .

Cat wanted to scream: Joel wouldn't kill anyone. But he would,
she thought. Oh, yes. Pushed hard enough, he would.

"What happened?" she forced herself to ask. "What made him
do. . . what you say he did?"

Cat shifted her eyes from man to man. Tom looked as if his
world had narrowed to the patch of floor just in front of his boots.

"Tom?" she said.

Campbell did not give him a chance to answer. He said, "We
came across evidence of recent poaching activity. You've seen it,
you know how it is. What we saw was worse. Your brother was

pretty upset by it. The next afternoon we ran smack into Reitholder and about twenty men." He stopped. "Jesus Christ, you don't want to hear this."

"I do. Tell me," Cat insisted.

"They'd taken down an entire herd with machine guns," Campbell said harshly. "They were still hacking off tusks, but several of the elephants were not yet dead. Reitholder was laughing, watching them—"

Cat put both hands to her ears. "My God, what are you saying?"

"You have to understand what happened, Cat," Campbell went on. "Joel had been under a strain for days, he looked terrible, wasn't sleeping or eating. Maybe it was the extent of the slaughter we'd seen. He'd taken a lot of pictures—really grim stuff. You've seen them. We're used to this kind of life, we don't talk about it afterward." Campbell ran a hand across his mouth. He was sweating. "At the time, it seemed the best thing to do was to let him alone. Maybe that was a mistake. It turned out, he was more affected by it than I realized."

He must have found the terrorist camp around that time, Cat thought, horrified. "I saw a terrorist's poaching camp that he'd seen," she said. "I recognized it from the sketches he sent me. They arrived weeks after his funeral." She looked at Campbell. "I told you about the sketches, but I didn't tell you I'd found the place. It's close to Maasai Springs."

She thought of the pile of dead lion cubs she'd seen at that terrible camp on the escarpment. The drying racks. The bloody tusks. What that would have done to him. "If it was like the camp I saw with you, he must have been..." She stopped, and the men waited. She felt crowded by the sheer physical presence of them. They stood, watching her. Even Tom had his eyes on her now.

To get over the moment of terror, she told them about the papers printed in Chinese blowing across the bare ground. The scraps of rope like that used by Reitholder to bind tusks.

N'toya gave a dismissive grunt. "Too bad Joel chose not to mention all this. We could have told him something to reassure him. The fact is that we knew about that camp. We'd had an eye on it for months, hoping General Francis would show up there in person. He never did, unfortunately. So our people—" he gestured at Tom and Campbell "—attacked it and it was dismantled. Just about the time you arrived in Nairobi, as a matter of fact. What you found was the skeleton."

Joel didn't tell them because he knew he couldn't trust anyone, Cat thought. He must have been so alone.

N'toya was looking at her with something like sympathy. "I regret we had to deceive him, Cat. I met him the night before he left Nairobi. He hadn't changed much. We sat up late, and I told him I'd join him for part of his safari so we could take pictures like we used to in our college days. He never questioned it."

"You've made some terrible accusations against my brother," she said to him. "But you still haven't told me what happened."

N'toya started to answer, but Campbell cut in. "Your brother was a brave man," Campbell said carefully. "When we came across Reitholder, I couldn't just let the bastard go on, it was too good a chance to put him away. But we were outgunned. Suddenly Joel became a different man. Completely rational, cold, businesslike, clear about what needed to be done. He insisted on taking part. He proved he could handle weapons, so..." Campbell shrugged. "We needed the help. I armed him and told him to watch our backs. He took orders, carried them out without argument. The trouble started when it was over. He wanted Reitholder executed, right there in the field. Unfortunately, there were political implications I couldn't tell him about. We took Reitholder alive because we can prove he is a serving military officer, a colonel in the army of South Africa, part of a secret cabal. I ordered Joel to turn in the weapon he'd been issued and he refused. He had to be disarmed. He didn't make it easy."

Stephen N'toya said, "He shot and killed two men."

Cat looked at Campbell. Her lover. She felt sick and weak. "So you shot him."

"No," Campbell replied. "Of course not. I had him bound and roped to the wheel of a Land Rover. But when the watch was changed at 2:00 a.m., three guards were found with their throats cut—"

"No. No. No. Joel did not…" Cat started to shake her head, back and forth, back and forth, trying to eradicate the image. "He did not do that—"

Quickly, Campbell broke in. "No. No, Cat, listen. Joel was not there. He was gone. Reitholder had taken him as a hostage. We followed their tracks. Unfortunately, we found his body the next day, well into Tanzania." He picked up one of her hands. "Reitholder had shot him," he said gently.

Cat remembered the vultures she had seen circling above the kills, the bones picked clean, the scavengers scurrying away with what was left until no trace remained. She thought of the ugly gray metal carrying case containing Joel's plain wooden coffin being lowered from the 747. Had his body really been in there? She couldn't ask…couldn't speak. Stricken, she stared at Campbell.

"Your brother's blood was avenged." The voice was Tom's, but deep and harsh, torn from his chest.

"Tom," Campbell said warningly. "There is no need for any more. It is enough."

Tom ignored him. "We found the knife used to slice through the ropes and the throats of the guards. It was in the possession of the fifth man in the picture you saw. And we found money, also. A great deal of money. You are right. That was my brother in the photograph. He dishonored his people and himself. He dishonored me. It was he who took a bribe from the Afrikaner. He cut the throats of men who trusted him. So I killed him. I killed him in the ancient manner of our mother's people."

"Tom, that's enough," Campbell said.

Tom's face was gray, beaded with sweat. He spoke only to Cat. "No one dared interfere with what I had to do. I was heavily armed."

Campbell was staring at the floor. Cat looked uncertainly at Stephen N'toya. He gazed back impassively.

"I took him into the bush," Tom said, "and I killed him by tearing out his heart with my hands. Then I threw his body to the hyenas."

Cat leaned her forehead on one hand. In her mind she could see how it must have been—Tom threatening the circle of men to keep back, the flickering light playing across their faces as he dragged his brother into the darkness, away from the watch fire. She could hear the screams.

"Your brother's blood was avenged," Tom said again. "His spirit is appeased."

Cat could say nothing. She couldn't nod. Couldn't acknowledge his words. Her body was numb.

Campbell broke a long silence. "Blood money was paid to the families of the men killed. It is the traditional way, and they were satisfied. All of the deaths were attributed to poaching activity. Joel, as an American, was reported as being trampled to death by buffalo. Stephen's presence was not mentioned."

"This is politically sensitive, I think you can see that," Stephen said. "No charges can be brought in connection with Joel's death. I'm deeply sorry. Joel was my friend. But I hope you understand that there can be no further investigation." He paused, then said, "I am sure you don't want Joel branded as a killer."

She looked at him numbly. "I don't need that warning from you."

The sound of the telephone tearing through the room was a relief.

Thirty-Eight

Campbell grabbed up the phone, barked his name.

"We are under attack," Moses yelled. Behind the voice, Campbell heard the grind of machinery, the rattle of gunfire.

"What's their strength?" he asked urgently, but the line was already dead.

He banged the receiver down. "The barn's under attack. Tom, rouse the men at the compound." He crossed the room, wrenched open a gun cupboard, took an AK from the rack inside, tossed it to Tom as he spoke. "Stephen, get Jock, tell him to come armed. Tell him I don't know who it is or their strength. The line's been cut." He slammed a couple of AKs and extra clips on the desk, shoved ammunition in his pockets. He started toward the door.

"It's Reitholder," said Stephen, following. "Francis is there, too. This brought him out, I knew it would. It's the chance we've been waiting for, see if this bastard is who we think he is. I don't know their strength. I thought I had time to find that out, another week, ten days." His eyes glittered with excitement. "But we've got them.

We've got them together. It's what we've been waiting for. I knew they'd come for it."

Campbell and Tom were already at the front door. Campbell turned. "What the hell are you talking about?"

"My people found out that Reitholder is being recalled to Johannesburg. This was the only way. I dropped a word about our ivory into the right ear and——"

Campbell did not let him finish. "You brought a gang of murderous thugs down on Erukenya? On Erukenya? On Cat and Morag and Mary?"

"I didn't think they'd attack so soon. That's what I'm here to warn you so you would be ready for them."

"You lethal bastard!"

Swiftly, Tom moved between the two men. He shoved an AK into Stephen's hands. "Take this. You're going to need it."

Campbell threw a glance at Cat, saw the AK in her hand. "Good. Let's hope you won't need it. Go rouse the household. N'kosi will know what to do. Stay with him."

Jock raced from the interior of the house, rifle in hand, pistol thrust into his belt, his jacket weighed down with ammunition. Campbell did not waste time on explanations. He knew his father didn't need to be told what was happening.

"Don't worry about the compound," Jock said quickly. "I'll take care of the ammunition, send up reinforcements. You get to the barn. N'kosi's got Morag and Mary safe. You go with them, Cat. N'kosi knows what to do here."

"Good, Jock. Right," Campbell said. "Send Aaron with four men to me at the cedar grove south of the barn. You come in from the north with Zama and his people. Then move west, toward the main doors. We'll come up from the south. We'll hold them between us."

Jock waved, disappeared into the darkness. Campbell got behind the wheel of the Land Rover in front of the house, Tom and Stephen hard behind him. The vehicle was already moving when Cat hurled herself into the back seat. N'toya grabbed her shirt, hauled her in as the vehicle rocketed down the drive.

Campbell stood on the brake. "Cat, get back to the house."

"I'm coming with you."

Campbell jumped out, jerked the door open, reached to drag her out. Cat fumbled in the pouch of her sweatshirt. The crump of a heavy-caliber weapon came from the barn, and Tom got himself behind the wheel, threw the Land Rover into gear, started it moving. For a breath of time, Campbell looked at a pistol wavering in Cat's hand, then at her eyes. The pistol wavered uncertainly, but her wide eyes were steady.

"Dan! Come on!" The vehicle moved faster. Campbell slammed Cat's door, ran to the passenger seat, jumped in as Tom floored the gas.

"It can't go wrong!" N'toya raised an excited voice to be heard above the engine. "They've broken cover. Reitholder's out there with Francis because I told them. We flushed them. They've come after our ivory. I knew they would. We've got them."

Tom skidded to a stop in a thicket of trees. Campbell was out of the Land Rover before it halted. Over his shoulder, he yelled at Cat. "Stay with the Land Rover." He thought for once she'd have the sense to do as he said. The night was filled with confusion and noise—shouting men, the whine of engines, the crack of gunfire. "For God's sake, Cat. Keep down."

An assortment of battered trucks—pickups, vans, panel trucks, matatus—ground over the white-rock road, past the farm buildings. Innocent business names, untraceable and bogus, decorated the door panels: Singh Bros. Electricals; Nairobi Sweet Spice Co.;

Victoria Falls Carpet Co. Headlights blazed. After the first round had been fired from the barn, Reitholder had abandoned all attempts at stealth and gave the order to switch them on.

The operation had started with bad luck. The Thika Coffee and Tea Co. van drove into the barn's lot, the driver scratching his head in puzzlement, rolling down the window to ask directions to the main house. Instead of exchanging pleasantries, a bit of gossip, giving the men in the back a chance to slip out, garrotes in hand, Campbell's Maasai had opened fire, killing the driver and the men in the back before retreating inside the barn.

Men he needed for loading ivory. And now he had one fucking truck out of commission.

The night's work was not going to be easy.

Ignoring the firefight around them, Reitholder kept the trucks moving into the barn clearing. Now that they'd lost the element of surprise, there was only one way into that barn.

"Moshi!" he shouted to his boss *kaffir*. "Take over here. Keep them moving, get them under as much cover as you can. But keep them away from the barn doors, we can't afford to lose any more of them."

General Francis ran across the clearing. "Colonel, get the trucks closer," he shouted. "They don't have a field of fire from inside. Their reinforcements won't chance blasting the trucks if they're close to the building—"

"What reinforcements? You said no one would be up here—"

"We don't know that for sure."

"We're going to take that building from the roof, man," Reitholder shouted. "You're going to have a chance to use one of those toys we bought you. Make a nice big hole."

"Colonel, that's foolhardy—"

"Don't fuck with me," Reitholder shouted. "That barn's tighter than a virgin's arsehole. We can't blast those doors open without

blowing the fucking ivory to kingdom come. Get your man in position. Aim at the ridge line. Be sure nothing gets inside to blow
the tusks."

General Francis hesitated. Reitholder grabbed him. The operation had been planned down to the last minute. Surprise the Maasai, cut the lines, overpower the guards at the barn, load the
trucks, get out before anyone at the house knew they'd been there,
disperse, make their way singly to the collection point in Mombasa. Several trucks carried extra gasoline to enable them to take
circuitous routes.

Plan B had been to blast their way in.

Francis nodded, ran back down the line of trucks to give the order.

Cat stumbled through the trees. She was alone, Stephen gone,
Tom and Campbell lost in the smoke. Someone grabbed her,
pulled her to the ground. She brought up the AK, struggling to
turn to face her assailant.

"Where do you think you're going?" Campbell pushed the barrel of her AK away from him. "Why didn't you stay where you
were, for God's sake."

"I'm just trying to keep up," she hissed. "What are you going to
do?"

Beyond Campbell, Tom crouched against a boulder, Stephen beside him. Other men, four or five, knelt among the rocks. They
didn't look at her, their eyes locked on the barn. They were on the
far side of the building from where she'd been earlier that night.

"We are going to take Reitholder and this bloody general alive,
and hope the rest will run," Campbell said. "It's our best shot. We
don't have enough men to take them all. Jock is coming up on the
other side with Zama and his men." He pulled her toward him,
his arms close. "If you don't stay down, you could get caught in

the crossfire. You understand? You must stay here, in this spot so that we know where you are. I can't protect you—"

"I don't need you to protect me. No one has to protect me."

Tom nudged Campbell's arm. From beyond the barn, a flare burst skyward, throwing a brief, eerie artificial daylight over the scene.

"Tom." Campbell pointed. "Simba Heavy Equipment. Dead center. Tell Aaron and his men cover us. Kill anything that moves in those trucks. We'll make as much noise as we can when we break. The bastards have to think we're an army."

Tom turned to the men behind him, spoke in Swahili. They got to their feet.

"Jock's in position. Tom and I are going after the white lorry. Stay here." Campbell turned Cat's face toward him, put his lips against hers. "I love you. You know that, don't you?"

Cat heard the words through the noise of weapon fire. He loved her? Yesterday it would have meant everything. Now they were just words he used.

"Go!" Campbell yelled.

Howling like the hounds from hell, men burst from the trees. In the harsh light of the flare, panic stained the faces of Reitholder's men turning to meet them. Campbell and Tom raced across the open ground, firing at the heavy truck.

Then a force of energy surged through the air, sucking breath from fragile human lungs. Trees tossed like maddened mops as an explosion rocked the landscape and flames shot into the night sky. Evil-smelling smoke rolled through the woodland. The truck disintegrated. Flaming figures staggered through the metal frame of what had been the rear doors, threw themselves down, rolled frantically in the dust. Their screams escalated into high, thin, inhuman shrieks.

The small judas gate in the doors of the barn slammed open. A burst of fire sprayed over the jerking bodies, mercifully silencing them.

Reitholder ran forward, AK spitting. "It's open," he shouted. "Take the fucking door. It's open—"

Firing a fusillade to rip open the wide blank doors, half a dozen of his men charged toward the barn, into a storm of answering fire from more of Campbell's people, hidden low against the wall of the building, waiting for them. Men dropped, screaming.

"Come on," Reitholder shouted. His *kaffirs* were breaking. The bastards were turning back. "Come on. Take it." But he was alone, the survivors crawling toward the cover of the trucks waiting on the perimeter of the clearing.

He tore after them, grabbed an arm to drag a bleeding man upright. "Get on your feet," he yelled in Swahili. "There's enough ivory in there to make you rich. We'll take it from the roof. Get ready."

A few men, five, six, came forward, the rest, hunched between the trucks, stayed where they were. Reitholder stared around him. Where the fuck was that black bastard Moshi?

The operation had turned into chaos. Gunfire came from every direction. From inside the barn. From reinforcements outside. From the north and south. It had turned into a rout. Where was Francis? The fucking *kaffirs* had lost their balls. Only Francis's men, politicals, would do it now. Fanatics, all of them.

Half a football field away, Tom pointed at the running, yellow-haired figure. Campbell nodded and yelled, "I'll take him. Find Francis."

Tom veered off at a run. Campbell raced along the edge of the trees, firing short bursts to prevent Reitholder from crossing the line of trucks. If he got into the trees, he could slip away. The urge to kill him throbbed in Campbell's veins like a fever. It took all he had to aim low, not to blow the bastard to kingdom come. Then Reitholder changed direction and was lost behind the corner of the building.

Adrenaline pumped through General Francis's veins. Not fear. Never that. As usual in action, he felt only the rightness of his mission. The stink of burning fuel was sweet in his nostrils, the screams of men, the explosions, the chatter of bullets, all were the music of revolution. Tonight was a minor skirmish.

Francis tapped the shoulder of the man kneeling beside him. The man steadied the rocket launcher on his shoulder.

The smell of charred flesh and burning fuel filled Cat's nostrils. An explosion knocked her to the earth. Then another. Minutes passed before she was able to force her way through the thick underbrush to the edge of the treeline.

Sixty feet away, a tall, slim camouflaged-clad figure was framed by the flames of a burning truck, his voice inaudible above the roar of gunfire, the crackle of flames. He ran a hand through a mane of iron-gray hair in a familiar gesture, then turned. She saw his face, the Roman collar beneath his battle fatigues. Dazed, almost disembodied with shock, she sat back on her heels, muscles slack, uncontrollable tremors shaking her body.

Father Gaston raised a hand, the white cylinder of a cigarette plain between his fingers. In a sharp motion, he brought the hand down. Another edge of the roof fragmented and he nodded, patted the shoulder of the skinny man kneeling beside him, the rocket launcher on his shoulder.

Isaac. The gardener. The beggar.

* * *

Campbell broke from the trees, charged after Reitholder, through the line of trucks, across the open yard. A rain of bullets followed him. Zigzagging, jumping the bodies littering the clearing, he reached the cover of the barn, crouched against the wall, searching for the Afrikaner through the smoke. Then above his head, the corner roofline of the building fragmented, debris exploding like giant, deadly hailstones. He ducked. Splintered wood thudded into his back. He leaned against the building, trying to pinpoint the source of the attack. He caught a glimpse of Tom, Aaron at his heels, racing toward the sound, east of the building. He could see Tom's open mouth, knew he was roaring threats, knew, too, they could take care of it. His job was Reitholder. Another blast shook the structure, and beams hurtled through the air like matchsticks.

A strange metallic taste was in her mouth. Joel had told her nothing was as it seemed. Why hadn't she understood? *Nothing* was as it seemed. Numbness gave way. The tremors subsided into relentless shivering. Another rocket smashed into the roof. Father Gaston was blasting his way into the barn.

Cat looked at the AK in her hand.

Reitholder wanted to scream. Smash. Kill. It was over. Gunfire swept the clearing, scythed through the men, turned trucks into torches. Only one thing was left. He charged toward a truck with an extra petrol tank and found Moshi behind the wheel.

"Get out," he screamed. "Get out of there." He pulled open the door, dragged the skinny body out. "Fire the fucking barn."

Moshi stared at him, terrified. Reitholder struck him across the mouth. "You hear me, you black bastard. Fire the fucking barn. Burn the ivory."

Moshi raised his Uzi, smashed the butt against Reitholder's shoulder. Pain shot through his arm, his weapon dropped from numbed fingers. Screaming in an incoherent mixture of Afrikaans, Swahili, English, Reitholder lunged forward to grab the black throat. He could smell the blood he wanted.

Moshi raised his Uzi, finger curled around the trigger. He hesitated, then he smashed Reitholder's shoulder again. He stepped back, turned, faded like smoke into the trees.

Reitholder hurled himself behind the wheel of the truck, slammed into gear, wrenched at the wheel, shoved his foot down. The truck gathered speed, roaring toward the barn. He jumped before impact, rolled to his feet in a run. The truck smashed through the double doors of the barn. Walls bulged as gas tanks exploded. The roof lifted. Fire grabbed the wood, roared through the building.

She'd jumped straight into the arms of the devil, Cat realized, taken in by lies wrapped in the trappings of a cassock, a Roman collar, kind words about Joel.

A long, brutal, eardrum-shattering burst of gunfire erupted, then stopped. For a moment she thought silence had been restored, then shouts and gunfire began to penetrate the echoing emptiness in her head.

Gagging on great sobbing gulps of the foul air, Cat pressed her face into the earth. Then she scrambled to her feet, jerked the safety off the AK and crashed through the brush.

Almost dizzy with relief, she saw Tom M'Bala swing his AK toward her.

"It's me," she shouted. "Cat."

Tom turned the weapon back to cover Gaston kneeling in front of him. The rocket man, gardener, beggar was spread-eagled, his life's blood spurting in great arcs from the bullet wound in his neck.

"At least let me tend to him," Gaston shouted. He reached toward the dying man.

Tom shoved him back with the AK. The gardener's legs drummed convulsively in his death spasm. Gradually the drumming lessened, then ceased. Lips moving in prayer, Gaston made the sign of the cross in the direction of the body.

In a crouch, Stephen N'toya ran across the smoke-filled clearing. Exultant, he yelled, "Where's Reitholder? Don't let him get away!"

"Dan's after him," Tom shouted. "He can't get away. Jock's at the road with Zama." A spray of bullets cut through his words. With a shriek of splintering wood, the tops of trees crashed to the ground, air whining through falling branches. "Get back," he yelled to Cat. "It's not over."

Still kneeling, Gaston twisted, looking behind him to stare into her face. *"Mademoiselle."* He nodded as if they were meeting for tea at his church in Nairobi. Then he shrugged in his curiously Gallic way, managing to encompass the burning van lighting up the half-wrecked barn, the running men, the bullet-riddled trucks careening toward the narrow roadway. "This is a dangerous place you find yourself in. Do as our friend here asks."

"You never knew Joel, did you?"

Gaston shook his head.

"Then why the playacting?"

"My regrets. We did not know what he had told you about the camp in the hills. He thought no one knew that he had been there. But we knew. As our friend here knows, our ears and eyes are everywhere. As it turned out, it did not matter." He shrugged again. "The camp was attacked."

"Nyamaza!" Tom's finger tightened on the trigger.

N'toya jumped forward, jamming his own AK against Gaston's ear. "Get after Reitholder," he said urgently to Tom. "I'll take over here."

"If he moves, shoot him,"Tom shouted. He raced toward a Toyota pickup careening in the direction of the roadway, fired directly into the windshield. The vehicle veered off, crashing into the side of the barn. The screech of a stuck horn added to the din.

An explosion rocked the south side of the barn. Flames shot into the air, crept along the line of the roof, eating at the wood, consuming the structure and its contents.

"Well, all for nothing, I see," Francis said. He laughed. From beneath half-lidded eyes, he studied N'toya. There had to be a way to turn this situation around. It was useless to waste regrets on the lost ivory. Elephants were still out there, younger, their tusks smaller, but still useful. Until the last of them were gone, the great beasts would continue to be what they always had been—the resource that drove the engines of war in Africa. Cash for recruitment, training, arms. The need was as acute as it had been since he'd heard the call of Marxism as a young activist priest in the Congo.

Testing the limit of N'toya's resolve, Francis rose to his feet. He felt safe enough. He'd guess this man did not have the belly for a killing. He reached into his pocket.

"Stop!"

"A cigarette," Gaston said calmly. "A last smoke is permitted?"

"Get back on your—" N'toya did not finish the sentence. Gaston's hand emerged from his pocket holding a tiny handgun. He raised it. N'toya fired a burst from the AK.

Instinctively, Cat jumped backward, away from the bombardment of sound. Then her scream died, strangled by an arm tightening around her throat. She struggled to keep her feet. She could smell the sweat, the same foul breath she'd smelled before.

She knew who it was.

Thirty-Nine

Campbell choked on searing black smoke that was thick with the stink of burning ivory.

Screams rose from men falling in the deadly crossfire, caught between Jock and Zama at the road, Aaron on the north side of the barn, Moses and Sambeke, the rest of the Maasai outside the fired barn.

He thought like the man he was hunting—and knew. Reitholder would make for the east, the only way open, then swing south through the cedar forest. And that way, he would stumble across the Land Rover. Even without it, in that direction lay the house. Hostages. The wild slopes of Mount Kenya.

Campbell started running across the open fire-filled clearing. The group of figures appeared through the flaming, smoky chaos.

N'toya, the priest on his knees in front of him. General Francis. It didn't matter. All he could see was the yellow head pressed against Cat's, the pistol at her temple, her precious body pulled across the Afrikaner, shielding him.

Reitholder was going to drag her into the trees, to the Land Rover. She was the hostage he needed.

A head shot, Campbell thought. Sudden, without warning. If Reitholder had even an instant's suspicion Campbell had him in his sights, the bastard would take his last pleasure on this earth by killing her first.

Campbell took in the orange glow from the burning barn, the roiling black smoke, the sudden bursts of flame shooting into the black night, the erratic play of light and shadow. And the Afrikaner's head, as close to Cat's as if it was part of her body.

Reitholder slammed the Beretta against Cat's ear. He jerked her back, braced against her weight as her feet went from under her. She struggled for purchase but she was helpless, upright only because of his arm across her throat, forcing her head back. She tore at his arm with both hands, gouging his flesh. He tapped the Beretta against her skull. She had slipped away before, but now she was a gift from God.

"Struggle, missy, and I end it now. Stay quiet, and maybe you live."

"Reitholder, you're making it worse," N'toya shouted.

Reitholder ignored him. He dragged her backward, toward the haven of the trees. "You have a Land Rover." He loosened his hold to allow her to speak. "Where?"

Cat tried to swallow. He intended to kill her. This was the same terror that Joel had felt, at the hands of the same man. She'd get the same fate, a bullet in the head. She could not answer. Her throat was closed with terror, with the smoke from the blazing barn, the stink of charred flesh and burning elephant tusks.

"Where is it?" Reitholder shoved the gun hard under her chin. "The Land Rover. No heroics, missy."

"Reitholder, let her go." Stephen N'toya looked at Gaston, on his knees, blood oozing from between the fingers clutching his right arm. Stephen took a breath, spoke through his teeth as if unwilling to let the words escape him. "Let her go, and you can take him with you."

"Kill him, *kaffir*. Save me the trouble."

Reitholder tightened his arm around Cat's throat, dragging her backward. One of his arms was weak as if he'd been injured.

Cat fought to keep her feet. Then a sudden eruption of gunfire deafened her. Bullets exploded among the trees—survivors firing as they tried to escape that way. She couldn't let him drag her into the trees. She'd be finished.

Now. She had to make a move.

She jerked as if shot, then slumped heavily against the weak arm, every muscle loosened, making her body a dead weight.

Reitholder grunted, struggled to maintain his hold on her sagging body. "Get up!" He tried to drag her upright. "You bitch! Get up!" For an instant, he released his hold to try for a better purchase.

It was all she needed. Cat twisted from his grasp. She could hear Campbell's voice shouting at her to get away. She aimed a kick at Reitholder's genitals, felt the solid connection of her booted foot. He doubled, grunting in agony. She grabbed the Beretta from his hand.

Aimed.

Fired.

A cloud of brain tissue erupted. The Afrikaner's torso pitched forward.

For an instant, savage joy swept through her. Joel...Joel. Her mind screamed his name. Then she opened her fingers, jerked her hand back and released the Beretta from her grasp as if tossing away something unclean.

In the second before she tightened her finger on the trigger, her father's face had melted into Reitholder's, covering it like a death mask.

Forty

"That's it, then." Doug Jones threw down his pencil, leaned back, stretched and grinned at her. "We'll knock 'em cold."

Cat swiveled in her chair, stared out into the coral trees on San Vicente Boulevard. Still November, yet some of the trees were already budding. Soon they would be covered in the flaming color for which they were famous, the red flowers massed on bare branches almost the exact shade of an elephant's hide, no leaves to soften the contrast. She liked that.

"Guitterrez just got back from Thailand," she said. "He may have found something they'll like better. But if they decide to go for Africa, I think they'll go for Maasai Springs."

"I don't know. What about these others?" Doug sorted rapidly through the original drawings covering her side of the ebony partner's desk. "These are staggering. This place is a primo site."

Slides of the sketches were part of her upcoming video presentation, but copies had been made and bound into separate proposal folders, together with the photographs she had taken. The folders would be placed in front of each of the five men at today's crucial meeting of the full Bluebonnet board.

The preliminary presentation the day after she got back had been enough to buy her the time she needed for a formal proposal. From Nairobi, through the stopover in London, and from Heathrow to LAX, she'd worked nonstop, then gone straight from the airport to the office, showered, worked without sleep for another twenty hours pulling everything together.

Only the work had kept her sane.

Without it, all she could see was Reitholder's body, blood still pumping from the severed arteries in the neck. She'd staggered over to a tree, sank to her knees. While she threw up, strong hands had steadied her, kept her from falling. Crazily, she'd thought it was Joel. Then she'd realized he was dead and it was Campbell holding her until the spasms were over.

It was strange how she remembered the rest of that night with such clarity. The intermittent gunfire tapering off. Campbell watching the tusks burn. Moses directing the collection of the dead, his impassive face as Sambeke's body was placed with the rest of Campbell's men who died that night belied by the track of tears coursing through the dirt on his cheek. The occasional shot that meant one less prisoner. Tom's hand squeezing her shoulder, his reassuring words about the death of Reitholder gentle in her ear, as if he'd thought a loud voice would shatter her equilibrium like glass.

And the delight of N'toya, her old friend Stephen, hustling Gaston, hands bound behind him, into an army helicopter idling on the great lawn of Erukenya. Morag's white face. Her own icy calm. She saw everything about that night clearly. Except Reitholder's face...

Doug found the sketch he was looking for, one of many she'd

done at the site, and held it up. "This meets every criterion we set up." He studied it, elephants in the foreground, the cave mouth yawning above. "Except accessibility. And handled right, that will turn out to be a plus. We'll bring the airstrip at, what's the name of that little town? Kitale? Yeah. We'll bring that airstrip up to a standard to take a fleet of small planes. Widen the road up the mountain. An exclusive, killingly expensive hotel. People love that. It'll be good. Very good."

She didn't turn to look at the drawings. She didn't need to. The day she'd got back, John Rifken had dropped by the office while she was working, the sketches and photographs she'd had developed pinned up around her drafting table. He'd riffled through a pile of paper she'd set aside, glanced at some quick pencil studies of Campbell—asleep in the sun, hunkered down building a fire, drinking coffee while he looked out over savannah wreathed in the mystery of early-morning mist—and put them aside without comment. Then he'd picked up the photographs and drawings of the caves at Kitum.

"You including this?" he'd asked.

She'd taken the sketches out of his hand, replaced them in her portfolio. "No."

"Why not?"

"I saw the site too late to get any data. No feasibility, no figures. Nothing to impress a consortium of land developers."

He retrieved the photographs. "So, today just keep their interest in Africa alive with Maasai Springs. Tomorrow, I'll talk to people in Kenya, government people, start to get some figures together for you on this site. Include it in your formal proposal, you could kick Guitterrez's ass. If it's financially viable, I can promise you, the job's yours."

Why look back? she'd thought. Her choice had been made at Erukenya.

She'd nodded. "Okay."

"So, what do you think?" Doug was saying.

"Think?"

"Are you listening to me?" Doug asked patiently. As usual, his sandy hair stood up in spikes, twiddled by nervous fingers. He started the day slick as a seal, and by midmorning looked more like a porcupine. "What do you think about choppering in building material? At least until we improve the road enough to bring up supplies."

Cat thought of the baboon challenging Campbell, his outrage and her laughter. Francolin and cold tomatoes dripping on bare skin, Tusker beer in the middle of a burning day.

She swung her chair around, planted her feet securely under her desk. "I think we're going to have to be very careful not to destroy what we're trying to showcase. Any building we do has to be well distanced from the caves. I'm going with a rammed earth system."

"Sure. We can look at that. Maybe the tribal people…what's their name?"

"The Nandi. It's their tribal land."

"Yeah, Nandi. We'll get them working on it. This African tongue-and-groove design in terrific." Doug smacked a hand on one of the detail drawings. "So let's go with it. When we get the go-ahead from Bluebonnet, first thing we ought to do is get permission to fell local lumber, have these Nandi people dress it in their traditional way so it can mature while the preliminary work is being done. Good PR. Their government will love us for providing jobs. Governments always love you when you do that. They'll eat out of our hands."

He had not heard a word she'd said about rammed earth. She said, "Don't kid yourself. They're more likely to chew them off at the armpit."

"And we'll use local stone."

"Local stone doesn't have any compressive strength. It's too soft for bearing walls."

"Use it for facing, then. We can use local artisans."

"Doug, the Nandi are pastoralists. They don't work stone."

"So, we'll introduce a new skill."

Mave Chen's head appeared around the door. "You've got half an hour to get over to Century City. You'd better get moving."

Doug got to his feet. "This presentation really shows what we can do, Cat. Lets them know nothing fundamental has changed at The Stanton Partnership. We've got two distinctly different treatments for two distinctly different sites. Compared to us, Guitterrez is a cookie cutter. He hasn't got a chance." He clapped his hands together. "Right. Let's go get 'em."

At a nod from John Rifken, Charlotte Buller, his assistant for twenty years, went to the wall of glass overlooking Century City. She pressed a button. Heavy lined drapes swung together, closing out the sun and plunging the conference room into darkness. A large screen descended from the ceiling. Cat pressed a switch on the multimedia projector.

The mist-wreathed image of Maasai Springs sprang to life, illuminating the room.

"This is the site as it now appears," Cat said. And in an ideal world, how it should be left, she thought. The image changed. "These aerials were flown six weeks ago, and you can see the natural boundaries of the project. This will be the last major building on the Mara, so the government reserves the right of architectural review. This is what I propose."

The rest of the slide presentation for Maasai Springs took just over fifteen minutes. She concluded with a shot of a sunset over the Mara, flat-topped thorn trees, a black silhouette of a single gi-raffe against the crimson-streaked sky. Hokey, but effective. She clicked the button on the projector. The room went dark.

The next slide would be of the elephant caves of Kitum. Camp-bell's place of renewal. The gift he had given her because he loved her. In some deep part of her being, she'd known that even then, with the words unspoken. But when he'd finally told her how he felt, it was too late.

Her fingers were still. She felt paralyzed. She couldn't do it. She couldn't press the button on the remote that would bring the ele-phant caves of Kitum into the conference room in Century City.

The moment lengthened. "Hey, if there's a glitch, I'll take an-other bourbon and branch while you get it fixed," a voice said.

"Cat, is there something wrong with that machine?" John Rifken asked.

"No. Nothing's wrong. The presentation is complete. Char-lotte," Cat said, "will you open the drapes, please?"

Daylight flowed in. Doug, in the chair next to her, leaned forward, confusion plain on his face. Cat raised a hand. She left her seat, walked to John Rifken halfway down the conference table, bent to murmur in his ear. "I can't continue with Kitum, John. I'm sorry."

"What the hell do you mean?" Rifken ground the words between his teeth. He turned to look at her, his one gray eye glittering. "It's already in the folder. I've talked it up. Do you intend to make a fool of me in front of these people?"

"I'm sorry."

John shoved back his chair and stood. "Charlotte, let's have an-other round of drinks here. Gentlemen, just tell Charlotte what you want while I—"

"Does the sun ever shine there, honey?" Lorne Tollet asked.

Cat looked at him, a small skinny man with the pasty complexion of someone who rarely sees the light of day. She was hard put to conceal her dislike. He looked as if he'd sway if she breathed on him, but from the moment she and Doug had come into the room, he had been overly solicitous, jumping up to help her as if she might be too weak to hold a pencil without assistance. One of Guitterrez's supporters.

"Seems an awful lot of rain in those photographs." Tollet shook his head.

Charlotte set a glass of bourbon, light on the branch, on the table in front of Rifken. He hesitated, looked at Cat, then sat down in his chair.

"The rains come twice a year," she said. "The rain is intermittent even then, and I saw Maasai Springs during one of those periods. However, you can see that neither the beauty of the site, nor the pools, are in any way diminished during the rainy season, which of course is not limited to Maasai Springs." She touched John's shoulder, then walked back to her own place. She picked up her copy of the document she had placed in front of each man. "You will see I have covered the annual rainfall and average daily hours of sunshine in the area. Page seven."

"American capital is being withdrawn from Kenya. I got the figures here," Tollet said.

Before the presentation, he'd droned on about the crash of the Texas real estate market—he wasn't getting his balls caught in that wringer again, pardon me, honey. He'd watched to see her reaction, as if the word *balls* had never been spoken in mixed company before, and seemed disappointed when she didn't have a reaction.

Cat glanced at John Rifken scowling into his drink. When this meeting was over, there was going to be one hell of a reckoning.

Rifken came to a decision and looked up. "I spoke with Mr. Joseph N'gonga, the minister of tourism, just last week."

Cat started to breathe again. He was going to try to sell them on Maasai Springs. John was a businessman. He was backing her because he had no choice. Not if he wanted to show Guitterrez, and the rest of this board, who held the power.

"I was assured that the government will do all it can to facilitate this project. The country desperately needs long-term commitment of foreign capital. They're prepared to make us a very sweet deal."

"Get it in writing," Tollet said.

"I did, Lorne. Page thirty-six."

"The figures are okay. More than okay," Bubba Nelligan said. Bubba had once played tight end for the Texas Aggies and looked as if he still could. "But my daddy always said, hell with the figures, go with the gut. My gut tells me Africa is bad news. Who the hell's going to want to stay at some hotel in the middle of a country with an AIDS epidemic?"

"AIDS is a reality of life everywhere," Cat said. "The government of Kenya would welcome regular health checks of all employees."

"I bet they would, on our payroll. Bubba here goes by his gut. My daddy believed in his accountant, and so do I." Brett Hardinge struck a wooden match on the sole of a lavishly tooled boot and held it to his cigar. He rolled the cigar around in his mouth to thoroughly moisten the end, speaking between puffs. "I'm gonna take a real good look at this proposal. Real good. We don't want to buy into problems we can't solve. I like your design, Cat. Nothing personal, you're a talented little gal."

Cat wondered what his reaction would be if the little gal responded to that remark as she wanted to. She stared at him without smiling. Another supporter of Guitterrez.

"We gotta face the political instability," Greg Hayakawa said. "One rich, connected tourist gets his head blown off before we sell out to investors, and we're in the hotel business. Bluebonnet's not geared up for running hotels."

"Figures are not everything, John," Hardinge said. "Greg's right. Those elephants are gonna draw poachers. Stands to reason. Someone's gonna get killed, sooner or later."

Cat smiled to herself. He still held the wooden match in his hand. Charlotte, an ardent reformed smoker, always managed to forget ashtrays.

"What I think is, John here has got his head up his ass, pardon me, honey," Tollet said.

The discussion dragged on. A power struggle in Bluebonnet, Cat thought, little to do with the project at hand. They must have gone over all this before Joel left for Nairobi—terrorism and poaching, AIDS and the constantly changing business climate, how much they could rely on the government of Kenya. The sides were clearly drawn up. Tollet and Nelligan. Hardinge and Hayakawa wavering. John Rifken pushing for Maasai Springs.

Outside, windows were beginning to glow in the high-rise buildings in Century City, and the hills were dotted with lights.

Greg Hayakawa looked at his watch. "I got a plane to catch." He flipped through his folder. "What about the rest of this?"

Doug leaned forward. "Cat—"

She put a hand on his arm. Expensive cigar smoke wreathed the air. Around the table, the men looked at her expectantly, John scowling from beneath his eyebrows, one manicured finger tapping the black patch over his eye. "Cat?"

He was giving her another chance. Doug put the projector remote on the table in front of her.

She put her hand over it. "I studied another site. You will find the details outlined. Kitum is on Mount Elgon, on the border with Uganda, a country struggling even more acutely with the problems discussed this afternoon. With that in mind, I have to conclude that Maasai Springs is the site that most clearly meets the criteria set up prior to Joel Stanton's visit to Kenya, and my own follow-up. It is, therefore, the only recommendation that I can make." She leaned back.

"You've just handed this job to Guitterrez on a silver platter," Doug Jones said in her ear.

The minute the goodbyes had been said, the handshakes over, John exploded. "Okay. Let's hear it."

"It's personal—"

"Don't give me that schoolgirl bullshit. This is business. If you don't want to chop cotton, girlie, get out of my cotton patch. You were paid for that study. I bought your talent and you fucked up. Now, *what the hell happened?*"

She turned to Doug, sitting at the conference table, staring into a glass. "Doug, will you excuse us? We'll talk in the morning."

"I'll go back to the office—"

"Let's make it in the morning, Doug. Okay?"

"Sure." He gathered his papers together, murmured a good-night to Rifken, closed the door softly behind him as if closing it on a funeral.

John walked to the bar, poured a couple of fingers of Chivas into a glass, then filled it with ice. "Here. You're gonna need this." He re-filled his own glass, dropped in one ice cube. "Okay. I'm waiting."

"Dan Campbell showed me that site when my safari was over. He had no intention of it being part of the job he undertook to do."

"So what? It's a great site. We can make it work. Or at least, we could have done before your little speech."

"It should be left as it is. Kitum is, I don't know…a special place." She shrugged. "Not many like that are left now."

"And that's it?"

She slugged down a healthy gulp of whiskey and shuddered.

"That's it."

"Why didn't you tell me that earlier? Before you decided to make a damn fool of me?"

"I don't know. I thought everything was up for grabs. I just found out that it wasn't."

"So what you're saying is that you fell for Dan Campbell?"

"That's none of your business. I'm not ruled by personal considerations—heart, hormones, whatever you want to call it—any more than any architect would be, if that's what you're implying. Comments like that are out of line. I didn't want to break a trust. Even you should understand that."

"Well, you certainly found your moral center at an awkward moment. I hope you can afford it."

"Your fee will be refunded."

"Damn right it will."

"I'll have Mave cut a check for that part of the work done on Kitum here in Los Angeles."

John grunted. "You know you blew this job?"

"You know I don't care? Maasai Springs should be left as it is. If you don't build this hotel, it's not likely to get done. The government will find hard currency some other way. You've lost nothing. Guitterrez will get the project in Thailand, or somewhere else. You'll make money."

"You're damn right. That's what I'm in business to do. And so are you."

"My professor at Harvard used to say architecture was an ego-driven profession. His advice was, if you want to make a fortune, go into another line of work." She put her glass on the table, prepared to gather her papers together. "But I'm not hurting."

"So why are you crying?"

She hadn't realized she was. She ran a hand over her face, smearing tears and mascara. "I mean, I've got a lot of work."

"I know what you mean."

John walked to where she was perched on the edge of the conference table. He put an arm around her and pulled her toward him. "Come on, kiddo. Come on. What is this?"

She put her head on his shoulder, not easy since he was shorter than she was. "I don't know, John. I seem to be doing this a lot lately."

She wondered what he would say if she told him that when she was in Africa doing his work, she'd killed a man. For a moment, she was tempted, but the urge passed. Committing murder was not something easily discussed.

John shook a snowy handkerchief free from its folds, dabbed clumsily at her face. "Good. I never saw you shed a tear for Joel before this. This is good."

"No, it isn't." She couldn't breathe. Her sinuses were clogged, her throat ached. She took the handkerchief, wiped away streaks of mascara, handed it back to him. "I hate it."

"Ah, hell. You've got to learn to let yourself go more often. It doesn't do for a woman to get too detached."

She gave a small half laugh. "That's a sexist remark, John."

He continued to pat her back. "Sure is."

"I've got to get back to the office. I've got a lot of work to do tonight." She leaned against him for a moment, pressed her lips to his cheek. "I'm sorry about today. I know how much you wanted to stop Guitterrez."

"Ah, hell, honey. It ain't over until the last dog howls. That little bastard has met his match. He just ain't rolled over yet."

Cat nodded. He was feeling better. Texas was back in his voice.

* * *

The drafting room looked bleak under fluorescent light, the tables empty, the constant blare of the radio silenced. Even Mave Chen had gone home, leaving a note on Cat's desk: "Call me with the good news." Cat crumpled it, threw it in the wastepaper basket and dropped into her chair. She wanted to sleep for a week.

Her office was dark, lit only by the light filtering in from the drafting room. Cat stared out at San Vicente Boulevard, teeming with traffic and people walking, everyone in couples it seemed, on their way to dinner.

She turned back into the room. Her phone glowed, inviting. She rested her hand on the receiver, imagining the sound of a telephone pealing through the early-morning quiet of the house in Nairobi. What did she want to say? That in the search for the truth about Joel, she'd discovered some more pieces of her own puzzle? That the only trouble was, she hadn't been able to fit them all together yet?

That she just wanted to hear his voice?

She removed her hand, turned on the light over her desk and opened a folder containing a pile of bills Mave had left for her to check.

He wouldn't be there, anyway. He'd be out in the bush, killing or being killed.

A week later, John Rifken called. "You got your wish, honey. The government of Kenya is going to have to do without hard currency from Bluebonnet. We're scrubbing the Maasai Springs project."

"Well. Win a few, lose a few. You don't sound too upset."

"I got what I want. Guitterrez is out. We're going with a program of building in Morocco, Tunisia, Algeria. Warm-weather vacation destinations for frozen Europeans. And to start with, we're looking at a luxury hotel in Nairobi. That job's yours if you want it."

"Thanks, John, but I can't run a job in Kenya from Los Angeles."

"What? Did I hear right? Joel would have grabbed at this."

"I'm not Joel."

"Last call, honey. It's a plum job."

"No thanks. But give me a chance at the rest of the work."

"Yeah, well, there you'll have to compete. We're going to be looking at architects from all over the country."

"I'm not afraid of competition."

"Maybe you should be."

She put the phone down without a tinge of regret.

Forty-One

Even without Rifken's project, the office was busy. Spring Street Plaza had its share of problems and there was a new golf course tract in Palm Springs—just what Palm Springs needed, Cat knew, another golf course to deplete the water table, saturate the desert air with moisture that nature didn't intend to be there. But it was a job. And an old client, Mike Isenstein down in Del Mar, wanted more work done on his spa and country club near the racetrack.

She was working on Isenstein's dinner theater when Mave's voice crackled through the intercom.

"Cat, pick up line two. You're going to love it."

They were alone in the office. It was the end of the day, tomorrow was Thanksgiving and most people had already started the long weekend. Eyes locked on the elevation she was working out, Cat leaned back and flipped the switch.

"If it's Isenstein, tell him I've gone for the weekend."

"No, it's not Mad Mike. You'll want to talk to this guy. Believe me. Line two."

The pit of Cat's stomach started to quiver. That last night at Eru-kenya, Campbell had told her that he loved her, never more than at that moment, bloodstained, her sweatshirt and cords splashed with brain tissue. He'd asked her to stay. They had to have time together, he'd said, calm, quiet time to regain what they'd had. He'd held her, told her that he needed her.

She couldn't listen. All she'd wanted was to run—from the rage that had erupted from deep within her. From him, from Africa, from the violence in his life that was a reminder of what she couldn't face in herself. That night, she had gone back to Nairobi with Tom.

She had not spoken to Campbell since.

Cat smoothed back her hair as if he could see her, put out a tentative hand, then grasped the receiver firmly. "This is Cat Stanton."

"You sound like a woman who needs someone to take her out to boogie the night away. How're you doing, sweet thing?"

Cat took a breath. Then she laughed shakily, feeling foolish and disappointed. Glad. Thankful she was alone and no one had seen her face. "Paul!"

"Your very own bad penny."

"When did you get in?"

"An hour ago. I'm on my way to Washington, but made it by way of Los Angeles just to see you."

"And I suppose you haven't seen civilization in months and are raring to paint the town."

"Sure. But I'll settle for a quiet dinner for two. Can you make it tonight. Better yet, the weekend?"

No. Yes. No. Why not? "Where are you?" She played for time.

"Just checked in at Loews in Santa Monica. Pretty luxurious digs after what I've been living in these last few months. What about it?"

"Not the weekend. Why didn't you let me know you were coming into town, give me a chance to clear my calendar?"

"Last time I called you from Sarajevo, and you went to Africa, anyway. What about tonight, and we'll negotiate the weekend?"

"Sounds good."

"I was thinking I'd order a fancy pizza from Spago, a bottle of champagne, and we'll spend a cozy evening at your place, exchanging news. And whatever else occurs to us. Okay?"

She hesitated. Always, when he came in after a long absence, they made love first. Afterward, they'd potter about her kitchen, or get dressed, go out to eat, make love again before he went back to his hotel. She never let him stay the night.

"Nothing doing. You haven't seen me in months. The least you can do is feed me a decent meal."

He laughed. "Okay. Michael's on Third. Shall I pick you up?"

"I'll meet you there. Eight. Okay?"

His voice lost its usual bantering note. "I can't wait to see you, Cat. I've missed you."

It was time to pick up her life. "I've missed you, too," she said.

She left the office just after seven, leaving herself enough time to get home, shower, change into a soft black dress that Paul liked and get to Michael's by eight. At five minutes past, she drew up outside the restaurant, nodded to the parking valet opening her door. His mouth was moving but she was unable to hear his words over the blast of rap from an open Jeep tearing past. Everywhere trees were strung with lights. The city was deep in its annual holiday mania. Every year it seemed to start earlier, streets festooned with Christmas decorations by Halloween.

Cat thought of weaverbird nests hanging like ornaments from the branches of trees silhouetted against an endless melon sky. The cry of a jackal over a lonely plain.

She walked into the tiny bar and saw Paul unfolding his long, lean body from behind a small table.

"Thought you'd never get here," he said. "I felt like a kid waiting for his first date." He took both her hands, standing back to look at her. "You're wearing my favorite dress. How are you, Cat?"

"Wonderful. What about you? How's the world of the combat reporter?"

"Well, I'll never be out of a job." Paul smiled his charming, diffident smile, brushed back the spill of brown hair from his forehead. "You look fabulous. You always look fabulous."

He settled her into a chair next to him. He was drinking a gin martini and Cat ordered the same.

"Last I heard from you was a postcard from Jeddah."

"Yeah, and I got a picture of an ugly little animal from Africa."

"Only one? I sent you a dozen. Where did you go after Saudi Arabia?"

"Back to Bosnia. Got in this morning."

She laughed. "By way of Los Angeles?"

"I didn't want to get bogged down in Washington. It's been too long since I've seen you."

She smiled, toyed with the olive in her glass. They both looked up at the maître d' announcing their table was ready. He led them through the restaurant, original art on white walls, light gleaming on crystal and silver. She'd forgotten how romantic it was.

They ordered, sipped wine and chatted casually until smoked salmon and toasted brioche bread had been placed before them and the waiter had retreated to a discreet distance.

Paul reached across the table, laid his hand on hers. "So, did you manage to search out any more about Joel's death?"

She turned her hand over so that she could respond to the pressure from his.

"What makes you think that's what I was doing?"

"Give me some credit, Cat. I've known you for a while."

She extricated her hand, forked some smoked salmon into her mouth. "Mmm. Good. Tell me about Bosnia."

He looked at her, then started to eat. "Nothing you'd want to know. The usual story. Psychopaths with guns given license to kill by psychopaths with political power. Apart from Joel, how was Kenya?"

"Okay. Interesting. A lot of animals. A lot of killing."

"Well, you didn't have the usual tourist trip, I take it."

"Not exactly."

"You don't want to talk about Joel?"

Paul was gazing at her with a quizzical look in his eye, and she knew she sounded strained. "No. Later, maybe."

She looked up gratefully as the waiter chose that moment to remove their plates, then place double lamb chops in front of Paul, and broiled salmon for her, garnished with a few tiny vegetables only just out of the bud stage.

While eating, she told Paul about Thomas and Moses, Olentwalla's drumming, Sambeke's quiet presence, trying to keep the wobble of grief out of her voice when she spoke of him. She talked about the beauty of the savannah after rain. No mention of Stephen N'toya or Tom. No Gaston or Erukenya. Nothing about Dan Campbell. But they laughed over Brian Ward, the bumbling colonial.

She didn't say that on the way back to Nairobi with Tom, she'd told him about Ward's mysterious appearance in the Indian grocery store. A loose end to be tied up. Tom had laughed. Ward was nothing to worry about. He was exactly what he seemed—a leftover from another era with a network of informers in the villages who sold him bush gossip. Nothing sinister, but sometimes he struck gold. Made people nervous. Ward liked that. Made him feel important.

Paul refilled the glasses. "Did you get a site for your hotel?"

"No. The hotel job's dead," Cat said. "Nothing will come of it."

"Ah, Cat. That's too bad."

"No, it's not. I like to think of the pools at Maasai Springs left as they are." A place to restore the soul, if you believed it would.

Plates were cleared, and they turned to discussion of dessert, decided on one order of rum-raisin tart and ate from the same plate as they always did, then lingered over espresso and brandy.

It was after eleven when they got home. Cat had kept the drapes open before she left, and from her darkened fourteenth-floor living room, a sparkling Palos Verdes Peninsula wrapped the bay to the south, and out on the black expanse of the Pacific the lights of fishing boats bobbed northward toward Point Dume in Malibu.

Paul put his arm around her, and they walked into the bedroom. He pulled her to him. Cat slipped her arms around him, the feel of his ribs unfamiliar to her, the prominence of his vertebrae alien, as if she had never felt them before. She opened her lips to him, felt the touch of his tongue. Slowly they went through the ritual of undressing each other. He ran his hand over her belly, and she parted her legs, reaching for him.

A little later, Paul rolled over onto his back. "Sweetheart, you're supposed to be enjoying this. It's not something you should have to work at."

"I am enjoying it."

He propped himself on his elbow, picked up a strand of her hair. "Liar, liar, pants on fire. Or rather, pants very much not on fire."

"I'm sorry. I guess it's not my night."

"It'll be fine. Let's give it a minute."

"No. Maybe you'd better go, Paul. I'm tired. Down to my bones, I'm tired."

"You want to tell me about it?"

"What? Being tired?"

"No. The guy you met in Kenya. The guy who means something to you. The guy whose name you didn't mention."

She didn't answer. They'd always had a tacit agreement. No questions, no strings, no commitment. But she couldn't lie. Paul deserved more than that.

He swung out of bed. He was tall, slim, elegant, without Campbell's solid musculature. Would she go through life, she wondered, comparing every man to Campbell?

"Okay, sweets. Have it your way." He dressed, hung his tie around his neck without knotting it and leaned over her. She felt his lips on her hair. "Unless I hear from you, I'll go back to Washington in the morning. You know where to reach me."

She heard the front door close behind him, then turned on her side, drew her knees up under her chin.

She wouldn't call him.

Forty-Two

Dusk was falling, Christmas lights were just beginning to come on in front of some of the houses. Cat drove down Malibu Road, past the old beach house in which she and Joel had been brought up. There were no ghosts there for her anymore.

Cat entered the garage of Jess's house, let herself in, fending off the little gray terrier Jess had found three years ago, starving and cowering in her garage. When she and Mike were away, Jess bribed friends to stay with him, refusing to put him in a kennel. This year, for their annual visit to show Rosie off to grandparents, she'd zeroed in on Cat. He'd be company, she'd said. Christmas was going to be hard this year, the first without Joel. She'd put her arms around Cat. They'd clung together, both knowing she spoke for herself, as well as for Cat.

Cat rubbed the terrier's ears, submitted to his sloppy affection. "Scroungy, you've got it made, buddy."

The Christmas Eve staff lunch had been longer than usual, and bittersweet. After a lot of thought, she'd offered Doug the partnership he wanted—sixty-five thirty-five. They'd settled at sixty forty. This morning the contract had been signed, and at lunch she'd announced the new name of the firm. Stanton and Jones. A break with the past.

But Joel had been very much present. After a few toasts, talk had turned to him, his humor, his formidable talent. They'd mourned his loss. For the first time since his death, she'd been able to talk about him, even found herself laughing about some of his idiosyncrasies with the people who'd worked with him and had known him well. If that could be said of anyone, apart from herself, and maybe Jess.

The terrier followed her while she closed the curtains, shutting out the night. This morning when she left, the ocean in front of the windows had been wreathed in mist. Now the mist had deepened into a dense sea fog. Cat plugged in the tree lights and switched on some Christmas carols. Waves boomed as they struck the beach, water hissing as it flowed back across the sand into the sea. The house had the distinctive smell of old beach houses, familiar from childhood, the sea and wood smoke, and now with Christmas, the resinous scent of Rosie's tree.

Determinedly humming along with the carols, she poured a glass of white wine, puttered about in the kitchen, opening a can of dog food and pouring kibble. "Just you and me, babe, for the whole weekend." She put the dish down in the service porch. "Yum, yum. Home cookin'."

It hadn't been hard for Jess to persuade her to stay. The three-day weekend stretched ahead, alone with the dog, a little work, long walks on the winter beach, the sound of the waves soothing her to sleep. She was exhausted from the running she had done since being back—every minute filled with activity, the days so empty. Occasionally, in the depths of the night, the thought came to her that she'd killed a man, but not very often anymore.

Gradually, Reitholder's face had come back to her, in dreams at first, then later she'd been able to conjure him up at will. Stare at him with her mind's eye, allow her father's face to be superimposed over his, know what she had done. Mostly she felt as if a great weight had been lifted from her—a weight that had pressed upon her for as long as she could remember. As well as Reitholder, she had killed her father that night, and she was at peace with what she had done. Sometimes she wondered if she ought to be worried about that.

Given time, work would be fulfilling again, becoming the reward it always had been. Campbell would fade into the past. He'd made it plain there was no going back.

A couple of weeks ago, alone in the office late, she'd dialed the number of the house in Nairobi. She'd listened to the phone ring a dozen times and had been about to hang up when a deep voice answered.

"Campbell."

She'd licked dry lips with a drier tongue. "Hi. It's Cat."

"How good to hear from you, my dear. How are you? Recovering?"

Her heart bumped with disappointment. Their voices were so alike. "I'm fine, Jock, thanks. Working hard. How are things in Nairobi?"

"Well, behind the scenes, a great deal of turmoil. There is a real determination to clean up poaching, but a lot of pockets are lined by the slaughter. Did you see that President Moi publicly burned three million dollars' worth of tusks taken from a ship inside our territorial waters?"

"It was front-page news here," Cat said.

"Good. That could have been sold for hard currency the country needs, so it sends a message. If he hadn't done it, the Kenya

Wildlife Service was going to torch what they had been stockpiling for that purpose. The president had his hand forced, but it was better for him to do it."

"That was the ivory in the barn?"

"That was only part of it," Jock said. "Publicity is what's needed. Stephen's going to get plenty of that when he brings Gaston to trial. A lot of people in Johannesburg will be very uncomfortable."

"That's good. Stephen must be pleased." She was suddenly tired of it, the danger and the blood. "How's Morag?"

"Busy working with her math tutor. Still says she's going to be an architect. She's over at the Terrys'. She'll be sorry she missed you."

"Give her my love."

They chatted about the project in Maasai Springs. Jock didn't seem too saddened it wouldn't go ahead. Tembo had adjusted to the new herd. The eland project was doing well, a lot of females in calf, but the white peacock had been taken by a lioness. Neither mentioned Reitholder's death. Conversation petered out, and there was a pause. She couldn't bring herself to ask for him.

"Dan isn't here, Cat," Jock said at last. "He left Erukenya just after you did."

"Oh. Just tell him I called, will you, Jock?"

She waited for him to tell her where Campbell was, when he was expected, but he volunteered nothing and she didn't ask.

Campbell had never called her, and that itself was the message.

Piling a plate with the tiny English mince pies Jess had left for her, Cat took her wine and the mail, kicked off her shoes and stretched out on the sofa in front of the fire. Scroungy jumped up beside her, settled across her feet, sighing noisily. Cat wiggled her toes, scratching his belly as she slid the brown paper sleeve from a newsmagazine, riffled through the pages.

A headline leaped at her.

Richard the Lionheart under attack.

The subtitle read: Attempt made on life of head of the Kenya Wildlife Service.

She sat up, spread the magazine on the table and leaned over it, scanning the printed page.

Richard Leakey, recently appointed by President Daniel Arap Moi to head the Kenya Wildlife Service, the agency that oversees all of Kenya's conservation efforts, was severely injured when his small aircraft came under rocket attack while flying over Tsavo National Park, an 8,000-square-mile territory southeast of Nairobi that is the last refuge of some 7,000 elephants.

The pilot, Tom M'Bala, also injured in the attack, managed to land the damaged plane, but Mr. Leakey suffered broken legs and other unspecified injuries.

A full-scale battle later erupted between a highly secret commando unit of the Kenya Wildlife Service and a well-armed company of the regular army equipped with rockets and a helicopter gunship. Heavy casualties are reported to have been suffered by both sides.

Last night, General Josephus Kalinda, a long-time supporter of Mr. Moi, was arrested at his home in Nairobi. General Kalinda is said to have extensive financial dealings involving poached ivory with South Africa's Afrikaner Broederhood, an organization that is said to have officers on active duty in South Africa's military, as well as cabinet ministers of the de Klerk government among its membership.

In Nairobi, Mr. Moi reiterated his support for the shoot-to-kill policy to curb poaching in Kenya's national parks. He issued a clear warning that no one should assume they are above the law.

Johannesburg refused comment.

Cat ripped the paper sleeves from the rest of the newsmagazines and fumbled through the pages. Two more magazines covered the action, one giving an analysis of the political implications for Kenya. She scanned it—three hundred million dollars in loans secured from the World Bank...half earmarked for the KWS to improve wildlife conservation, now jeopardized unless Leakey remains at the helm...democratic multiparty elections tied into loans. She threw the magazine aside.

Her imagination jumped from one terrible scenario to the next. Campbell maimed, his body broken. She tried to calm her fears, and full-throated terror roared back at her. Maybe he was dead and no one had thought to call her. And Tom? Would anyone call her about Tom, or Thomas, or the others?

Her hands refused to obey her, the telephone seemed to jump, clattering to the floor as she reached for it. She forced herself to move with deliberation. Her fingers felt thick, almost nerveless, as she punched out the number of the house in Nairobi. The ringing went on and on, but she couldn't bring herself to hang up. Frail and nebulous though it was, the sound seemed suddenly the only connection she had with him—a telephone ringing in his home.

Finally she forced herself to hang up so that she could call Erukenya. The same. She redialed the house in Nairobi without result. Then she remembered it was Christmas.

The terrier pushed his head under her hand. Cat looked down at him. Seven o'clock on Christmas Eve was an impossible time to find someone to take care of a dog. Everyone she knew well enough to ask was out of town. Tomorrow, though, she would hammer on the door of every kennel in Malibu until someone took him in. As soon as that was done, she would get on a plane for Nairobi.

The decision made, she felt marginally better. On every hour, she called both Campbell and Stephen N'toya. On the half hour, she dialed Erukenya. At midnight, finally, Stephen's machine answered with a message in Swahili. She asked him to call and left Jess's number.

Cat opened her eyes. The gray light of early dawn filtered through the drawn curtains. The fire had burned out, the room was cold and she was stiff from falling asleep on the sofa, and from the weight of the dog across her legs. Her mouth felt like ashes.

Scroungy jumped down and stood patiently at the door. She let him out, watched him scamper down the wooden steps to the beach and disappear into the mist. She turned back into the house, relit the fire, plugged in coffee and called American Airlines. She booked a flight to London, trusting the Kenya Airline flight to Nairobi leaving an hour after her arrival at Heathrow would have a seat available. If not, she'd find something. At least she was in action.

When she got out of the shower, Scroungy was reminding her with small plaintive yelps from outside that he needed his breakfast. She let him in and opened his can, drank some coffee and ate a mince pie from last night, then put on her old gray running sweats.

The tide was low, ripples in the hard sand gold in the rising sun, and she turned east into an opalescent dawn. Mist hung low over the sea, gulls sounded their plaintive call. Cat swung into an easy rhythm, the dog at her side.

As she ran, she thought of the last few months. John Rifken was right. It wasn't good for a woman, for anyone, to be too detached, as she and Joel had been. As children, they'd needed that distance. She didn't need it anymore. It was not only her father from whom she had to be free. She had to be free from Joel, too. He could not be the other half of herself. Not any longer.

Her stride lengthened, and sweat bathed her body as she got her second wind. Ahead of her, Scroungy ran barking at a flock of terns and gulls settled on the sand, and they rose, wheeling over the sea. Her bare feet splashed through pools, and she picked up pace, running faster, the fresh, salt-laden air cold on her face. Certainty replaced the terror and anxiety of the night. He was alive. If he had died in that skirmish in Tsavo, she would know it.

At the end of the Malibu Colony, she turned back. The sun was higher, touching the mist with pink, spreading a silver gilt path across the water. Waves lapped over her feet, soaking her sweats to the knee. She swung down, scooped up a branch of giant kelp, hurling it ahead of her. The dog raced after it.

Close to the house, she slowed to a walk, damp with sweat and seawater, gritty with sand. Scroungy bounded up the steps and stopped at the top, the hair on his back ridged from neck to tail. He looked around, saw her right behind him and began to bark.

Her eyes took in the tall figure rising from a chair on the deck. Later, she would wonder why she wasn't surprised to see him.

"I called John Rifken from the airport," Campbell said. "He told me where you were, but he didn't have the telephone number."

He looked older, with more silver in his hair, unshaven and haggard, as if he hadn't slept for a week.

"I read about the attack on Leakey. Is Tom okay?"

"He will be. Olentwalla is dead. Zama. Many others."

She went to him, put her arms around him, fitting her body into his, knowing she didn't want to change him, or the life he had chosen. She held him close, remembering the comradeship she had shared with the men who'd died, Sambeke's calm reassurance, Olentwalla's laughter, the intricate rhythms he had woven on his drum.

"I called you," she said. "I wanted to tell you that I love you."

"And I thought I'd love you enough to let you go back to your own life. But I find I can't do it. There's a lot I want to tell you."

She felt the secrets of the past breaking loose.

"Yes. Both of us. Come on, my love, I'll make you some breakfast. We've got a lot to talk about."

For a moment, Cat watched him sleep, then quietly slipped out of bed. He stirred restlessly, and murmured something unintelligible, but didn't awaken. She put on her old terrycloth robe and made some coffee, took a mug into Mike's small study off the living room. She picked up the phone on his desk and punched in a number.

"What the hell time is this to be calling?" John Rifken's voice growled in her ear.

"Merry Christmas, John."

"You're a bit late. It's almost over."

"Well, Happy Hanukkah, anyway."

"I guess he found you okay."

"Yes, he's here. I called to thank you."

John grunted.

"I also wanted to talk to you about the Nairobi deal. Have you decided on an architect yet?"

"Got anyone in mind?"

"I might."

"So talk to me."

"My fee is fifteen percent of the cost of construction."

He snorted. "In your dreams, sweetpea."

Cat laughed, then turned as she felt Campbell behind her. She'd heard nothing—he'd entered the room with his usual animal silence. Cat moved her head to rub her cheek against his hand on her shoulder and leaned back against him.

"John, I'll call you in a couple of days. We'll talk about it."

"Okay, but you'd better sharpen your pencil, honey." He hung up.

"Was that John Rifken?" Campbell asked. "I'd like to thank him for telling me where to find you."

She stood to put her arms around him. "I already did."